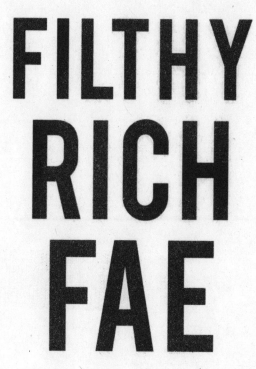

FILTHY RICH FAE

FILTHY RICH FAE

GENEVA LEE

NEW YORK TIMES & INTERNATIONALLY BESTSELLING AUTHOR

Entangled Publishing, LLC
644 Shrewsbury Commons Ave., STE 181
Shrewsbury, PA 17361
rights@entangledpublishing.com

Amara is an imprint of Entangled Publishing, LLC.

Visit our website at www.entangledpublishing.com.

Edited by Liz Pelletier
Cover art and design by Geneva Lee
Stock art by Adobe: Marinavorona/Adobestock, Anna/Adobestock,
Chansom Pantip/Adobestock, jmagico/Adobestock,
WONGSAKORN/Adobestock, prin79/Adobestock
Interior formatting by Britt Marczak

Trade Paperback ISBN 978-1-64937-577-3
Ebook ISBN 978-1-64937-578-0

Manufactured in the United States of America

First Edition June 2024

10 9 8 7 6 5 4 3 2 1

ALSO BY GENEVA LEE

FILTHY RICH VAMPIRES SERIES

Filthy Rich Vampire
Second Rite
Three Queens
For Eternity

THE ROYALS SAGA

THE RIVALS SAGA

The Sins That Bind Us

To the readers who would take the apple

CHAPTER ONE

D eath was business as usual, and tonight, business was…good? No, not good. More like unrelenting. Time didn't really exist inside a place like Gage Memorial's emergency room. Maybe that's why death visited so frequently.

It was a stark, nearly windowless maze of beds and machines, sterilized extensively by bleach and four-foot ultraviolet light bulbs. But by ten hours into my shift, I navigated it instinctively, pausing at the nurse's station to pull a new chart.

Haley, the charge nurse, passed me one. She was only a few years older than me, but she wore every one of them in the circles rimming her eyes. She tossed her box braids over one shoulder and peeked across as I skimmed the paperwork. "Pediatric blood draw and IV," she informed me. "You have all the luck."

I stuck my tongue out at her. Important but boring work. Not that I'd ever wish for something more exciting, exactly, but this late in my shift, I was starting to feel the hours. Sticking a kid wasn't going to keep the adrenaline pumping. "Tell that to the kid in about five minutes."

She tried to grin, but her lips flattened instead. "I just sent another overdose downstairs. That's the third one this week."

"Trinity?" I asked.

"What else would it be? I miss the old days when clover didn't kill everyone," she said with a sigh. "Fuck, I just miss being able to hit some myself."

I bit back a frown. I'd learned my lesson about messing with shit like that the hard way. Now I just worried about kids like my brother, Channing, making a mistake that might cost them their lives.

"Times have changed," I reminded her.

New Orleans's favorite street drug, clover, had once been as harmless as the tequila shots slung on Bourbon Street, almost beloved for its ability to turn any night into the best one of your life—without the risk of addiction. But the criminal syndicate that ran New Orleans must not have been making enough money on it or were greedy and wanted more, so they altered the formula. In the last six months, clover had been responsible for nearly half of the overdoses in the entire city. We'd dubbed the new strain "trinity" because if someone went looking for the high of a four-leafed clover and got trinity instead, their luck would run out.

"I heard that we're getting funding for more beds to help," Haley said.

Like that was going to solve the problem. The worst part was that no one was doing anything about it—not when the criminals selling it bankrolled every institution in town, including this one.

"It's something," she added when she saw my face.

I couldn't stop myself. "Or maybe someone needs to lock the monster selling it away."

"Shhh. Don't forget who pays the bills."

"Paying a hospital to keep quiet doesn't absolve sin."

Haley's face softened, and I braced myself for her usual apologetic gymnastics about making tough decisions for the greater good.

But all hell broke loose instead as a blur of blue scrubs rushed toward the entrance.

One caught my eye and shouted, "Full trauma coming in from first district—two males; gunshot wounds, one to left shoulder, one intracranial; estimated blood loss unknown."

"Get this down to the lab," I ordered an intern who looked a little too excited by the prospect of seeing actual gunshot victims.

He opened his mouth to protest, but the charge nurse cut him off with a stern, "Now."

"Bourbon Street?" I shouted to the nurse who had taken the call.

He shook his head. "Waverly."

The single word told me all I needed to know. If the shooting had occurred on Waverly Avenue, it wasn't tourists caught in a drunken altercation. Tourists stuck to the well-worn, fabled streets of the French Quarter and its booze and beads. Waverly, farther south, was tucked next to the residential Warehouse District. Waverly's bars and nightclubs served a rougher clientele, and if two victims were on their way, there was every likelihood more would follow. Even in my delinquent days, I'd avoided that neighborhood. Even now, no one I knew went down there. But for native New Orleanians, there was only one family's name that struck fear deeper than Waverly.

Gage.

Maybe it was because Waverly could be avoided—and usually was—but for those of us stuck here, the Gages were synonymous with the city itself. Not just because their name was plastered on a dozen businesses scattered around the Big Easy, including the trauma center I was currently standing in, but because it ran through the very veins of the city and into its sinew and bone. The outside world knew us for the French Quarter and the Garden District, voodoo and jazz and food. Tourists were welcome; protected, even. But those of us living here knew the true darkness of the city. We felt it watching us. And the heart of that darkness was Lachlan Gage.

A man I'd never met, never even seen. And now I'd be cleaning up another one of his messes.

Haley's muttered curse snapped me to attention.

I dropped the kid's chart and bolted toward the fray, picking up snippets of information from the EMTs as they stood over a gurney. Blood soaked the white sheet beneath the man's head, his skin waxen and his breath labored and shallow. That much blood coupled with the way his dark hair clung together with a matted, oily sheen was a bad sign. I started toward the gurney just as my eyes snagged on the tip of his ear...and stopped. What the hell was wrong with it?

I blinked as Dr. Garcia, the chief of medicine, stepped into my path with an air of authority completely undermined by his inside-out lab coat. "My team will handle this one."

I opened my mouth to argue, trying to crane my neck around him for another glimpse at the man's strange anatomy, but he held up a hand.

"Cate, why don't you take a break?" He shot me a look before he was off.

A break? We didn't have the staffing for anyone to take a break. What—

Ice filtered into my blood as the doors opened a second time. Haley was already there, barking instructions, but her gaze found mine a second before the world stopped.

It took me a moment to find my center as I stared at my brother's body being wheeled inside—mostly because my center was right there on that gurney. Channing was as pale as the sheet covering his shaking body. An oxygen mask clung to his pain-stricken face.

I didn't process taking the steps to reach him even as every word of the EMTs sank through my carefully controlled panic.

"Stable."

"...hit in the shoulder with a Gage special. Friendly fire."

"...fragments missed the subclavian and axillary arteries."

And finally, *"Lucky."*

He was *lucky*.

My panic shifted to relief, then something darker. He may have been lucky compared to the other man, but that luck was about to change because I was going to kill him. With my hands. My stethoscope. I hadn't decided yet.

He wasn't just in trouble—he was in with the Gages.

He had the pieces of a Gage special—one of their custom-made bullets lodged in his shoulder as proof. And if it was friendly fire, that meant he wasn't just mixed up with them. He was working *for* them.

I was going to vomit.

Haley moved to my side. "Cate, he's okay," she said gently. "Let them—"

"I've got him," I cut her off.

Haley opened her mouth before clamping it shut. She glanced at Garcia, who was now completely focused on the other victim. "You can't go in with him," she warned me.

I already knew that and gave a quick nod. I wouldn't go in, but I wasn't leaving his side until I absolutely had to do so. Haley held my gaze for a breath and then fell back to speak with Garcia.

I jogged alongside Channing's gurney, surveying the bloody gauze on his shoulder. The result of the iron slug bullets Gage and his men preferred. The bullets were a brutal, inhuman choice due to the way they shattered into splinters when fired. If Channing had been hit even a few inches over... Heat pricked my eyes, and I drew a steadying, if reedy, breath. This wasn't my first night on the job. It wasn't even the first time he had shown up injured.

But it *was* the first time it involved the Gage family.

Channing shoved the mask from his face, drawing a ragged breath. His blue eyes met mine, their gold-flecked irises a pale contrast to my brown eyes. By appearance alone, it was clear we weren't related by blood. Where he was fair, I was tan despite my long hours in the hospital. His dirty-blond hair was getting a bit shaggy, but it wasn't long enough to cover the scar on his right brow. He'd still had stitches there the day he arrived at Gran's with all his belongings shoved in a threadbare pillowcase. Lately, Channing had gotten a few more scars, but this...

His pupils were dilated as they tried to focus on me. "Hey, sis."

My own eyes narrowed. "Do not *hey sis* me."

"Come on, I'm bleeding. Have sympathy." His lopsided grin did nothing to soften the sharp edge of my rage.

When Gran died, we'd made a pact to keep her memory alive, look out for each other, and stay far away from the Gage family. Like most, we were raised on horror stories of people who had crossed the city's oldest, richest, and cruelest family. They never had happy endings. Since I'd come to work at Gage Memorial, I'd witnessed enough of them firsthand. Channing *knew* this.

"Uh, where should we put him?" the EMT asked, eyes darting to his partner's.

"In jail," I snapped. Maybe that would teach him the lesson he clearly needed.

"Room two," Haley said, pointing to the north side of the ER.

My heart flipped, but I refused to let it show as they wheeled him toward the private rooms reserved for what we all grimly considered our VIP guests. The real reason the Gage name was on the side of the building was because their crew were our best customers. That meant they'd endowed the hospital, not just with money but also state-of-the-art equipment, so that they would receive special treatment when their people showed up bloodied, battered, and beaten.

And tonight, my brother was a VIP.

"What happened?" I demanded as soon as the EMTs left us alone to wait for an attending to assess my brother.

He tried to grin and failed. "I got shot."

Well, that was clear as mud. I glared at him.

"I owed someone some money."

"Gage?" I guessed.

He turned his head as if he couldn't bear looking at me. Answer enough. "I couldn't repay the debt. It doesn't matter now."

"Shooting you was enough?"

"He didn't shoot me. We were dealing with some guys. They got away."

I swallowed. "Dealing with?"

Channing avoided my eyes. "I have to pay Gage back."

Icy fear splintered through me. Paying him back? I searched for the calm I usually mustered at work and found none. Nothing—not even Channing's previous trips here—had prepared me for hearing those words. "What the fuck were you thinking?"

"*You* try finding a job around this city that doesn't eventually involve working for the Gage family," he snapped.

The blood froze in my veins. Being involved with the Gages,

owing them, was bad, but working for them was a death sentence. He was on borrowed time. "How hard did you try?"

"I get it. I'm a fuckup." Resignation weighed down his voice.

I closed my eyes and tried to remember that he was still a kid. That he was only nineteen, five years younger than me, and that I'd once been in and out of trouble as often as him. But I didn't want him to grow up like I did—abruptly and traumatically. "You're not a fuckup. You're just success-challenged."

Laughter was a survival skill people like us needed in this world. It was usually Channing's job to deliver it, but tonight he didn't even crack a smile. A muscle twitched in his jaw, and he attempted to sit up. Pain etched his features, and I held out a hand.

"Don't," I warned him.

He groaned, eyes locking on mine. "They own everyone in this city. You're working in their fucking hospital, Cate."

"It's not the same thing." I couldn't accept that. I was helping people. I was undoing the Gage family's damage. I stared at my brother. "You need to get out."

His laugh was hollow. "You think it's that simple? There's only one way out, but unfortunately, it looks like I'm going to live."

Cold fear twined around my heart until I thought it might shatter. "Channing—"

The arrival of the surgical team cut me off. I backed out of the room, trying to remember how to breathe.

Haley stepped beside me, assessing me like *I* was in triage. "They'll take care of him." She wrapped one arm around my shoulder.

I knew that. Here, he was safe, but out there?

"He's involved with the Gages." I needed to say it. I needed to hear it.

"I know." She hesitated for a moment. "You know there's nothing you can do, right?"

There's nothing you can do should be tattooed on her forehead. It would save her the trouble of saying it, which she did *a lot* when it came to Channing. But this time, it was different. This time, there was no coming back.

"Why don't you take off?" she suggested.

I squeezed my eyes shut and shook my head. Leaving would be worse. My thoughts couldn't wander too long at work. Here, I needed to be focused on what was right in front of me. "I need to do that blood draw."

"You sure?" Her lips pinched when I nodded, but we were too short-staffed for her to argue.

I felt numb as I made my way to the other side of the ER. Each step I took away from the surgical suite, my heart raced faster instead of slowing. I ignored it as I gathered the child's chart and headed to do my job.

That was all I could do. There was no other choice. Not that I was ever very good at making choices. One of the many reasons I was good at what I did. There wasn't a second guess in emergency medicine. Lives were on the line.

Like Channing's life.

I shook the thought from my head as I stepped into the exam room. The little girl, only four, was cuddled in her mother's arms on the bed, eyes glued to the television in the corner. Her mom looked up, sighing with relief. They'd been waiting a while. Normally I might feel badly about that, but tonight I envied their safe cocoon.

"Sorry for the wait."

"It's okay," the mom said, but she sounded tired. That's how I'd felt before shit hit the fan tonight.

Behind me, the bright sounds of a cartoon were completely at odds with my pounding heart. I asked a few routine questions as I pulled on a fresh set of gloves.

The little girl burrowed into her mother's arms as I took the stool by the bed.

"What are those for?" she whimpered, studying the tubes in my hand with suspicion. Her eyes widened as I leaned to tie the tourniquet around her tiny arm and she jerked away. "It's going to hurt! What is it?"

Probably. Needles, like much of life, stung. Like finding out your kid brother had been shot. That he was a corpse walking. Because owing Lachlan Gage was a death sentence. I forced a smile. "I'm going to tell you everything I'm doing, okay?"

Her dry lower lip trembled. *Suspected dehydration*, I reminded myself. A life I could save. Right here in front of me. Unlike the one down the hall.

The one I was responsible for now that Gran was gone.

"This is going to pinch just a little but will make you feel better, okay?" I asked the girl, holding out the rubber tourniquet.

When she eventually nodded, I gently reached out and wrapped it around her small arm, careful to keep the rubber over the sleeve of her shirt so it pinched less. I tugged one side over and under the other, and the girl's chin quivered but she didn't jerk away again.

I took the time to explain everything I was doing, gaining the little girl's trust inch by inch, and eventually we were done. Blood drawn and IV fluids dripping.

"Thank you," the mom said softly. Her shoulders sagged.

"The hard part is over," I promised.

The little girl cowered into her mother, and my heart broke a little. It would pass. Tomorrow, she wouldn't even remember this. She would be home. She would be safe. But for kids like Channing, like *me*, there had never been a home. There still wasn't. Channing was the closest thing I had to a family—to a home. And tomorrow, he would be recovering in a hospital bed, and he definitely wouldn't be *safe*.

Haley appeared as I dropped off the specimens I'd collected. Her face was drawn, and my heart nearly stopped until she said, "They got everything. We're just waiting for a bed to open up."

"Can I talk to him?" She was the charge nurse, and I was on shift. I waited for her to order me to another room or to encourage me to head home for the night, but thankfully she didn't.

"He's out of it," she warned me. "Garcia gave him morphine."

"Good," I said grimly. "Maybe he'll be honest for once."

Getting him to confess to how this happened was the only way I might find a way to help him. I yanked off my gloves, balled them up, and tossed them in the waste container nearby. I sucked air into my lungs until they burned before turning to walk slowly toward the VIP rooms.

He owed Lachlan Gage money. If this was about debt, we could figure it out. I wouldn't allow Channing to lose his life over money, and that's what working for the Gage family meant. I didn't have much. I didn't have any savings, really. But I did have one thing that might be valuable. I wasn't sure it was enough. I wouldn't know until he opened up.

A security guard nodded at me as I approached the recovery room, and I forced myself to swallow, my mouth dry, before walking in.

I reached his side, and Channing gave me a weak smile from under his oxygen mask.

"How much do you owe?" I asked, my voice calmer than I felt.

He fumbled for the mask and lifted it to speak. "It's too late."

Because he was already in too deep—the wound on his shoulder proved it.

"Let me worry about that." I rubbed the inner band of my ring.

Channing's eyes tracked the movement and narrowed. "Cate." He shook his head, guessing what I was thinking.

My mother's ring. It was special. The only possession I'd had after the accident my parents died in when I was two. The ring was the only piece of that life. It had passed from foster home to foster home, tucked safely in the bottom of whatever trash bag I'd been given for my latest move. I had never dared wear it until Gran had spotted it the night she took me in. She'd encouraged me to unpack, even given me a dresser—the first I'd ever had. It was the worst and best day of my life. She had seen the ring and told me to wear it, to never take it off. I'd tried to explain why I couldn't bear to see it. Why I'd hidden it in every home, afraid it would be lost or stolen. Afraid that the only piece of who I truly was would be taken from me, too.

And then she had said the words that changed my life. "You are safe here. Wear the ring to remember that. Wear the ring because you survived."

I'd never had the heart to get it appraised. I didn't want to know if the emerald in the center was genuine or how much it was worth. Knowing that might make it too tempting to do precisely what I was considering now, especially during those times when the only food in my fridge was pickle juice. The ring reminded me that I could survive anything in those moments. I never took it off like she said, but for Channing…

"I can get the money. How much?" I repeated.

His already pallid face blanched. "You can't get involved with Lachlan Gage."

I shook my head, crossing my arms. "*You* got involved with him, so what choice do I have?"

"Cate, no. You don't understand." He lifted his head, panic on his face. His mouth opened and closed several times before he finally choked out more nonsense. "Gage isn't what people think he is."

"He's not a rich asshole with more guns and money than human decency?" I snorted, but he didn't answer. He just sank back onto the bed and stared at the wall with vacant eyes. The change in his demeanor was enough to make me dare to ask one more question. "What is he, then?"

He wasn't making sense. His jaw tightened, eyes glazing slightly. Morphine in action. So much for it loosening his tongue.

I couldn't lose Channing. I refused. We would survive. I would give up my ring for that. I would give anything to ensure that.

I set my shoulders in determination. "Fine. Don't tell me. But I'm not going to let you get killed."

"Cate!" He tried to shove himself up, but pain sent him crumbling back down. He called my name one more time as I left the room.

I marched toward the nurse's station, where Haley was bent over, deep in conversation with one of the EMTs who had brought Channing in. A gun was sealed in a plastic bag on the counter. As I approached, I saw Channing's name written on its label. It was evidence. Not that it would ever wind up in the hands of the police.

Just one of the many accommodations Gage Memorial and its private
EMS made for their deep-pocketed benefactor. No. My brother was
working for the Gage family, which meant that gun would be given
back to him when he was deemed well enough to go and try to get
himself killed again. I had to do something.

"We found a bed for…" Haley trailed away when she saw my
face.

"Where was the shooting?" I asked the medic.

He shared an uneasy look with Haley. "Waverly."

"Specifically." I had no idea where to find Lachlan Gage or the
rest of his family. No Gage had ever been treated here despite the
alarming number of their associates that wound up in our beds—or
in the morgue. Tracking any of them down was a long shot. I probably
wouldn't even get close enough to see Gage himself, let alone speak
with him. He was notoriously private. No photographs. Not when
the Gages owned the newspapers and everything else. But even in
the age of everything being on the internet, they weren't. People
who spoke out about his family business had a habit of disappearing.

So no one ever did.

"Crossroads of Waverly and St. Charles. In front of the Avalon
hotel." He paused, a battle waging in his eyes. "You do not want to
go down there. Gage owns the Avalon."

What didn't Gage own in this city?

The medic held out a hand. "Look, it's not safe. You—"

"Thanks," I stopped him. Reaching over the counter, I grabbed
the phone and punched in a number.

"What are you doing?" Haley asked quietly.

I ignored her question. When this came down on me, I didn't
want her caught up in it, too. She asked again as someone picked up
on the other line. "This is Cate Holloway at Gage Memorial. I need
you to send an officer down here."

Haley cursed. I half expected her to disconnect the call, but she
didn't. "I hope you know what you're doing," she said when I hung
up. "When Garcia finds out…"

"When Garcia finds out what?" his baritone interrupted from

behind us.

I tilted my head for her to go. I would take the fall for this. Spinning around, I faced him. "I reported my brother for being involved in a shooting and for possession of an unregistered firearm."

I had no idea how deep Channing's debt to the Gages went, if they would care enough to get the charges dismissed, or if the police would drop them on their own. But for now, Channing would be protected—at least long enough for me to do what I needed to. I would find a way to pay his debt. Whatever the cost.

Fury gripped his features. "That's against policy."

"I do not give a shit whose name is on the side of this building or what deal your team has worked out with those monsters," I hissed at him. "You might be okay with having blood on your hands, but I am not going to let my brother get sucked into this."

I waited for him to speak, his face growing redder with each second that passed. "I think you need to take a few days off, Miss Holloway. Your recent trauma is affecting your ability to think clearly."

I'd expected that. In fact, I was hoping for it. "I'll finish my shift."

"No," he said firmly. *"Now."*

Even better.

CHAPTER TWO

Waverly Avenue wasn't what I expected.

I stood on the southeastern corner of where it crossed with St. Charles and stared up at the Avalon, a hotel I'd avoided my whole life. This was where the medic said Channing had been shot. I'd always pictured this part of town as dismal, seedy, *dangerous*. And it had been...until I reached the crossroads.

There, the smell of the city had shifted from exhaust and grease to the florid citrus of the sweet olive bushes planted in oversize pots outside the hotel.

The hotel's glazed white terra-cotta facade gleamed like a bright jewel in the ink-black night. Stone garlands draped the arched entrance. Gold carpet swathed its massive stone staircase, and half a dozen windows with gilt etchings glimmered on either side of it. I looked around for signs of the shooting, for some indication that I wasn't hallucinating, but the street was eerily quiet. The silence crept across my skin, urging me toward the safety of the Avalon's golden lights. But it was the anger still burning in my stomach, as hot as a yawning pit in hell, that spurred me toward the door.

My brother was lying wounded in a hospital bed, and this place had the nerve to look like the Ritz.

I'd made it to the top step, only feet from the entrance, when the rotating door spun and a tall, dark-haired man with a square jaw dusted with stubble stepped into the night air and looked directly at me.

Fear gripped my chest, and I froze. Shit. I'd at least hoped to make it inside before getting caught.

The man was dressed entirely in black, his jacket hooked over his shoulder with his index finger. He didn't say anything—just polished a glossy red apple on his sleeve and studied me with an intensity that sent a shiver down my spine.

I glimpsed a flash of white teeth as he took a bite. The apple's flesh snapped with a *crack* that sent another thrill through me—a side effect of being in dangerous territory.

Or maybe it was the man himself, because I couldn't tear my gaze away from his hooded eyes. From his mouth. The way he leaned ever so slightly in my direction. Was he a hotel guest? That was probably wishful thinking, given where I was. My heart fluttered like butterfly wings in my chest, waiting on what felt like the edge of a cliff for…something.

Say something.

But I couldn't speak, couldn't move. I was riveted to the spot.

The handsome stranger cocked his head as if he was waiting, too, giving me a better glimpse of high cheekbones as sharp as his brutal jawline and a pair of full, sculpted lips. Green eyes, the color of soft jade, raked down my body. His gaze, while still assessing, was so intimate that it felt like he was slowly stripping me of my white romper and sneakers.

I swallowed, shifting on my feet as he studied me. At least I'd changed out of my scrubs. But in my casual clothes, it was clear that I didn't belong anywhere near what was obviously a five-star hotel.

When he took a step toward me, I spotted tattoos curling under his rolled-up sleeves. Broad shoulders that hinted at the muscled torso hidden under his shirt caught my attention next for an entirely different reason: the harness strapped over them. My throat knotted when I saw twin pistols holstered under his arms.

A guard. My stomach dropped to my toes. I'd walked right up to a guard—an *armed* guard.

"And who might *you* be?" His voice was deep and smooth, as

though he was delivering a sinful invitation rather than a simple question.

I just stared at him, trying to decide if I should lie. Everything about this man screamed *dangerous*.

He arched a dark brow, drawing my attention back to those searching, wary eyes.

"Cate." My name burst out of me like he'd ordered me to tell him instead of simply asking. "Cate Holloway."

Why the hell was I telling this man my full name? He was armed, and I was in Gage territory. I supposed he'd know what to engrave on my tombstone.

"Are you lost, Cate Holloway?" His teeth clicked on my name, and I found myself biting my lower lip. Was it just second nature for him to ooze danger and sensuality, or was he trying to lower my defenses?

Lifting my chin, I looked directly into his sparkling eyes. "I'm looking for Lachlan Gage."

"Really?" He blinked, and that grin flattened into a line. "About what?"

I swallowed. "A personal matter."

"Personal?" His eyes lit with interest.

"Yes. As in, it's none of your business."

"In that case"—he took another suggestive bite of apple—"*no*."

Irritation blazed through me, temporarily liberating me from my uneasiness. "I'm not leaving until I see Lachlan."

He shrugged. "Then tell me why you wish to speak to him."

It wasn't like I could force my way around him, even if he wasn't armed to his perfect white teeth. I took a deep breath. "My brother," I said. "I need to talk to him about my brother."

"Tonight?" He waved a hand around, giving me a view of another tattoo, this one covering his forearm to his knuckles. I'd never seen anything like it. Symbols and words in a language foreign to me. "It's hardly business hours. Make an appointment."

I doubted Lachlan Gage offered those.

I crossed my arms, trying to look impatient. "This can't wait."

"Can't wait?" he repeated in a bemused voice.

My brother was lying in a hospital bed while this asshole acted like tonight was completely normal. Had he been here during the shooting? Did he even care that people had been hurt? He had to know. Fury blazed in my chest. "That's why I'm here. It's a matter of life and death that we come to an understanding."

"I see." He thought for a moment as he stretched his neck. Then he moved closer, and my breath hitched. Would he grab me? Throw me back into the street? Or maybe drag me inside?

He smirked as if he'd heard my thoughts, then tossed the apple in a nearby waste bin.

This man was *thoroughly* aware that he was messing with me.

He turned toward the door. "Follow me and *don't* wander off."

I scrambled after him before he changed his mind—or I lost my nerve. This might be my only shot to save my brother. He paused as the door started to spin, waiting for me. My heart stuttered, but my brain knew better than to trust that gentlemanly gesture. He worked for Gage. He was no gentleman.

I didn't dare to look at him as he pressed into the compartment behind me, but in the tight space I was acutely aware of him, of the guns under his muscled arms, of the cedar-and-spice scent that surrounded him. I stumbled out, and he strode behind, unrolling his sleeves one at a time and refastening his cufflinks. Men like this didn't exist. The kind of men that walked through the world like they owned it. I kept sneaking glimpses of him like he might actually be a figment of my imagination.

He paused to slip on his jacket. "After you."

I mumbled a quick "thank you," stepped into the foyer, and stopped.

Seeing the hotel from the outside hadn't prepared me for how big it was inside. White marble floors so glossy that I could see my reflection stretched before us. Columns held up a ceiling that had to be at least thirty feet tall, and at the center of the cavernous foyer, a staircase curved to an upper level. Guests milled about, crossing to a bank of brass elevators or disappearing down corridors. Diamonds and pearls glittered everywhere I looked. Past the wealthy guests, beautiful paintings hung in gilded frames. Everything was elegant and timeless, far from the sleazy front for illegal activities I'd imagined.

"It's like a palace," I whispered.

He snorted, obviously amused at my assessment, but didn't say anything.

A server in a white jacket drifted toward us, extending a silver platter with a gloved hand. "Canapé?"

My stomach rumbled, reminding me that I'd been too busy to eat a damn thing all night, but I didn't trust anything here—not even the food. Before I could shake my head, my companion shooed the server away. He paused to face me. Looking deeply into my eyes, he warned me, "Don't eat or drink anything here."

I almost laughed before I realized he wasn't joking.

"Why?" I planted a hand on my hip and tipped my chin. "Because I don't belong at your fancy party?"

"Just…don't. This way," he murmured, pointing toward the elevator. "Stick close."

"I'm not going to run off."

"You would if you were smart," he said, his eyes flashing for a moment, "but we do stupid things for our blood, don't we?"

I shook my head. "He's my foster brother."

There I went again, giving him too much information. What was it about this guy?

"*Foster* brother?"

"He's family to me." I didn't say anything else this time. Let him make what he wanted of desperate orphan Cate Holloway and her troublemaker foster brother.

"I see," he repeated as if compiling mental notes on me. He pressed the down button. "Then I hope you make a strong case for him."

I held my breath as the doors slid open, half hoping he wouldn't join me in another enclosed space.

He did.

I trained my eyes on the elevator panel, watching the lights illuminate as we descended to the hotel's lowest floor, increasingly aware of my pounding heart. I was actually going to do this. I was going to go toe to toe with Lachlan Gage and save my brother.

Or die trying.

The doors opened, but he didn't step out. Instead, he held an arm across the threshold to keep them from closing.

I stared at the open doors, at his tattooed forearm, at the gold ring he wore, at the ink-black stone in its center, and my confidence flickered. I hadn't thought I would get this far. I'd been going purely on adrenaline and resolve.

"You just made it," he murmured. "He's only taking requests for the next hour."

"Requests?" I frowned. What the hell was he talking about?

"You aren't here because of the Equinox?" he asked slowly, adding, "Mabon?"

Now he was just talking in riddles. "I'm here because my brother is lying in a hospital bed with a gunshot wound he got in front of your fancy fucking hotel a few hours ago."

He went utterly still.

"And you already mopped up the blood."

A muscle worked in his jaw. "That was a regrettable situation but a misunderstanding."

"Was it?" My anger sparked back to life, and I grabbed hold of it before the ember faded. "I doubt it. But since I'm sure you're concerned, the other man that was brought in is in the *morgue*."

"Unfortunate." He glanced out the open doors. "A word of advice? Consider what you're willing to offer in exchange for your brother's life. My kind doesn't deal in mercy."

His...kind? *Criminals*. I swallowed and stepped out of the elevator. "What do you deal in?"

He swept one final look over me, and his lip curled ever so slightly before he answered, "Desire."

The word was dangerous on his lips. But as seductive as it sounded, warning prickled across my skin. I didn't have to ask what he meant by that, and he didn't bother to clarify. He strode out of the elevator. For a moment, I hesitated. I could get back in and push the button to the lobby. I could run. From here. From him. From everything that one word implied.

But I'd walked through hell before. I could practically be a tour guide. Clenching my hands at my sides, I followed him into the very depths of it.

Neon sconces illuminated the black walls, casting the armed guards lining the perimeter in garish light. He lifted a hand, and for a moment the room seemed to shimmer—likely the result of the smoke that curled from the many lit cigars, choking the air with a sweet, heavy scent. The room pulsed with an intoxicating energy from the mass of bodies crowded around tables and bars. Glasses clinked, and cards rustled. Cages hung from the ceilings, and dancers wearing nothing but strings of pearls danced to the low, sensual music that crept under it all, although no one seemed to notice.

I kept close to him as we wove our way through the crowd. Eyes followed us, a few patrons even opening their mouths to speak but falling silent at his stern face. Each step made my pulse and my thoughts race faster. My ring couldn't be worth much to a man who lived like this. I didn't have anything else. I doubted he wanted my shitty car, and I could barely pay the rent with my salary. I couldn't even afford to fix my broken air conditioner. But maybe the guard was right and Gage wasn't after money. Why would he need money when he had this?

But desire?

I tried not to think about what that meant.

We walked to the back of the room toward a heavy oak door. Two men, also dressed entirely in black, straightened as we approached. The shorter of the two was a redhead; the taller had silver hair shorn close to the scalp on one side, long on the other. He was about the same height as the man accompanying me, with an equally impressive build, even more tattoos, and a lip ring that matched his hair.

"I was wondering where you went." Lip Ring ran a hand through his hair, his eyes straying to me. He raised a brow but didn't ask.

"What are you doing here, Shaw?" my companion asked the red-haired man.

"Same thing you are." Shaw grinned at him. "It's—"

But he didn't so much as smile. "Get the fuck out of here. You were supposed to stay clear tonight."

Shaw squared his shoulders, his face twisting with a retort, but he didn't speak before he stalked away. When he was gone, the silver-haired guard held up his hands.

My guide barked at the other man, "Roark, I told you to keep him away tonight."

Roark shrugged. "He's not a kid anymore."

He didn't look pleased at that, but he tilted his head toward the closed door. "Are they in there?"

Roark looked at me one more time before he answered, "Yeah. The client is here."

Finally, he nodded at me. "Check her bag."

I gripped my purse tightly. "No fucking way."

He looked at me, a smile ghosting across his face before vanishing. "I can take you back upstairs, if you prefer." We stared at each other before he inclined his head toward my purse.

I held it out, pinning a glare on Roark as he rifled through it. "Nothing," he pronounced and handed it back to me. "Should she be—"

"She asked for an audience. I can't refuse." He seemed annoyed about this, like I'd tricked him into bringing me down here.

"Now is not a great time," Roark warned him.

But he gripped my elbow and steered me toward the door. "Sounds like the perfect time."

There was no turning back now.

CHAPTER THREE

A man lay crumpled on the floor under a single flickering overhead light. Two men in dark clothes—more guards, by the looks of them—stood over him.

A massive executive desk sat in the middle of the room, completely bare save for a bowl of apples placed in one corner like a macabre version of a classroom.

But it was the men gathered on the other side of the desk that stopped me in my tracks.

A collection of brutal beauty, each was dressed in a suit, as though they could hide their true natures behind fine clothing. They were all younger than I would have expected. Not a single one looked a day over thirty. No wonder they had no issue getting kids like Channing mixed up with them.

The one at the center of the group scanned us as we entered. He was handsome, in a cruel way, except for the sneer he wore. He looked powerful. Savage. Was this who I'd come to see? I waited for him to take a seat behind that desk, waited for him to pounce.

But he looked at the man beside me. "It's about time, Lach."

It took me a moment to process what he meant. My eyes widened as it hit me. The man I was with was not a guard. He was not some obedient lackey.

"You're…" *Lach.* He was Lachlan Gage.

Horror laced with icy fear slithered through me. Unhinged. Vicious. Merciless. That's what they called him. I'd followed him blindly, and now he had me trapped.

A smirk hooked his lips. "You really didn't know, did you?"

I couldn't speak. I simply stared.

He knew what I wanted. He knew why I was here. But he leaned closer and whispered, "I'll be with you in a moment." He winked. Straightening, he crossed the room and settled into the desk chair like a throne. "What is this about?"

One of the men moved closer and whispered in his ear. Gage's eyes darted to the other men in the room as he listened, his expression unreadable. When the man stepped away, Gage sat back, his fingers steepled under his chin.

"Do you know what happens when you break my rules?" he asked the man on the floor in a surprisingly soft voice.

He whimpered in response, rising to his knees with clasped hands. "Please. It was a misunderstanding."

"Now, Martin, you know that isn't true." Gage shook his head and nodded to the man standing next to him. "You broke the law."

"Please. I will never do it again." Martin switched tactics. "If you give—"

"I suspect you won't, because another offense will mark you for the Hunt."

Martin shrank toward the floor, his face contorting with pure horror at the strange threat.

Gage lifted his hand to the other man I'd initially thought was him. "Would you like to decide his fate, MacAlister? You are a guest."

MacAlister stepped forward, brushing an invisible fleck from his suit jacket. In the dim light, he looked like a lawyer approaching the stand. He frowned as he gazed down at Martin. The other man shrieked, which seemed a little like overkill. What was MacAlister going to do? Force him to give a statement? Cross-examine him?

"Right or left?" he asked, and my heart began to race. "You must have a preference."

"*Please.* I'll do anything."

MacAlister chuckled, shaking his head like it was some inside joke.

My stomach clenched. Were they going to kill this man in front of me?

One of the guards yanked Martin to his feet and shoved him forward. He folded in half onto the desk, his begging turning to desperate sobs.

"Choose," MacAlister said. "Or I will choose for you."

Martin began to shake. "*Please*. Don't. My family…"

"Your family would agree with me," Gage snarled.

"I guess he doesn't have a preference." MacAlister pulled something from his pocket, and bile rose in my throat when I caught a flash of steel.

"N—" I started to cry out, but the protest died in my throat when Gage shot a sharp look at me. Ever so slightly, he shook his head.

I clamped a hand over my mouth, even as every instinct in me screamed to stop this.

MacAlister pinned Martin's hand to the desk and brought the knife to it. I squeezed my eyes shut, trying to keep myself still. But I couldn't block out the sounds: Martin pleading, then screaming. The wet splintering sound of blood and bone. And then…silence.

I forced myself to open my eyes, forced myself to look. Blood pooled on the desk, dripping onto the floor where Martin's unconscious body lay. This time, I couldn't stop myself. I moved without thinking. Dropping to the ground next to him, I swiftly unhooked the strap of my purse. I felt their eyes on me as I wrapped it around Martin's wrist like a tourniquet to slow the bleeding.

"Interesting," MacAlister said with a laugh. "Is she next?"

I looked up at him. "Fucking monster."

The men began to murmur, but Gage held up a hand. "The matter has been dealt with. Get rid of him," he ordered like he was telling them to take out the trash. Then, his attention shifted and landed directly on me.

"What about her?" MacAlister pressed.

"She is mine." He held my gaze for a long, heated moment, then looked to them. "The night is young. Enjoy it. *Elsewhere*."

No one argued as they made their way from the room.

"Careful," I barked as one bent to pick up Martin. I looked at Gage. "He needs medical attention."

"He'll have it." He nodded to his man.

I barely trusted myself to speak as the door shut behind us. I steeled myself as I stood, determined to be brave. But as I approached his desk, the scent of blood overwhelmed me.

"If I wanted him dead, he would be dead," Gage said as if reading my thoughts.

It was a fact and a warning rolled into one. One order was all it would take, and I would be the next body carried out of here.

I ignored the warning. "You maimed him!"

"I did not touch him."

"You allowed that bastard to maim him."

"MacAlister." His lip curled on the name. "He has a taste for cruelty, but custom dictated I allow him to step in. It's hard to explain."

"Try impossible." I shook my head. "You could have stopped him."

"Perhaps, but if you knew the crime that man committed, you would be reaching for the knife yourself. However, you didn't come here to condemn my customs. You came to make a deal." He sat back in his chair, completely unconcerned with the bloody mess before him. "Let's hear it."

"You already know why I'm here," I said through gritted teeth. "My brother."

He shook his head. "But now you've had time to consider your offer."

"Channing owes you something. Money, maybe?" I took a deep breath. "I came to pay it."

"Channing sent you?" he asked, a little surprised.

"No." I gave him a cold smile. "As I told you, he's in the hospital, and after that, he'll be in jail. So it might be easier to work with me than him."

Gage lifted a brow. "The hospital doesn't call the police. If someone there—"

"*I* called the police," I interrupted. "And they suspended me for doing it. I'm sure once you call them, I'll be fired."

"Doctor?"

"Nurse." I squared my shoulders.

He studied me closer. "I should have guessed from your medical theatrics. Unfortunately, your brother has sealed his own fate. I can do nothing."

"What?" It exploded out of me. I'd just watched this guy order someone to cut off another man's hand. I didn't buy that excuse for a second. It was just another twisted game.

He continued, "Channing should have followed orders."

Something reckless took hold of me. I lurched a step forward and pointed to the blood on his desk.

"Orders like that?" My voice shook, but I was past caring.

"He broke the rules." For a moment, he almost looked apologetic, but I knew better than to trust that. "Channing stole food. He didn't deny it. Not that it would matter. He is guilty, and there's nothing I can do."

My mouth dropped open. "Food," I repeated. Even after what I'd witnessed, I refused to believe that...to believe anyone could be so cruel over so little. "He stole *food*, and you're going to kill him for that?"

"Kill?" Gage looked up at me, his tone shifting to bitter amusement. "I have no plan to kill Channing. Is that what he told you?"

Not exactly. "Well, he's already been shot."

"The shooting was a misunderstanding."

"Because that makes me feel better. What else do you *plan* to do to him?"

"He will pay the price. He knows what he owes."

"And what is that?" I demanded.

"His life but not his death."

I stared at him, waiting for the punch line. When it didn't come, my mouth hung open. "You can't be serious. You think he owes you his *life*?"

"I am serious." He pushed back in his chair and stood, rising to his full and considerable height. "You should leave."

Every instinct in my body shouted at me to shrink, but I held my ground. I wasn't weak, regardless of what he thought. Being horrified at what these men had done to Martin wasn't weak. It was human. I could feel, unlike these monsters. And *I* had walked into Gage's office. *I* had faced him. I had survived worse than this brute. I was strong, and he wouldn't cow me.

His head tipped, interest lighting in his eyes at my defiance. "Will there be anything else?"

I swallowed, forcing myself to voice my deepest fear. "Please," I said softly. "He's all I have."

"Then I would advise you to be more careful with your possessions, Cate." He plucked an apple from the bowl on his desk, tossed it in the air, and caught it. "Let's try again, shall we? What would you offer for your brother's life?"

My hands shook as I touched the ring. I'd vowed to never give it up, but I would. For Channing. I held out my hand. "I have this."

His eyes flashed, his gaze dropping to the ring with faint surprise. He took my hand, stroking a thumb across my skin, and paused at the emerald ring. He studied it for a moment, eyes narrowing, something unreadable moving behind them. Hope blossomed in my chest, only to wilt when he said, "It's worthless."

"It's valuable to me."

"Then I suggest you keep it on before you offend me by offering cheap trinkets in exchange for a life. Besides, as I said, Channing doesn't owe me money." He leaned over the desk, tattooed hands splayed across the wood. "You said this was a matter of life and death—now act like it. What would you give in exchange for your brother to be free of his debt to me today?"

"Anything." Tears slipped down my cheeks. "I would give *anything.*"

"Even your soul?" he asked quietly.

"Don't be ridiculous—" I started, but he cut me off.

"Would you trade your life for your brother's? Would you trade your soul?" he pressed.

"Yes." In a heartbeat.

"And you're sure about that?"

I smashed my palms into the desk, bringing my face level with his. "I would do anything to save him from *you*."

"In that case..." He tossed me the apple. I barely caught it. "Eat something. Your stomach is growling so loudly, they can probably hear it upstairs."

I looked at the apple. All of this trouble, and all I was getting was a stupid *apple*. "Are you fucking serious?"

"Do you resist every effort to help you?" he asked.

My eyes narrowed. "What happened to don't eat or drink anything?"

"We're past that now, don't you think?"

I was done with this twenty-questions bullshit, done with this brutal world. If a stupid apple was all I could take from Lachlan Gage, I would.

I bit into it ferociously and glared at him, but he simply folded his arms across his chest, his smile wolfish. A strange sensation, like I was being watched from behind, prickled across the back of my neck. I looked over my shoulder, but no one was there. The prickle deepened as I chewed. I reached up to rub it, but it didn't go away. Instead, it burrowed like a hook, and I gasped, dropping the apple as I nearly choked.

"I should tell you that I prefer that you call me Lach." He picked up the discarded fruit and studied it for a moment before lifting it to that sinful mouth and sinking his perfect white teeth into the bite I'd just taken.

My heart nearly climbed into my mouth. The sight was both erotic and infuriating. I backed up a step, catching the edge of the desk when the room spun. "I'm leaving."

"No, you aren't," he said. He swallowed, and I watched his throat slide, watched that hint of shadow on his jaw tense and release, watched his tongue lick the juice lingering on his lower lip. "We need to discuss the terms of our arrangement."

"There is no arrangement." My heart pounded in my chest, beating faster and harder until I felt it everywhere. I steadied myself, but when I tried to turn away, I couldn't. My feet might as well have been encased in concrete. The tingle on the back of my neck returned, sharpening to a sting as though an invisible hook had caught me. My breath sped into shallow pants that heaved with my speeding heart. "What is happening? What have you done?"

"You made a bargain." Darkness glittered in his eyes as he watched me strain, trapped like a butterfly caught in a spiderweb. "Your soul for his—and now, you are *mine*."

Then, he snapped his fingers.

CHAPTER FOUR

I didn't have time to panic as a tapestry of colors wove around me, shimmering rainbow strands glinting with an edge of gold. I tried to scream, tried to move, tried to do anything, but I couldn't. My stomach dropped like a trapdoor, my arms splaying to catch my fall while the whole world transformed around me, and when its threads knit together once more, I was no longer standing in front of Gage's desk. I was standing in a garden.

It was not a well-kept garden, tended and orderly, or the polished halls of the Avalon. This was more like wandering into the Garden of Eden. Plants with large, fernlike leaves as tall as me grew in wild clumps around the bases of enormous willow trees. Their branches wept overhead, sunlight breaking through and falling in dappled patches over a plush blanket of grass. Vines covered with exotic crimson blooms as large as my hand snaked around the trunks of the trees. The air was humid but not suffocating, and the wind carried the herbal scent of flowers. Their perfume filled my lungs as I sucked in a deep breath—

Something jolted me out of my shocked state. This time, my legs moved, and I stumbled.

Or, rather, nearly fell on my ass.

A strong arm caught me, and I looked up to find Gage assessing me. I clutched him until the world felt solid beneath my feet again, until my head stopped spinning. But when it did, I opened my mouth to demand answers only to find myself once again shocked into silence as *he* transformed before me.

He was even more beautiful now, so beautiful that it almost physically hurt to look at him. New tattoos swirled into place, only to blink away again without settling onto his skin. His shoulders were broader, his cotton dress shirt barely containing them, and I swore he was a few inches taller. Except that would be impossible, right? His green eyes sparked with feral amusement as I gawked at him. And as I watched, his ears sloped into long, elegant points.

At that final transformation, I jerked out of his hold, needing to put as much distance between us as I could. "What are you?" I gasped, my eyes skittering around me but never quite letting him out of my sight. "Where am I?"

"You're in the Otherworld."

"The? Other? World?" I repeated haltingly, as if breaking the words apart might help it make sense. It didn't.

"My world," he clarified. "Although I suppose it's your world now."

His…world? No. I was hallucinating. Had to be. Because this wasn't happening. Things like this *did not happen.*

I gulped down the fear that shot into my throat and scanned his muscular body, his pointed ears. What *was* he? I resisted the urge to reach out and touch those ears, even if it would prove I wasn't hallucinating. Nothing good could come from touching him. I didn't really care what he was or where we were. I only cared about one thing. I planted my hands on my hips and forced myself to sound more defiant than I felt. "Take me back."

"I'm afraid that's impossible."

"Make it possible," I demanded.

"You made a bargain, or did you already forget?"

Wicked delight danced in Gage's jade-green eyes. He was a cat playing with a mouse. Any minute now, he would pounce.

The thought slashed a white-hot line through me. More magic or whatever trickery this was. I clamped down on the heat it produced, determined to channel it into something useful: anger. I could use it to keep moving forward, keep focusing on getting out of this situation. "I didn't—"

"I asked you what you would give for your brother's life," he reminded me. "You agreed to give yours."

Yes. I had. But I hadn't known what, exactly, he meant—or who I was dealing with. I still didn't know. "Okay, but I never agreed to this. Who goes around *actually* collecting souls as collateral?"

He waved that off. "I asked you three times," he said as if this fact alone sealed my fate. "You exchanged your life for your brother's." He paused and regarded me with lethal quiet. "Do you regret your choice?"

Yes. But also no, because I'd saved Channing. I bit down to keep my lip from trembling, to hold back tears that might douse that flame fueling me. Something told me not to show this man—or whatever he was—weakness.

"I can see you do." His shapely lips pressed into a line, but then he shrugged, his corded biceps straining against his shirtsleeves. "Unfortunately for you, it's nearly impossible to break a fae bargain."

My thoughts snagged on *nearly*. It took a minute to process the rest.

"F-f-fae?" I tripped over the word. Wrapping my arms around my middle, I stroked my ring with my thumb. I couldn't fall apart. Not now. Not *here*. "Like cute little garden pixies with wings? Is that what you are?"

His upper lip curled to reveal his sharp teeth, a guttural snarl rumbling from him. Fear flooded through me, and Gage's nostrils flared. My arms tightened as if I could physically hold myself together.

"Some of us have wings. Some of us do not," he said, the words tight and clipped. I didn't dare ask him which category he fell into. I didn't think I could handle it if he sprouted wings, too. "Few of us are cute…or little. And even those who are can be deadly. No one but humans would mistake us for little or cute, and the humans that do tend to *die*."

I drank in his massive body again. *Fae*. He was fae. I turned the word over again and again, but I still couldn't process it.

"It's best to remember that here."

My head bobbed again. "Here?" I blurted out. "You mean, the Otherworld?"

"It is always wise to remember that in the Otherworld, but especially wise to heed it at the Nether Court."

"There's a *nether* court? You're making that up."

Gage lifted a brow, looking like he was seriously considering strangling me. Then, he turned and walked away without another word. Perhaps because it was the last thing I'd expected him to do, I darted after him. Or tried to. I made it one step before my shoe caught in the mud and stuck. I cursed loudly enough that Gage paused, turning to watch as I pulled my foot out of the stuck sneaker. I didn't bother to salvage it. I doubted I needed footwear in a prison cell. Instead, I reached down, ripped off the other one, and tossed it on the ground before stalking toward him.

"I could carry you if you're having trouble," he offered in a low voice that sent my traitorous body clenching. More of his fae magic, screwing with my fight-or-flight response by targeting my hormones.

"I can take care of myself," I grumbled.

He looked down to my bare feet. "Noted."

He continued walking, but this time, I kept pace with him. The grass was cool and damp against my skin, almost pleasant enough to soothe me, but I surveyed the world around me with suspicion. A low-hanging willow branch drooped in our path, and before I could duck, Gage lifted it with one tattooed hand and gave me my first real glimpse of where he'd taken me.

I'd been impressed by the Avalon, but it was nothing compared to what lay ahead of me. It was a palace, constructed of black stone that sprawled in every direction, especially up. A pointed spire rose from its center like a spear thrust toward the sky, as if to keep heaven out—as if the two couldn't bear to touch.

Half walls and arcades extended to outbuilding after outbuilding. The compound spread as far as I could see like a never-ending labyrinth. Lancet windows glowed with green light, the colored glass a shimmering field of emeralds. It was like nothing I had ever seen before, and the sight of it hit me squarely in the gut. My eyes skirted to Gage, to those elegant, inhuman ears, to the power that shimmered around him like an aura. He belonged here in this strange world. He belonged to the same dark energy filling the air.

"This is the Nether Court," he said as I continued to stare. "Your new home."

I whipped toward him, his words snapping me from my daze. "I am not living here!"

"Is it not up to your standards?" He prowled a step toward me, the movement both graceful and lethal. "Is there a *problem*?"

"I can't." I forced the words out. "I can't stay in the Otherworld. I have responsibilities. A job. People who depend on me." The prickle at the back of my neck returned, digging deeper, until I reached up to rub it away.

"I believe you were on the verge of being fired and your brother was on his way to jail. It doesn't sound like you have much going on at the moment," Gage drawled, stalking closer. His tattoos swirled and moved distractingly on his skin. "Be honest, Cate. You're here because of your *foster* brother. You're an orphan. No family. You came alone to do something you knew was dangerous, so that tells me you have few friends, if you have any. No one knows you're here. I can do whatever I please with you. You would do well to remember that."

His words pressed in on me like a hand shoving me underwater, holding me there just to prove how vulnerable I was. He could save me, or he could drown me.

"And let's not forget Channing."

"Just leave him out of it." The words tasted like defeat, bitter and foreign.

"I will so long as you remain here." He nodded. "We can discuss the terms of the arrangement later."

I scowled back at him, but he only laughed and strode toward the front entrance. He didn't wait for me as he pushed open the arched door and went inside. I followed, stopping to stare at the twenty-foot-high doorframe and the massive oak door that he'd just opened like it was any normal entrance. Reaching for it, I tried to push it closed. It didn't budge. I might as well have been trying to move a brick wall. Giving up, I pivoted to the foyer and gasped.

I'd walked into a fairy tale. The entry opened into a large foyer two stories tall. Gold veins split the black marble floors, and a sweeping staircase with brutal spindles spiraled to the second story. Hanging in the center was a golden chandelier with a thousand points, each ending in a tiny orb of light. To the left was a sitting room of some sort, its black leather couches spaced evenly before an unlit hearth so large I was sure I could walk inside it.

Before I could investigate further, Gage coughed impatiently.

I turned on him. "Is there a problem?"

"Tonight is the Equinox."

I looked at him blankly. This was the second time he'd brought up this nonsense. "You might as well be speaking in Greek."

He glowered at me. "It is the autumnal Equinox, and we are hosting, hence why I have the distinct pleasure of entertaining assholes like MacAlister. I'd rather not leave him to run amok in my city."

"Don't let me stop you. Just point me in the direction of home."

He snorted. "I will show you where you can wait for me."

I folded my arms. "I'm not following you anywhere."

"I don't have time for this," he muttered. "If you want to stand around and wait—"

"I've never been kidnapped before," I cut him off. "I'm sorry if I'm inconveniencing you."

His mouth twitched. "Kidnapped? What an *ugly* word."

"It fits," I snapped back. "Where shall I wait, *my lord*? The dungeon?" But despite the fire in my voice, icy dread filtered into my veins.

This time, his lips lifted into a smile. "We don't have a dungeon." He paced toward me. "If I decide to keep you shackled, I have far more interesting ways to bind you."

I blanched under the weight of his gaze, uncertain if that was a threat or a promise. Gathering up the remaining shreds of my courage, I lifted my chin. "If you expect me to sit around and wait for you like a dog, you'll find yourself disappointed."

I would remain until I could find a way out, but I wasn't going to let him see my fear. Showing fear was more dangerous than showing weakness. Fear could be exploited. Another hard lesson learned.

"Such a sharp tongue"—his eyes studied my mouth, darkening slightly as wisps of shadows swirled around us—"for such a weak creature."

"Oh, I forgot that I'm supposed to be cowering in fear." I smiled at his blink of surprise. "Would you like me to fall on my knees and grovel for your mercy?"

"That won't be necessary. Although, if you want to get on your knees..." He swept a hand toward the floor in invitation.

"You're a pig!"

"I've been called worse, princess." He shrugged. "Feel free to explore. I'll find you when I get back."

Was he actually going to leave me here in this strange place without any clue where I was *or* where I was going?

"What if I get lost?" I hated the tremble that splintered my words.

"You won't." A hint of that sinful, unnaturally beautiful smile.

"What if I escape?"

He didn't even blink at the suggestion. "You won't."

"You can't just—"

He snapped his fingers and vanished.

"Asshole!" I hurled the insult at the empty space where he'd stood a moment ago.

Couldn't escape? We'd see about that. I started toward the door, making it two steps before it snicked shut with an ominous *thud*. I rushed to it, yanking on the knob but finding it as immovable as before. I smashed my fist into the oak as hard as I could. And nearly broke my hand.

Pain sliced through my arm as I cradled my throbbing hand to my chest. The door wasn't an option, but there had to be another way out.

This was no time to panic. No, that was probably about fifteen minutes ago when he'd stolen me away to a fae underworld. All because I'd let my guard down for a moment, blinded by a heady combination of desperation, curiosity, and his stupid smirk. I wasn't sure what was more dangerous: my circumstances or that smile.

CHAPTER FIVE

With no idea how long I had until he returned, I didn't waste any time. Dashing into the adjoining sitting room, I grabbed a candlestick from a table near the door and hurled it at the green glass window. It bounced right off. A string of curses fell from my mouth.

Just then, a soft howl whispered through the air, and I whipped around only to find myself alone. I shivered as my unease sent me out of the room and deeper into the house.

My footsteps echoed through the empty, cavernous rooms, each colder and more elegant than the last. I stumbled into a dining room with a black stone table that stretched to fit twenty seats. Silver candelabras dotted its center, surrounded by crystal bowls spilling over with ivy and cream-colored peonies in full bloom. Their powdery scent filled the air, the softness at odds with the brutal, polished beauty of their surroundings. I started toward the hall joining the far end of the room, but as soon as I took a step closer to the table, a shimmering aura glimmered around me, and out of nowhere, gold platters laden with plump strawberries, velvet-kissed peaches, and glossy apples appeared. I didn't dare touch any of it. I'd learned my lesson about taking food from the fae. Hurrying forward, I heard another soft wail whisper through the room and froze.

"Is someone there?" I called out. Silence answered me, somehow more disconcerting than the creepy, invisible laughter that seemed to be following me.

I continued through the great rooms and sprawling corridors, looking for any way out and finding none. And if the front door was locked...I was stuck.

Gage hadn't needed to put me in a dungeon because this place was a prison.

And he was a fae. But not like any of the books I'd read. Those fae didn't carry guns. They didn't live in cities like New Orleans. But they *did* steal humans away to their world and trap them there.

What had I done?

"You saved Channing," I said to the empty hallway, but it did little to boost my resolve. I wanted to be angry at my foster brother for not telling me the truth about Gage and what he really was, but would I have even believed him? I barely believed myself. But my still-throbbing hand was proof that this wasn't a nightmare, and even though part of me wanted to sink to the floor and cry, it wouldn't do me any good. I'd been in terrible positions before, and I'd gotten out of them. I knew the company of monsters well. I wouldn't let him scare me.

I was just considering trying my luck at climbing over a balcony into the wild garden surrounding the house when I heard something. Not the hollow, aching wail from before, but a low, amused chuckle that scraped across my already fraying senses and sent me whirling around to find Gage watching me. His tie hung loosely around his unbuttoned collar, giving me a glimpse of more swirling, shifting tattoos. His smile spread as our eyes met, and the sight of it turned me liquid.

No. *Molten.*

It was rage, this fire burning inside me, and some dark, unnatural magic. It had nothing to do with Lachlan Gage and his smug grins and his stupid, perfect face.

"I wouldn't advise that. You're far safer in here than out there."

He was back. Not that I could be sure he was any less dangerous than that disembodied laughter I kept hearing, but at least I could see him. "Party over?" I asked in the chilliest tone I could muster.

"Unfortunately, no, but Roark is handling things." He scanned me as if looking for clues about what to do with me. "I didn't want to be rude and leave you here all alone."

I frowned. "Don't pretend to worry about me. I'm a prisoner, remember?"

"You aren't a prisoner, Cate." He had the audacity to look amused at the thought.

"I. Can't. Leave." I bit out each word, since he seemed to struggle with understanding simple concepts. "That is the definition of prisoner."

Gage leaned against the wall, playing with a cufflink like we were discussing the weather. A tattoo snaked around his neck and disappeared under his collar. "There are matters to discuss. Arrangements to be made. I assumed you'd want a say in the terms of our bargain. You seem...opinionated."

"I didn't make a bargain with you. You tricked me."

His sculpted lips curved into a smile that nearly knocked the wind out of me. How had I ever mistaken him for human? No one looked like that. He was so beautiful that it was terrifying.

"You have a lot to learn about fae."

Like *everything*, but I wasn't about to let him distract me. "So, you admit that you tricked me?"

"I didn't say that." He raked a hand through his ink-black hair. "I didn't trick you, Cate. You offered yourself to me."

Fighting him was getting me nowhere, I realized. I had no idea why he'd traded Channing's soul for mine, but maybe somewhere very, very, *very* deep down, there was a shred of decency below that cold beauty. It was all I had to work with until I found a way out of this bargain.

"I was desperate." The words fell from my lips with resignation.

Gage shrugged a broad shoulder. "I know."

The question burning inside me leaped out before I could stop it. "Why?"

He mumbled something I didn't catch, then, "Why not?"

I waited for more, waited for some explanation as to why Gage had bothered helping me at all. If that's what he was doing. I couldn't be certain. Not while I was trapped in some Otherworld with no way back to my real life.

"Are you ready to discuss our bargain now?" he asked after a moment. "Or do you plan to continue demanding release?"

"Would it matter?"

"No."

"This bargain means Channing is free from you, from *this*." I stretched my arms to the strange world surrounding us. "Swear that you won't go after him ever again, and then we can discuss terms."

"It's a little late to be adding conditions," he said with dark amusement, "but very well. I swear I will not go after him as long as you uphold whatever terms we come to. Does that satisfy you?"

My end of the bargain. Belonging to Gage, giving him my soul. I raised my chin and met his gaze. "Better me than him."

Something dangerous flashed through his eyes, but he blinked, and it was gone as quickly as a bolt of lightning. He pushed off the wall and started down a corridor without another word. I stared after him for a moment before following. Gage stood a full head taller than me and walked twice as quickly, so I had to jog to catch up. My bare feet slapped against the dark marble, and he slowed but didn't stop.

"Where are you taking me?" I called after him.

"Stop dawdling, and you'll find out."

"Excuse me for not having fae superspeed."

He finally stopped, turning just enough to offer a feline smile. "My offer from earlier stands. I could carry you."

I glared back at him, ignoring the dangerous uptick in my heart rate under his scrutiny. *Deadly*, I reminded myself. "My legs work just fine."

"Debatable." He slowed his pace until we were walking side by side. "I'm showing you to your bedroom."

"Bedroom?" I repeated with a swallow.

He peered down at me. Had he smelled this good in the real world, or was it more fae fuckery?

"It's a place where you sleep," he said.

"Has anyone ever told you that you're a dick?"

His lips lifted at the corners. "Many a time. I've even let some of them live."

My stomach tumbled twice, but I merely returned the slight smile. I refused to blanch at his words, refused to give him even an ounce of satisfaction that he'd unnerved me. But I'd seen the holster he wore, even though I doubted he needed guns. Not with the strange magic he wielded, so powerful that he'd taken me into another world. Still, gun or magic, I was at his mercy here.

"Killing me now wouldn't be a very good return on investment."

He barked a laugh and gestured toward arched double doors that were intricately carved with intersecting vines and those strange symbols inked on his skin.

"Your quarters," he said. When I didn't budge, he sighed impatiently, pushed the doors open, and strode in. Warm light spilled into the dark corridor, easing my trepidation enough for me to follow.

A small gasp escaped my lips at the room that greeted me. It wasn't a dungeon. It was a sanctuary.

The walls were painted a warm, earthy green, and a huge, thick rug softened the marble floors. Gold sconces with real burning candles hung every few feet, explaining the glowing light. Overhead, the ceiling rose to a dizzying height, curved beams crisscrossing one another like the vines on the door. On the far side of the room, a bank of ivy-covered glass doors with arched points led to a stone balcony. And next to the doors…a bed.

A huge bed.

A bed that was not made for humans.

Four posters curved into a coronet over the massive bed. Gauzy curtains draped from the center to each rail, each held back by silk ropes. Rich, velvet bedding and dozens of pillows in shades ranging from emerald to dark evergreen were strewn in artful order over it. Across the room, a welcoming fire crackled in a stone hearth.

I stared at that bed, my hands clenching at my sides. It was beautiful. This entire place was beautiful in a horrifying, exhilarating way. Just like Gage himself. Just like the moment you realize you're in a nightmare but can't quite wake up.

If I was going to survive in this place, if I was going to survive him, I couldn't let my guard down.

"The bathroom is this way." He took a step toward an arched door.

"Wait!" I took a deep breath, steeling myself. "Let's just get this over with."

Gage stopped. His eyebrows knitted together as he studied me. "Get what over with?"

"Sleeping together," I said in a rush.

He blinked. "Excuse me?"

"I'm not stupid." I crossed my arms over my chest to cage my pounding heart. "There's only one reason you made that bargain. I know what terms you're going to ask for. You said you deal in *desire*."

"Oh?" He cracked his knuckles, and the tattoos twining his fingers fled at the sound.

"That's the arrangement we need to discuss." A lump knotted my throat, but I forced myself to speak, pointing to the bed. "So, if we're here, let's just get it over with. Please."

He didn't move. Nothing flashed in his eyes now. His features remained stony. Finally, he asked in a slow cadence, "Do you wish to sleep with me?"

"Does it matter?"

"I'll take that as a *no*." He fell silent for a moment. Finally, he snorted, continuing to survey me. "I suppose that's one term we can agree on. Sex is not part of our arrangement. No offense, but you're not my type."

My knees wobbled beneath me, and I fought the urge to collapse. Not from relief, exactly. I shoved the feelings down only to discover a new one burning on my cheeks. "I thought...the bedroom..."

"You are bound to me," he said seriously, "and my interest in you lies elsewhere, so I can assure you, I do not expect sex." He smirked. "Besides, do I look like I need to trick a woman into bed?"

Humiliation raged through me. I was going to catch on actual fire and burn to a crisp in front of him. It took sheer force of will to not bury my face in my hands and hide.

"There's another more practical purpose for taking you to your room," he said, breezing on. "Our Mabon celebration will continue at the court shortly. I assume you…don't want to attend."

I followed his gaze to my bare feet and fought a frown. "I do not. So what am I supposed to do? Just wait here for everyone to leave?"

"If you wish. They should all be gone in a few days."

My mouth fell open. "*Days?* I can't. I have to get back—"

"To your very important human life," he finished for me.

"It *is* important." Without thinking, I advanced on him, getting close enough to jab a finger into his chest. "I have a job."

"You no longer need one," he said breezily. "And as we've already established, you will not be going anywhere."

Panic gripped my heart. I couldn't just stay here. Bargain or not, he couldn't keep me here forever. "Please let me go," I whispered, allowing some of that desperation to leak through. Maybe that was the key to unraveling him.

He paused for a moment, his lips pursing like he was seriously considering the request. "No."

"Dick," I spat at him.

He smiled. Not the arrogant grin from earlier but a dazzling smile that lit up his whole face and made me forget for a second that I hated him. "Congratulations, princess. You're the first person to call me a dick twice and live."

"Stop calling me princess."

"Stop making demands."

We glared at each other, neither of us willing to look away.

"We'll finish this conversation in the morning." He sounded tired. Good. Maybe I could wear him down. Maybe he'd get so sick of me that he'd dump me back home.

If he didn't… My eyes lingered on the holsters under his arms. There had to be a reason that he carried them. Maybe even magic couldn't survive guns.

"You're staring," he accused.

My eyes snapped to his. "What am I supposed to do?"

"Take a nap? Unless you wish to throw more things at the windows? They're all warded." My mouth dropped open. How had he known? I thought of those hollow wails in the halls and shivered.

"It's up to you. I really don't care."

"Dick." I held up three fingers and smiled around the knot forming in my throat. I wouldn't let him see me cry.

"Charming," he muttered, already turning toward the door.

The tears came before it clicked shut.

CHAPTER SIX

I spent the night fighting sleep, terrified of what might happen when I closed my eyes. But I had pulled a full shift before coming here and barely slept before that. When the call of sleep became too heavy to resist, I dragged a heavy velvet armchair in front of the door, locked it, and collapsed on the chair. A sharp knock startled me awake what felt like a minute later, and I forgot where I was for a moment.

I stared at the door, wondering if I'd imagined the knock in the dreamless state between sleep and waking. But a muffled voice called, "I'd prefer not to break the door down. It's an antique."

Something told me he would dare to break it down, so I shoved the chair away from it. Drawing my shoulders back, I unlocked it.

Gage filled the doorway but didn't enter. His eyes skirted to the chair, his brow raising slightly, a smile ghosting over his lips. "Was there a problem with the bed?"

Heat flooded my cheeks. "Better safe than sorry."

His nostrils flared. "Locking your door will suffice."

"Will it?" I crossed my arms. "Why should I trust you?"

"You shouldn't." He shrugged, tipping his head in silent request.

I groaned and stepped to the side. "That was refreshingly honest."

"Not honest. A simple fact. I will assume that if your door is locked, you do not want it to be opened. Besides," he added, a wicked gleam in his eyes, "I can nip inside regardless of locks or whatever fortress you contrive."

"Nip?" I asked faintly.

He grinned and snapped his fingers.

The world swept from under us, but before I could scream, my feet found solid ground. My stomach churned as I stared around the dining room I'd explored yesterday. It wasn't empty now. Guards were stationed in the doorways, hands folded, eyes trained to some vacant spot in the distance. There were no guns in sight, but I suspected they had them holstered under their black jackets. The fact that they looked almost bored made them more menacing than if I could see their weapons.

Gage ignored them as he walked to the far end of the black stone table, where three place settings were laid. The silver-haired guard from last night at the Avalon—Roark, I recalled—looked up from his phone and gave me a silent nod hello. He was as huge as Gage now, maybe bigger, and he had those same pointed ears and strange tattoos. Handsome in a brutal way. He looked like he'd been chiseled from ancient stone, hewn from the primordial elements that made up the world. Gage stopped at the seat across from Roark and pulled out a chair but didn't sit. It took me a moment to realize he was waiting for me.

I didn't quite trust my legs yet after he'd used that finger-snapping trick on me. "Let me guess. Nipping?"

"It's more convenient than walking. We nip from here to there with a snap of our fingers." He held up his hand, and I shrank back a step, waiting to be whisked to another place, but he only laughed and gestured to the chair. "Breakfast is getting cold."

Platters heaped with sausages, eggs, and pastries appeared, and hunger rumbled inside me. I knew how long a human could survive without food. My stomach did not. "I think I prefer walking," I grumbled but started slowly toward the table.

"You'll get used to it."

Some of my appetite evaporated at the implication of those words. I'd get used to it because this was my new life, my new world. By the time I reached the seat, I no longer wanted to eat at all.

Gage piled his own plate full of food, frowning when I didn't do the same. He waved a hand, and a bowl of strawberries appeared between us. He picked it up and held it out.

I didn't move.

"It's perfectly safe to eat." He plucked a particularly large berry and bit into it as proof.

"I'm not hungry."

Across from me, Roark watched over his phone but didn't say anything. He also wasn't eating. I got the impression he was holding back a smile, though.

Gage took another strawberry. "Is that your plan, then?"

"Plan?" I tried to sound innocent.

"I assume you've been plotting how to get out of our bargain." He tossed a stem onto his plate. "I'd be disappointed if a hunger strike is the best you'd come up with."

The truth was that I'd come up with nothing. I had no idea where I was or how to get from his world to my own. That made plotting an escape damn near impossible. And then there was the matter of this bargain. Even if I could get out of here, what would stop him from tracking me down? Or going after Channing? I was stuck. For now.

I should let him think he won. Maybe he'd let his own guard down, let something slip. But I refused to act broken. "Do you really think I would tell you?"

I snatched up my fork and speared a sausage. But I didn't take a bite.

"So, you claim that you aren't pixies or garden gnomes," I mused out loud.

Roark, who'd just taken an unfortunately timed drink of coffee, spit it across the table. Gage frowned at the mess. With a wave of his hand, it vanished. "I thought we cleared that misapprehension up yesterday."

"Fucking *gnomes*?" Laughter choked Roark's voice.

"We didn't clear up anything." I brandished my fork at Gage. I still hadn't touched a bite. "You told me you were fae, which means jack shit to me. I'm just going off what I've seen in fairy tales."

His knife clattered to the table, a half-buttered scone forgotten on his plate. "Fae existed long before human stories. Our world was civilized millennia before yours—"

"You expect me to believe that?" I interrupted him.

"No." His mouth twisted. "I do not, considering that you've seen the truth with your own eyes and you're still acting like a brat."

A brat? I smiled widely at him. He had no idea. "I'm just trying to understand what you are and where I am and why the hell I never knew about any of this."

"Why?" Gage's eyes narrowed.

"Speed up the Stockholm syndrome?" I shrugged at his annoyed expression.

Roark barely covered a laugh with his hand, but Gage's gaze remained pinned on me.

"One question," he said finally.

I lifted a brow.

"You may ask one thing about us or our world," he said in a tight voice. It sounded like he was begrudgingly offering a kidney, not agreeing to something as simple as answering a question.

But I had gotten the short end of the stick with this bargain, so I shook my head. "Two."

"Two?" Gage repeated. "Are you *negotiating*?" He cursed under his breath.

"Would you rather I remain confused on the difference between a fae and a gnome?" I asked with mock sweetness.

He grimaced as he picked up his scone. "Fine. *Two*."

"What are fae, exactly?" I asked before he changed his mind and threw me back in my room.

"A species," he said dryly.

"That's not really an answer."

"A *magical* species." He sighed when I continued to stare. "How would you explain being human?"

Damn, he had me there. I studied the sausage on the end of my fork. "So, you're a *magical* species, but so far all I've seen you do is snap and move from place to place. Is that as far as your magic goes?"

"Pray that you never find out everything we can do, princess." The predatory smile that oozed across his face sent my pulse racing, my entire body tensing at the implied threat. "That was two questions. Happy?"

He hadn't really explained anything, but I found myself nodding anyway. Sooner or later, I would find someone willing to talk to me. For now, I zeroed in on Roark, pointing my sausage in the direction of his phone. "Does that actually work down here?"

"Hoping to call for help?" Gage guessed.

I ignored him. "My phone died. I couldn't charge it."

"No electricity but also no data." Roark leaned back in his chair, dropping the phone next to his empty plate. His tattoos barely moved, unlike Gage's, but he wore a similar ring. Maybe some type of family signet? Did every Gage associate wear one? Would Channing have?

Would I?

"That doesn't stop him from playing games on it all day," Gage said as he shoveled some eggs and toast onto my plate.

I continued ignoring him. "How do you charge it?"

"I don't actually live—"

"Enough," Gage cut him off. I wondered what Roark was about to let slip. Interesting. Maybe it would be easier to get information from him.

Gage redirected his annoyance at me. "You don't have more pressing concerns than your phone? I'm disappointed."

I bit off the tip of my sausage. He winced. Appeased, I glared at him. "If you really didn't kidnap me, let me leave."

"In such a hurry to go?" He reached for a gold-rimmed goblet.

"Yes."

"You offered your life in exchange for your brother's freedom," he reminded me…again.

I gripped my fork a little more tightly. "Are you saying I can never leave?"

"Since you seem intent on returning to your human life—which sounds rather boring, by the way—"

"It's not," I interjected. "I'm a fixed air conditioner away from total happiness."

"Whatever you say." He rolled those gorgeous green eyes. "Given your plea yesterday, I'd expected you to be slightly more grateful for my mercy."

I should never have let him know what Channing meant to me. Gage might be all but a stranger, but now he knew exactly which of my buttons to press.

Roark cleared his throat and rose from the table. "I'll leave you two to…talk."

Gage shot him an incredulous look, but Roark responded with a grin as he backed out of the room.

"What is he? Your bodyguard?"

"Bodyguard?" Gage repeated, lips twitching. "Do I need protection?"

My eyes fixed on the other armed guards in the room. "You tell me."

"You get used to them." He waved a hand. "But no. Roark is my penumbra." He sighed at my confused expression and raised the hand that wore the matching ring.

"Are those, like, your version of friendship bracelets?" I asked slowly.

He looked to the ceiling like he might find a fresh supply of patience there. "'Penumbra' means shadow. When an heir to the throne is born, a child born on the same day at the same time is chosen to be raised alongside him as a companion."

"And his family just…?"

"It's considered a great honor to be taken as a penumbra. He has lived here his entire life." He shrugged as though this was perfectly normal. Then again, he'd taken me. Apparently, the fae had no issues with abduction.

I pushed some food around my plate. "Sounds like he didn't have a choice."

"Don't feel sorry for him. A penumbra is second only to the one he serves. He is my right hand; moving against him is akin to treason. In my absence, he acts as me. He has as much freedom as I do."

That didn't sound like much, actually. I kept the thought to myself. "Must be nice."

Gage grimaced at my jab. Setting down his goblet, he reached into his pocket. "For you." He held out a black box.

Taking it tentatively, I opened the lid to find a gold chain. Hanging from it was a pendant of interwoven loops, at the center of which lay a sparkling black stone like the one in his ring. Up close, it seemed to drink the light into its endless depths.

"Is it onyx?" I asked, not touching it.

"The stone is an abismine. It's from my world."

Alarm bolted through me. Accepting anything from him was dangerous, but this... He wore this stone, as did Roark. Was this to mark his ownership over me in a way others could see?

"It's not dangerous," he said, picking up on the tension in my body. "And it serves a purpose."

He rose and stepped behind my chair. My hands shook as I reached back and lifted my hair, allowing him to slip the chain around my neck. My heart pounded when his fingers brushed my nape, my whole body too aware of that single touch. As soon as the clasp closed, I dropped my hair and angled myself away from him.

"And what is its purpose?"

"It connects you to me," he said. "Touch the stone, and you can call for me. Whatever you think, I will hear."

My eyes widened, but I quickly rearranged my face into a more neutral state. "Why would I want to do that?"

"Because you'll need a means to contact me when you are in your world—unless you wish to stay in the Otherworld forever and keep me company."

Hope bubbled inside me, but I tamped it down, afraid to let it show on my face. I'd seen enough of Lach to warrant caution about showing him my hand. "So, I *can* leave the Otherworld?"

"As long as you return as expected."

These were the terms of the bargain, I realized, and I needed to tread carefully. Speaking without thinking, without considering the consequences, had gotten me into this mess. "And when am I expected? Every week? Once a month? Once a year?"

Mischief glittered in his eyes. "Human life spans are far too short for that. You gave me your soul, remember? I expect you to be here every night."

"Every night?" I touched the necklace. If this fairy asshole thought I was giving up every night of my life to amuse him, he needed—

"I can hear you," he reminded me, those eyes of his now dancing with wicked delight.

I snatched my hand away from the necklace like it might bite. I was going to have to remember that.

"I can't think of any other agreement that would work for me. Do you have a better plan?" He waited for me to offer one.

But planning was not my strong suit. Reacting? I was good at that. Thinking long term was a luxury I'd never been afforded, and now he wanted me to make a decision that would affect the rest of my life? "How about you just let me go? It's not like you need me around with your guards and big, empty house and important fae bullshit."

His mouth flattened, the spark leaving his eyes. "I do not agree to those terms. You promised your soul."

"So you keep reminding me," I grumbled. Maybe one day I'd understand exactly what he needed with my soul anyway. For now, I sighed. "I can't come every night. I might have a shift." I swallowed. That was, if I didn't get fired. "Once I'm reinstated."

"If you wish to continue working—"

"I wish," I snapped. "People depend on me."

"Like Channing?"

My eyes narrowed. "Not just Channing. I work at Gage Memorial. Someone has to clean up your messes."

For a long moment, he didn't say anything as he weighed my words. "As I said, I will settle for your nights. I will speak to the hospital regarding your availability."

Of course he could do that. His name was on the trauma center. He could do whatever he wanted. But still, the more I understood about this, the better off I would be. I pointed to the necklace he'd just given me. "So, I will use this to come back here?"

"It's also spelled to send you to your world at sunrise. At night, when you are ready to return, just think it, touch the necklace, and it will be done." He waited for me to object, but I didn't. Not with so many lovely loopholes to work with. But as if he'd just realized that, too, he added, "I expect you within an hour of sunset."

"Wonderful," I said through gritted teeth. "And if I forget?"

"The necklace is a courtesy."

"And if I don't want to wear it?"

"I will know if it's removed. Would you prefer one of these?" He pointed to his tattooed arm, and some of the ink fled at the attention.

Revulsion flooded me at the idea of something so permanent—at being marked by him forever. Suddenly, the necklace seemed like a really good idea. "I'd rather not."

"Then do not take it off," he warned me. "I can always use the bargain's bond if you forget, but that way is rather unpleasant."

I touched the back of my neck, remembering the prickle I'd felt when the deal was struck. "The bargain's bond?"

"It's like a leash—"

I narrowed my eyes. "I dare you to call it a leash again."

"I suppose *collar* isn't better?" The smirk was back.

"Getting colder," I bit out.

"A *connection*," he said carefully, still smiling. "Our lives are bound now, after all."

"So, that's it? You just get to claim every night forever?"

"Not forever." But before I could cling to that, he added, "After all, you are human. There can be no bargain with the dead."

"At least I have something to look forward to."

"Has anyone told you that you're delightful, princess?"

I smiled with mock sweetness. "Rarely." I paused. "And if you die? Do I get passed down in a will or what?"

"Fae can live for thousands of years. I wouldn't worry about it."

He sighed at my raised brows. "Death breaks the bargain for both parties. Happy?"

I shrugged. Happy wasn't the word I would use, but it was useful information. A bargain could be broken. It wasn't much, but it was something. And fae could die—or be killed. I thought of the other man who'd been wheeled in with Channing. I'd seen his pointed ear and thought it was my imagination, but he had been fae. He hadn't survived the gunshot wound. Gage carried guns; so did all of his guards. If that—

"I mean, I could gift you to another court," he added, tearing me from my thoughts. "But I'm not sure any of them deserve dealing with you."

I bristled at the insult, so annoyed that I nearly missed what he was implying. When it hit me, I forgot how to breathe. "Gift?" I repeated, unable to hide my horror. "I don't belong to you."

It was his turn to shrug. "Your soul does."

"Would you give me away?" I forced myself to ask.

"Unlikely." There was nothing reassuring about his answer.

"Till death do us part." I grimaced at the thought. "Why did you do it?"

He was more talkative than he'd been yesterday. Maybe I stood a chance of getting an answer.

I needed to find a way out of this bargain that didn't involve me dying. What if he just decided to keep me here forever? What if he got bored with me? I would never be safe in the Otherworld, but what choice did I have? I belonged to Gage as long as I lived. Escaping wouldn't help. He could summon me to him with that unstoppable magic. I felt sure of that. And if I messed up, he might go after Channing in revenge. I thought of what had happened to that man in the room last night. Gage had no issue with violence, and neither did any of the other men there. I had to find a way to not only break the bargain but also escape the Otherworld and keep Gage away from Channing.

"I have my reasons." He sipped from his goblet, but his shoulders had seized slightly and his knuckles were white around the cup.

"About this evening."

I went cold, but I forced myself to take another bite.

"I'd like you to join me. There is a party at midnight—"

"No," I cut him off.

He blinked several times. "Excuse me?"

"The terms don't say I have to spend my evening with *you*," I pointed out.

"It wasn't a request." His voice was low. *Lethal.*

I reached for my own goblet and lifted it to my lips, pausing to repeat myself. "No."

He pushed his chair back with a loud screech. Rising, he planted his palms on the table and glared down at me. "You will attend, or I will drag you."

My heart began to pound, but I didn't look away from those murderous eyes. "I dare you to try." I lifted my chin. I'd done what I had to do to protect Channing, but I drew the line at spending time with this monster. "I want to go home now. That is the arrangement."

His jaw worked for a moment like he was chewing on a decision. "I will see you tonight, princess."

Before I could argue, he snapped his fingers, but he didn't send me home. Instead, I found myself on the floor of my new bedroom, still in the Nether Court.

I grabbed the pendant. *Send me home now.*

When the demand didn't work, I closed my eyes and wished myself home. No luck there, either. It was clear he was ignoring me despite the stupid necklace. I'd gotten under his skin, and that was a dangerous place to be. I'd seen what Gage was capable of, and that left me little choice in what I did next. He had told me exactly how to break the bargain and protect Channing at the same time.

I had to kill Lachlan Gage.

CHAPTER SEVEN

G age's total disregard for upholding the terms of our bargain on day one made planning his demise easier.

It helped that I was well aware of the number of lives his brutal business had claimed. He was responsible for putting trinity on the streets. The drug claimed lives daily. He didn't deserve to live thousands of years.

Which meant tonight was the night. Right now, Gage and Roark were the only people—or fae, rather—who knew who I was here. How long would that be true if I had to come here every night? And if there were others visiting the court tonight, everyone would be distracted, especially if the party was anything like that smoke-filled bar at the Avalon. It was now or never, most likely.

I would wait until the party started before slipping out. I'd explored the living areas of the house yesterday while trying to find a way to leave. No one had followed me or watched me. I guess I must not seem like much of a threat. Tonight, though, I planned to find the other bedrooms through whatever means necessary. I needed Gage to be alone and unguarded, and since he even ate breakfast with armed guards, that was going to take some arranging.

Once the party started, I would find his private quarters and hide there. And when he was asleep, I would take the gun from his holster right before sunrise and...

I didn't think about that part. I could do it. I had to. And as soon as the magic sent me home, I would run. Haley would keep tabs on

Channing for me, and when he was better, I'd get him out of New Orleans, too. I had no idea if the plan would work, but I couldn't trust Gage. He'd tricked me once. I couldn't make the same mistake twice.

I didn't bother to leave my bedroom. It was better if he thought I was sulking.

But staying inside was an exercise in patience because everything about the space tempted me to relax. If the bedroom was show-stopping, I didn't have words for the bathroom. There were the obligatory sink and toilet on one side, but on the other, there were more tall, elegant windows, and buttressed beneath them waited a sunken stone bath surrounded by four pillars. The ivy that clung to the exterior balcony had crept inside, covering the walls and wrapping its lush tendrils around the columns. Candles flickered from a bronze fixture overhead, as if the room had been waiting for me. But that bathtub…

Grumbling over the unfairness of having all of these things at my disposal when there was no way I'd ever use them, I stuck my head under the sink's faucet and quickly washed up. The only thing worse than letting my guard down would be being naked while I did. At least my hair felt clean if not the rest of me.

I paced the bedroom until twilight. The sunset was unlike anything I'd ever seen, as if to remind me that I was in another world. The sky faded into bottle green, stars winking into existence while a sliver of light divided night and day on the horizon. I stepped onto the stone balcony to watch it. As if on cue, music spilled into the night along with the sounds of laughter and conversation. Lights twinkled in the growing dark.

The party was starting.

I stretched over the railing, trying to catch sight of the guests, but the wild vines blocked everything save for those dancing lights.

It was time.

But before I reached the door, someone rapped on it. Anger flamed inside me. He really thought he could just show up and drag me to this party. I marched to the door and threw it open, poisoned words on my tongue, only to find a fae woman standing there, holding an armful of delicate pink silk. Her long, black hair was at odds with her ice-pale skin, a faint rose flush the only color on her striking face. She surveyed me for a moment, her lips pursing with unmistakable disapproval.

"You look like a wet dog," she muttered as she pushed past me.

I tucked a strand of damp hair behind my ear and forced a tight smile. "Can I help you?"

"I got the short straw," she informed me, holding up the gown in her hands. "I'm here to dress you for this evening."

"I'm not going. He knows that."

She rolled her eyes, turning her attention to the dress as she began fussing over a few wrinkles. "You'd really rather spend all night pouting in here?" She gave a disapproving cluck. "Fine. I'll tell your guard. He'll be thrilled to hang out here and miss the Equinox."

Guard? My heart sank as the foundation of my plan crumbled. Until I figured out a new way to get Gage alone and unprotected, there was only one option. Maybe I should play along—hopefully I could lose my guard in the chaos of the party.

Crossing to her, I thrust out my hands. "I can dress myself."

"Maybe." She shrugged a petite shoulder. "But it will take magic to do anything with that hair."

"Tell me something I don't know." I grabbed the dress and waited for her to leave. When she didn't, I nodded toward the door. "A little privacy."

She rolled her eyes, muttering "humans" along with a few choice expletives, and turned around.

Apparently, that was as much privacy as she was going to give me. Ducking into the bathroom and closing the door behind me, I laid the gown on the marble counter. There wasn't much to it. I stripped out of my clothes and slipped the gown over my head. The fabric glided over me like a delicate second skin and fluttered to my feet. Two long slits in the skirt allowed my legs to slip through, and veins of black branched across its pale silk. I turned toward the mirror, and the dress moved like butterfly wings skimming through the air. The door cracked open, and she peeked inside. The fae had serious boundary issues.

"It suits you," she told me, but it didn't sound like a compliment. She handed me a pair of heels. "He will be pleased."

I barely held back a laugh. If she knew how little Gage was interested in me, that he was probably already considering giving me to one of his enemies as revenge, she wouldn't think that. Instead, I reached for a towel to dry my hair, but she stopped me.

"Don't bother. You'll make it worse." She stepped closer and lifted her hands.

I braced myself for her touch, but her fingers ghosted around my head without making any contact.

"I'm Cate, by the way," I said to break the awkward silence.

She didn't introduce herself. "I know. Everyone knows about Lach's new stray."

I decided a change of topic was in order. "Will there be lots of f— I mean, people at the party?"

"Fae? Yes. Humans? No. Well, except for you." Her mouth twisted, telling me exactly what she thought about that.

I nodded, my mouth going dry as I realized how much I would stand out in a room full of fae. "And tonight is the Equinox. Is it a big celebration?"

I'd heard the term before, but it meant little to me.

"The fae celebrate all the old holidays," she told me, tucking up a loose strand of my hair.

"The old holidays?" I frowned.

"Tonight is Mabon. There's Samhain, Saturnalia, Yule." She sighed heavily at my blank look. "Mabon is the autumnal Equinox. That's tonight. You call the others Halloween, Thanksgiving, Christmas."

I could tell from her tone what she thought of that.

"I have no idea why he wants you there," she said, "especially with the other courts visiting."

I plastered my lips into a bland smile. "And the other courts are here because of this Equinox?"

"It's tradition. The fae courts gather to discuss new bargains and alliances to advance trade, political influence, and becoming even more filthy fucking rich. They party for days and shower one another with gifts."

I barely contained a flinch. What if Gage decided to dump me with one of them like he'd threatened, claiming I was a *gift*? I had to find a way to dispose of him *soon*, especially if everyone was going to be focused on the celebration.

She stopped scrutinizing me and met my eyes. "They'll also punish anyone who breaks their agreements without cause on this day."

I pretended to fuss with my gown, but my mind was racing. Was that why they'd taken Martin's hand yesterday? My stomach turned over as I considered what they might do to me if I was caught killing Gage, but what choice did I have? I couldn't stay indebted to him. Couldn't risk being traded to another monster. Gage had the power to destroy my life and hurt Channing. This might be my only opportunity to break the bargain and stand a chance of escaping.

But maybe more important than any of that, killing Gage would be doing my world a favor. I'd seen the bloody toll of his power in the city. If that meant facing fae punishment, so be it.

"It sounds boring." I trained my face into disinterest. "A bunch of men getting out their measuring sticks."

Her lips curved slightly, as if she might agree with that assessment. "That's how it works here. Don't be surprised if he trades you for something he wants."

My knees buckled, and I barely stayed upright. Even *she* thought he might send me to another court.

"Deals and alliances," she continued. "He wants to strengthen his ties with the Infernal Court, so he'll need to *entice* their prince."

Sweat slicked my hands, and I resisted the urge to wipe them on the beautiful gown. I felt sick. I had to get out of the Otherworld. There was no time to waste. I forced myself to laugh, trying to sound nonplussed. "I doubt he'd force me to attend this party with him if he planned to give me away."

She paused and studied me for a moment in a way that told me she was assessing not her work but me. "Gages don't marry for anything but power or status. You should remember that."

It wasn't what I expected her to say. I blinked, puzzling out what she meant before shock dropped my jaw. She assumed I meant he wouldn't trade me because he was *attached* to me. "I'm not interested in Gage, and he's *not* interested in me."

She let out a slight *hmph* that only made new questions form in my mind but changed the subject. "You were stupid to make a bargain with him."

I gritted my teeth. It wasn't like I needed the reminder, but I wasn't about to argue that I hadn't actually intended to make a deal with him. I doubted she would be sympathetic to my cause, especially since she clearly disliked me. "I don't know. That bathtub is pretty spectacular."

This time, she actually smiled. "Enjoy it while you can."

That sounded like a threat if I'd ever heard one. I tried not to let fear take hold, but its oily tendrils snaked through me, and I forced myself to turn around and look in the mirror—to do anything but meet her cold eyes. But what I found was nothing like I could have imagined.

The delicate dress clung to my curves, its pale color bringing out the warm hue of my skin. My usually unruly hair was up in a pile of curls, tendrils spiraling around my face, which was bright with highlighted cheeks and red lips. My lashes, thick and fluttery, framed my eyes so that they seemed larger and brighter than normal. I wouldn't have been able to make myself look like this with hours of trying, and she had done it in minutes.

"How?" I breathed.

"I said it would take magic. It's a light glamour."

"Glamour?"

"Think of it like a veil. It can hide or disguise, but in this case, it just accentuated what was already there."

"Like magical makeup?" It had to be what made Gage and the others look like humans in the real world.

"But better for the skin. It will fade overnight, so don't stay out too late," she warned me. "It's simple magic that can be done when you wish. You just have to ask."

I was slightly relieved that I wasn't expected to look like this all the time. I couldn't imagine going to work looking like a TikTok filter. "Thank you," I said, actually meaning it. If I had to get close to Gage tonight, I needed every advantage I could get.

"Any servant can help you. I'm not around the court much. I'm only here for the Equinox."

I might have been disappointed if I planned to stick around.

"Your escort is here," she announced, drawing me from my doomed thoughts. How she knew, I didn't ask. Maybe those fae ears, so different from my own, heard things I couldn't.

I braced myself for Gage, for enduring his insufferable presence, but another woman waited at the door. Unlike my annoyed attendant, she squealed when she saw me.

"I could not believe it when I heard my brother had a date!" She threw her arms around my shoulders, dragging me into a suffocating hug that was nearly as shocking as her words. I knew the Gage family by their names only. That meant she was either Ciara or Fiona. She pulled back, a dazzling smile on her face. She was a delicate version of her brother, all curves and softness swathed in a sheer lace gown. Her hair was pinned half up to cascade over her bare shoulder, a few glossy black curls escaping to frame her heart-shaped face. But it was her eyes that she shared with her brother—brilliant, glittering green that glinted with secrets like the facets of cut emeralds.

"Ciara." My attendant said the name with disapproval. "You'll fuck up her glamour."

Ciara released me with an apologetic grin, but it soured as she looked at her.

"Fiona," she said coolly. "Why are you here?"

No. It couldn't be. Not some random fae sent to assist me with my hair. His sister. My head started to swim.

"I volunteered. The servants were busy with the party, and if I have to spend one more minute with Oberon and his sanctimonious bullshit, I'm going to murder him. I figured I'd find something more constructive to do before I got marked by the Wild Hunt. Getting to meet Lach's new pet was just a bonus."

I blinked. That was way too much information to unpack. Half of it might as well have been in another language. Probably the one scrawled across Gage's skin.

Ciara's eyes narrowed. "And what lies have you told her?"

She laughed. "I didn't need to tell her anything. She reeks of fear. Good luck with that one."

"You aren't a servant," I accused.

Ciara shot a glare at Fiona. "We're Lach's sisters."

That confirmation transformed her before my very eyes. The dress she wore, while simple, was elegant...*expensive*. The bracelet that hadn't been noticeable before now glittered in the light, showcasing its large diamonds. And Fiona herself, still lovely and cold, now radiated a regal beauty. Something clicked into place. "You wore a glamour."

"At least she's a quick learner," she said not to me but to her sister. "Maybe she'll live longer than usual."

I didn't dare ask what she meant by that. Not when I was smart enough to deduce the truth: I wasn't the first woman to find herself trapped in the Otherworld. I added the info to my list of reasons I needed to kill Gage.

But now I'd met both of his sisters. That complicated my escape plan.

I couldn't dwell on it. There were fates worse than death, and what Fiona had said about the prince from the other court... Even if I didn't escape, I would rather die than endure that.

"You should go," Ciara said, causing Fiona's eyes to roll.

Fiona glided toward the door, tossing out a sarcastic "you're welcome" at me.

"I hope she didn't scare you," Ciara said, looping her arm through mine. "She can be a bit of a bitch, but she's all bark and no bite."

As if there was a need to scare me. As if Fiona hadn't made me into a beautiful butterfly just to prove how trapped I was.

I focused on the annoyance I felt to keep my fear from showing. "It was fine. Informative." I gawked at where Ciara was clutching my arm, unsure what to make of her. At least she was friendlier than her sister. The two were like opposite ends of the spectrum. "Your brother couldn't be bothered to drag me to this himself?"

I looked around the corridor for signs of a guard but found only shadows. A moan so soft I might have imagined it drifted through the air, and I stepped closer to her.

"He's taking care of something," she said brightly as we started down the hall.

"Something or some*one*?" Ciara might act like a ray of sunshine, but she was still a Gage.

"Our reputation precedes us." She sighed heavily but didn't release her grip on me. "Let me guess—you've been warned about the Gages your whole life."

I nodded. Even the crowd I'd run with as a teen had steered clear of them.

"And that kept you away, right? You didn't come to Waverly Avenue? You didn't publicly criticize our family for fear of us retaliating or—even more terrifying—of one day needing a favor from us?"

Another nod, even if admitting to the last bit stung.

"That's the point." Another big smile. "It's part of the whole glamour, so no one looks too closely."

But I had seen the truth firsthand. Maybe Ciara Gage stayed in her own perfect bubble, maybe she could avoid the reality of who and what they were, but I couldn't. "So you don't run the city and kill anyone who gets out of line?"

She glanced over at me, her mouth sliding into a frown. "I didn't say that."

"Why bother with New Orleans when you have this place?"

"Fae are territorial," she explained. "We don't like other creatures."

Curiosity got the better of me. "What creatures are there besides fae?"

"Vampires—"

"Vampires?" I gaped at her. "Vampires are real?"

"Yes, and werewolves, gods, nymphs, witches, sirens. Basically, anything you believed was from a storybook is actually real."

My head spun. If fae were real, why couldn't there be other magical creatures? Something about the realization made me feel very small, as though my place in the world had shrunk from its already negligible space.

"But why not just stay in your world?"

Why bother ruining mine?

"There are cracks in the veil between your world and ours. Some call them portals, entrances, whatever. Since we don't want just anyone slipping into the Otherworld, each court's power extends to one of your mortal cities where the veil is thinner, where there are those entrances. Our magic is stronger there than other types of magic, too."

"Other types of magic?" I murmured, feeling a little faint. I pushed aside my unease and focused on the information. Anything I learned would help me escape. Freaking out would not. "There's more magic in my world?"

"Of course. Every creature's magic is different." She shook her head like she couldn't believe I didn't know any of this. I refrained from reminding her that until yesterday I hadn't even known that fae actually existed outside of stories.

I was still thinking about it when Ciara stopped in front of two black doors, carved and gilded in that strange, ancient language that was inked on Gage's skin. "Ready or not…"

Not.

CHAPTER EIGHT

It wasn't a party. It was a spectacle.

I tried to keep myself from gawking as we made our way into a ballroom that looked like it belonged inside Buckingham Palace—although its size and opulence were the only similarities.

Chandeliers wreathed with ivy hung overhead, pillar candles in glass orbs sending warm light sparkling over silk-draped tables laden with platters of succulent fruits and vases of large, blooming flowers. A heavy perfume of rose petals and something sweet and herbal filled the air along with the melodic chatter of the gathered crowd and soft, luring music from unseen musicians.

Despite my best attempts, I kept catching myself staring at the other guests. The fae moving around the space radiated an ethereal unearthliness. Their skin was too polished to be human, their eyes glowing too brightly, their movements too graceful and otherworldly, making goosebumps ripple over my skin. My body instinctively understood that even with their beauty and grace, I was in the midst of predators.

"Stick close to me," Ciara advised. I didn't object, aware of the potential danger surrounding me. "Would you like something to eat?"

"I'm fine." But my stomach grumbled at the lie, and she raised a coiffed eyebrow. I gave up. "Sure." Then paused, thinking better of it. "I'm not going to be punished for taking your food, am I?"

"No." Her forehead bunched like she was being tested. "You are my brother's guest here."

I didn't bother to argue I was more of a prisoner. I'd lost that argument too many times already. But the mention of food had made me uncomfortably aware of how famished I was, the hunger gnawing at me for attention. I'd barely eaten breakfast. "Is it safe to eat?"

She only laughed and grabbed my hand as she led me toward one of the banquet tables. I stayed close to her as people watched us. I definitely didn't want to get lost among the strange, beautiful creatures surrounding us.

Their attention faded as we approached the food. My stomach had been knotted this morning, making it impossible to eat, but there was something about Ciara that almost put me at ease. I refused to trust a Gage. But I *was* hungry.

If I managed to go through with this plan, I'd either be on the road by dawn or in a cell—because this place definitely had a dungeon somewhere, no matter what Gage said—and this might be my last meal. I grabbed a gold-rimmed plate.

Ciara dropped my hand and stepped to the side, seeming to sense she shouldn't stand between me and the food. She chuckled softly and tipped her head toward the feast. "Help yourself."

I didn't need to be told twice. Some of the dishes were full of food I recognized. Bowls of ripe fruit, beckoning with their sweet scent, the aroma more pungent than I'd ever smelled. Chafing dishes full of roasted meats that dripped with juices. Bread and cheeses of every shape and variety. But among them were things I didn't recognize. Fruit the size of an apple with nearly translucent skin that revealed purple veins in its flesh. Something that was definitely not chicken. And a sauce wafting a smell that was completely foreign. I avoided them all and piled my plate with the normal food I knew from the human world.

Ciara appeared beside me, picked up one of the strange fruits, and plopped it onto my already heaping plate. I gave her a questioning look.

"Trust me."

No one else was eating. Maybe they were used to lavish buffets every night. Maybe food never ran out in the Otherworld. Maybe they never knew hunger. As I stepped away, I caught sight of the dessert table and whimpered.

Ciara tracked my gaze and laughed. "We can come back for another round."

Appeased, I smiled. "Lead the way."

She steered us to a small alcove off the main ballroom. She hadn't bothered with a plate. Instead, she watched as I dug into my food. It was like nothing I'd ever tasted, like…magic. Each bite made me crave more, and I found myself eating so quickly that I was glad no one was near us. I made myself pause between mouthfuls. "Why is no one eating?"

"They will when they've had enough wine. There's no rush. The party will go all night."

Exactly like I expected. I just had to find Gage alone and hope they were all too drunk to notice he was missing until after sunrise.

"Do you want any?" I gestured to my plate, feeling a little rude for eating in front of her.

And for planning to kill her brother. Because honestly, Ciara was genuinely nice.

"I'm not certain it's safe to take anything off it."

I grinned at her and plunged on until there was nothing left but the strange fae fruit she'd added.

Ciara picked it up and held it out. "It's not poisonous."

A warning clanged in my chest. The last time a fae had offered me fruit, I'd wound up bound to him in a bargain. I shook my head. "I'm full."

Her lips quirked, and she pushed it toward me. "The food here won't ever fill you up. It's nourishing," she added when she saw my wide-eyed look, "but you can never eat too much."

"Is this heaven?" I asked.

Her smile dimmed for the first time since we arrived. "Far from it."

I accepted the strange fruit with some hesitation. Ciara was sweet, but there had to be other differences between the fae and humans. I just didn't want to find out through my tastebuds.

She sighed. "Just try it. I promise nothing bad will happen if you do."

I hesitated still, but that felt like a fae bargain I could live with—and curiosity was slowly winning over my reluctance. I braced myself and took a bite. It melted on my tongue, its syrupy sweetness oozing like honey but with a sharp, bright tang. Warmth flooded through me, flushing my cheeks, and I couldn't help taking a second bite.

"It's a blood apple," she told me with a smug grin.

I nearly dropped it.

"Not real blood," she assured me. "It's just the extremely clever name some ancient fae gave it based on its looks."

As unappetizing as the name was, I couldn't deny that she was right. "I've never tasted anything like it."

"It only grows in the Otherworld. It's forbidden to plant in your realm. I'm not certain it would grow anyway. There's so little magic in your earth."

But there was *magic*. It was impossible to wrap my head around it. How would I look at my world the same after this? Especially if what she said was true about other creatures.

Before I could pry more information from her, a shadow fell over the table, and I looked up to find Gage glowering down at us. He wore a tuxedo, his tie knotted at his throat, and there was no sign of his holsters bulging under his arms—the guns I was going to need later sadly missing.

The suit made him look almost civilized, but there was something of that predatory fae that remained. I sucked in a jagged breath, struck again by that terrible beauty and that supernatural aura that called out to me.

Monster. I had to remember what hid beneath that perfect face.

I returned his glare. "Lovely impression of a caveman." But his sneer faltered as I stood up, a momentary look of surprise ghosting across his face. "Do I meet your approval now?"

His gaze skirted along me as if determining just that, pausing a little too long in spots that told me he was definitely not a gentleman. *What happened to not his type?*

Gage arched a brow, lifting a long, tattooed finger and spinning it slowly. I scowled but turned, trying not to trip over my own feet. Maybe the glamour extended past the surface because I moved smoothly, *gracefully*, as the skirt of my gown fluttered around me like wings. He didn't speak when I stopped and faced him. After a moment, he cleared his throat slightly and shrugged. "You'll do."

My cheeks burned, but I refused to cower. Instead, I scanned him from head to toe, sighed, and said, "I guess I can be seen with you, too."

His lips twitched. "Is that so?"

I pinned a bland smile on my face. "It's not like I have a choice."

Ciara coughed politely, and her brother's mouth drooped into a frown.

"Yes, dear sister?" he said through clenched teeth. "Is there something you feel you have the right to add?"

She rose to her feet, tossing me an irritated eye roll—but not before I saw a flash of hurt cross her face. "Try not to kill him," she muttered to me, and I almost snort-laughed. But then she turned on him. "Lach, you can be such a prick. You should tell her she's gorgeous."

She didn't wait for a response before she disappeared into the crowd.

I scowled at him. "Are you rude to everyone?"

Shadows darkened his eyes. "I don't have to explain myself to you." He crooked his arm. "My sister will recover. She always does."

He sounded almost…jealous, which didn't make sense. "You should be nicer to her."

"And why is that?" he asked, arm still extended.

"She's your family."

His brows nudged together. "So?"

"Not everyone is so lucky." I didn't know why I was bothering. It was clear that Gage was blinded by his overly inflated ego.

But something flickered in his eyes at my answer. "Come on. I need a drink."

I blinked. "So, go get one."

That thing prickled and sharpened at the back of my neck.

He smirked. "You were saying?"

"Don't even think about it." I thrust my arm through his, keeping the rest of my body as far from his as possible. "I guess you don't need to do a caveman impression. You *are* one."

"Delightful," he muttered as we made our way to the next chapter of this nightmare.

We wound our way through the crowd, Gage nodding at others as we passed but not pausing to talk to any of them. Many dipped their heads in slight bows, their eyes following us through the room. So much for avoiding attention.

"What exactly are you?" I murmured as I caught them whispering behind our backs.

"Fae," he said tightly, as if he didn't enjoy being here, either.

"I know that." I frowned at him, even if I was still processing that fact. "Why are they staring at you?"

"Perhaps they're staring at *you*." His voice lowered. "The glamour suits you."

My head whipped toward his. He couldn't be serious. What happened to *you'll do*? "Don't flirt with me."

"I wouldn't dream of it," he said smoothly, aiming us toward the back of the room, away from anyone else. "It's simply called a compliment. No need to get testy."

"*Testy?*" He had not just said that. "I suppose I should be honored to hang on your arm?"

He paused to cast a sharp look at me. "It's not exactly an insult to be seen with the Prince of the Nether Court."

I lost my footing, but he was quick to right me, not even breaking stride as we continued to move through the room. *Prince?* I mouthed the word like I was chewing on it, not sure how it might taste. My confidence in my plan faltered. How was I going to kill a prince?

No choice.

Gathering myself back together, I forced my features into

indifference. "I guess that explains your unearned arrogance."

Darkness flashed in his eyes, but he leaned closer, so close that his lips nearly brushed my ear, his breath ghosting across its shell, sending goosebumps rippling along my arms. "It's not unearned, princess."

I jerked away from him, from the heady rush his nearness sent charging through me, and regarded him with cold eyes. "Stop calling me that."

"Would you prefer queen?" Laughter coated his voice.

"Don't even think about it," I warned.

"I believe that means I can call you whatever I want." He chuckled at my glare. "Besides, I don't think there's a more fitting title for you. Not when you give orders so boldly. You'll need that courage to survive here."

It was almost another compliment, but I wasn't about to let it go to my head. I couldn't afford to let him get to me in any way. Because I suspected the thing that would be hardest to survive about the Nether Court was its prince himself. That was exactly why he couldn't live, so letting him charm me... I couldn't.

"But if you like, I could call you something else. Gertrude, perhaps?"

I blinked, a laugh spilling from me before I could stop myself. So far he had glowered and flirted and taunted, but *that* had been an actual *joke*. "Just call me Cate."

He inclined his head, but from the mischief glinting in his eyes, I doubted he would.

Since he seemed to be in a good mood, I seized the moment. "Your necklace didn't work. I was stuck here all day."

I had to be certain of how the magic worked before I...

Gage didn't look at me. "It works."

It took effort not to attempt murder on the spot. "If you aren't going to uphold the bargain—"

"The terms were set today," he interrupted me. "Hence, they start today, and since you received the necklace after sunrise..."

"You're unbelievable." A few heads turned toward us, and Gage hurried me along.

"I swear it will send you home at sunrise. Happy?"

"Ecstatic."

A slight rumble rose from his chest, his nostrils flaring, before he gestured toward the bar. "I really need that drink."

That made two of us.

We were a few steps from the bar when he placed a hand on the small of my back. I opened my mouth to protest and found him staring over my shoulder, a frown deepening on his face even as his hand remained possessively in place, making me more aware of him, of the warmth and steadiness of that hand, of how every nerve in my body seemed to narrow to that point of contact. I wondered how many humans had unwittingly bound themselves to fae under the influence of that strange, seductive magic he wielded.

I was still preoccupied as we reached the bar. His hand fell away, and, instantly, my head cleared. Further proof of his magical, fae fuckery. He held up two fingers. I took a step back, needing more distance between us, and bumped into the man behind me.

"Watch it," a rough voice said.

My blood chilled as I recognized the deep timbre and whipped around to find the man from last night glaring at me.

"Manners, MacAlister," his companion said, a trace of London on his tongue as he adjusted the sleeve of his tux.

MacAlister continued to glower at me, but the other man nodded. He was both ruggedly handsome and infinitely bored, his white hair as icy as his light-blue eyes. Gage stepped next to me, pressing a champagne flute into my palm before moving his hand to rest once more on the small of my back. I didn't shrink away from his touch this time, even if I didn't know what he was playing at.

"Bain." He spoke to the other man. "I'm pleased you were able to make it."

Bain scoffed at the greeting. "Liar. I hear I missed out on yesterday's fun."

I swallowed as I recalled the fun he spoke of, but I must not have kept my disgust from showing. His companion returned my stare, his lip curling back when he recognized me.

I lifted my chin. "That's your idea of fun?"

That caught Bain's interest. He turned his attention from Gage to me, but I didn't shrink under his glare. I returned it.

Gage's fingers dug into my back.

MacAlister chuckled. "He deserved what he got."

"For breaking a bargain?" I asked.

MacAlister's eyes flicked to Gage. "Do you always let them speak so freely?"

Oh, he did not just say that.

"He doesn't *let* me do anything," I shot back hotly. "I'm a person. Not a pet."

Gage tensed next to me but didn't step in.

Bain did. "And how does your kind deal with rapists?"

The question rang in my ears, the floor suddenly unstable beneath me. Gage moved closer, his strong body bracing mine as if he sensed the sudden shift. A hand closed over mine like a warning. My attention riveted to the whorls winding over the back of it, the ink streaming down to where his skin touched mine. Gage cleared his throat. "As I've said before, scum like that deserve far worse." The words sawed out of him. "Cate is new here."

Something sparkled in Bain's quicksilver eyes. "Ah. That explains it. Our ways must seem monstrous to you."

I felt all their eyes on me as he dangled the bait and waited for me to bite.

Instead, I cleared my throat. "I didn't know."

Bain inclined his head. "And now that you do?"

"I agree. He deserved worse," I said to everyone's surprise, even my own. Gage glanced down at me, his expression unreadable.

Before we could debate the merits of the fae justice system further, Ciara sauntered over. "Why is no one dancing?" she demanded, then winked at me.

I breathed an inner sigh of relief, grateful for her interruption. Not only was I meeting more fae than I wanted, I was drawing attention to myself—so much for remaining anonymous. But my respite was short-lived.

Gage held out his hand. "We've been ordered to dance."

I stared at his outstretched palm.

Ciara nudged me with her shoulder. "Go," she whispered, and if I'd had any doubt about her timing, it vanished.

"We'll join you," Bain said, extending his hand to Ciara. Her throat slid at his implied command, but she smiled and dropped her hand in his.

I forced myself to do the same, giving my hand to her brother. I needed to get Gage to drop his guard. Dancing might help, I reasoned. But I barely registered anything as he led me onto the dance floor, every eye in the room following our every move.

His grip tightened on mine, and I tried to ignore the way my heart rate ratcheted up when he drew me against his broad chest. I slipped my arm around his waist only to discover the hard outline of his gun.

No holster tonight but tucked somewhere more accessible, as if he expected he might need to draw it more quickly. So, he didn't trust his own guests. I couldn't blame him for that.

His mouth tightened. "Careful," he warned.

I moved my arm up, resting my palm on his strong shoulder, hoping I hadn't given myself away. That gun was mine the second I found an opening.

"You're thinking," he accused.

"Is that a crime?" I asked. I didn't dare look at him, didn't dare risk seeing what was in his eyes. But looking at our audience was somehow even worse. "Do they ever get tired of staring at you?"

His dark laugh rippled down my neck and settled deep inside me. Up close, his scent filled my nose—the deep, woody aroma of cedar laced with warm spice. It smelled as dangerous as the rest of him.

"Can you blame them?" he murmured.

I snorted, determined not to fall under his spell, even if I was grateful for the distraction. "Cocky bastard."

"There are many women who would be happy to dance with me."

I turned my face up to give him a wolfish smile. "Why don't you find one of them?"

"That would be rude of me. You are my guest." I opened my mouth to protest, but he cut me off. "Don't start in again about how you're my prisoner. I did you a favor."

"Do you expect me to thank you?" I shook my head at the arrogance. He could spin it however he wanted, but we both knew he'd tricked me. Had I known, I might have made a different decision, tried to find another way to help Channing. Or packed my brother up and run to the ends of the earth.

"You would do well to remember that I have the power to make your life pleasant..." Gage traced a finger up the length of my spine, sending an unbidden thrill fluttering through my body. He smiled down at me as if he knew exactly the reaction that touch had produced. "Or miserable, every night for the rest of your life."

Defiance sparked inside me, and I refused to cower from that beautiful face or his cruel manipulation. "The way I see it, I can do the same."

He studied me for a moment, and then he laughed. The warm sound cascaded down my body and pooled somewhere low and forbidden. He leaned closer, his mouth brushing my ear. "Should I be watching my back, princess?" I tensed at how close his words hit to the mark, but he didn't seem to notice and I didn't reply.

One dance led to another, until my feet hurt from the spinning. Normally, I loved to dance, but there was nothing normal about tonight. Even time seemed to slip away as he pressed me against his body, one song bleeding into the next. Until finally, Gage straightened, his eyes sweeping the room before they found mine. His next words sealed his fate. "Let's get out of here."

CHAPTER NINE

Neither of us spoke as we made our way through the deserted corridors, the sound of our footsteps on the stone floors echoing the ominous beat of my own heart. Lit sconces cast long shadows that stretched and shifted with each step.

My brain teemed in the emptiness, as if my mind needed to fill the stillness. I had to kill Gage.

I swallowed the bile rising in the back of my throat. I was a nurse. I saved lives. But death was the only way to break the bargain, and he'd intentionally misled me to trap me. Probably to "gift" me to someone for more power.

All the reasons to take his life were right in front of me. But spending time with him, even when he was insufferable for half of it, had forced me to see a tiny glimpse of the man behind the monster. I would be ending them both. But what other choice did I have?

As we reached my doors, I opened them and waited for him to follow me inside. A quick glance at the clock on the mantel told me it was already past three in the morning. Only a few hours until sunrise. I turned to find him stopped on the threshold, the warm light of the hallway silhouetting his body. He had practically walked into my trap. Now it would be easier than I thought to get his gun. Everyone else was at the party, getting wasted.

I opened my mouth to invite him in, my decision made.

But before I could, he spoke, his face half obscured by shadows. "Earlier. When Bain told you about Martin…"

His words halted my rising determination. I didn't want to talk about this. Especially not with him. Instantly, I was numb. I wished I had shut the door as I retreated a step into the bedroom.

Gage planted a hand on the doorframe, as if to stop himself from following. "I don't need details. Just…give me a name."

I only stared at him, numbness melting to panic. It took me a moment to find my voice. "It was a long time ago."

His jaw clenched, rage flashing in his eyes. "That doesn't matter." He sucked in a breath. "When you're ready, then."

I forced myself to nod, my plan forgotten in the face of his offer. He turned and started down the hall as his words sank in. I had no doubt what would happen if I gave him that name. But that couldn't change my plans. If anything, it should prove to me what kind of a man he was. It should make what I had to do easier.

It *had* to.

I closed my eyes and called out, "Wait." He turned toward me, and I pushed the bedroom door open wider. "Do you want to come in?"

Even in the dim hall I saw his eyes narrow. "I don't think that's a good idea."

I swallowed and forced away a sudden surge of guilt. I had to do this. "I thought I wasn't your type."

A grim sort of smile carved his mouth. I counted my breaths as he considered until, finally, he stalked toward me. At least fae males were as predictable as human ones.

I twisted around, unable to face him as I tried to ignore the accusatory voice inside me. *Liar. Liar. Liar.*

Was I any better than him if I did this? Could I live with myself? I tried convincing myself by thinking of everything I knew of him so far. Gage might be more than the sins he'd committed, but that didn't erase the things he'd done. It didn't change the fact that he'd trapped me. It didn't mean that he would keep his promise not to hurt Channing. And I shouldn't be moved by his offer of vengeance.

"Have you changed your mind?" he asked gruffly, stopping only a few steps behind me.

Awareness prickled like electricity through my body in a way that had nothing to do with the push and pull of my conscience. His unearthly magic at work again.

He cleared his throat, but his words sounded heavy when he finally spoke. "About the name, I mean. The man who...hurt you."

Somehow he knew that I was anxious. Could he hear my heart racing? Probably. But he'd mistaken why I was worked up. I closed my eyes and remembered what was at stake. He could trade me to someone like Bain or MacAlister. He could take the necklace and trap me here. And as long as he was alive, he could hurt the person I cared most about in the world. I had no choice. The fact steeled my resolve. "No, but I have something else to offer you." I willed my voice to remain steady. "Something you want more."

"Oh?" He moved nearer, close enough that I felt his heat through my thin gown.

It would be so easy to turn in to his body, to surrender to this strange, terrifying attraction he compelled from me. But that wouldn't save me or Channing.

I just had to get the gun.

And pull the trigger.

"And what is that?" he asked gruffly.

"Me," I whispered.

"I thought I made myself clear." I heard the strain in his voice as his finger traced the sweep of my shoulder. It hesitated on the strap of my gown, and for a moment, I thought he was seriously considering what I'd offered. Every nerve in my body tuned to that singular touch, tuned to his raw, brutal energy as if it was a command. The finger disappeared, and I gasped at the ache its absence triggered.

But then his hands caught my shoulders, and he spun me around. "It's not part of our arrangement," he reminded me, his eyes burning into mine.

"Because I'm not your type," I murmured, casting my eyes away from the intensity of his scrutiny.

He chuckled softly, moving his index finger to tilt my chin up.

He studied my mouth with that magnetic concentration, and I found it opening, knowing what he was thinking. This was part of my plan, wasn't it? Under the heat of his stare, I couldn't remember, couldn't remember why I'd invited him in, couldn't remember how to think.

"What game are you playing, princess?" He leaned close enough that I thought he might kiss me. Instead, his breath caressed my lips. "You haven't changed your mind. Or do you get off by fucking men you hate?"

I *did* hate him. The reminder snapped me out of my daze, made me recall what I had to do and why I'd lured him here in the first place. I pasted a lazy smile on my face and moved closer to him, molding my body to his and slipping my hand under his jacket. My fingers trailed along the hard ridges of his chest, moving lower.

Gage didn't stop me as I explored.

I could do this. I had to do this. Flattening my palm against him, I lifted my eyes to his as I slid my hands around his waist, drawing him closer. Shadows moved in his eyes, a curse dropping from his mouth as he bent and lowered his mouth to mine. It hovered there for a delicious second, and…I grabbed his gun.

He froze as I lurched out of his arms.

His brows raised as I pointed the gun at his chest. I tried not to think of how his body had felt beneath my fingertips or the darkness that stirred inside me when our eyes met. For a second, he just stared, and then…

He *clapped*.

Motherfucker.

"I'll admit I was starting to buy it." A grin hooked his mouth as he took a step closer. "But I should warn you, I am immortal."

"Don't," I commanded, curling my finger over the trigger. "Even immortals bleed."

"Do you really think you're capable of shooting me?" he asked, taking another step. "Your hands are shaking."

I was breathing hard and fast now, my entire body focused on keeping my hands steady. I knew I only had one shot. I just had to take it. "You have absolutely no idea what I'm capable of," I bit out.

"And I've seen what these bullets can do. I don't have to be a good shot. I just have to aim a little." That made him pause. Gage looked at me like he was seeing me for the first time, and I swallowed. "I've faced monsters before."

A slight growl escaped him. "I gathered."

He took another step forward despite my warning. And another. And another. I didn't even realize I was backing up with each one until I bumped against the wall. There was nowhere to turn. I kept the gun aimed at him, but he didn't try to seize it. Instead, he gripped the barrel and pressed it directly over his heart. His eyes never left mine. For once, those tattoos didn't move, didn't even flicker.

"Slay the monster, princess."

My chest heaved as I searched for that final shred of courage.

And found it.

My finger pulled the trigger.

And nothing happened.

Gage's movements were a blur as he disarmed me and tossed the gun on the floor. It clattered ominously, sliding out of reach for either of us. His hands closed over my wrists and pinned them to my sides. "I can't decide if you failed that test." The tip of his nose brushed mine, and a pang shot through me. "Or if you passed it."

"I would have killed you," I breathed, letting him see the truth of it in my eyes.

"Oh, I know." His rough laugh rasped over my feverish skin. "Remind me to show you how to turn off the safety."

My eyes flashed. "Don't fuck with me."

Another low laugh. "I wouldn't dream of it. You'll have to earn a weapon before I teach you. I'm afraid you'll need to redirect your homicidal urge before that happens."

"That might be a problem." I pulled against his hold on me, but he held me fast.

"How about a little help?" Was he actually fucking smiling at me? I couldn't tell. He was so close. His eyes. His lips. Him. "I assume you think this is the only way out of the bargain you made. I'll look past your ingratitude."

I glared up at him, keenly aware of everywhere our bodies touched.

"And I will tell you how to break it," he added.

I went utterly still.

"I thought that might get your attention." He snorted softly. "Fae bargains are based on desire."

"I don't want you." But my cheeks burned, my body burned, I *burned*.

"Clearly," he said dryly. "But you did want something *from* me, and I gave it to you because there's something I want in return."

My stomach pitched as his words hit me. "What do you get out of it?"

I couldn't imagine what he could want from me—what could motivate a man like him to make a deal with a woman he didn't even know?

He clicked his tongue in disapproval. "It won't be any fun if I tell you. You have a month and a day to break the bargain. Before then, if you can prove to me that you not only know what I stand to gain from this bargain but also that I will never get it from you, I will release you."

I swallowed. It was too good to be true. I narrowed my eyes. "And Channing?"

I had learned my lesson about bargains.

"I'll leave him alone. You have my word." He paused, squinting down at me. "And contrary to what you believe, my word is unbreakable. Until then, you will come to me at night *and* you will stop trying to kill me."

I knew that wasn't an optional condition. I took a deep breath. "Fine."

His tongue swept over his lower lip, his eyes straying once more to my mouth before he released me. I slumped against the wall, adrenaline still coursing through me. Gage bent and picked up his gun. He slid the magazine free, and I stared as he drew gold-plated bullets out of his pocket.

"You said you knew what these bullets did. I assume you've seen them in the hospital." He reloaded one into the magazine before holding another up. "The slugs are iron, which is lethal to fae if it hits the right spot. These slugs splinter when fired for maximum effectiveness." He looked over at me. "They're meant to kill us. We coat them in gold so we can handle them."

"Why are you telling me this?" I asked quietly.

"You have no idea who you're playing with, princess. Now you do." He finished loading, and then he strode toward the doors without looking back at me. "And now I know about you."

"Know what?" My voice shook. He'd baited me, knowing I wanted to kill him.

He stopped, a hand on the knob. "I told you it was a test. Good night."

I was still trembling as he strode from my bedroom, but I could have sworn I heard a smile in those final words.

CHAPTER TEN

I bolted awake but relaxed as my tiny bedroom greeted me. My clothes were still strewn on the dresser alongside stacks of books with no homes. Maybe it had all been a dream…

My fingers fumbled to find the chain around my neck, the pendant solid and real, and I moaned, "No."

Not a dream at all. I had been at the Nether Court. I had made a bargain with a fae prince. And even though I felt the heart pounding in my chest, it was no longer my own. I was the property of Lachlan Gage. At least according to some magically binding contract.

Forcing myself from the bed's warm cocoon, I gritted my teeth and yanked off yesterday's dress to find something warmer to wear. That wasn't a problem I was used to having in New Orleans, thanks to my landlord being too shitty to fix my AC. I glared at the working window unit blowing icy air across my skin, knowing it had to be Gage.

It took a fair amount of digging to find my robe in a pile of unfolded laundry that had probably been sitting in the basket since last fall. In the bathroom, I couldn't avoid the proof of what I'd done. My eyes were dry and scratchy from lying awake trying to puzzle out the cryptic and confusing challenge he'd set. I didn't remember falling asleep or how the necklace's magic had worked.

The pendant taunted me from the reflection as I brushed my teeth, catching the light and winking at me like the arrogant fae asshole who had given it to me. I wanted to take it off, to drop it down the drain, but since Gage had warned me he would know, I did not. If I didn't return to uphold my end of the bargain, Channing wouldn't be safe.

And I owed my brother more than I'd ever been able to give him.

It wasn't until Gran took me in that I found somewhere I belonged. But that hadn't happened overnight. Even after she'd convinced me to put on my ring, I didn't trust her. Despite the dresser she'd given me, it had taken months before I'd stopped keeping my few personal belongings in a trash bag, ready to move at a moment's notice. When Channing had come along a year later, I'd decided I would be someone he could count on, too. Gran's house was the first place I allowed myself to think about life, about my future. She'd encouraged me to apply for college, even driven me to a few local schools to go on tour. And when she had gotten sick, she'd held on just long enough to see me graduate. To make me promise to watch over Channing.

If there was a heaven, she was probably up there shaking her head over how badly I'd screwed that up. She had warned us about Gage, and I had let Channing get mixed up with him. *That* was on me. I twisted the emerald around my finger to hide the stone, as if she was watching me with it. Maybe it was better that she wasn't around to see my colossal failure.

Still, part of me was relieved that the gun hadn't been loaded.

That I hadn't killed Gage.

I might have failed Channing, but what would Gran think if I had become a murderer?

I found my purse and clothing on the nightstand like I'd been dropped off and tucked into bed instead of whisked away by a magic necklace. Because a working air conditioner wasn't creepy enough—and proof that Gage was paying attention to every word that I said. My phone had died, because the Otherworld might have fantastic fucking food but no power outlets. I went to find a charger while I contemplated the medieval torture of it. How was I supposed to vanish every night and put up with shit like that?

Not that I was living in luxury here.

My house was a small rental with only two bedrooms and one large room that served as a kitchen, dining room, and living room all rolled into one. Everything inside was worn and dated, from the kitchen cabinets to the cheap, beige carpeting that was so old it felt like sandpaper on my bare feet. I'd filled it with secondhand furniture from local thrift stores. Library books covered the water rings on the coffee table. A blanket was thrown over the couch's thin upholstery to cover its sags and creases. Everything was utilitarian. There to serve a purpose, not look pretty.

The only decor I'd bothered with was a collection of pictures on the fridge. I'd snipped them from magazines so long ago that their edges were curled and yellowing. Paris. Venice. London. Hong Kong. Prague. Places I had never been that I wanted to remind myself existed—places outside of New Orleans. The closest I'd ever gotten to any of them was in the pages of a book.

When I finally got my phone plugged in, it powered on to show a dozen missed calls and texts—all from the hospital.

I dialed Haley directly, because if they'd been calling to upgrade my suspension to a full-blown termination, I'd rather hear it from her. She didn't answer, and she still hadn't called back by the time I was out of the shower. Channing's phone went straight to voicemail. I threw on some clothes and decided I couldn't avoid the real world any longer. But I was dragging ass by the time I turned the radio up in my Volvo, ignored the engine warning light for the thousandth time in a row, and headed a few blocks to the hospital.

The waiting room was already full. A quick visual sweep told me it was the usual mix: overly cautious parents with sick kids, a woman doubled over with what was probably food poisoning, and a man holding a bloodied rag to his head. It took effort not to check on them. But the only thing worse than kissing Garcia's ass to get my suspension lifted would be doing it if he found out I'd been treating patients in his waiting room.

Pausing at the desk, I flashed my badge to Barb, who grimaced.

"I know you're suspended." She peered over the thick rim of her glasses. "But I *might* have forgotten to turn off your badge. Are you sure you want to go back there?"

I screwed up my face. "No, but I'm going to do it anyway."

"Good luck," she called as I swiped my badge. The door buzzed open with an ominous, echoing *click*.

Haley caught sight of me as soon as I was on the other side and beelined my direction, her long braids swaying with each step. As she reached me, she grabbed my arm, her brown eyes wide. "Where the hell have you been?"

"I was dealing with something." Not a lie, exactly.

She frowned, her fingers digging into me as she dragged me into an empty triage room. "You went to see the Gages, didn't you?" she asked in a low voice even though we were alone. "You think I don't know what you were up to when you left the other night? Christ, I've been losing my mind. Tell me you didn't do anything reckless."

Define reckless. I bit the words back. "More reckless than getting suspended?" I fingered my badge before sliding it into the back pocket of my jeans. "Or am I fired?"

"No clue. Garcia has been dealing with the police." Her eyes widened with accusation, like I needed a reminder of who had involved law enforcement.

"A crime was committed." Now that I knew the truth, I questioned that call, but I wasn't about to admit that.

"Well, Channing hasn't been very cooperative. They sent some rookie down here, and he's making Garcia jump through hoops, trying to get statements from all of us. He even stationed someone outside Channing's door."

I sighed. "So, I'm in deep shit all around?"

"I don't think you're getting employee of the month." She shook her head and wrapped an arm around my shoulder. "Maybe bring Garcia some of the beignets from that place on Canal?"

She was probably right, but even though Dr. Garcia held my career's future in his hands, he wasn't the reason I was here. "How is Channing?"

Haley released me, a bemused smile flashing across her face.

"Not speaking to anyone. The only time he says anything is to ask for pain meds or food."

My jaw clenched on a few choice words, frustration bubbling inside me. He could be mad at me all he wanted. He was the one who had gotten shot, and if I did regret getting the police involved, it was only because I now realized how truly powerless they were against Gage. Though none of that was a good enough reason to be rude to the people who were helping him. "Is that so? Let me see him."

Haley swept a hand toward the door. "Be my guest. I need to get back out there. We're short-staffed."

I winced, her words lodging directly in my gut. The hospital's staffing issues were only worse with me gone. I drew a deep breath as I followed her into the organized chaos of the emergency room. Weaving my way through the white coats and scrubs, I made my way to the nurse's station to check his room number before heading upstairs.

A uniformed police officer greeted me at Channing's room with a gruff, "No visitors." He looked back at his phone.

"I'm not a visitor. I'm a nurse." I showed him my badge. "He came through my department the other night. I wanted—"

"Whatever." He waved me inside, either sensing the lie or not caring enough to argue. I shuffled past him with an overly sweet thank-you.

Despite spending most of my adult life in a hospital, I wasn't prepared for the sight that waited for me. I'd been too freaked out to absorb what had happened the other night. But now?

Tubes snaked from Channing's arms and his chest, connecting him to IV bags and monitors. He was as pale as the sheets tucked around his body. But his chest rose and fell peacefully as he slept. He looked small again, like he had when he was a kid. That wasn't what stopped me in my tracks, though. It was the handcuffs.

His eyes fluttered open, blinking in sleepy confusion as he spotted me. I smiled, and his confusion shifted to cold anger.

"What are you doing here?" he demanded.

"I work here."

He angled his head. "Do you?"

"Good news travels fast," I muttered as I approached the bed. "I came to check in on you."

"Why? Wanted to see if you could fuck up my life a little more?"

I flinched slightly, covering my reaction by reaching for his chart. I flipped through it, reassured to see that he was truly stable. "You'll be released from here soon," I told him as I hung it back up.

"To a waiting cell?" he asked bitterly.

This was going well. "Better than a coffin." I glared down at him from the end of the bed. "What did you expect me to do?"

"You called the police!" A monitor beeped loudly as his heart rate shot up. "They won't leave me the fuck alone. They have me on illegal possession of a firearm, thanks to you!"

"The other guy died!" I reminded him. "It could be worse. You'll get probation."

He shook his head. "They think I'm going to turn on the Gages."

Fear opened a pit in my stomach. What would happen if he did tell them about Gage? Would the bargain I'd made for my soul be enough if trouble showed up on the Avalon's doorstep? I doubted it would matter. Gage probably had plenty of people in the police force in his pocket, but he might resent cleaning up another mess for me. "I'm sure nothing will happen," I lied smoothly, but I felt anything but certain. "Gage can buy his way out."

"You don't know him," he said darkly.

I swallowed. If Channing knew what I'd done, he would lose it. That's why it was better if he spent a little time incarcerated while I found the answer to ending the bargain. "I know how the world works. Or at least how New Orleans works. I wouldn't worry about Lachlan."

"Lachlan?" he repeated.

Shit. Shit. Shit. Why had I called Gage *that*? "That's the asshole's name, right?"

"Cate." Channing scooted up a little, studying me carefully. "Where the fuck have you been?"

"Home." Blood roared in my ears, my heart racing even as my face betrayed nothing. One of the few life skills being a foster kid taught me was how to lie. The trouble with that was Channing had the exact same skill set. It was a lot harder to lie to him. "I was suspended, remember? Where else would I be?"

"I tried to call." Suspicion colored his voice. "You—"

"You aren't the only one allowed to be angry," I cut him off, crossing my arms. I couldn't let him find out about the bargain, and there was one sure way to keep him from puzzling this out. "I called the police because you broke your word. If you won't stay away from Gage, I will keep you away from him."

He muttered something that sent my eyebrows shooting up. I waited for him to explode again, but he simply slumped into the bed. "Yeah, thanks for your help."

I waited for a minute, torn between trying to reason with him and giving in to my own anger. In the end, I opted for the latter. "You're welcome."

Silence sat heavy between us. How had it come to this? My chest tightened. Channing was the one person I could count on to always have my back, and now we were keeping secrets from each other. But I didn't know what he would do if I told him the truth. It was better to keep him away while I found a way out of this mess for the both of us.

Eventually, I said I was leaving, and he didn't try to stop me. By the time I reached my car, my hands were shaking with the effort not to give in and cry. But crying wouldn't help anyone, least of all me.

Climbing into my ancient Volvo, I turned the key, and the engine sputtered, followed by a *thunk*. I closed my eyes and tried again, opening them to discover smoke billowing from the hood.

"No!" I jumped out of the car, but before I could hit the latch button to open it up and see what the problem was, I saw the first flame. "Nooo!"

My car was on fire. Of course it was, because my life was hell—a flame's natural habitat.

I tried to stay calm as I bent to rummage in my purse for my phone. The pendant fell into my line of sight, and I shoved it out of the way. Spotting my phone on the front seat, I silently cursed and prayed to the gods for help as I opened the door to grab it.

But a god didn't answer.

CHAPTER ELEVEN

"That can't be good," an amused voice murmured in my ear, the heat of his breath tickling its shell.

I whipped around, colliding into Gage, who caught me smoothly. "What are you doing here?"

"You rang."

"I didn't."

But he tapped the pendant. "Your prayers have been answered. You were asking the gods for help."

The stupid necklace. "They couldn't send a fire extinguisher?"

"Clearly, you need me."

"Believe me, you are the last person I need." I opened the back door and started digging around until I found an old sweater. Grabbing it, I started toward the front of the car.

"I don't think it's cold." Gage leaned against the side of the car and watched me. Fantastic. A fae jerk had arrived to heckle me.

"I. Need. To. Put. Out. The. Fire." I might have imagined the hood was his stupid, perfect face as I smacked my sweater against it. Tears smarted my eyes, but I blinked them away. I wouldn't cry in front of him, even if my life was literally going up in flames. My brother wasn't speaking to me, my job was on the line, and the man responsible for all of it was watching the whole thing go down like he wished he had a bucket of popcorn for the show.

"I'd let it burn," he suggested.

"Leave or be helpful!" I shouted at him. I wasn't certain what was worse: that my car was on fire or Gage's unwanted commentary.

But he didn't move. "I am being helpful. This car has lived a good, long life. Let it burn."

I ignored him and kept beating at the flames, but the fire only spread. I didn't realize I was crying until his arm wrapped around my waist and dragged me to the safety of the sidewalk. Once we were there, he muttered something under his breath, snapped his fingers, and the fire died out.

But the damage was done. The entire hood was charred black, and if it looked that bad on the outside... Whatever hope I'd had smoldered along with it, but I fanned the last ember into red-hot rage.

"Why didn't you stop it?" I hurled the question at him as I stared at the ruins of my car.

"You didn't ask." He shoved his hands into the pockets of his jeans. For a second, I only stared up at him, part of me processing the fact that he was here in the real world, wearing a black T-shirt and jeans and looking far too much like the god I'd been calling upon even with his human glamour. Apparently, his sexy magic worked even in my world.

Finally, the rest of me caught up with his words.

"I didn't ask? Are you fucking kidding me?" I threw the ruined sweater at him. He caught it before it hit his face. "So you'll only help me when there's something in it for you. Is that it? You've already got my soul. Why help me? I've got nothing of value unless you want to bargain for the shirt on my back!"

"Now that could get interesting."

I hated his arrogant smirk, hated how completely unapologetic he was even now; mostly, I hated him. The hatred boiled inside me until I was shaking, words spewing out of me. "Why did you even come? I tried to kill you last night. Did you honestly think I was calling for you?"

He snorted, stepping away even as his body remained angled between me and the street. "I never know what to expect with you, princess."

"That makes two of us," I grumbled. "Why don't you just kill me and get it over with?"

It was the only logical course of action after I'd tried to take him out. He had to have reached the same conclusion. And if that's where this was heading, I'd rather he didn't toy with his prey for too long.

"I considered it." The sheer boredom in his voice coupled with that endless smirk told me he actually had.

And maybe it was a couple nights of lost sleep or watching my car's Viking funeral or just the mere fact that Gage wouldn't leave me alone, but I tilted my face up to the sky and screamed.

"Cate, it's just a car," he said, the smile finally dying.

"'Just a car'?" I repeated, nearly choking on the words. "*Just* a car?" I jabbed a finger at the scorched mess. "I spent two *years* saving up for that car." The only reason I'd been able to buy it was because the windows didn't roll down. Some days, I could barely afford the gas. More than once, the insurance had lapsed because money was too tight that month. But it was my car, the closest thing I'd ever had to a ticket out of New Orleans.

And he had let it burn in front of me.

"You can have one of mine," he said.

I detonated. "I don't want your car or you or any of this!" I ripped the necklace off and threw it at him. It bounced off his chest and landed on the street.

Some of his glamour slipped, his tattoos shifting as he glowered at me. His jaw tensed, shadows filling his eyes. "We've been over this. The bargain cannot be broken, and you are required to wear that to fulfill your end of the bargain. No exceptions."

"I thought you were some powerful fae prince, but you couldn't grant Channing's freedom without stealing mine? Your bargain doesn't work without some stupid necklace?" I planted my hands on my hips. "I think you're full of it. I think the Gage family—"

"Be careful what you say about my family in this city."

"What do you care?"

"I care because I own New Orleans. Because someone is always listening," he hissed, grabbing me by the shoulders and yanking me closer. "What you say matters—"

"Like that I hate this city almost as much as I hate the family that runs it?"

He winced.

"Or that you prey on—"

"Careful," he interrupted, the word drawn out low and deadly as he leaned closer, his dark gaze fixed on mine. A shiver raced down my spine but not in fear.

It was a testament to how stressed I was, because all of a sudden what I wanted was for this man to make me forget. Forget my shitty car. Forget my shitty suspension from work. Forget the shitty lies I'd told my brother. Even forget this shitty little bargain. I just wanted to say "fuck it" and give in to the need pulsing between us and forget.

Our eyes met, and for a second I swore I saw understanding, as though he knew exactly what I wanted but would never ask for, before his mouth smashed into mine. The kiss cut off my breath and stole the words from my lips. And then my senses lit up like a live wire and instinct took over.

If I'd thought I'd reacted to him before...

Stupid, fucking, sexy magic.

My body melted into his hard one as Gage claimed my mouth. He tasted like the sweet fire of wine and spice and wild things, and his fingers tightened possessively on my shoulders. Wrong. It was so wrong. Somewhere in the back of my mind I knew that, but I didn't care. Not as his hands swept up to cradle my neck and his fingers tangled in my hair. Not as I lost myself to him. Not as the line between my anger and my attraction to him blurred. Until he drew back and pressed his forehead to mine.

"Watch your mouth," he rumbled.

I balked, pulling a little against his hold, but he didn't let me go. "Or what?"

"Or I will watch it for you. I might find your little threats and insults amusing—endearing, even—but you will not speak poorly of my city. Don't test your luck."

That's what this was about. His city?

"The city that you're poisoning with trinity?" I glared at him. "If you cared about New Orleans, you wouldn't let that shit on its streets, let alone be the one responsible for putting it there."

"You think you have me figured out, don't you? I promise you have no clue, princess," he shot back.

I knew what I'd witnessed at the hospital and what I'd seen on the streets. But it was hard to believe that Gage was responsible. Was he an unbelievably arrogant, selfish ass of a fae? Yes. Definitely. But his worst behavior since we'd met didn't quite add up to evil, even if I wished that it did. Still, he needed to be held accountable.

"Let me go," I said through clenched teeth. Or maybe I was just being influenced by the heady combination of his proximity and my hormone-clouded brain. "Stop using your sexy magic."

His grip loosened in surprise, but he didn't let go. "*Sexy* magic?"

"You know what you're doing, asshole," I hissed. "Stop using your magic to fuck with me."

He chuckled, the rich sound burrowing under my skin. "I'm not using any magic on you."

I didn't believe him, but what was new? He couldn't be trusted.

He studied me for a moment. "Have you learned your lesson?"

"Yes." I squirmed under his hard gaze.

Gage fully relaxed his grip, and I slid away from him, all too aware of my trembling legs, the sweat slicking my skin, the racing of my heart. The lines of his face remained stony as I retreated and put some very necessary distance between us.

"You kissed me." The words were half accusation, half confusion.

"Don't let it go to your head."

"*My* head?" I spluttered, instantly regretting any doubt I'd had about him being a grade-A prick. "Do you think I *wanted* you to kiss me?"

He shrugged. "You didn't seem to mind."

My mouth hung open, every rational thought emptying from my brain, which was busy imagining a target right over his arrogant face. Closing my eyes, I took a deep breath. I wouldn't let him get to me. "Don't do it again."

"I won't." But those sinful lips twitched, sending a rush through me. "Not until you ask me to."

I dared a step closer. "I wouldn't hold your breath. Because I will never ask you to kiss me."

"Never is a long time."

"Not long enough," I snapped. Forcing my hands to stay at my sides, I backed away from him. "I have to go."

"How?" He squinted at my car.

"I can walk." Anything to get away from here, away from him.

He bent and scooped the necklace off the ground. "What are you really mad about?"

I glanced at the burned husk of my car. "That, to start with."

He nodded. "And?"

"This bargain," I shot back. And the fact that I was no closer to guessing what his secret was—why he'd agreed to the deal in the first place.

"And?" he pressed. "It's something beyond that."

"I think that's more than enough." I narrowed my eyes. He was trying to get into my head. It was probably another fae trick. But there was a glimmer of something in his eyes, foreign to him but familiar to me. It wasn't possible that he actually cared, though. "But if you're keeping track, the hospital is short-staffed because people are covering for me. Because I got suspended for breaking the shitty policy they agreed to in exchange for your money."

He rubbed his lips thoughtfully. "I see." He was going to see my foot up his ass, but before I could cheerfully follow through, he pulled out his phone. "I already told you the job was unnecessary. I can see now that it will only be a problem."

"What are you doing, Gage?" I lunged for the phone, but he turned away. He only had to make one call to get me fired. "Don't. I have student loans. I have bills."

He held up a single finger, his back still turned to me. "Garcia, please." A pause. "Make him available."

He was making a power play. I'd pressed too many of his buttons, and now he was going to press one of mine. Unfortunately, it was the one that sent my entire world into self-destruct mode.

I tried again, the fear in my voice making it thin and needy. "I'm begging. Please don't—"

"Garcia." He didn't bother to tell him who was calling. I barely managed to stay on my feet. "I wanted to let you know I've taken on a private nurse."

Private *what*? "What are you—"

The finger went up again to silence me. Forget our new deal; I was going to kill him.

"Miss Holloway works for me now. You may have her back when I decide or when she wishes to return. In the meantime, I'm concerned about your staffing shortage. I nearly couldn't lure her away because of it. If the hospital is that underserved, you should have told me. I rely not only on your discretion but on your services, as does my city. Hire more nurses," he said swiftly. "I don't care how you find them. Try doubling the starting salary." He waited, and I just stared at him. "Then double the salary of the other staff, too. And Garcia? Don't risk my city again, or the next position we hire for will be yours."

He hung up with that threat and finally turned to face me.

"You just threatened the chief of medicine," I said, feeling a little numb.

"I dealt with a problem. That's what I do for my city."

But it wasn't for his city. Not really. It was for me, and that was… disorienting. "You told him I was your nurse." Apparently, I was going to work out my confusion aloud and in real time. Fantastic.

"How did you put it? Even immortals bleed?" he asked tightly. "You know that Gage Memorial exists to provide care for my kind and for our associates. Perhaps it's time I had someone on call in case of an emergency."

I couldn't tear my eyes from his. Nothing about him made sense. "You have an entire hospital on call for you."

"But I don't trust them." He slid his phone into his pocket.

"Why would you trust me?" I blurted out. "I pulled the trigger." I really shouldn't be reminding him of that right now—or ever.

A slow smile spread over those lips. "I trust you *because* you pulled the trigger." He stuffed his hands in his pockets, his eyes straying past me. I looked over my shoulder to where my burned car sat forgotten. "Sure you don't want a ride home?"

"You didn't drive," I reminded him, my brain still trying to catch up with the dizzying events of the last twenty minutes.

But he only laughed. "Later, princess."

He snapped his fingers and was gone before I remembered the necklace. He'd taken it with him and left me with more questions instead, but I kept coming back to the same one.

What was he getting out of our bargain? There was something in this for him, and I needed to find out what.

Okay, maybe I had *two* pressing questions.

How was I going to keep myself from asking him to kiss me again while I figured it out?

The second question should have been easier to answer than the first. The trouble was, it didn't feel that way.

CHAPTER TWELVE

I didn't know what to do when the sun slipped below the horizon, the day dying in a blaze of fiery orange and crimson. After throwing the necklace at him, I'd waited for Gage to summon me. When the stars punched holes in the velvet night, I began to wonder if he wouldn't—if he regretted that stupid kiss, too. As midnight approached, I gave up my vigil and poured myself a glass of wine to erase the taste of him lingering in my mouth. I was about to reach for one of my overdue library books when I felt heat prickle the back of my neck.

Then the world was yanked out from under me.

I landed on my ass in the middle of my Nether Court bedroom, wine splashing down the front of my Rolling Stones T-shirt.

Gage leaned against the wall, grinning down at me.

Getting to my feet, I flipped him off. His dark amusement flickered, but he didn't budge. He was back in his usual suit— probably to better hide his guns from me. His undone shirt collar revealed a whorl of ink that fled out of my sight to somewhere else on his hard body—the body that had been pressed against me a few hours ago. He raked a hand through his jet-black hair, leaving it a tousled mess. "Good evening."

"Is there something wrong with this place's foundation?" I snapped at him, swiping at the wine spreading across my torso nearly as swiftly as the heat flooding across my skin. "Or do you just stand around holding up the walls and brooding out of boredom?"

"You're in a good mood." He shifted on his feet and moved toward me. "I thought you might be a little nicer to me. I gave you a few hours off."

I stared at him. That was how he was going to play this? Like he'd been doing me a favor? "Sadly, in your case, absence doesn't make the heart grow fonder."

He placed a hand on his chest. "You wound me."

"If only." I suspected his heart was his least vulnerable target.

I brushed past him, depositing the empty wineglass on the table, and headed into the bathroom to search for a towel to clean up my shirt. He followed me closely. Too closely. The heat of his body, the scent of him—cedar and spice—his mere presence all dredging up memories of that stolen kiss.

I dropped the towel twice, completely flustered between his nearness and those memories. Being this close to him was unbearable. What if he kissed me again?

What if he didn't?

Oh no, I was not going there. He was definitely screwing with me. I didn't believe for a second that he wasn't using his magic.

I gave up on my shirt and whirled around to face him. "Clearly, *you* missed *me*."

"Did I?" His brow curved along with his lips, a tattoo creeping up the side of his neck.

"That, or fae have no concept of personal space." I took a step back.

He moved closer. "I'm just waiting."

My eyes narrowed. "For what?"

He leaned in, his mouth angled precariously over mine, his breath hot on my face. I bit my lower lip and waited, all too aware that letting him be this close to me was a terrible idea. If I wasn't careful, I might find him kissing me again. My breath hitched in my throat, but I didn't move. I didn't dare. Our eyes locked, and I knew we were on dangerous ground.

"An apology," he whispered.

I recoiled. "I'd sit down, then, because you are going to be waiting a long time."

He gave me that stupid smirk—the one that could probably melt panties. Gage knew exactly what he was doing, baiting me like this, waiting for me to explode. Probably so he could kiss me again and claim it was to shut me up. But I'd fallen for that trick before, and my panties were staying on, *thankyouverymuch*.

"I'll apologize when you do, Gage."

"Why would I apologize?"

"Exactly." I started around him toward the much larger bedroom, where there was more space for the three of us—me, him, and his enormous ego. "Are you done torturing me yet?"

His lip curled back, a soft snarl escaping him as he blocked me. "My mere presence is torture? Because I'm irresistible, or because you can't stop thinking about that kiss?"

I swallowed, reaching for every ounce of anger I could summon before he realized how close to the mark he'd hit. "Because every time I look at you, I see the biggest mistake of my life."

His shoulders went rigid, his tattoos moving so swiftly that they appeared to cloak him entirely in ink. He seemed even larger, as if he belonged entirely to those writhing words and symbols. He advanced one step toward me. "I assure you that the feeling is entirely mutual."

He relaxed, allowing his scowl to soften to a smile that spread so rapidly, I braced myself. "And to answer your question: the torture is just beginning."

• • •

There was torture and then there was a dress fitting.

Until this moment, the closest I'd come to one in my life was the time I'd gotten a zipper stuck trying on a skirt and the fitting room attendant had needed to use scissors to cut me out of it. I'd thought that was embarrassing. I was wrong.

I'd bypassed *embarrassment* an hour ago, when I'd stepped onto the stool and discovered Gage had claimed a chair to watch. Having two fae seamstresses pinning and sighing and debating in front of him was the definition of humiliation. I'd ratcheted straight to *kill-me-now-please* when he picked up a folder from the table, flipped it open, and began to read from it out loud.

"Truancy by age eleven."

My breath hitched.

He didn't seem to notice as he continued rattling off a list of my sins. "Trespassing by thirteen. Shoplifting that year, too. Now this is interesting: at fourteen, possession of clover *and* assault. I knew you had it in you."

"How did you get that?" I demanded in a hollow voice.

One side of his mouth crooked up. "I have my ways. I find it's smart to look into anyone who threatens to kill you." I fought a wave of nausea as he flipped ahead. "Such a *colorful* past, and you were worried about Channing."

My colorful past was exactly why I was worried about Channing. I'd paid a high price for those mistakes. I refused to let the same thing happen to my brother.

"Those records are sealed," I whispered.

"Yes, they are, but sealing them doesn't erase them." He tapped a finger on his glass. "But then at fifteen, nothing. It's a remarkable turnaround."

My stomach roiled as unwanted memories flashed in my mind, but I remained silent, keenly aware that he was watching me, assessing me. I tamped down my pain, swallowing it back to that dark place I kept it, and shrugged. "I guess I learned my lesson."

He took a sip, then slowly licked the lingering liquor from his lips. "Nothing happened after that?"

"No." I couldn't bear to look at him.

"Really?" he pressed.

Why wouldn't he let this go? Or had he found other records from the Department of Children & Family Services? Ones I never wanted anyone to see. But he only waited, so I shook my head, stars dancing in the corners of my vision.

"Just checking." He dropped the file onto the table. The

interrogation was over. I sagged with relief.

I picked at the gossamer fabric, earning a sharp rap on the knuckles from one of the women. "Why do I need this, anyway?"

"Because you're stuck with me every night for...well, forever." Gage swished the contents of his glass, sending the brown liquor swirling dangerously close to its rim. He was still on his first glass, as if he was savoring it as much as his little game.

"And I need ball gowns for this life sentence?" I groaned when he laughed.

"It's a little late to ask questions now, isn't it?" He stood and crossed the room in three long strides, pausing in front of where I was being measured and trussed.

I refused to look away despite the electric charge I felt under his dark gaze. "Then I won't ask where I'm wearing all of these fancy dresses."

"Good, because I'm tired of all your questions."

"You could leave," I said with mock sweetness.

He grimaced and lifted the glass to his full lips, finally downing the liquor in a single swallow. "But I'm enjoying your company *so much*."

"Why are you here?" It wasn't exactly riveting to sit through a dress fitting.

"I enjoy when they stick you with the pins."

I plucked one out, earning an annoyed shriek from the seamstress, and brandished it at him. "Say that again, Gage."

"Lach," he corrected me, but I glowered at him. His low chuckle slid between my bones. "You need the gowns for parties."

"Parties, *Lachlan*?"

That seemed to irk him more than calling him Gage, so I decided to stick with it.

"Did you think I wanted to dress you up like a pretty, pretty princess for my amusement?"

I peered down at the seamstress assessing my hemline and twiddled the pin. "Are these made of iron by any chance?"

She paled, but *Lachlan* snatched it from my fingers. "We've been over this. No murder allowed."

"With all the riddles and torment, who has time for homicide?"

"Your wardrobe isn't suitable for court events." He pulled a flask out of seemingly thin air and refilled his glass. "And unfortunately, we have company coming again."

I blinked at him, my bravado faltering. "Company?"

"I'm about to seal a deal with the Infernal Court that will help with my little clover problem."

"Problem?" The surprises kept coming. "Not ruining enough lives?"

The glass paused on the way to his lips. "Is that what you think?" He shook his head. "Clover was never meant to ruin lives. It's simply currency. A fleeting moment of happiness in exchange for money."

"Drugs don't work like that. You're thinking of chocolate."

"Clover worked like that," he said grimly, "but the magic... It's hard to explain. Something is wrong with it."

"Trinity?"

He raised a brow.

I didn't buy for a second that he actually cared, but if there was even a chance that he did... "That's what we call it at the hospital. Because it's not good or lucky or happy anymore. Not fun. Not safe. It's not four-leafed clover anymore. It only looks like it."

"Clever." His lips pinched, but he finally sighed. "Until we figure out what's gone wrong, I need to fill the gap."

"Yes, because different drugs are the answer," I said dryly. So much for him being part of the solution.

"Paint fae as the villains if you like, but humans are their own worst enemies. They crave happiness so desperately that they'll do anything for a moment of it, even if it's going to destroy them." His eyes examined me briefly, something unreadable moving in them. "Getting clover off the streets won't fill the hole it leaves behind. The Infernal Court has something that will."

"So, you're inviting everyone here to do a drug deal, and *that* requires formal wear?"

"It's much more complicated." He sighed and took another

drink. "It *requires* ritual fuckery and pissing contests and other bullshit."

I could tell what he thought about that.

The seamstress stood, casting one final weary look in my direction. "You can take that off. We're finished for now." Before I could thank her, she vanished along with her partner.

"I will never get used to that," I muttered, gathering my skirt carefully to avoid the pins before stepping down.

"Nipping?" he asked.

"Why not just call it teleportation?" I replied, plucking the glass from his hands.

He tracked me as I took a drink, his mouth twisting into a bemused line. "We've been nipping for thousands of years, but, yes, by all means, let's modernize it."

I took another swig, appreciating the way the liquor burned down my throat, and changed the subject. "So, ritual fuckery and pissing contests? Did you put that on the invitation?"

"Two of our most beloved pastimes, but don't worry, there will also be food and dancing."

I traced the cuts and grooves of the crystal glass. Did he really expect me to flutter around in a ball gown, making small talk and hanging off his arm? "That sounds fun."

"It isn't." He raked a hand through his hair, a tattoo winding its way around his knuckles. "However, securing an alliance with the Infernal Court is the only option we have."

"But all the courts have to come?" I sipped again. "Why?"

"Some would say tradition, but it's more superstition. When deals are struck between courts, especially shadow courts, everyone wants a say."

I shook my head, still trying to understand. A deal sounded simple enough, but Lachlan seemed to be dancing around something bigger. "Because the shadow courts are bad?"

His nostrils flared. "I'm afraid it's not that black and white," he said tightly. "Although, the light courts are pretentious enough to think they're better than us."

"So why the differentiation? Why worry about the opinion of the light courts?"

"Fae magic exists on a spectrum of lightness and darkness. It has nothing to do with morality," he added when he saw my confused expression. "Believe me, a Hallow Court fae is just as likely to hunt down someone who breaches his territory as we are. But each court's magic operates differently. At the Nether Court, we draw off the magic that runs deep underground in cold, dark places. The Infernal Court draws off the molten power at the Earth's core."

"And the other courts? The Hallow Court and the…?"

"Astral Court," he answered. "They draw off the energy above us. The sun. The stars. The Hallow Court draws off the air. If you ask them, their magic comes from heaven itself. That's probably why they think they're above us. In a way, they are. Quite literally."

"I thought the fae hated humans. Why make me go?"

"I assume you don't want to hang out here while everyone else is having a good time."

I did, actually. But the way he said it suggested he would not be having a good time himself. "We could just take a few nights off."

"That's the unfortunate thing about bargains." He took back his glass and poured another drink. "We're both beholden to the terms of our arrangement, even on nights when I have other guests."

"You can entertain anyone you want at night," I said lightly, even though the words felt heavy on my lips. "I don't *own* your nights."

Was the shadow moving in his eyes magic or something else? "I'll keep that in mind. Although, I doubt I'll have time while I'm negotiating a new trade alliance for the next month."

"Month?" I said faintly. "It sounds like you'll be very busy. Maybe…"

"I have other reasons for wanting you there." And there it was.

Reasons that had something to do with his motive to make the bargain with me in the first place? My pulse sped up, but I tried to look disinterested.

"I'm arranging a marriage."

It was possibly the last thing I'd expected him to say. My mouth went utterly dry, and I had to force myself to respond. "Oh, and who are you marrying?"

"Me?" His head tipped back, and he howled. When he finally quieted, his eyes sparkled in a way I hadn't seen before, but pain tainted it. "No one wants to marry me."

My hand reached for his shoulder instinctively and squeezed. He looked down at it, and I withdrew it quickly. What the hell was that? "What happened to the women you claim are falling all over you?"

"You misunderstand me." His voice was soft. "There are plenty who *would* marry me, but only for money or power or sex."

I flushed. "Sex?"

The smirk was back. "Sex," he repeated without further explanation, which was answer enough. "Thankfully, I cannot marry anyone to secure an alliance."

I couldn't keep my curiosity at bay. "What exactly is your type? Or is no one good enough for you?"

"Jealousy brings out your eyes." He chuckled roughly at my grunt of displeasure. "To truly secure an alliance, I would have to marry a princess. Not just a courtier. There are only four fae princesses. Two of them are my sisters. The other two are heirs to their own courts."

"Isn't that ideal?" I had no idea why I cared. I told myself it was simply curiosity, but the rapidness of my heart suggested otherwise.

"Heirs don't marry each other. Not anymore," he added, eyes fading to some distant memory.

"You're all princes and princess? There's no king or queen?" I asked.

A shadow passed over his face. "Not for a long time."

"So, you're forbidden to marry another heir?"

He licked his lower lip so slowly that I found myself staring.

Not. Going. There.

"It's not forbidden, exactly," he continued. "But it would be discouraged."

"Discouraged?"

He nodded. "*Violently* discouraged. The last time two heirs married, it ended poorly. The other courts would frown on it, and even if it were an option, Aurora and Titania are both from light courts."

"I don't get it. If you can't marry to secure an alliance…" I was picking at a loose thread on my dress when it hit me. "You're setting up one of your sisters."

"Ciara loves London. She'll fit right in at the Infernal Court." But he didn't smile. "She'll be happy there."

It sounded like he was trying to convince himself of that. I'd only spent a little time with Ciara. I didn't know her well enough to decide if he was right. "She knows about this?"

"Yes, which leads me to the reason I need you around." He lifted his eyes to mine. "She likes you."

I snorted before I realized he was serious.

"She could use a friend."

"Me?" I just stared at him. "I don't understand."

"Shop with her, hang out with her, keep her mind off it until it's over."

I sank into a chair near the window, wishing I could just swipe his flask. "You want me to distract her so you can force her to marry someone?"

I hadn't signed up for this. I liked Ciara, *despite* the fact that she was a Gage, and even if I didn't, this was the twenty-first century. I started to shake my head.

"She's already agreed." Was I imagining the regret coloring his tone? I had to be. "Marriage between courts is always political. Once she produces an heir…"

My eyebrows shot up, my stomach beginning to churn on her behalf.

"…she'll be free to do as she pleases. She can stay in London or return here. It's simply a transaction."

A bargain, I realized. That's how this world worked. But the desire the fae dealt in felt a lot more like desperation the more time I spent in the Otherworld.

"What about your other sister? Fiona?" I grasped for an excuse to get out of this. "Can't she come hang out with her?"

"Fiona will not be a distraction. She probably won't even come, since she already suffered through the Equinox. She avoids the court unless she's required to attend."

Gee, I wonder why? I bottled the comment up. "And you aren't going to require her to be here for Ciara?"

"Ciara would probably beg her not to come, and I'd rather not add listening to their endless fighting to my plate." He tilted his head. "That's why I need you."

"I'm not sure I'm the right person to ask." I was definitely *not* the right person. I might even be the last person who should be asked, except, apparently, for Fiona. "Why me?"

"Because I trust you."

This again. He must have a lot of enemies if he thought I was his best option.

"And because Ciara knows me best in the world, except maybe for Roark," he continued.

"So?"

He arched a brow. "I assume you're trying to figure out the answer to my riddle."

What did he want with me? What did he get out of our bargain? The two questions I kept asking myself over and over again. I'd do almost anything to answer them. *Almost.*

"And you think that dangling the person who knows you best is enough for me to pretend to be your sister's friend? That I'm willing to use someone like that?"

"I'm just trying to show it will be mutually beneficial." He shoved a hand in his pocket, but not before I saw those twisting tattoos. Why did they move like that? Was it another clue to how he worked? "You can say no. It's not part of our arrangement. I just... This will be hard for her."

And he didn't want it to be. That shouldn't matter. Not since he was the one putting her in this terrible position. But I knew a thing or two about doing something terrible to your sibling when options felt limited. Was sending Channing to jail any better than what he was doing? I recalled how my brother had looked at me earlier. I bet he wouldn't think so.

But there was one thing that didn't make sense about this.

"Do you want me to find out what you're after?" I asked. That's what I really couldn't understand. I knew that he was keeping something from me. This was about more than the bargain, but I couldn't begin to guess what. The thought hollowed out my stomach. "Because if Ciara knows what you want out of this bargain, she might actually tell me."

"Maybe I'm trying to play fair," he offered.

I shook my head. That definitely wasn't it.

"We all have to pay for our mistakes, princess." His smile made my stomach sink like a stone plopped in a pond. "Ciara doesn't know why I made the bargain with you. Not even Roark does."

Did *he* even know why he'd made it? I was beginning to wonder. Maybe spending more time here would reveal what he was trying to hide.

"But when you fail to break our bargain, I don't want you to accuse me of tricking you," he said. "I'm giving you a fair shot."

But was he really? Lachlan might not have been pure evil, but he was more than capable of getting his hands dirty.

"Fine." I was going to regret this. Maybe he'd known I wouldn't be able to resist the temptation, but it was more than that, more than seeing my own actions in his. It was about Ciara. I knew what it was like to have no control over my life, to have others making decisions for me. Even if Ciara had agreed, I doubted she felt like she had a choice. Maybe I could show her that she did. Maybe I could help her find a way out, and she could do the same for me.

He relaxed, his shoulders softening, and I realized for the first time how rigid he'd been until this moment. As if he couldn't have just forced me to do what he wanted. "I'll need you to stay here for the next month, of course."

"Here?" I blurted out. I hadn't heard him correctly.

"Why do you think I informed the hospital that you'd accepted a private position?"

My eyes felt like they were going to pop out of my head. Arrogant, selfish, lying fae prick. "Do you need medical care, or do I get the pleasure of seeing that you do?"

His lips twitched. "I thought we were on the same page about your homicidal urges."

"I can inflict plenty of pain without killing you," I promised.

He had the good sense to look concerned. "I need you here."

"And I need electricity and data. You freed up my schedule." A dubious claim, to be sure. "But I can't just take a vacation to the Otherworld. I need to be reachable."

He considered for a moment, and I braced myself for him to say no, for him to remind me that I had no one in my world who would even notice. The hospital didn't need me. He'd seen to that. The closest thing I had to friendships was with my overworked colleagues, who would have been told about my new position by Garcia. And if Channing didn't want to speak to me now, he'd be even less inclined when he was released into police custody.

"You make a good point," he said, surprising me. "There's an easy solution. You'll move into the Avalon with us. I assume you can suffer staying in a five-star hotel."

"Does it have internet?" I wasn't agreeing to anything that easily. Not with his track record.

"And electricity and running water," he said dryly.

I was about to cave when I processed the rest of what he'd said. "Wait. What do you mean, move into the Avalon *with us*?"

"We don't live in the Otherworld." He sounded amused at the idea. "No electricity, remember? It might kill Ciara and Roark if their phones died."

My mouth fell open. "You don't even live in the Otherworld?" I cursed under my breath. "But you made *me* sleep here."

"I thought it was better if you remained in the Otherworld the first few nights. No data, remember?" He unscrewed the cap of his flask and refilled the glass. He handed it to me. "I didn't need you calling the police on me."

And I might have tried to do just that. "That's what Roark started to say at breakfast." I clutched the glass to my chest.

"He has a big mouth."

I made a mental note of that. If Roark was the other person who knew him, I needed to get to know him as well.

Lachlan kissed like a god, but the devil ran through him. He might not be evil, but he was ruthless. If he was willing to use his favorite sister as leverage, it was only a matter of time before he turned our bargain to his advantage.

"So, I don't have to stay in the Otherworld every night," I said slowly.

He rubbed his temples like I was giving him a headache. "I just want you...nearby."

And the Otherworld was nearby in his eyes. I'd spent the last two nights sleeping in a chair in front of the door, and the bastard hadn't even been in the same *world* as me.

"The Avalon is directly over the Nether Court, which means it's nearly as secure. We can draw from our magic more easily there," he admitted, "and there's your blessed electricity. Any more objections?"

At least the Avalon was in my world.

"What should I pack?" I asked, wringing my hands together.

"Obviously, your wardrobe is being arranged." He gestured toward where I'd been poked for the last several hours. "Bring whatever you like, but feel free to leave your attitude at home."

"I'm afraid that's part of the package," I said sweetly.

He pursed his lips, but he turned slightly toward the door. "I'll leave you to change."

I was still in my gossamer gown. Right. I pasted an irritated smile on my face. It was getting late, but I had no idea what to do with myself in his strange world. "And then what? Tea in the garden? A slumber party?"

"Are you inviting me to share your bed?" he purred, something feral prowling behind his beautiful, deadly face.

I flushed from head to toe, anger heating my blood. "First you

kiss me without permission, and now you're trying to sleep with me."
I crossed my arms over my chest, ignoring the tightness of my skin,
my breasts. I needed a glamour against his sexy magic. "I thought I
wasn't your type."

He glowered back at me. "Maybe not, but I'm willing to try new
things."

I gagged, even as my cheeks burned. "Thanks, but you aren't
my type."

"Really?" He continued to chew on his lip, his bright eyes
gleaming. "That's odd, because you seem flustered."

"Flustered?" I sputtered the word, backing up a few steps.

"Agitated. Nervous." Each word was clipped and crisp as he
stalked toward me. *"Worked up."*

"I am not *worked up*." My back hit the wall, and my heart shot
into my throat as I realized we were right back where we'd been last
night. So why did it feel so different now? "You have no effect on
me."

"I don't?" He cocked an eyebrow and closed the space between
us. Lachlan planted his hands on both sides of the wall, caging me in
place. "What about my *sexy magic*?"

Fuck, why had I called him on that? Because something about
the way he was looking at me expectantly, half amused and half
arrogant as fuck, told me there was no magic at work.

"That was a joke." Worst excuse ever.

"Why are you lying to me?" And he wasn't buying it.

"I'm not lying," I whispered.

A warm laugh rasped past his lips. His head fell forward, and
a loose wisp of hair tickled across my face. Cedar flooded my nose,
and I clamped my mouth shut, trying to hold my breath, trying to
keep my body from responding to his nearness. He lifted his head,
eyes sweeping from my feet upward and lingering on my hips, my
breasts before continuing slowly to my neck, my lips, until his eyes
found mine. He was so close I could count the gold flecks in his
irises. If he got any closer...

"If I have no effect on you, why is your heart racing?" he

murmured, tilting his head so that his mouth was angled over mine. He closed his eyes, and I forgot how to breathe. "I can hear it."

"You scare me." Not exactly a lie. He terrified me. Not only because of who he was—a Gage—but because of what he was. At least that's what I kept telling myself. But deep down in a place I refused to look, I knew that wasn't what scared me about him.

He remained silent, but he didn't let me go. His hand ghosted along my throat, a single finger tracing softly down my collarbone. I moaned at the unexpected touch, and a slow grin stole across his mouth as he opened his eyes and stared into my lying face. "Yes, I can see I have *no* effect on you." He leaned closer, his lips tickling my ear. "I'll remember that *I'm* not *your* type."

"Good." The word came out breathless. "I'm glad we cleared that up."

He flicked the pendant around my neck, chuckling when my hand shot up to find the broken necklace returned. "You'll need that to reach me, but it won't send you home at sunrise anymore. Someone will take you when you need to leave."

I swallowed, managing a nod. My fingers rested on the pendant. That's why he had touched me. He was simply putting the necklace back on. It wasn't because he needed to feel his skin on mine. It wasn't because my scent was clouding his thoughts and dissolving his common sense. It wasn't because he wanted me.

"And, princess." He stared at my lips, licking his own in a way that told me he knew how to use that mouth for more than arrogant banter. "Later tonight, when you're in bed *not* thinking about me, feel free to touch that necklace while you touch yourself."

I dropped my hand in disgust. "You think very highly of yourself."

"I don't think." He grinned down at me. "I know."

I glared at him. "Why would I think about you?"

But the damage was done, and even if my contempt had been believable, I knew those fae ears heard the truth in my speeding heart. He pushed away from the wall and straightened. "I'll have a car take you to gather your things in the morning."

That cleared my head. "Morning? I can't—"

"Yes, you can."

"I need to go by the hospital." I stood my ground. "I left some things there."

"The car will take you wherever you want to go. Take as long as you need."

Spoken like someone who had all the time in the world. How old was he? I was too busy studying him to realize he was waiting for an answer.

"That is…acceptable."

He didn't look at me again, and I wondered if I'd imagined the tension between us or if it had all been another one of his games. He walked toward the door, pausing on his way out. "I'll see you later." His eyes strayed to my neck—to the pendant, I realized. I reached up and flicked it, hoping he somehow felt it, but he only laughed.

I watched him leave, but my heart didn't slow. It kept racing for hours as I considered the challenge before me. My head was clearer with him gone. Maybe that was the real reason he wanted me to stay at the Avalon: so he could keep confusing me with his flirting. I had a month to figure him out, to figure out what he wanted from me—and then I had to make sure he could never get it. It was absurd but surely not impossible—*if* I believed what he'd said about playing fair.

The trouble was, that kiss told me we both might be better at playing dirty.

CHAPTER THIRTEEN

I had no idea what time it was when I finally gave up on sleep and slipped from the bed to look for a book. I considered touching the necklace and waking Gage's ass up to bring me one, but calling for him in the middle of the night might send the wrong message.

To both of us.

The hall outside my room was dark as I crept out in search of distraction that did not come in the form of thinking about six-feet-plus of purely masculine fae arrogance.

"Can I help you?"

Cursing, I spun around, one hand on my chest to keep my heart from jumping out of it. I squinted as a red-haired fae stepped from the shadows. His hair, glinting in the corridor's dim light, was a stark contrast to his tailored black suit. He'd been there that first night at the Avalon, I realized. The guard Gage had cruelly dismissed.

He tossed me a sheepish grin. "Shaw," he reminded me, seeing the recognition in my eyes. "Sorry. I didn't mean to scare you. Do you need something?"

Apparently, the Nether Court wasn't entirely abandoned. It made sense that Lachlan would have left guards and household staff. "I can't sleep."

"Is there something wrong with your bed?"

"It's…comfortable."

He studied me for a moment. "And that's a problem?"

I sucked in a deep breath. I doubted he really cared, but it wasn't like I had somewhere to be tonight. Or any night, for that matter. "I'm used to something a little less heavenly," I admitted. "That thing is like sleeping on a cloud."

"Heavenly?" He grinned at my choice of words. "No one has ever mistaken the Nether Court for heaven before."

For a moment, I thought of Ciara. She'd said something similar. After I'd learned her brother's plans for her, I was inclined to agree, and it seemed Shaw felt the same.

"It's better than what I'm used to." I shrugged. "I was just looking for something to do. I need to remember to bring a book."

Shaw crossed his arms. Ink covered every inch of his hands. It wrapped itself in intersecting symbols and swirls around his neck. But unlike Lachlan's constantly shifting tattoos, Shaw's remained solidly in place. I took a step closer, as if I might spur them to transform. They didn't even shimmy.

"Your tattoos don't move." I looked up at him.

"They do sometimes, but only when I'm thinking."

I lifted one brow. "You only think sometimes?"

It was a rude thing to say, particularly to someone who was probably packing under his suit jacket, but Shaw chuckled. "If I can help it. I only think when I'm worried, and I try not to worry."

I snorted. "Must be nice. I worry all the time."

"Worrying is expensive. It costs you the one thing you can't get back. Time."

I frowned. Shaw looked like he was in his early twenties. Far too young to be spouting that kind of wisdom. But to be honest, I had no idea how old any of them were. I hadn't seen a single fae that looked older than thirty yet. For all I knew, he could be hundreds of years older than me. "That's very wise for someone who doesn't think."

"I think, but I try to stop while I'm ahead." He tipped his head toward the empty corridor. "You said you wanted a book. I'll show you to the library. It's this way." He gestured for me to follow.

I kept a careful distance from him as we wound our way through the night-dark corridors. The only illumination came from candles perched on thick, gold sconces, their flames dancing in the shadows and their warm wax scent comforting under the drafty, vaulted ceilings that seemed to swallow most of their light. Next to me, Shaw maneuvered easily, probably due to his Fae eyesight.

We walked until I forgot what direction we'd come from. I would never find my way back to my room at this point. "Does this place ever end?"

"The court?" he asked, glancing over at me. "It does."

I looked toward one of the windows and the endless night beyond it. "What's out there?"

"Gardens, and then beyond those, the city."

"There's a city?"

Shaw looked like he wanted to pat my head. "There is. There's an entire world," he said as he opened a door. "More cities and villages, but it's safer to stay at court."

My gaze swept around the unfamiliar room, cataloging the overstuffed shelves filled with books and knickknacks. Strange art hung on the walls, the paintings seeming to glow with some internal light that must have been magic. A pair of plump velvet chairs were wedged into the corner, more books piled around their legs. It wasn't the formal, regal library I'd expected to find at the Nether Court. It was cozy and welcoming and so much better for it. "I'm still wrapping my head around this place."

Shaw nodded and lit a brass lamp. "Take anything you like."

"I'm not going to get you into trouble?" I picked up a novel and flipped it over to read the title.

"My brother might be pissed, but what's new?"

My fingers tightened on the book. "Brother?" I flushed and was suddenly grateful that the dim light likely hid my face.

He smiled. "Shaw Gage. The baby—the unwanted, unplanned, *unwelcome* baby."

I hadn't put two and two together until now. Not with mishaps like accidentally selling my soul and dress fittings and car fires distracting me. I needed to spend some time stalking the Gages on the internet. Yet another reason I needed the modern amenities of the Avalon. "I know that feeling. Look, your brother is a prick. I wouldn't take it personally."

"He forgets about me. I was at school until recently." He sounded almost wistful, and I thought about what Lachlan had said about Fiona keeping her distance from the Nether Court. "But all good things must come to an end."

"And why are you here now? I thought everyone stayed at the Avalon." Everyone but me and Shaw, it seemed.

He frowned. "Not tonight. I've been ordered to hang here while Lach and Roark deal with some stuff by the docks."

"You mean you've been left to watch me."

He shrugged. "That's Lach's excuse, but he doesn't want me around while he's dealing with business."

I studied him for a moment. "He's trying to keep you safe."

But Shaw snorted. "Lach doesn't worry about safety, or he wouldn't be out there tonight."

I decided I didn't want to know more about what his brother was doing, because I suspected that whatever it was was likely very illegal. "He must think about safety sometimes, because he didn't leave me to my own devices."

Shaw's eyes twinkled. "Troublemaker?"

If he only knew. "Not anymore." Was that a fact or a reminder?

I stared at the books, drinking in the woodsy, worn scent of them. Some of the titles, I recognized; many, I did not. My eyes skipped over spines emblazoned with strange characters, the same language that was inked on Lachlan's flesh. I bypassed those, perusing the shelves until I found a leather-bound collection of Jane Austen novels. I reached for one and paused.

"If I borrow a book from your library, you aren't going to make me give you a kidney or something, right?" I asked.

Despite the frost coating my voice, Shaw snorted. "No. Read as many books as you like." He dropped his voice to a whisper. "Lucky for you, I'm not the type to make bargains."

"So you wouldn't have tricked me out of my soul?"

"Unlikely," he admitted with a contagious laugh. Shaw was

different than his older brother. He was more like Ciara. It would be easy to be friends with him, to trust him, to like him. I couldn't say any of those things about his brother. If likability was a genetic trait, it must have skipped Lachlan and Fiona in favor of their siblings. "It's only worth making a bargain if you know it won't be broken. Otherwise…"

"Oh?" I fixed a neutral stare at the book in my hands, but my heart raced. "What happens then?"

Shaw leaned against the shelving, tracing the gilded spines of the tomes. "Our magic relies on bargains, especially with humans. It balances our world, since…" He trailed away.

"Since what?"

But Shaw waved off the question with a forced smile. "That's not important. It's just risky to enter a bargain that might be broken. It can warp our magic. It *has* warped our magic."

If that was true, why would Lachlan point me in the direction of breaking ours? Unless he really believed I wouldn't be able to figure it out. I tried to keep my voice steady. "But it can be broken?"

If Lachlan had lied to me, all bets were off on my promise not to kill him.

"If both parties agree that the conditions can't be met." He nodded. "It's just like when the bargain is made. Both parties have to mean it."

"Why?" I asked, completely forgetting to stay composed.

"Otherwise, what's the point? Without magic, it would just be a promise—and promises are broken all the time." He shrugged.

"Fae don't seem very trusting."

He raised a brow. "And humans are better?"

He might have a point. "So magic means you can't break the promise?" Or change your mind.

"Doesn't stop people from trying," he admitted. "Like I said, it's not worth the hassle."

"Your brother seems to think it is." Relief flooded me, tinged with a little guilt. The magic had sealed our bargain because I'd agreed to exchange my life for Channing's. Lachlan hadn't tricked me. He'd just conveniently failed to mention that magic was involved. And once I proved to him that he was never getting his end of the bargain, there would be nothing to prevent breaking it. As long as he left Channing alone, there was nothing more I wanted from him. "Does he make a lot of bargains?"

"Lach?" Shaw snorted his brother's name. "Never. He doesn't do anything for anyone. He relies on other people to do it for him. You must have something he wants very badly."

But I didn't. I might have thought it was about sex, but he could have had me that first night and sealed my fate. It wasn't that simple. I suspected that whatever Lachlan wanted would prove very dangerous. But I kept that thought to myself. "I think he just wanted to screw with me."

"He excels at torturing people, and someday he's going to get rewarded with a one-way ticket to hell for it."

"Does he have a lot of enemies?" I asked before I could stop myself.

"He doesn't have anything else." Shaw straightened, reaching under his unbuttoned jacket to adjust his holster.

"Even his family?" It was clear that there was no love lost between Shaw and Lachlan, but Ciara…

"I know I sound like an asshole." He forced a smile that held none of the warmth of his others. "But if I was on fire, Lach wouldn't piss on me to put it out. The hazard of being a fae royal. We're a dysfunctional bunch, even in the light courts."

Well, that was colorful. "I'm sorry," I said, meaning it. "I think I romanticize family. It's the hazard of not having any."

"Want some of mine?" he asked dryly. "Maybe a disapproving brother or a reckless sister or two?"

I couldn't help smiling. "You aren't exactly selling me on them. And I'm already stuck with your cocky, dickhead brother, remember?"

Shaw answered with a wry grin that crinkled his golden eyes. "Definitely the worst of the lot." He tipped his head toward the shelves and the books I'd mostly been ignoring. "I feel like I'm distracting you."

"No," I said quickly. "It's nice to have someone to talk to." Someone who didn't delight in tricking and toying with me. "I've read all of these, but this is my favorite."

Shaw scrunched his nose, looking around the stacks. "Maybe—"

"What the hell are you doing in here?" A lethal voice cut through the room, and we swiveled to find Lachlan watching us.

"Lach, I didn't expect you back tonight." Shaw's eyes bounced from him to me.

I shoved the novel back into its place and took a step away from the shelf.

When I looked, he was already staring at me. "I can see that."

"I wanted something to read." I couldn't tear my gaze away from his eyes. The bond thrummed between us, the bargain a gentle caress on the back of my neck. Lachlan stalked closer, stepping between me and his brother. He slid the book I'd been holding free of the shelf and held it out to me.

"Don't write in my books."

I frowned. "*Your* books?"

"This is *my* room." He dropped into a velvet chair, sweeping a hand toward the other half of the room. My stomach plummeted as I looked around. I'd been distracted by my conversation with Shaw, only half paying attention to the room in the dark. Now I saw what I'd missed: a bed nestled in an alcove. There were two more shelves extending to the arched ceiling on either side of it and an arched window lined with heavy, black drapes at its head. The sheets and pillows were strewn across in haphazard fashion, as if sleeping was the last thing that Lachlan Gage ever did in that bed.

My blood heated as I stared at it. "I thought you lived in the Avalon."

"I stay at the Avalon, but this is my home." He shot a sharp look at his brother. "Do you ever do as you're told?"

Shaw took a nervous step forward. "I didn't think you would mind."

"I asked," I interjected. "If you want to be angry, be angry with me. I asked for a book. Shaw was being nice. It never occurred to me that they were yours."

Lachlan paused. "You seem surprised."

"I am," I said coolly. "Who knew you could read?"

His eyes sparked with amusement. "There's a lot you don't know about me." He draped an arm over the back of the low-slung chair. "Now, if you don't mind, I'm going to bed." He paused and raked a feral gaze over my body. "Unless you want to join me."

I clamped my thighs together to smother the ember his words had stoked. That was his second invitation tonight. He was giving my body mixed signals with that sexy magic—and apparently he wasn't even wielding it consciously. My brain was getting the message to stay away, but how long before the rest of me overruled it?

"I think I'll pass." I willed my voice to remain steady as I backed closer to Shaw.

"Sorry we bothered you," Shaw said tightly. He placed a hand on my back, guiding me toward the door.

Lachlan's attention narrowed on his brother's touch, and his face darkened. "Shaw, in the future, ask permission before you touch *my* things."

My fingers tightened on the book, preparing to launch it at his cocky face, but Shaw hustled me out of the room with a curt apology. He cursed as soon as we were outside. I added a few expletives of my own.

"Does he always treat you like that?" I asked him. Lachlan had been dismissive of him that first night, but now I saw that the rift between them ran deeper.

He took a deep breath. "I'm pretty sure Lach would prefer to be an only child." He shook his head. "I've never been able to figure him out."

That made two of us. I placed a hand on his shoulder. "I'm sorry if I got you in trouble."

"He's my older brother. I'm always in trouble with him." He forced a grin that didn't quite reach his amber eyes. He was quiet for a second. "Did you really make the bargain with him to save *your* brother?"

My throat tightened, but I managed a small nod. "I did."

Shaw's face fell as he studied the ground. "You must really love him. No one would do that for me."

I didn't know what to say. Part of me wanted to tell him he was wrong, but I wasn't sure that was the truth. "Thank you for risking your brother's wrath to get me a book."

Maybe Ciara wasn't the only one who needed a friend. Though what they really needed was someone to call their brother on his shit.

"Want me to show you back to your room?" he asked, stuffing his hands into his pockets.

I shivered at the thought of getting lost at the court, of those disembodied wails that haunted the halls. "Yes. I don't want to run into the ghosts."

"Ghosts?" he repeated with a surprised laugh.

"This place is definitely haunted." I explained the sounds I'd heard every night since I made the bargain with Lachlan, but as I spoke, Shaw's grin widened. "You think I'm imagining it, don't you?"

"No. I think you're hearing the wraiths. They guard the court."

"Wraiths?"

"Lost souls that are bound to the Otherworld. They're invisible to everyone but the ruling family. I don't know why magic decided to bestow that perk on us."

"You can see them?" Something in the way he spoke told me that I was glad I could not.

"Unfortunately." He grimaced. "Because I'm a member of the royal household, they answer to me, which means I can see their disgusting, rotting asses."

"Rotting?" I said faintly. Hearing them was bad enough.

"Some of them. Most of the ones at the Nether Court look like half-rotted corpses cloaked in shadows."

I rolled my eyes even as an icy shot of fear filtered into my blood. "That sounds like ghosts to me."

"They aren't ghosts, exactly." He chewed on his lip as though it might help him with whatever minute difference there was between a lost soul and a ghost. "In the Otherworld, only fae pass to the next life at death. If another creature dies here, they are caught in the veil between this world and the afterlife. They become wraiths, beings of pure light or shadow, and are forced to serve the fae royals. It's why we're so careful about allowing access to our world."

"Other creatures? Like humans?" I swallowed, trying to dislodge the dread sitting like a lump in my throat.

Shaw bobbed his head, his eyes darting in my direction. "Humans, witches, vampires..."

"So, if I die here"—I tried to keep my voice from trembling and failed—"I become a wraith." A dead, rotting, ageless creature of shadows. This just got better and better.

"In the light courts, I'm told they can be quite beautiful. What a human might call an angel." He gave me a lopsided grin. "I bet your soul would find a light court."

It was a sweet thing to say, which only made me absolutely sure that if I died here, I would not wind up at a light court. Not if it was down to what was in my soul. Because I'd already agreed to help Ciara for my own purposes, and if getting close to Shaw would help me, I wouldn't hesitate.

"I think I'll try to kick the bucket in my world," I said.

"Probably a good idea."

We smiled at each other. Despite my commitment to hating the Nether Court and everyone in it, I liked Shaw. He reminded me of my own brother, and just like Channing, Shaw was caught up with a bad crowd. Not because he was a bad person but because he was a decent person who didn't have a choice. I wouldn't hold it against him, but that wouldn't stop me from using it to my advantage—just like Lachlan would.

CHAPTER FOURTEEN

I wasn't surprised when I woke in the Nether Court to find the sky filled with a lavender haze as the sun chased away the moon. Lachlan had warned me the necklace wouldn't send me home. And part of me didn't mind. Instead of wailing sirens, birdsong drifted on a sweet-scented breeze through the balcony door I'd left cracked last night.

It was...nice.

Lachlan had made it clear that he expected me to stay in the fae world while they prepared the Avalon for the visiting courts. And there were perks to the Otherworld that I doubted the hotel would have—and my own place definitely didn't. Namely, the bathtub I'd been avoiding but which called to me after another long night of tossing and turning.

I made a point of locking the door, not caring what Lachlan said about his intentions, before I tore my clothes off and turned the golden tap, shaped like a winged serpent, to fill it.

At home, I was lucky if my shitty boiler kept the shower hot for five minutes. Here, the water seemed to operate with some of that strange magic Lachlan used, because it came out the perfect temperature, smelling slightly sweet and herbal, and filled the tub impossibly fast.

I groaned as I took the steps into the water, the bath more a pool than a tub. Sinking onto a built-in bench, I felt my muscles relax as the water lapped against my skin, its heat seeping into my bones and erasing the lingering tension. I shouldn't let my guard down, but I would enjoy this.

Too bad my brain had other ideas. A constant loop of questions played in my mind along with dangerous thoughts, like *maybe this wasn't so bad*—especially if Lachlan's big plan was to lock me up in a five-star hotel room.

I laid my head against the edge of the bath and stared at the candles glowing overhead and sorted through my thoughts. That nothing more had happened with Lachlan was both a relief and mildly insulting. Not that I would ever admit that to any living soul. Nor would I admit how hot that kiss had been. He may have started it, but my traitorous body was more than willing to finish it.

The memory sent me sinking under the water. I needed to stop thinking about it or I'd have to do something to take the edge off. He'd know. I was sure of it. And what would be worse—the cocky smirk he'd give me or him whispering that he wished I'd called him?

I blew bubbles into the water. Maybe he was just trying to keep me flustered so I couldn't figure out his end of the bargain. What did he want with me? And what if it was sex and he was just buying time until my deadline came and went? Maybe it'd be better to bang him just in case.

I should have opted for a cold shower because I definitely didn't need to warm myself up to that idea.

I pushed out of the water, my racing thoughts driving me from the bath far too quickly. But that was probably for the best. The last thing I needed was to get comfortable here.

I didn't bother to dry my hair before I pulled on my clothes from the night before, scowling when I spotted the wine stain in the mirror. There wasn't much I could do about that. A glamour would be handy right about then.

When I opened the door ten minutes later, Roark lounged outside in a hall chair. Apparently, I warranted an armed guard at all times now. I might be the only person Lachlan trusted, but it was clear he was out of practice with the concept. Not that the hulking, tattooed fae he had assigned to watch me was very intimidating, given that he was always glued to his phone.

"I want to go home," I announced.

He slid his phone into his pocket. "I was told to accompany you."

My eyes narrowed. "He owns my nights, not my days."

"I figured." He held his hands up. "Is there anything you want me to tell him?" He blinked at the string of curses that fell out of my mouth, but he smiled. "Do you want me to repeat that word for word?"

"Please." I started to turn but remembered I did need Roark to get me out. Damn it.

He stepped to my side. "Ready?"

I locked my knees and sucked in a breath. "Yes."

Maybe I was getting used to nipping, because it wasn't nearly as bad as the other times. We appeared in a quiet corridor, and I recognized the polished marble floor of the Avalon. Activity hummed in the distance, the hotel already stirring for the day.

"Car is out front," Roark told me. He must have seen the surprise on my face that he was actually going to respect my desire to leave alone. "Look, I think he's worried you'll vanish."

"I don't know why," I said sourly. "He can yank me back here whenever he wants."

Roark's jaw worked for a second, like he was chewing on how to respond. "He would never forgive himself if something happened to you."

I blinked. "Nothing's going to happen."

But he only nodded and gestured toward the lobby. He didn't follow me as I hurried out of the Avalon, but his words did. They niggled at me as I left the hotel and chased me down the front steps. For a second, I considered walking past the long, black Mercedes idling at the curb, but I'd already made a stand about having a chaperone, and it was quite a walk from here to my place.

The driver opened the door as I approached, and I slid into the back seat. For a minute, I simply drank in the quilted leather seats and the silver-plated champagne flutes and bottle of Cristal waiting in the center console. The touch screen on the back of the passenger seat welcomed me with a selection of massage settings.

The driver got behind the wheel and looked back at me. "Home, Miss Holloway?"

I didn't ask how he knew my name or where I lived. If I had armed guards in the Otherworld, it was safe to assume that Lachlan was going to be overbearing in my own world. It was one of the reasons that I shouldn't get comfortable here, but for now, what choice did I have?

I smiled politely at the driver. "Actually, I need to make a few stops first."

• • •

At this hour of the morning, the streets of the French Quarter were empty of the tourists who came out at dusk for the bars and restaurants and music. Elsewhere in New Orleans, the real world had already risen, but most of the Quarter was sleeping off its hangover. I loved the city when it was quiet and deserted. It was easy to imagine I'd stepped back in time, looking at the wrought iron galleries dripping with ferns and flowers, the rainbow of cottages and shotgun houses, and the cobbled sidewalks. But today I couldn't help seeing the wrought iron as a danger. A man playing guitar on the corner had eyes too dark to be human; even the very air seemed to shimmer with barely suppressed magic.

My world wasn't my own anymore. It was bigger, fuller, *scarier.*

I could have cried with relief when we reached our first stop and it looked exactly the same as it always had, the air heavy with the tempting aroma of sugar and oil.

Haley sat at the nurse's station, looking like she'd been through hell. She spotted me and tried to tuck a loose braid into her now limp bun but gave up with a weary groan.

I swallowed, wishing I could jump in my scrubs and give her a break. "Back already?"

"Never left." She yawned, stretching her arms over her head. "Why are you here?"

There was no bite to her words, just exhaustion.

"I popped by to see Channing, but I took your advice." I held up the bag I'd brought for Garcia.

Haley glanced around, then waved for me to follow her. She lowered her voice as we headed into the staff lounge. "The police took Channing into custody this morning until his hearing—or someone bails him out."

The news hit like a punch to the gut. I'd known it was going to happen, but the reality of my choice was entirely different. I reminded myself that, according to the internet, illegal possession of a firearm wasn't as serious an offense in Louisiana as in some states. Channing would probably get probation for a first offense. The thought didn't quite soothe me.

Haley eyed me as she grabbed two cups and filled them with coffee. She passed me one before sitting at the table.

"Good," I managed. I hated the idea of him being in jail, but I hated the idea of him being caught up in this more.

"You look tired. Wild night?" Haley took a drink from the Styrofoam cup and scrunched her nose in distaste before taking another dutiful sip. "Were you with Lachlan Gage?"

I hid behind a huge swig of coffee, my eyes widening as it scorched my tongue and throat. I blinked back a few tears from the burn as I dumped the rest. Boiling hot coffee and Lachlan didn't mix. I probably should also avoid heavy machinery. "Why would you ask that?"

"Because you've got a wine stain on your shirt, a Mercedes just dropped you off in the ambulance bay, and rumor is that a *Gage* told Garcia to replace you," she added meaningfully, waggling her eyebrows. "Care to confess your sins?"

"I remain pure as the driven snow," I said dryly.

Haley lounged back in her seat, crossing her arms and tutting under her breath. "Pure as the driven snow? This has all the hallmarks of a walk of shame."

"Do you really think I would date someone like him?"

"A billionaire who owns half the city?" She rolled her eyes. "If he was anyone but a Gage, I'd hope you would."

I ignored the flutter I felt at her words. "You forget that he's dangerous."

"True, but being with him is safer than being against him."

I hated that she might have a point.

"Come on. Spill. What is going on?"

"I swear, nothing happened." I opened the white cardboard box next to the coffee machine, praying there were still a few donuts left. "It's not like that between us."

"Us?" My back was turned, but I could hear the mischief in her tone. "What *is* it like between the two of you?"

"Lach did me a favor. It's complicated." The donut box was sadly empty. I considered dipping into the paper bag of beignets I'd stopped for on Canal Street, especially if kissing the boss's ass was a lost cause.

"Lach, huh? Already using a nickname. That's *friendly.*" Her tone bypassed suggestiveness in favor of something north of accusation.

Fuck, now I was slipping and calling him Lach? I needed to reassert some boundaries fast.

"We aren't friends." I didn't know what we were, but it definitely wasn't *that.*

"Look, I haven't left the hospital in..." She paused and counted on her fingers. "I actually have no idea when I last left. I need news of the outside world. Tell me about him."

"Black hair. Tattoos. Green eyes." The thought of those eyes sent me reeling to last night when he'd put the pendant back on me.

Haley let out a loud whistle. "Oh, you're in trouble."

"Did I mention the guns and that he is disgustingly arrogant?" And confusing, hot and cold, thoughtful and thoughtless. I plopped onto the lounge's beat-up couch. "I would never go for someone like him. Even if he's hot—"

"So, you admit that you think he's hot."

"That's just a fact." I could admit to that much, at least. "How many bodies in the morgue right now are there because of trinity?"

I fought back a wave of guilt. *Lachlan* was concerned enough about the effects the drug was having on the city to try to negotiate with the other courts, but that didn't excuse him from responsibility for his part in it.

She frowned. "Point taken, but damn, you're a lot stronger than I am if he's as hot as you say *and* rich."

"I doubt it." If she knew how close I'd come to giving in to my attraction to him, she wouldn't think that.

"Sexy billionaires do not grow on trees." She shook her head as if she knew this from wasting time looking for one. "Have you considered that you might be able to influence him?"

My brows shot up. "I know I don't have the best track record with men, but I do know that you can't change them."

"I didn't say *change him*." She rolled her eyes. "But no one gets close to Lachlan Gage. Even Garcia has never actually seen him. You mentioned the staffing shortage, and, boom, we're getting nurses."

"Your point?"

"Maybe you can do something about trinity." She paused as if waiting for me to rebuff her. When I didn't, she breezed on. "I know you didn't want to leave the hospital, but you might be able to save more lives this way."

She was right. If this meeting with the other courts was the only hope of fixing the trinity problem, making sure it went well was more important than being here. It was more important than breaking the bargain. I'd been so caught up in my own shit, I'd never stopped to really consider that.

"Maybe you're right, but things are complicated. I don't know what I think about Lachlan."

She leaned against the couch, propping her head onto her hand. "In that case, can I give you some advice?"

I snorted. "Don't you always?"

She ignored me. "If he wasn't worth the effort, you would know. The fact that you're uncertain how you feel about him tells me that you feel a lot."

The truth of her words knotted my throat. "What if he's not a good man?" There had been a time when that mattered to me. I was sure it still *should* matter.

Her face softened, empathy shining in her brown eyes. "There are no good or bad men. No black or white. We are all just a shade of gray. A collection of our choices, our hopes, our desires. Trying to stick him into one narrow end of the spectrum won't help you figure out how you feel about him. Only seeing who he truly is will allow you to do that."

"What if I don't like what I see?"

She tilted her head. "What if you do, Cate?"

And that was exactly the problem.

CHAPTER FIFTEEN

arrived at the Avalon a few hours later, on my feet this time, with suitcase in hand. I'd exchanged my ruined clothes for a pair of jeans and cropped white tank, opting for comfort if my near future included countless gowns. I braced myself for judgmental looks from the wealthy clientele only to find the hotel vacant.

But any relief I felt vanished when I spotted Ciara and Lachlan arguing in an alcove near the front entrance. His head lifted, a grin ghosting his face when he saw me. Before I could catch what they were saying—or rather, yelling—Shaw approached from my left, his strong hand gripped my elbow, and he dragged me into a sitting room off the lobby. A clock ticked faintly over the stone mantel, its steady rhythm at odds with the rising pitch of the disagreement outside.

"I'd give them a minute," Shaw advised me.

Roark sat on a leather stool nearby, examining his nails with an intensity that told me he was listening to every word being hurled across the lobby. He grimaced at whatever he heard, adjusting the signet ring on his right hand.

I opened my mouth to ask Shaw what they were fighting over, since I could only pick up snatches, when Ciara shrieked, "You didn't tell me we were hosting a bacchanalia!"

It sounded like things were going well in there. That meant Lachlan would be in a foul mood. Then again, it was a day that ended in *y*. As far as I knew, he only had two modes: ill-tempered or drunk on his own superiority.

"Should we intervene?" I had no idea what kind of damage they could do if magic got involved.

Shaw moved closer, keeping his voice even more hushed as the argument rose to a fever pitch. "Ciara is just blindsided."

I felt the blood drain from my face. "I thought she knew about his plans."

"She agreed to the betrothal." Glass shattered in the lobby. I flinched, but Shaw continued smoothly. "She just wants to get things over with, but the Infernal Court wants to do things the old-fashioned way. A dowry and calling the banns and all the feasts and parties. Lach knew, and he forgot to mention it until now. I don't see why she's so upset, though. It's all an excuse for everyone to get rip-roaring drunk, smoke cigars, and make bad decisions."

At least he was being honest. "Bad decisions, huh?"

"Several, and usually at the same time," he admitted.

"While drunk? That seems smart."

"That is the problem with immortality. You can do a *lot* of stupid shit." He pushed a hand through his copper hair. "Well, that and trying to figure out what to eat for dinner every night."

"I guess things aren't that different for fae and humans after all," I teased, but I understood why Ciara was upset. I had my own deadline looming, at the end of which was either freedom or a life sentence. She had to feel the same way. I didn't blame her for wanting to get it over with.

Ciara stormed into the sitting room, halting when she saw me. Her lower lip trembled slightly, but she forced her mouth into a bright smile. "I suppose he told you everything."

I didn't know what to say.

She swiped at a renegade tear and waved her manicured hand. "I'm not mad at *you*." From the way she said it, I knew exactly who she was mad at. "At least this nightmare will give me a chance to finally get to know Lach's new friend. He's been keeping you all to himself."

I was about to correct that misapprehension, but Lachlan did it for me. "You do love to hear yourself speak."

Ciara stuck her tongue out at him. It was such a sisterly thing to do that I nearly laughed. "No one asked for your opinion, but I *do* want to know what spa Cate prefers. If you're forcing her to attend a bacchanalia, the least we can do is spoil her first."

"She's a person, not a doll," he warned her. "Perhaps you could ask her what she'd like to do."

"It'll be fun," Ciara said primly, "which seems to be something the rest of you struggle with."

He rolled his eyes. "You mean that you know how to blow through a bank account."

"We can't all sit at home, brooding and waiting for something to kill." Ciara turned to me expectantly.

Oh, right. Spas. I twisted the necklace awkwardly. "I, uh...I don't have a preference." Spoiling myself at a spa hadn't exactly been a priority when I'd been struggling to survive.

Lachlan glanced at me, something tightening around his eyes, and I knew he'd heard what I hadn't said. "Do you want to go?"

I dropped the necklace like it was on fire.

What was he playing at? Was he looking out for me? If so, that was surprisingly...thoughtful.

The last thing I needed in my already confusing life was a thoughtful Lachlan. I needed him to be arrogant and annoying or my hormones would win before I made it a whole month.

"Are *you* going to be there?" I asked him, trying to reverse course. When he shook his head, I smiled. "Then, yes. I'd love to go to the spa with you, Ciara. And shopping to spend all your brother's ill-gotten gains. And whatever else you want to do."

Shaw, who'd been hanging back—probably trying to stay out of his brother's way—coughed to hide a laugh. Lachlan's mouth tightened into a thin line. I felt bad for half a second, but Ciara giggled as well. "I think I'm going to like her. We'll go first thing tomorrow."

Maybe it was guilt, or maybe I was being played, but I decided in that moment I wasn't just going to pretend to be Ciara's friend—I was going to actually be her friend. And Shaw's, too, if he let me.

"What about Fiona?" I asked. "Will she be coming to this bacchanalia thing?"

Ciara's smile faded, and she shook her head, dark curls spilling over her shoulders. "No. She got out of it."

Oh. Maybe someday one of them would tell me why Fiona avoided her family or why everyone tensed at the mention of her name. I certainly wasn't going to risk asking and dredging up that shit myself.

Roark unfolded himself from the armchair and joined us, clapping his hand on Lachlan's shoulder in sympathy. "Fiona isn't the heir to the Nether throne. That comes with perks."

"Thanks for reminding me," Lachlan grumbled.

Roark shook him a little. "Cheer up. You can still get in plenty of trouble. We've doubled the usual amount of security. Even the crown prince can let loose with whomever he chooses."

Did I imagine Roark's eyes flashing in my direction?

I crossed my arms. "I'm beginning to think I'm going to be everyone's babysitter for the next few weeks." That was probably for the best. It wasn't like I hadn't let loose plenty when I was younger. But I'd paid dearly for it.

Lachlan took a step closer, his mouth curling softly as it lifted with his mood. "What? You aren't interested in a little trouble?"

My heart dipped dangerously at his words. His eyes smoldered into mine, the very embodiment of *trouble* standing before me.

I resisted the urge to retreat. "Unlike you, I don't need trouble to have a good time."

"But that's the best kind." He leaned so close that I saw the gold flecks in his irises for what they really were: sparks of mischief. "I could give you a few pointers."

"I'm pretty sure all you'll ever give me is a headache."

"Maybe you should keep an open mind."

He was so close, I could taste his breath on my lips. Why did he have to be so fucking beautiful? With his stupid, sexy magic and those eyes? "Maybe you should—"

Ciara coughed, and we snapped apart. Lachlan looked as startled to remember we weren't alone as I felt.

"Thank the gods," Roark muttered behind us. "I was beginning to suffocate with all the sexual tension."

Lachlan flipped him off. "Choke on this."

I groaned. "Infantile."

"Come on," Ciara urged me, shooting one final scowl in her brother's direction. "We'll hit the spa later. For now, let's go raid the bar."

Finally, a plan I could get behind. But before she could drag me away, Lachlan snagged the waistband of my jeans and hauled me close enough to whisper, "You know, princess, I think trouble is exactly what you need."

I yanked away, cheeks burning, and forced a scowl. He only laughed as he turned to leave with Roark, and as he walked away, I couldn't help feeling like I'd made a big mistake.

I was at the mercy of Lachlan's charms for the next month. How soon before he convinced me he was right?

CHAPTER SIXTEEN

A few hours later, Ciara was still drowning her sorrows with the help of a second bottle of Scotch. I nursed my own drink and listened to her cry about all the things—and, to my uncomfortable amusement, *people*—she would never do.

At least it was a welcome distraction from thinking about Channing sitting in a jail cell. A reality I wasn't quite prepared to face, even if I was the person responsible for putting him there.

She picked up the bottle and tried to pour another drink only to discover it was also empty. She glared at it before tossing it over the bar. We were the only souls in the place. Without the neon and smoke and sin, the club felt smaller and less intimidating than the first time I was here. How had it only been a few days and not a lifetime?

"I mean, I don't have to be faithful." She hiccupped as she climbed over the bar and dug around for another bottle. "*No one* is faithful in the courts. Not anymore."

I nodded absently, wondering if that was true. I'd seen plenty of that in my world.

"But I'm only two hundred years old. Fiona is way older than me." She unscrewed the cap while I gawked at her. She bit her lip and grinned sheepishly. "Okay, I'm a *little* older than that, but not much!"

I just kept staring. Over two hundred years old? And Lachlan was even older than that.

"You didn't know how old we are, did you?" she asked, peering at me with glassy eyes.

I managed to shake my head.

"Lach's one of the youngest crown princes." She tapped the neck of the bottle against her chin. "I think Sirius is younger. He's the prince of the Astral Court, but he's not the heir. His sister is. Bain is older. I forget how much. And Oberon is ancient."

I wondered what counted as ancient to a fae. "Then, you just don't age?"

"We age like a human until we're out of puberty and into our twenties, but then pretty much no. Our bodies get to the perfect point and just stop." She actually looked a little sad about it.

"And you don't get sick?" I sighed. "Sorry. I guess it's all the nursing classes. I'm being rude."

She waved my apology off, sending Scotch flying out of the new bottle she'd grabbed. She giggled at the faux pas and placed it safely on the counter. "It's rare for a fae to get sick. It's not unheard of, though. There have been plagues that attacked our kind, but not for a very long time."

"So, you just never die?"

"We die," she said sadly, and I wished I could take the thoughtless words back. "The Otherworld is no paradise. There is always a push and pull between light and dark, peace and violence. It's been like that my whole life, but it feels worse now. More attacks. More death. Just more since…" She glared at my drink. "You're never going to catch up with me."

I'd been pacing myself, not wanting to lose an ounce of control in Gage territory. "I'll die of alcohol poisoning before I catch up with you. Human, remember?"

She waved that annoying detail away and topped off my glass.

"And your parents?" I asked. No one I'd spoken to mentioned them. If Lachlan was a prince, there had to have been a king and queen at some point, but if he was arranging Ciara's marriage…

"Fae royalty have a slightly shorter life expectancy than non-royals, *especially* those who wear the crown. My parents were killed."

"I'm sorry," I said and meant it. I knew the pain of lost parents, but it had to be different—*deeper*—to have known them.

"It was a long time ago." She capped the bottle as if losing interest in it. "But sometimes I wish they were here."

I reached across the bar and took her hand, squeezing it gently.

She shook her head as if clearing it and smiled through her tears. "I swear I won't always be this morose. I'm a lousy drunk." Her eyes widened. "Ohhh, what about clover?"

My grip on her tightened. "Are you sure that's a good idea?"

"I've had my stash for decades. It's safe," she reassured me, but I politely declined. Ciara didn't push me. Instead, she recounted the last two hundred years of her sex life. We'd only reached the 1980s— a decade she referred to as her vampire era—when she fell silent. A moment later, she was slumped against the bar, snoring.

Ciara was petite, but there was no way I was getting her upstairs. I probably couldn't even get her to the elevator. I closed my eyes, wishing I had any other option, and touched my necklace.

Lachlan appeared next to me instantly.

"You got her to sleep." He sounded impressed. I tried and failed not to stare at him. It must have been late, because he'd changed out of his suit into a ribbed, cotton T-shirt that stretched taut across his chest and biceps and showed off an impressive amount of tattoos. But it was the pair of silk pajama bottoms that hung low on his narrow hips that nearly undid me. The loose black fabric did little to hide the powerful muscle of his thighs, and it took effort to keep my eyes from moving inward to see what else was on display. His hair was wet, as if he'd just gotten out of the shower, a few strands dripping onto his broad shoulders. I itched to reach out and comb them back with my fingers—

I cleared my throat and focused on his sister. "I can't take all the credit. The three bottles of Scotch and hundred-year-old clover she just took probably knocked her out." I studied her peaceful face more closely. "Is she going to be okay?"

"She'll sleep until noon, but she'll be fine." He scooped her into those arms, tattoos winding and flashing around them.

I followed him into the elevator, realizing I had no idea where she actually lived. Or, for that matter, where I was expected to stay. Once we were inside, he nodded to the panel. "Top floor."

That made sense. I punched the button for the thirteenth floor and shifted to the opposite side of the compartment. He tracked the movement but didn't speak. When we reached the top, he angled his body to keep the doors from closing, cradling his sister carefully. "Welcome home."

I started to remind him that the Avalon was not my home, but the retort died on my lips when my gaze turned to the stunning foyer. A round mahogany table sat in the middle of the gold-veined marble floor, the extravagant arrangement of white roses, lilies, and peonies at its center filling the air with their perfume. On one side of the foyer were two corridors. I couldn't see the ends of them. It was as if they stretched infinitely, but that would be…impossible. On the entry's other side was a single black door.

I took a small step toward the table, not quite trusting whatever magic was clearly at work. Lachlan just strode past me and began down one of the long corridors to the left. I scrambled to keep up with him, nearly tripping as the floor shifted to plush ivory carpeting. Eventually, he stopped and nudged a black-lacquered door open with his bare foot.

Ciara's bedroom was actually fit for a princess. A tufted bed framed with ornate gold carvings sat in disarray, piled with pillows and blankets in a palette of elegant blush shades. Two arched windows rose above it on either side, their long, gold curtains tied back while still left to pool on the oak floors. Moonlight seeped through the glass and glinted off the dark chandelier that hung in the center of the coffered ceiling. The powdery softness of rose petals filled the air, either from Ciara's natural scent or the numerous perfume bottles arranged on an antique vanity in the corner. A gilded mirror was propped against the wall, the pink slipper chair by it strewn with lacy bras and several pairs of heels. A few magazines and a half-eaten box of chocolates lay on a cream fur rug that extended past the bed's tufted footboard.

Lachlan placed her on the bed, removed her shoes, and then

pulled a soft sheet over her.

"Maybe I should stay with her?" I brushed her hair back so it was easier to see the steady rhythm of her breathing.

"She's absolutely fine. The wraiths will watch over her."

I shivered. "They're here, too? How?"

"The Avalon exists half inside my world and half inside yours."

The wraiths were one thing I wished stayed in the Otherworld, especially if they liked to watch people sleep. But I supposed that existing between our worlds might explain the hotel's strange layout. A yawn overtook me.

"I'll show you to your room." He moved to the door and waited as I stood and tucked the blanket around Ciara's shoulders before joining him.

Lachlan was quiet as we made our way back to the foyer, but before we reached it, he broke the stony silence, his voice low and rumbly. "Is she okay?"

"She's unhappy." I wouldn't lie to him. Not about this. Maybe Ciara understood his reasoning, maybe the alliance with the Infernal Court would get trinity off the streets of the city, maybe I could live with it, but I wouldn't sugarcoat the truth. "She doesn't want to get married."

"If there's any other way, I can't see it."

I stopped a step short of the foyer's marble floor. "Why are you really doing it?"

"I told you. An alliance with the Infernal—"

"No, that's not it." I planted my hands on my hips and studied him. Not his muscular body or his crushing green eyes but *him*. The way his wary, guarded eyes never seemed to match his smirking, arrogant mouth. The fact that his broad, strong shoulders were defined by the weight he had to carry and never show. The fleeting, changing tattoos that told me he might not be speaking but he was thinking—I had Shaw to thank for that knowledge. "Do *you* even know why you're doing it?"

He stared back at me, the look piercing straight through me. What did he see? "If—"

"Ciara finally out?" Shaw strolled into the foyer and stopped to pluck a petal from one of the roses.

Lachlan's nostrils flared slightly, but he turned to his brother. "We just tucked her in."

Something twisted inside my chest at the way he said "we"—at the implication that seemed to lace that single word.

I was still trying to decide what the hell that meant when he placed his palm on the small of my back. "I was about to show Cate to her room."

Shaw frowned as Lachlan led me toward that single black door on the other side. "Shouldn't she stay in the eastern wing?"

The eastern wing? How could he tell which way was east with the floor's nonsensical architecture?

Lachlan's hand slipped lower, to grip the curve of my hip. "She will stay with me."

My eyes flashed to his, a rebuke poised on the tip of my tongue. Like hell I was going to share a room with him.

Shaw seemed to notice my discomfort. "There are plenty of empty bedrooms for her to use."

"Your concern is noted."

I sucked in a deep breath, twisted the pendant in my fingers, and let him have it. But if Lachlan heard the string of curses I was shouting at him through our magical connection, he didn't so much as blink.

So I added a few more.

"Maybe you should…" Shaw trailed away as Lachlan left my side and strode toward him, grabbed his elbow, and hauled him across the foyer.

Gran used to tell me to count out my frustration when she sensed the anger I bottled up was about to shatter free. I started counting as Shaw and Lachlan whispered heatedly, the former's eyes straying to mine every few seconds. By the time he threw his hands in the air, shot me an apologetic look, and nipped out of sight, I was at 111 in my count.

Lachlan muttered something uncharitable before flourishing a hand toward the black door that apparently led to his private wing.

"I meant what I said before. You should be nicer to your family."

"And why is that?" He rubbed his temple.

"Because you're lucky to have them." My voice shook slightly. "Not everyone gets a family."

The lines of his face softened along with his tone. "I know that." He nodded toward the door. "Let me show you where you're staying."

I braced myself for another fight as he opened the door.

A bedroom didn't wait on the other side. Instead, I stepped into a massive living room that oozed pure masculinity reminiscent of the male who called it home. Black-paneled walls were broken on one side by a large picture window that looked over the lights of New Orleans. The faint thrum of the traffic was punctuated by the pop of logs in the marble hearth. On either side, bookshelves were built into the walls; firelight danced on the paperbacks that were crammed onto the shelves. A long, leather couch and two club chairs occupied the space, a brass coffee table situated on the thin, woven rug beneath them.

He strode across the living room, straight to an antique bar cart brimming with various bottles of liquor. He frowned when he reached it and waved a hand, and a bucket of ice appeared, mist curling over its frosted edge. Now *that* was useful magic. He tossed a few cubes into two glasses and poured amber liquid from a crystal decanter before stretching one out to me.

I hesitated. If he expected me to share his quarters, and it was obvious that he did, maybe we needed to establish a few ground rules before we added alcohol to the mix.

"It's not poisoned."

I accepted it with a sigh but didn't take a sip. Not until I knew why he'd insisted on me staying with him. I clutched the drink, my thumb tracing a pattern in the condensation sweating through the glass. "I'm sure I'll be fine in the eastern wing."

Better, even. Something kept that thought locked in my mouth. Maybe I was developing a sense of self-preservation.

"That's debatable." He took a languid drink that drew my attention to his mouth. "Don't worry, princess. You have your own bedroom."

I dared a glance down the hall, relieved to see several doors. At least he didn't expect us to share a bed. "Do you all have your own wing?"

"Shaw and Roark share. I personally prefer to be at least a mile away from my siblings at all times." He took another swig of his whiskey, and I wondered if it burned down his throat the way his touch seared across my skin. "As for why you'll want to be in *my* wing, these events have a tendency to get a little debauched."

It was my turn to raise my eyebrow. "Debauched? Do I want to know what that means?"

"I told you there would be lots of ritual fuckery," he reminded me. "Believe me, you don't want to be sharing a wall with Roark if he brings guests home."

"Guests? As in plural?"

Lachlan's answering smile was wolfish. "Fae appetites are insatiable—all of our appetites."

Oh, holy shit. I was suddenly glad I had a drink in my hands. I hoped he didn't notice the way my fingers trembled as I raised it to my lips. The whiskey scorched a line of fire through me, giving me the courage to ask what I really wanted to know. "And will you be taking part in this debauchery? Because if so, I think I should stay on another floor."

If he was planning on bringing people home, I wanted my own zip code.

"Would it bother you if I did?"

Something twisted in my gut at the idea of Lachlan in these great, big rooms, surrounded by beautiful fae intent on serving the prince in whatever fashion he desired.

"No." I schooled my face into indifference. "Do *whoever* you want."

His smile told me he knew I was lying. "I'll keep that in mind."

"And I'll do the same." I knew I was creeping too close to the line we'd drawn before, wondering if he would reinforce it or erase it entirely.

"Unfortunately, I'm unlikely to enjoy myself at all during the festivities. There are details to be worked out." He rattled the ice in his glass, the sound of it wearing on my already frayed nerves. "I'm afraid I won't have as much fun as the *others*."

The *others* would have fun. Not him. Not me. There was no mistaking the implication of that single word. Another test or perhaps bait. I wouldn't bite. "So, you're just going to sit in smoke-filled rooms and do what, exactly?"

"I told you there would be pissing contests." His mouth set in a grim line, and he poured another drink. "And, as for the smoke-filled rooms, we are not actually in hell, contrary to whatever you believe. However, there will probably be cigars."

"Of course there will be." I shook my head. "And while you are doing that and the others are doing…each other, what am I supposed to do? Sit around and wait for you?"

"I suppose the idea of you pining for me is out of the question," he said flatly. Lachlan crossed the room and dropped into a worn leather armchair. He shifted his legs, the rippling silk of his pants catching his groin just enough to make my mouth go dry. "You won't be alone, but it's safer if you stick near me at night."

I studied him for a moment, studied the slight tick of his jaw, how his fingers drummed on his glass. Not as calm and collected as he pretended to be.

"Should I warn you if I…meet someone?"

I was paddling into dangerous water. On the surface, it looked calm, but nothing was ever as it seemed with him. Not with that dark magic that poured off him, magnetic and alluring. His fingers tightened around his glass, but his face betrayed no emotion. "There's no need."

This was becoming dangerous, but I pushed forward, testing his boundaries. "Why? Because I'm not allowed to participate in the debauchery? You seemed to imply earlier that I needed to get into trouble."

"You have to crawl before you can walk, princess."

"Is that a yes?"

He studied the ice cracking in his glass a little too intently. "Hoping someone will catch your eye?"

"I'm just asking," I said coolly. "I wouldn't want to upset you if I invited someone back to your quarters. Or multiple someones."

"That is entirely up to you. I wouldn't want you to get…bored."

I could feel it tugging at my core—the riptide that wanted to drag me under. Even as Lachlan continued to glare at his drink, I felt the current changing around us, shifting. My body responded instantly, heat and danger swirling through my limbs and settling into a low simmer. I shifted, but the sensation only grew.

"Noted," I said, unsteady. "I will endeavor to entertain myself."

His dark gaze trailed from my head to my toes, undressing me slowly like he had the night we met. And just like that night, I needed to stay in control. I hated that he had this effect on me. Hated it—and loved it. To have this powerful man focused solely on me was…intoxicating.

His eyes bored into mine, the battle he was waging clear on his face. *"Cate."*

My name on his lips undid me completely.

I needed to get out of the room immediately, before I did something I couldn't take back, like actually remove my clothes and beg *him* to be the one who entertained me. In any and every way. I cleared my throat. "Good. If that's settled, I think I'll find my room."

"Mine is the first on the left," he told me. "But if you want to share…"

He'd known exactly what I was thinking, as usual. I couldn't let him get the upper hand. "Pass." I pinned a saccharine smile on my face. "I'll make sure to choose the room that's farthest away. You know, in case I bring someone back. I wouldn't want to keep you up."

I fled before he could respond. I was bluffing—I knew it, and likely so did he—but I still chose the farthest bedroom anyway. That felt…safer.

The room was different than the one I'd been given in the Otherworld but no less luxurious. I barely noticed the thick cream rugs as I paced the polished floors. Barely glanced out the windows that stretched from floor to ceiling, draped with ivory silk curtains. I had a view of the river that bisected the city, which wasn't possible. Just more proof that while I might be in my world, the Avalon itself was built with fae magic. For all I knew, every room in the Avalon might have been wound up like a ball of string, crisscrossing over one another.

I flopped onto the bed. It was large and carved from oak, its strong pillars stained black. Layers and layers of blankets and linens and pillows in a welcoming palette of ivory and gold were piled on top of it. A fire chattered merrily in a hearth across from it, the mantel carved from one mammoth slab of stone.

I grabbed one of the pillows and buried my face in it. What was I thinking, going toe to toe with a fae prince? Was I *trying* to get burned?

I pulled my knees to my chest and tried to ignore the feeling that something was missing. The room was too big. The bed too empty. I knew exactly what—or rather, *who*—I wanted in it with me.

But that was one itch I refused to scratch.

CHAPTER SEVENTEEN

I spent the following few days being plucked, polished, and massaged within an inch of my life at not one but four of the city's spas. The only one Ciara hadn't seemed interested in visiting was the one at her family's own hotel. Instead, we spent our days being pampered and our nights closing down Bourbon Street—something I hadn't done in years.

I'd been more than happy to avoid the Avalon and my new roommate.

Some nights, Shaw and Roark joined us, but Lachlan never showed. I suspected he didn't want to put a damper on Ciara's final nights of freedom. But the light in his bedroom was always on when I dragged my aching feet down the hall to my own. More than one night, I lay awake and listened for his footsteps. Once or twice, I swore I heard them, but the door never opened.

By the end of the week, I knew he wasn't just avoiding his sister. He was avoiding me.

The morning the other courts were expected to arrive, Ciara bounced between the Avalon and the Otherworld, dragging me with her until my legs were jelly from all the nipping. Understanding her frantic energy, I didn't complain, but when she finally announced it was time to go upstairs and change, I nearly wept at the promise of solid ground beneath my feet for longer than ten minutes.

Two dresses had been prepared for the day's events, laid out by the discreet household staff who kept the place neat and tidy while never showing their faces. I just hoped they weren't wraiths. I assumed the gossamer ball gown was meant for this evening's party and changed into the other dress. Its fitted style clung to my curves like an embrace, and the silky fabric—a green that was more vibrant than the ink-soaked jade I associated with the Nether Court—was soft on my skin. It dipped low enough to showcase a swell of décolletage, a single strap curling over my left shoulder like a tendril of ivy. It seemed impossible that something so lovely was also comfortable.

I didn't want to risk stressing Ciara out by asking her to glamour me, so I pinned my hair back, taming my loose curls as best I could, and spent a few minutes applying mascara and lip gloss. A peek in the mirror confirmed I was presentable. It wasn't quite as good as the glamour Ciara effortlessly applied in seconds most nights, but I wasn't here to impress anyone. I wasn't the one with an arranged marriage on the line.

Ciara was already waiting in the foyer. The bodice of her dark dress was covered in black silk roses that stood out against her pale skin. Its tight, ruched skirt tapered at the knees to show off her shapely calves and a pair of sky-high patent leather platform heels. Her long hair cascaded in a glossy curtain over her shoulders. She would definitely make an impression on the Infernal Court prince.

As I joined her, she sized me up with a sigh. "You should have asked me to glamour you."

"That bad?" I touched my curls lightly, wondering if I should have put my hair all the way up.

"No!" She threw her arms around me, enveloping me in a cloud of rose-scented perfume. But unlike her usual bone-crushing hugs, this felt like she was clinging to a life preserver. "You're beautiful. I just should have helped you get ready. I've been completely self-absorbed today. I'm sorry."

"Maybe I should have been the one helping you get ready. I'm new to this friendship thing. It's your big day," I pointed out.

She looked a little green at the reminder, but she shook it off and grabbed my hands. "You are great at this friendship thing." Warmth spread through me as we shared a smile. "How am I doing?"

I'd begun to realize that despite the money and cars and magic, in some ways her life was as isolated as mine. When we went dancing, it was with a security team or Roark and Shaw, not other fae. Even when she'd bought shots for the bar and danced on top of it with strangers—that's what they remained. Strangers. Maybe it was because people visited New Orleans and left while she stayed, a problem likely exacerbated by living in a hotel. Maybe it was because she was a princess of the Nether Court.

But deep down, I knew it was because she came home every night to check on her older brother—the only person here more isolated than her. I suspected that's how she'd sold herself on the betrothal to Bain. London would free her from that silent obligation to Lachlan that she shouldered and open new doors, even if it closed a few.

"I might move to London with you," I warned her, wishing it was true. Like Ciara, I wasn't eager to leave New Orleans when I had my brother to look out for.

"Don't tease me." Tears glinted in her eyes. She wiped them away. "But I know you can't. Not with Lach…"

I hadn't told her about his promise that he would break the bargain if I figured out his riddle. How could I when I knew part of the reason she was willing to strike out on her own was that she thought I would be here to keep her brother in line?

My mouth was dry, my tongue sticky and thick with emotions that threatened to ruin my mascara. "We better go."

Ciara took a deep breath and nodded, but her shoulders shook slightly as we stepped into the elevator.

Every room at the Avalon had been reserved for the next three weeks to accommodate the other courts, each of which, I was told, was traveling with an extensive retinue. It seemed there was no trust between any of them, and the place would be full of armed guards and fae aristocracy. The Nether Court itself would host some of the events; others would take place in the Avalon's private club and ballrooms, fae moving freely between worlds. Meanwhile, I'd been

instructed to stay close to Ciara, Shaw, and Roark, who would see
that I didn't get stuck in either place.

I still hadn't heard a word from Lachlan despite my room being
only a few doors down from his.

The men were already waiting when we stepped off the elevator,
along with a dozen security guards. I had no doubt more were on
call nearby, tasked with surveilling every public space in both
worlds in an effort to keep the peace. I'd been too confused during
the Equinox to really take stock of their security measures. Now,
my pulse skittered as we made our way to meet them in the lobby.
Lachlan was closer to the door, his back to us, and if he heard our
approach, he didn't turn.

Shaw and Roark were dressed in their usual black with their
collars buttoned tightly, tattoos static on their necks and knuckles.
Shaw had slicked his copper hair back, making it look darker
than normal, and Roark's silver hair was swept hard to one side,
showcasing a freshly shaved design on the other. He nodded hello,
his tongue fiddling with his lip ring. Shaw, however, let out a low
whistle when he saw us.

Ciara preened, but I just rolled my eyes.

"Finally. You two are late. They'll be..." Lachlan trailed off as
he finally turned. His eyes raked up my body, loitering shamelessly
when they reached my hips, my breasts, my neck, like a winner
assessing his prize. When his gaze at last found my own, the intensity
stole my breath—straight up sucked the air from my lungs as if he'd
won that, too, and would settle for nothing less than every piece of
me.

Roark groaned. "Why do I suddenly feel like I need a cigarette
and a nap?"

Lachlan ripped his eyes from mine, offering his penumbra the
finger before strolling toward us. My focus dropped to the floor
as I breathed deeply, but it wasn't only my lungs on fire. Ciara
elbowed me in the ribs, but I ignored her. So far, she hadn't been
nearly as obnoxious as Roark about teasing us about our bargain.
Roark seemed to get a special thrill at poking Lachlan over it, but I

wondered how long it would be until Shaw or Ciara caved and joined him.

"You both look lovely," Lachlan said, the words as stiff as his rigid shoulders.

"I believe your instructions were *dress to impress*." Ciara's mouth puckered as she spoke. Her brother stared her down, and she forced a grim smile.

"It's not a funeral," he murmured more gently than I would have expected.

But she rested her head on my shoulder, refusing to look at him. "Tell that to my sex life."

They were still ignoring each other when guests began to arrive. The Infernal Court was the first to show, each one from the royals to the courtiers to the guards looking like they had a very long, hard stick up their ass. All of them were inhumanly beautiful, more like statues meant for museums than living, breathing creatures.

I recognized the crown prince from the Equinox. Bain waited in the center of the group as his security took positions on either side. At his left, MacAlister sneered in our general direction. I had no idea if his nasty smile was directed at one of us in particular or all of us equally. A small ring of guards, some Infernal Court and some from ours, circled us as Bain strode over to shake Lachlan's hand. He didn't acknowledge anyone else.

In case we weren't sure where we ranked.

Bain was the white-hot tip of the Infernal Court's flame, and Lachlan was the deadly, untamed wild of the Nether Court's dark. The princes of the shadow courts, though equal in standing, were so very different in every other way.

"Lachlan." The prince bowed his icy head slightly.

"Bain," Lachlan greeted him smoothly, not returning the gesture.

It seemed the pissing contests had begun.

Lachlan's mouth lifted at the corner, and I realized I was fiddling with my pendant. But this time I didn't drop my hand, letting him hear my thoughts. In this room full of fae, of strangers that I knew were as deadly as they came, he was my lifeline. *Even if he is an insufferable prick*, I added so his ego wouldn't become dangerously overinflated.

Lachlan cleared his throat of what I thought might have been a laugh.

Bain's smile bared a little too much of his teeth, and I wondered if this was just posturing between two fae males near the top of their food chain or if there was bad blood between them. If Lachlan thought his sister would be enough to resolve it.

"You're the first court to arrive," the Nether Prince drawled.

"Because we're the most important guests." Bain smiled at his own joke, glancing once at Ciara before his eyes flickered around the lobby. "Or, I am, at least."

Lachlan simply stared back at him.

"Ciara," Bain continued, something feral creeping into his eyes as he beheld his future bride. She inched closer to me, her hand slipping into mine. "I look forward to this evening, don't you? One final hurrah before the first calling of the banns."

She swallowed. "As do I."

Bain's gaze moved to where her hand clasped mine, and he frowned. "Don't tell me that you've grown attached to a human."

My mouth fell open, but before I could retort, Ciara glared. "I forgot how—"

"Not as much as I have," Lachlan interjected smoothly.

Bain looked mollified. "I just wondered if I should be expecting her to join us in London."

Ciara's hand tightened on mine, but Lachlan shook his head. "Only when I'm there." He nodded to his sister. "Ciara, will you show Bain and the others to their floor?"

Her chin raised, her smile a little too bright to be believed. "Please follow me."

I started to join her, but Lachlan held up a hand. "You'll forgive us for staying to greet the others. Tradition."

"Tradition," Bain echoed.

I shot Ciara an encouraging smile as she released me, my hand clammy from how hard she'd been holding it. She motioned for Bain and MacAlister to join her, and I fought the urge to go with her despite Lachlan's words. I relaxed a little as two of our guards followed. There would come a time when she would be on her own at the Infernal Court, but this first night, I knew she needed the extra courage.

Shaw and Roark moved beside me. I doubted their slightly protective stance was a coincidence. It seemed I had inherited two bodyguards in Ciara's absence.

"So, are they friends, or do they hate each other?" I whispered to Roark when Lachlan went to speak with one of his men. It was always impossible to tell where Lach was concerned.

"So you noticed." He grinned down at me. "A little bit of both. Bain and Lach tolerate each other's existence a little better than some of the other courts do. The Astral Court should be arriving from Prague shortly."

I hung back when they did, asking more questions under my breath and wishing I'd done more to prepare.

Aurora, the Astral Court's crown princess, was as beautiful as her name, her dark-brown skin offset by the deep amethyst shade of her column dress, which was the same color as her jewel-bright eyes. She spoke warmly to Lachlan, her hand touching his arm lightly every now and then. He actually returned her smile, leaning closer to speak with her in a low voice, and something twinged in my chest. I forced myself to look away, and my gaze collided with one of her companions. He grinned nervously at me. They looked enough alike that it was clear they were related, but he had none of the princess's effortless confidence despite being her equal in beauty. Instead, he occasionally shuffled his feet and sent anxious looks in my direction. They had fewer guards than the Infernal Court but more courtiers. Something about that put me at ease.

"Who is that?" I murmured to my companions.

"Sirius," Shaw answered this time. "Good guy. A bit young."

Considering how old they were, I couldn't imagine what *young* meant to them. He looked about my age, but for a fae, that could mean he was twenty-five years old or a hundred. Before I could ask more, the Hallow Court made their appearance.

It was immediately clear why Roark had mentioned heaven. While the guards who accompanied them ranged from burly to squat, the royals and the courtiers simply looked like angels. The two fae at the head of the group shared the same rich mahogany hair and deep amber eyes, and both had high cheekbones. The woman's features, delicate and lovely, were complemented by the airy summer dress she wore, its long skirt dusting the ground. Her male counterpart was equally handsome with a wide, strong jawline and broad shoulders that strained under his gray suit jacket. They didn't walk so much as float across the marble floor like their feet didn't need to touch the ground.

"Oberon. Titania." To them, Lachlan inclined his head.

"Twins," Roark whispered.

It took effort to look away from them, but when I did, I frowned. The rest of their retinue hung back in two distinct lines: courtiers and guards.

"Where are their penumbras?"

"They don't have them," he explained. "Only the true firstborn would be granted one. It's rumored their parents decided either might claim the throne. No one knows which was born first, so they still both claim the crowns, though everyone assumes it's Oberon. They're the oldest among us."

Oberon was the one Ciara had referred to as "ancient," but she had failed to mention his sister. My hands balled at my sides as she stepped forward to greet Lachlan with a kiss on each cheek.

"Titania." Lachlan stepped away quickly.

She bit her lip a little as she grinned at him, the gesture so unabashedly coquettish I felt a stab of jealousy. "It's definitely been too long, Lach."

I hated the way she said his name. The familiarity that oozed off her tongue. Which was silly, since they'd probably known each other for centuries.

But how *well* did they know each other? Was *she* his type?

Her bountiful curves and delicate features were a clear contrast to myself—and the way she held his attention so easily. I could never do that. I was so preoccupied that I didn't notice Oberon looking at me.

"And who is this?" His voice was warm and rich, like liquid gold itself poured from his lips.

My mouth nearly fell open, and I barely managed to hold it closed.

"You mean my newest acquisition." I bristled at the casual ownership in Lachlan's voice as he stepped between us, breaking Oberon's eye contact. "She is lovely, isn't she?"

I twisted my ring around my finger, torn between not being rude and hating how he spoke of me like I wasn't here.

Lachlan swiveled toward me, the grin on his face stretched as though he was forcing it. "Cate Holloway, allow me to introduce Oberon and Titania."

I forced myself to stop gawking and speak. "It's a pleasure."

Despite Lachlan's careful positioning between us, Oberon stepped smoothly around him and took my hand. He lifted it to his lips. "I hope we can get to know each other."

There was absolutely no mistaking what he meant. A flush swept over my body at the implication. Maybe he looked at every woman like he wanted to worship her. Maybe that's why his court was associated with heaven.

Lachlan's hand found the small of my back, and the touch grounded me. I drew away from Oberon gently. He might be handsome and tempting, but like it or not, my nights belonged to the Nether Court. I waited for the sting of disappointment as I realized that, but it didn't come. Instead, it took effort not to inch closer to Lachlan's steady warmth.

Oberon's smile faded slightly. "Will I see you at the feast tonight?"

"*We* will be there," Lachlan answered tightly, his palm pressing down as if to pin me to the spot. He nodded to his penumbra. "Roark will show you to your floor."

Before I could say goodbye, the hand on my back steered me

toward the bank of elevators, remaining on me possessively as the doors slid open. Lachlan didn't bother to wait for anyone else to join us, bypassing courtesy as though a swift retreat was necessary. After faking a smile for the last hour, I didn't argue with him, especially given the weary set of his shoulders. Still, the compartment felt too small as it carried us to the top floor. His hand remained firmly in place, but his demeanor had changed from the possessive bravado he'd displayed in the lobby to something closer to nervousness.

He didn't speak when the elevator deposited us on our floor, didn't bother to look around to see if his sister had returned, didn't even glance in my direction. Instead, he seized my hand and dragged me into his private wing.

And then the Nether Prince shut and locked the door behind us.

CHAPTER EIGHTEEN

My heart was a drum roaring in my chest as I stared at the lock, trying to decipher if Lachlan meant to keep them out— or me in. He braced his palms against it, tension radiating from him.

"I forget how insufferable they are," he gritted out.

I blinked, realizing he meant the other royals. That his agitation was about them, about their presence, their posturing, their fucking *pissing contests.* "Everyone seemed polite." Except Bain, perhaps.

"Until you turn your back," he said darkly. "They all have their own agendas."

"And you don't?"

His head dropped. "I've never been as good at hiding mine as the others."

I doubted that. I still didn't know what he wanted with me.

"Don't let them get under your skin," I said as my own pulse finally began to calm.

I studied him, the way his suit jacket strained against his muscular torso as he held that door like his life depended on it. Maybe I'd misinterpreted our hasty departure as jealousy on his part when, in reality, he'd used me as a means to escape. That…hurt.

I backed away. No. It shouldn't hurt. I shouldn't want him to be jealous. Shouldn't want that hand on the small of my back to mean something. There were at least three other men in this very hotel who were kinder and better choices than him. Four, if I counted the young Astral prince. Why did I have to react to Lach's every touch, to his presence, to *him*? I couldn't resist even his smallest request. I was a single star in a vast, dark sky, and Lachlan was the black hole that would devour me. I couldn't escape his gravity.

And worse, there were times I didn't want to.

"Don't let them under my skin," he repeated with a hollow laugh. "I'll try to keep that in mind."

When he turned to face me, I edged toward the hall, wanting to hide in my room, afraid that this stupid, foolish rejection I felt was written all over my face. But he just leaned against the door and pushed a hand through his ink-black hair, leaving it loose and tousled and begging to be touched. He looked vulnerable. It was unsettling enough to tamp down my panic.

"You hate them all," I said carefully.

"Not Aurora," he admitted.

Jealousy speared through me, but I swallowed it down. I had no idea where it came from. "She's pretty." It was easy enough to say, since it was true.

"Is she?"

I crossed my arms over my chest, over my heart. "You know that she is."

"The fae are beautiful." His eyes traced along my face. "All of them."

I knew he was looking at me and seeing a human, seeing that inconsequential star that he was bound to swallow and forget. The hurt flared back to life—more than it should have. I turned my face away from those prying eyes. "I suppose that's my cue to find Ciara and put a glamour on."

"Why?"

The soft question stopped me, but I just needed a few minutes, some distance to remind myself that Lachlan Gage had always been a very bad idea. And then tonight I would dance with Ciara, and maybe for once I would drink too much because I was actually safe here, I'd realized. Safer than I'd been in a very long time.

My mind replayed his lingering touch on my back. I tried to force myself to see it for what it was—a warning to the other fae that

I belonged to him. At least according to the terms of the bargain. I was a toy to play with when he was bored, but I wasn't to be touched by anyone else. He'd made that clear, but even so, there had been something in his eyes that suggested it was not so simple to him, either. It was a small thing to cling to, but I grabbed onto it and *clung*.

"Why do you need a glamour?" he pressed when I'd been silent for too long.

"I don't want to stick out. Better to blend in." Safer. Always safer.

His mouth tipped into a frown.

He was going to make me say it. He was going to make me face facts. "I'd rather look more fae tonight. Being the only human in the room is a novelty." I bit my lip. "Although, I think Oberon wants to fuck me."

Something lethal crept into his eyes at my last words.

"And do you want to fuck him?" Each word was careful, measured, and delivered just precisely enough that I felt a small spark in my chest.

"I don't know. Do I? You sure act like fucking a fae should be on the top of my bucket list." His answering silence felt dangerous, and somehow that was better than the nothing I'd felt before. Maybe because I was well-versed in danger and fear and anger. "What about Titania?"

"Fuck Titania *and* her brother? You are getting ambitious, princess."

But I wasn't going to let him ignore the bait, not until I'd forgotten that ache, not until I'd filled it with anger instead. "She wants you."

"Titania wants everyone."

"And you don't?"

His eyes blazed with fire I couldn't quite muster. "I think you will find that I have very particular tastes."

"I'm aware. She's gorgeous."

"I don't want Titania, Cate."

His fiery eyes dared me to push him harder, to drag one more confession from him. But I had learned my lesson. Any closer and I would get burned. Any closer and I might not be able to escape that magnetic force he exuded as effortlessly as breathing.

When I didn't respond, a muscle in his jaw twitched. "Be ready to leave at midnight."

"That's a little late for dinner, don't you think?"

His lips curled into a smile that made my toes do the same. "It's the Midnight Feast. And we won't be dining."

I shivered at the dangerous current running through his words, feeling it tug on me, feeling it pull me toward that unknown place again. I forced myself to swallow and nodded. "I'll be ready."

Something about his answering glower told me I wouldn't be.

. . .

The trouble with getting ready for a midnight feast that was not a feast—*whatever* that meant—was I didn't know how to prepare. I stared at the gown hanging on the closet door. I needed Ciara, not just to help me but to distract me, to pull me from my confusion. But I wasn't about to risk going to find her. I settled for sending her a text message and prayed that all the strange magic in the building wouldn't fuck with the cell reception.

It was almost laughable that I needed her to calm me down. That was supposed to be my job for her, especially tonight. Maybe I needed to steer clear of Lachlan or insist on taking one of the dozen other rooms on the top floor.

I wasn't thinking straight around him. I had to get my shit together. Now.

Less than a month. I had less than a month to figure out what he got out of this bargain if I wanted to break it, and now the Nether Court was full of visiting fae intent on distracting me from my task. I couldn't let them.

I took a quick shower to help settle my mind. But as I stepped out of the shower and reached for a towel, the door opened. My foot slid, and I careened, barely keeping myself upright. I snatched up the towel, draping it over my front as I spun around to find Lach.

"Don't you knock?" I tugged the towel more tightly around myself, wondering how much he had seen.

Hooded eyes skimmed over every bare inch of my dripping skin *not* covered by the towel. "I did. *Several* times."

"Well, obviously I didn't hear you." I huffed past him into the bedroom, hoping he interpreted my pink skin as a result of my shower and not his presence. If only I could do the same, but all the confusing feelings had reappeared in his presence.

"I was concerned for your safety," he said blandly. "What if you had fallen and hit your head? You could have drowned."

"I guess we're not that lucky." I threw open the closet and riffled through the hanging gowns until I found a silk robe. I'd barely tied it around my waist when the bedroom door flew open and Ciara rushed in, a collection of dresses gathered in her arms.

She deposited silk and tulle, satin and sequins onto the bed and turned to me, planting her hands on her narrow hips. "What are you wearing? Why didn't we plan this out?" She shooed Lachlan away with one hand. "Go glower somewhere else."

I bit back a laugh as his eyes narrowed, a tattoo winding around his knuckles as he cracked them.

"Try not to corrupt my..."

I waited for him to call me *possession* or *toy* or *pet*, my slitted gaze almost daring him.

But Ciara lost her patience, stomped over, and shoved her brother unceremoniously out the door before shutting it behind him. "Leering, obnoxious creep."

Sometimes, they reminded me so much of my relationship with Channing it hurt. Except my brother was in a jail cell and I was going to a party. I forced the thought aside, reminding myself that I was only going to the party to protect Channing and get us out of this mess. Eventually.

Ciara returned to the bed, picking up gowns and tossing them to the side. "I have no idea what to wear." She turned beseeching eyes to me. "And I don't want to sleep with Bain."

I sucked in a breath. "Then don't."

"You make that sound so simple." She dropped onto the bed, sending the voluminous fabrics into the air. The dresses settled around her, but she didn't look at them.

"Isn't it?" I asked carefully. Despite the time we'd spent together over the last week, she hadn't talked much about the betrothal. I'd followed her lead. But tonight was the eleventh hour.

"I don't know. It should be. I've had plenty of hookups." She picked at the hem of one of the dresses. "It's different because I don't want to. Not yet."

Her words squeezed my heart. I sat down beside her and took her hand. "Then *don't*. Spend some time with him. Maybe something will change."

"What if he doesn't understand?"

My blood ran cold at the fear lacing her voice. "I will shoot him myself."

Ciera stared at me, blinking several times. "You mean that, don't you?"

"I do."

Her fingers tightened around mine, and then she giggled. "Do not fuck with Cate."

I didn't feel like laughing, though. Not when I knew how concerned she was.

The smile fell from her face. "Shit. I scared you."

"I overreacted."

But she searched my face, as if she now suspected what I was sure Lachlan already knew. "Lach would never let him touch me. I'm safe here," she said softly, adding, "and *you're* safe here."

"Yeah, I know that." I'd shown too much, and now she was worried about me, which was the last thing I wanted.

But she shook her head. "Seriously, there's a code. The fae are a lot of things, but…"

I thought back to that first night in Lachlan's office, of what had happened to the man that broke that code. Each time I recalled it, my disgust diminished. Tonight, it was nearly gone.

I reached for one of the dresses. "All of these are pretty, and you'll look beautiful in any of them."

"I don't want to send the wrong message," she said in a breathy whisper. "Not just to Bain but anyone who might be interested."

"Anyone who might be—" My eyebrows lurched up my forehead. "What exactly is happening tonight?"

"Ever been to a bachelorette party?"

"Yes…"

"Like that but more…" She waved her hands around.

"Ritual fuckery?" I guessed.

She grimaced and picked up a dress, then tossed it back onto the pile. "One last fling before the ring, right? Except everybody joins in."

Wait, *what*? "Tonight is…is…an orgy?"

She rolled her eyes, the gesture reminding me of her brother. "I assume he didn't warn you."

"He most certainly did not!"

She sighed and hugged a dress to her chest as she rose to her feet. "The Midnight Feast is held the night before the first calling of the banns."

What did that have to do with an orgy? "I thought banns were a Catholic thing?"

"Where do you think they got the idea?" She shook her head, as if giving them credit personally offended her. "It's a fae custom to announce a marriage three weeks before the wedding, spend that time working up the courage to go through with it while secretly hoping someone intervenes, and then get it over with."

I blinked and waited for the joke. "Romantic."

"Vampires copied it, and the church followed them, but they always get the credit for our ideas."

"That's why everyone is here for three weeks?" Lachlan had told me that Bain had insisted on following tradition and that doing so would give him time to negotiate a solution to the trinity problem. There was a lot of his plan that I didn't like, but knowing why he was doing it would make it easier to show my face each night. "It sounds archaic."

"You have to be sure before you marry in our world. Marriage bonds are funny things. They trump all other bargains. After a year, they can't be dissolved, and fae…"

Lived a very long time.

"You don't have to go through with it."

"I know that." Her chin quivered a little. "But it's not a big deal. We're both doing this for our courts. He wants an heir. Once I give him one, we can go back to ignoring each other."

"But you'll still be married."

"A political marriage isn't about love. It's a transaction." The words were automatic, and I wondered how many hours she'd spent convincing herself of that.

"Should it be?"

Ciara sucked in a deep breath. "Love is a luxury royalty can't afford." Her throat slid like it was a bitter truth to swallow. "Believe it or not, I made the final call to go through with this. It's not Lach's sole responsibility to care about the Nether Court."

"And if he was the one who could get married, would he? Or would he make you do it?"

Ciara's eyes flashed, but she turned to survey my closet. "We're running out of time. We still need to figure out what we are wearing."

"I'm supposed to wear that one." I pointed to the gown that had been laid out for me.

She wrinkled her nose. "It's lovely, but tonight is not about looking pretty. It's about looking hot. Just in case, you want to…"

"I don't think your brother will like it if I bring someone back to my room."

"No, he wouldn't," she said wickedly. "But it's not up to him."

Yeah, right. "I'm not exactly looking for any action."

She paused, assessing me with sparkling interest. "I'm guessing you've never banged a fae before."

I nearly choked on my own spit. "No."

"Pity." She clicked her tongue. "I'm pretty sure Lach would be happy to remedy that for you."

My mouth dropped open, but she'd already abandoned my closet and started rummaging through her pile. Finally, she held one up with a triumphant grin. "This is the one."

I studied the petite dress. Ciara was nearly half a foot shorter than me. "That won't fit me."

"Please. There's magic for that."

I gaped at the breezy comment. "Magic? If there's magic, why did I spend an entire night being stuck with pins during a three-hour dress fitting?"

Ciara laughed. "Wow. My brother really is a dick."

The comforting prickle of irritation bristled through me. That was better. That was how I was supposed to feel when I thought about Lachlan Gage. Not only had he wasted my time, but he had also sat back and enjoyed watching me getting jabbed over and over again like some type of supernatural sociopath. A sociopath who apparently wanted me to play pretty, pretty princess so I would not attract too much attention this evening.

"Think of it this way. We're not dressing for action"—a dazzling smile oozed across her face—"we're dressing to get a *re*action."

Maybe Ciara was right. Maybe what I needed was to get a response—from everyone in the room. Because if Lachlan thought he had a claim to me, it was time to show him he was wrong.

CHAPTER NINETEEN

Ciara had remained cryptic on the specifics of the Midnight Feast, but based on the dress she'd chosen for me and the fundamental understanding of what an orgy entailed, I decided it might be best to be surprised rather than chicken out.

As promised, she had glamoured the dress to instantly transform it into something that fit my body. Although "*fit*" might be an overstatement. Not that its raciness was from a lack of magic so much as a lack of fabric. The gown consisted entirely of sheer layers of black tulle that swished across the floor with each step I took despite my five-inch stilettos. But other than length, there was nothing remotely modest about it. Its sheerness allowed nothing to be worn underneath it, and the only discretion it offered was by way of embroidered leaves that overlapped my breasts and my hips, a few fronds draping past my knees in various shades of black and bottle green. I couldn't decide which message it sent: that I was available or that I belonged to the wild, verdant heart of the Nether Court itself.

Every head in the room turned as we entered, and many of them bowed immediately when they saw the princess at my side. The guest of honor had opted for a rose-colored gown that gathered at the neck and flowed in a long, sensuous column down her body. Its color offset her pale, luminous skin, making the darkness of her hair and the subtle pink of her lips all that more stunning. But more than a few eyes tarried on me, including, I realized with a shiver, Oberon's.

He was standing near the entrance, deep in conversation with Sirius, the young Astral Court prince. A smile spread across Oberon's face as our eyes met, his entire being seeming to glow from within from the light court magic smoldering in his veins. Sirius, on the other hand, shot me a goofy grin.

Ciara noticed them looking at us and elbowed me in the ribs. Grabbing my hand, she dragged me over. "Oberon, I heard you met Cate, but I believe Sirius was being shy."

Sirius didn't look nearly as shy now. He straightened, showcasing his broad shoulders and impressive build.

"It's a pleasure." His voice was as deep and smooth as his flawless brown skin. He reached for my hand, and I allowed him to take it with some hesitation, blushing a little as he brought it to his lips. Another gentleman. Apparently, I had just needed to look to the light court for one. Who knew?

"It's a pity one of you is already spoken for." Oberon smiled at Ciara. "Best wishes, by the way."

"They haven't called the banns yet. I'm still single tonight," Ciara teased, but I heard the undercurrent of trepidation as she spoke.

Oberon turned his full attention to me, amber eyes gleaming. "In that case, perhaps we won't have to fight over Cate."

Sirius and Ciara shared a look as she stepped a little closer to me. "No one is fighting tonight."

That sounded like wishful thinking, especially with the number of armed guards stationed around the perimeter of the ballroom. I was about to point that out and then defuse the sexual charge to the conversation with a new topic when a familiar weight settled against the small of my back.

"I've been waiting for you," his dark voice rumbled.

I hadn't seen Lachlan approach, but my entire body was aware of him instantly. I dared to look up as he stepped to my side. His gaze whispered across my body, drinking in the see-through fabric of my gown and the provocative placement of its adornments inch by inch. I was sure I imagined the slide of his throat, the way his eyes shadowed, the shift as he angled himself between me and the others. He leaned closer, lowering his voice, although I had no idea why. The other fae could clearly hear him. "I don't remember picking out this dress."

"Yes, thank the gods." Ciara rolled her eyes and jabbed her brother with a perfectly manicured fingernail. "Were you picking out dresses for the Midnight Feast or a debutante ball? I already promised poor Cate I would take her shopping tomorrow so she has something decent to wear."

Her brother ignored her entirely, bending farther so that his lips grazed the shell of my ear. My breath hitched as he murmured, "Mouthwatering," then pressed a kiss to my neck.

I gawked at him, but he only smirked, as if that masculine arrogance that got under my skin so easily was second nature and not something he could help. But now it wormed its way deeper, lower, not stopping until I found myself shifting to squeeze my thighs together against the sensation.

Oberon studied us. "She would make an exquisite offering. Are you sure I can't change your mind?"

The request was enough to free me of my daze. I looked to Ciara, but she only shook her head slightly.

"Unfortunately, I already have everything I want," Lachlan said. His hand slipped from my back then, and I fought a surge of disappointment—until his fingers laced with mine and tugged. "There are more people I'd like you to meet."

First a kiss and now he was holding my hand? *He's marking his territory*, I reminded myself, but I was so rattled by the gesture that it took me a minute to remember why I was here. "I should stay with Ciara."

His hand tightened around mine. "This is her night," he said. "I'm sure she'll spend it wisely."

Sure enough, she'd slipped off to visit with another group. She spotted me, and I raised my brows in an unspoken question. She shooed me with one hand and winked.

"I won't let anything happen to her," Lachlan reminded me,

echoing what she had said earlier, and despite the uncertainty I felt about him, I knew he was telling the truth.

He led me away, deeper into the belly of the crowd. I suspected this had been Ciara's plan all along. The reaction she'd intended to provoke. Was it her revenge on Lachlan to play matchmaker? If so, she was going to be very disappointed.

We paused as a server stepped into our path, holding a gold tray laden with champagne coupes. Lachlan reached for two, passing one to me. I took it gratefully, already overheated in the crowd—at least that was what I was telling myself. But the first taste of the drink on my lips made my eyes widen. It wasn't like anything I'd ever tasted. It was much sweeter, like pure nectar, with none of the fire of whiskey or the warm fullness of wine. I found myself gulping more, relishing the honeyed taste of it on my tongue.

"Careful with that," he told me. "Ambrosia will give you one hell of a hangover."

"Ambrosia?" That was the name of this heavenly substance. The fae were really holding out on us poor humans, hoarding all these delicious delicacies in their world.

"And it's got a kick to it," he warned me.

"I can handle myself."

He drew a breath and pulled me closer—not so close that our bodies touched; just close enough to make me wish they were. "You'll want more," he said, "and you can have as much as you want as long as you're willing to risk the consequences."

He really saw everything, and somehow that made this strange, forbidden attraction to him worse. "Do I need your permission?"

"No." Sadness stole his smile. "Just know that you will be safe if you want to let loose."

The offer cracked something inside me open, and I clung to the pieces and tried to wrench them back together. "I thought you didn't want me to let loose."

"It's not about me," he said darkly. "It's about you, and since you're going to hide behind that sarcastic mouth I adore, I will spell it out."

Adore? Him? Me? The very mouth in question fell open because the way he held my gaze told me he'd meant what he said. He wasn't mocking or teasing.

"No one touches you—human, fae, or any other creature—without your permission." He definitely wasn't joking now. "So enjoy yourself, because if you say no, it will be respected, or I will personally remove the offending part from the bastard's body and choke them to death with it."

Every word eddied from my head. Lachlan snagged another glass of ambrosia from a passing tray and handed it to me. I gulped it down and instantly relaxed enough to nod.

He waited a minute. "Better?"

"I don't know," I admitted.

"That's fair." He scanned the room over his shoulder, his face tightening. "But I should warn you that things are about to get very interesting."

A hush fell over the crowd, and all around us, fae rippled apart, creating a wide chasm in the middle of the room.

Bain strode into the center, the chandeliers overhead catching his platinum hair and sharp features, making him look as dazzling and sharp as its crystals. Ciara stood on the edge of the crowd, hands clasped together. Everyone stilled as Bain addressed the room. "I regret to inform you that the rumors are true: the lovely Ciara Gage has agreed to marry me."

"I *regret* to inform you," I muttered along with a few choice words.

Lachlan hmphed. "I'm the one getting stuck with the bastard as a brother-in-law."

"Whose fault is that?" I bumped my hip against his. His thumb stroked the back of my hand, and my entire body tensed.

"Tonight, we partake in the Midnight Feast—a last supper, if you will." Bain's voice was smooth and wicked. Fae around us began to whisper, the entire room crackling with an electric energy that hummed over my skin and found its way into my blood.

That might also have been the ambrosia.

"Marriage is the binding of not only two souls but two families. It is not something I enter lightly," Bain continued. "I've had three hundred years to wait for the perfect woman to come along." He extended an arm toward Ciara. She strolled toward him, a smug smile on her face, but it didn't extend to her eyes. His speech might be winning over the crowd, but he was going to need to worry about her. When she reached him, he seized her hand. "I've found her."

I was going to throw up on her behalf.

Lachlan cleared his throat, and I realized I might have said that bit aloud.

"But before we spend the rest of our lives together, we're going out with a bang," Bain said. Ciara blanched under the light of the chandeliers, growing nearly as pale as her future husband. "Or ten. Who's counting?"

Everyone around us laughed and clapped, but my stomach began to churn.

Bain lifted Ciara's hand and kissed it. "Have a good time tonight, but try not to get in too much trouble."

He clapped his hands together, and the whispers around us turned into shouts and cheers.

This was getting weird.

Bain released her, and Ciara edged away from him, back to the safety of the crowd. I watched as a few fae stopped her to gush and gossip. I was about to pull away from Lachlan and go to her when Aurora moved to her side and whispered something. Ciara sagged with relief and nodded before the two of them vanished into the crowd.

Bain didn't seem to notice as he finished his speech. "To begin our delicious feast, offerings from all four courts."

I craned my head, watching for food to appear and completely unprepared for what happened instead.

Two rows of people filed into the room, taking up the empty space around him. I forgot how to breathe. They were all beautiful, bodies of every shape and size, some slender, others luscious with curves, others muscled and brawny, but all wearing nothing more than a shimmering coat of golden paint from head to toe. I blinked as I took in swaying hips and pert breasts and ready cocks.

Bain offered the onlookers a devilish smile, and instantly the lighting in the room shifted, lowering along with the space's energy into something sensual and inviting. The fae around me swirled and mingled. There was no shyness as many approached the gold-painted people at the center of the room. But I could only stare as I took in more details now that my initial shock was wearing off. Some of them had the tipped ears of the fae, but others did not. Humans? Or the other creatures that the fae claimed existed? My mouth went dry as two females approached the painted male closest to us. They offered him a coy smile, one of them leaning to whisper in his ear, the other reaching for his—

I jerked my gaze away. Nope. Definitely didn't need to see that.

Lachlan urged me closer to his side. "Maybe we should leave."

"I'm fine." Mostly. My brain felt fuzzier than ever. "Maybe we could walk around a bit?"

He offered me his arm, and I took it, no longer caring what message it sent, as long as that message included that I was not up for grabs.

We wandered toward the perimeter of the room, carefully bypassing interested eyes, their intentions so bald I felt a little queasy. But as we walked, I began to realize what he'd been trying to tell me earlier. "When you said *let loose*, you meant…"

"If you choose." He glowered at a fae who'd started in our direction, and the other man thought better of it.

"And you?"

"I'm exactly where I want to be."

Oh. My gaze snagged on one of the gold-painted women nearby. She laughed as the crowd gathered around her, flirting with them without reservation. What would it be like to be that free? "Did they volunteer?"

"Most of them."

There was no sign that any of this was making him uncomfortable. Then again, he had probably done this before. For all I knew, he might have been up there painted with the rest of them a few times. The thought made the sweetness of the ambrosia still lingering in my mouth turn sour.

"Others are repaying a debt," he continued. "But they are all here willingly."

I snorted. "I doubt that."

His gaze slid to mine. "The fae do not need to take anyone against their will."

"But you'll trick them," I pointed out.

He bristled and moved closer, catching my wrist. "I didn't offer you tonight."

I felt the blood drain from my face as I remembered what Oberon had said earlier. That was what he had meant. He had hoped that I would be among the painted people paraded out as a gift from another court to the happy couple.

"Am I supposed to thank you for that?"

"I might die of shock if you did."

"In that case, thank you."

His eyes narrowed, but before he could respond, Bain and Shaw approached us. "Lach," Bain began. "If you have a minute to discuss the matter of the—"

"Are you skipping your own orgy?" I blurted out.

"Why?" Bain purred. "Are you asking me to stick around? Perhaps business can wait."

I choked. Before the shock wore off, Lachlan stepped between us. His jaw worked slightly. "She is not. I'll be along shortly."

"Don't dawdle," Bain said in a clipped tone. "And do let me know if you change your mind, Cate. I'm afraid this is a limited-time offer."

"She doesn't wish to participate," Lachlan said through gritted teeth.

Bain shrugged as if this was no great loss to him but possibly one to me. "Then find a babysitter and hurry up."

I was vividly imagining shoving a champagne glass down his disgusting throat when Lachlan turned to Shaw. "Keep an eye on her. I won't be long."

His brother nodded, but his face fell a little. I couldn't blame him. If I was the orgy sort, I wouldn't want to get stuck keeping an eye on someone who wasn't.

Lachlan lifted his hand toward me, and for a moment I thought he was going to wrap it around my neck, drag me close, and kiss me, like he had that day on the street. Instead, he traced his index finger along my collarbone, trailing it to my pendant. "If you need me…"

I forced myself to nod, hoping that the noise of the crowd, which was becoming more salacious by the moment, swallowed the sound of my beating heart, the blood roaring in my veins, the slight gasp that escaped when that finger dipped slightly lower before it disappeared entirely.

As soon as they were out of sight, my legs buckled. Shaw's hand shot out to steady me, his palm ghosting over my shoulder only momentarily. "You okay there?"

"I'm just a little dizzy." I pressed a hand to my forehead and found it slightly feverish. "I haven't eaten anything. Probably shouldn't have had ambrosia on an empty stomach."

"All the nudity probably doesn't help, either," he pointed out with a grin.

I smacked him on the shoulder, and he laughed.

We wound our way through the crowd in search of something to eat.

"Are all fae traditions so…pornographic?" I asked.

He chuckled, raking a hand through his hair as his eyes landed on someone in the crowd. "No. Some are even family friendly."

Clearly, tonight was an adults-only event.

My gaze followed in the direction of his to find Titania tracking him from across the room. Apparently, she had eyes for both of the Nether Court princes.

"I think she likes you," I said dryly.

"Titania? We've…hung out before."

I refrained from asking him how long and hard they had hung out. It was obvious from the way he was looking at her that it was a memory he treasured. I shoved him slightly in her direction. "Go on. I can take care of myself."

"Lach would kill me if I left you alone," Shaw said, still looking at Titania longingly.

"I am just going to find something chocolate and hide in a corner to stress eat," I said. "It's an orgy. Live a little."

He cast a doubtful look in my direction. "I shouldn't—"

"You *should*. They don't throw these every week, right?"

God, I hoped not. If I was going to be expected to attend regular orgies, I was going to have to get a lot more comfortable in my own skin or start bleaching my eyeballs.

"Just don't go far. I'll be right back," he promised.

I shooed him away, glad that one of us was going to have a good night, then beelined for a dark alcove nearby, stopping only to swipe another glass of ambrosia from a passing tray. Lachlan had promised I was safe here. I might have relieved my conscripted chaperone from duty, but I suspected the order to protect me had been given to every Nether Court guard here, because no one approached me.

I just had to wait for Lachlan to return, and then…

And then I had no idea what would happen. He didn't want to be out there, and neither did I. Rubbing my fingers together, I wished his hand was still in mine. That had to be the ambrosia's fault. No wonder he'd given me that warning.

Leaving was a perfectly rational option, but if Ciara came looking for me, I'd feel terrible. I hoped she wouldn't. I hoped she was having the time of her life and checking several people off her to-do list.

Food would be a distraction, but apparently, this was a liquid-only feast. Which seemed a shame because, honestly, I'd read quite a few sexy scenes involving food in a romance novel or two. I wondered if the fae were open to suggestions. I giggled to myself as I imagined what an orgy comment box would contain.

A few interested parties roved my way, and I offered them apologetic smiles before slipping deeper into the alcove, allowing the shadows to cloak me as I sipped my ambrosia and tried to find a safe place to rest my eyes.

It turned out the only safe place I could look was the floor, because it didn't take long before casual flirting became more serious.

It wasn't all that different from reading a book, I told myself, taking in the scene. In fact, it reminded me a little of a fairy tale retelling that I'd burned through last year. But this time, I didn't have to imagine anything as fae coupled off around me, some even breaking into small groups. I watched as a few parties left the ballroom, heading upstairs to the massive beds that waited to welcome them and their partners for the evening. The less inhibited—and there were many of them—took to the walls or empty banquet tables along the edges of the room. Now I knew why no food had been laid out. I watched a male devouring a beautiful fae, the skirt of her gown hiked around her waist, her legs spread as he licked and sucked and nibbled. No man had ever touched me like that, devoured me like I was his last feast.

I could have that tonight, I realized—which was definitely the ambrosia talking. Lachlan had technically given me permission to take someone to bed. I didn't doubt I could find a willing partner or two. The thought rocketed through me and landed with a low, persistent throb between my legs. The problem wasn't having permission. It was that even as I watched, I knew I didn't want any of them. I reached up and touched the skin behind my ear, remembering Lachlan's stolen kiss. I belonged to someone else, like it or not. And I definitely did not.

Right?

"Mind if I hide with you?"

I startled as Oberon slipped beside me into the alcove. He was truly unspeakably hot, but I didn't trust him. I pressed myself against the wall, clutching my glass of ambrosia to my chest, and nodded.

"Not your thing?" he asked.

"Will you think less of me if I say it isn't?"

He chuckled. The laughter made his face look softer, almost human. Outside the alcove, someone moaned. Loudly. My eyes went wide, and Oberon chuckled again.

"Maybe we should find somewhere quieter," he suggested, holding up his hands to show he wasn't a threat. "No expectations."

"That sounds exactly like what someone with expectations would say," I pointed out. "You asked Lachlan to share earlier. Why aren't you out there enjoying all of..." I flourished a hand at the debauchery before us.

"It's not my thing, either," he confessed. "I was only interested in you."

A laugh burst out of me. *"Why?"*

"I'm doing this poorly." He hung his head. "The Hallow Court is a bit more isolated than yours."

My blood warmed at the idea that the Nether Court was mine.

"Honestly, I hate going to these things," Oberon said. "I don't have Lach's swagger."

Or his ego. I laughed at my own joke, and Oberon lifted a curious brow. "I was just thinking we could form a club for those of us who are not orgy regulars," I said to him.

"Unfortunately, I suspect we'd be the only members."

His voice was warm and welcoming, slightly musical, and it beckoned me. Not with the same magnetic force I felt when Lachlan walked into a room, but rather like the warm promise of a patch of sunlight on a cold day. My head spun a bit, imagining that the glow that seemed to emanate from his skin was sunshine itself.

He offered me his hand, and I stepped slightly out of the shadows, stumbling when my heel caught one of the sheer panels of my dress. How many glasses of ambrosia had I drunk?

"How did you get roped into coming here?" he asked as I tried to shake my heel free. "Something tells me you didn't know it was going to be like this."

I shook my head and yanked the fabric loose, which threw my already shaky balance into question. Oberon caught me before I landed face-first on the floor. He clearly hadn't gotten Lachlan's memo, though, because he didn't withdraw his hand. I liked the way it felt on my waist, warm and steady.

"I made a bargain with Lachlan Gage," I admitted to him.

His amber eyes widened. "Is that so? You don't seem happy about it."

"I got my brother out of trouble, so I guess it was worth it. It's just that the price is a little steep."

"Oh?"

"Every night in his court for the rest of my life." Somewhere deep down I knew I shouldn't be telling a stranger all my problems. Especially not a stranger that ruled a rival court. But while I was unclear on exactly what ambrosia was, it loosened my tongue as much as it did my inhibitions.

Oberon whistled. "That doesn't sound like Lach."

I grimaced. Apparently, no one knew Lachlan. Not his brother. Not his sister. Not the other princes. "I guess he needed someone to torture."

"I don't think that's why he made the bargain," he said carefully, but then he glanced up and his expression twisted, eyebrows knitting together.

Before I could look over my shoulder, a cold voice cut in. "Well, isn't this cozy?"

CHAPTER TWENTY

Lachlan stood behind me, arms crossed and murder on his face. He wasn't livid. No, he had blown somewhere past that to a terrifying place between DEFCON 1 and apocalyptic. Of all the times for him to walk up, he chose the moment another man had his hands on me, and not even in a sexual way when almost everyone around us was getting busy? The whole thing was hilarious, honestly. A giggle spilled from me, followed by more.

"Cate and I were keeping each other company," Oberon said smoothly, showing absolutely no signs of intimidation as Lachlan glared at him. I wasn't sure if I should be impressed or concerned about his self-preservation instincts.

"And where is Shaw?"

"I gave him the night off for good behavior," I said. The smile on my face felt a little sloppy, but I leaned into it—or rather, I leaned into Lachlan.

Instead of lecturing me, he wrapped an arm around my shoulders and pulled me closer. "Thanks for looking after her for me," he said in a clipped tone that contained no trace of genuine gratitude.

Oberon must have noticed the same, but he merely nodded. He turned to me. "Great talking to you. I look forward to next year's meeting. Perhaps we will grow our numbers by then."

Lach looked torn between asking questions and ripping his head off. Thankfully, he did neither.

"I'll make us shirts," I said happily.

My captor muttered something along the lines of "gods-damned nonsense," offered Oberon a curt farewell, and dragged me out of the ballroom. At least, he tried. We made it halfway before I planted my feet firmly, refusing to go.

He simmered. "It's time to leave."

I grabbed hold of his shirt. "What happened to *you will be safe if you want to let loose?*"

"If you get any looser, they'll be mopping you off the floor," he said dryly.

But I wasn't listening.

"We should dance." We had been too far away to hear the music in the alcove. Now it called to me, beckoned me, spoke directly to the blood beating in my veins. I *needed* to dance.

Lachlan stared at me as if I had grown a second head. He moved closer, searching my eyes, and frowned. "How much ambrosia have you had?"

I held up my hand, staring at my fingers as I tried to remember how to count.

"I'm going to kill Shaw," he growled.

"You shouldn't have asked him to babysit me."

"What else is he good for?"

He was seriously killing my vibe. "He's your brother." I poked his chest. "Be nicer to him."

"I'll be nicer when he stops fucking up."

Oh man, did I understand that feeling. "Maybe if you're nicer, he'll stop fucking up."

"Is that your strategy with Channing?"

I frowned. He had a point. Not that I was about to admit it. Besides, it wasn't like his strategy was working, either. But Lachlan seemed to realize his words had inflicted damage. He reached for my hand, but I snatched it back. The sharpness of my movement made my head spin, but I managed to stay upright.

"I'm sorry," he said. "Let's get out of here."

Normally, I might have rewarded him for his first-ever apology. Likely the only in his lifetime. Instead, I decided to use his newfound guilt to my advantage. Ciara and I had gone dancing on Bourbon Street, but I hadn't felt as free then, as safe as I did with him next to me.

"Make it up to me. Let's dance."

He bristled as his gaze swept the room, and I knew what he was seeing. There were a few couples dancing sporadically—if it could be called that. "Humping" was a more accurate description. Regardless, not everyone in the room was actively engaged in sex, and there was music. Since there was absolutely no way I was getting any tonight—by *my* choice—I needed to get some of my bottled-up energy out.

"Cate." His voice was laced with warning.

I ignored it. "I've spent the night watching other people doing it, and I need to work through that *physically*."

His lips twitched—the first sign that he wasn't going to continue acting like a deranged grizzly bear. "Is that so?"

"It's so," I said firmly. I grabbed his lapels and yanked him to me. "Now shut up and dance with me."

"Why were you hiding in a corner if you wanted to dance?" The question tiptoed along what I thought he really wanted to know: Had I been hiding or waiting?

I wouldn't give him the satisfaction of a real answer. Instead, I shrugged. "I didn't see anyone I wanted to dance with."

A smirk hooked his lips. "And you want to dance with me?"

Shit. I'd walked into that one. But I wasn't about to be defeated by Lachlan or his little temper tantrum. I pressed my body closer to his, rolling my hips to the beat of the music. "I sensed my opportunities were drying up, since you seem intent on not having any fun at all."

"I had business to attend to," he said stiffly.

"The boring meetings and cigar smoke, right?"

"You didn't answer me." He pressed closer, and I hummed at how good it felt to have his hard body on mine, how easy it was to melt against it and let him anchor me. "Did you want to dance with *me*?"

It really wasn't fair, because it was probably his sexy magic at work or the effects of their mysterious booze, but I couldn't tear my eyes away from his. I knew no matter what I said, he would see the truth in them. Lying would only be seen as weakness, and he already thought I was weak. He thought I needed protection. But tonight, I wanted to be a person I'd given up on a long time ago. And I was through with his insinuations. "I'm dancing with you now. Figure it out."

"So imperious." His lips tickled my ear again. Unlike before, they drifted over it a little, and I bit down on a moan. I knew he could feel the way my body responded to his. As if to prove me right, his fingers gripped my hips, sinking in so roughly that his nails scraped my skin through the tulle skirt. He dragged the tip of his nose along my jaw and whispered, "This isn't a dress. It's a sin."

I frowned. "Is there something wrong with what I'm wearing?"

"If you wanted everyone in the room to spend the evening eye-fucking you, then *no*."

Every clever retort dried up on my tongue.

"But you like that, don't you?" he murmured, his breath teasing my ear. I leaned into his dirty words, wanting more of them, wanting more contact. "Knowing that they would line up just to taste you." This time, his tongue retraced the line of my jaw, and I found my face angling, waiting, *anticipating* for that mouth to find mine. When it didn't, my eyes snapped open, and I scowled at him.

"You may continue."

Amusement flickered in those glittering eyes. "Continue what?"

"The dirty talk." Apparently, he needed me to spell it out for him. Why were men always so hopeless? "Proceed."

His low chuckle was pure masculine swagger. I bit my lip, feeling his chuckle bolt straight to my core.

He shook his head. "I think you've had enough to drink *and* enough dirty talk."

Before I could argue, the world swept out from underneath me. The effect was so dizzying, it took me a moment to process that I had been thrown over his shoulder. I pounded on his back as he carried me swiftly from the ballroom. More than a few people pivoted to watch us go.

"Put me down," I demanded.

"I would, but I think in your current state, marble floors are far too risky a proposition."

He might have a point. I wasn't going to tell him that, but I gave up trying to escape. Both because it was a free ride back to my room and because he smelled so damn good. His usual cedar scent was laced with tobacco and bourbon, and I breathed in the primal masculinity of him, barely resisting the urge to kiss his back just to see how it would feel.

"You okay up there, princess?"

Why did he have to go and ruin things by opening his mouth? Why couldn't he just be pretty and smell delicious?

"I am more than a piece of meat."

It appeared I had said that out loud.

"You did indeed."

And that. Apparently, I was narrating. Worse than that, I couldn't seem to stop. Which was humiliating, given that I currently had my face buried in his back, trying to decide if he smelled like actual sin or some forgivable derivative.

"I'm going to kill Shaw," Lachlan muttered again.

Considering I was spilling every filthy, carnal thought I had about him—which was clearly the ambrosia talking and *not* me—I was beginning to consider helping him.

He didn't put me down until we reached his wing, where Lachlan deposited me directly onto the floor. Probably because I started beating his back again and demanding it as soon as we were through the door. My ass hit the wood with a loud *thump* that temporarily knocked the wind out of me, and I glared up at him.

"You wanted to be put down." The gleam in his eyes belied the innocence he feigned.

"Since when have you done *anything* I wanted?" I swayed to my feet and stumbled to the bar cart, grabbing a bottle of tequila. I twisted the cap off before he stole it from me.

"I don't think that's a good idea."

"Why?" I demanded.

"Because you just spent the last five minutes ranting at me that you hated me while waxing poetic about the way I smell. I think you've had enough to drink for tonight and, for that matter, enough of my sexy magic, too. Which is *what* again?"

Thankfully, there was no level of inebriation that could get me to confess what I meant by that. Mostly because despite my current condition—or perhaps because of it—sexy magic was quickly being debunked.

I shook a finger in his face instead. "This is your fault. You left me down there. What was I supposed to do?"

"Hang out with my kid brother and stay out of trouble," he growled. "And you didn't manage either."

The thrill of victory shot through me. I had him. "Last week, you were the one telling me I should get into trouble."

"No, I said you *needed* some trouble."

I waved a hand in the air. "Tomato. Potato."

"I don't think that's how that goes."

God, he was beautiful when he smiled. Was it possible to have an oral fixation with someone else's mouth? Because those lips...

I really hoped I had managed to keep those thoughts inside my head. "What I'm saying is that I did not actually get into trouble. I had too much to drink. There's a difference. And secondly, you are a hypocrite."

His brow shot up. "*I'm* a hypocrite?"

I blinked at him, knowing I was walking into a trap but powerless to stop myself from ambling on like a deer into a clearing. I was leaving myself wide open for attack. "You say I need some trouble, tell me to let loose if I want, but you lecture me when I do. You act all hurt that I don't like you when you clearly hate me."

His mouth tightened. "And what about you, *princess*? You came to me, begging me to help you, and when I did, you accused me of tricking you, kidnapping you, and lying to you. None of which I did."

"Debatable."

Except it wasn't debatable, and somewhere deep down I knew it. Maybe it was the fairy wine muddling my brain, forcing me to see what I refused to acknowledge the rest of the time. Lachlan *had* helped me. He had offered me a bargain when, according to everyone who knew him, that was something he never did. He had fixed my air conditioning, which was a relief because it was the hottest autumn on record. He had shown up when my car was on fire, even if he hadn't helped me put it out. He'd even covered for my ass at work, although he was technically the reason I'd been suspended in the first place. And I didn't know why he had done any of it.

"Why did you offer me that bargain?"

He stilled, his face a stony mask. "You have to work that out yourself."

I scoffed. "Funny. I didn't peg you as a coward."

The dark aura around him shimmered, his tattoos moving in such a blur that I couldn't make out a single one. "Coward?" He stepped closer. "Well, then. Since you asked me so nicely," he seethed, "I will give you one more clue."

His hand shot out to grip my chin. It wasn't rough. It didn't hurt. No, his touch was featherlight. Despite everything I knew about Lachlan, this revealed something more to me. He knew his strength. He controlled it, just like he controlled everything else about himself—except for those telling tattoos. He knew he didn't need to use force to get my attention. Not when he looked at me the way he was looking at me now.

"I am not a man who shows his entire hand, nor am I one who acts without purpose," he said. "So trust me, princess, when I tell you that I have my reasons and that I know *exactly* what you have to offer me."

His gaze dropped, sliding along my lips, and suddenly, I didn't care if every soul downstairs had been eye-fucking me like he claimed. Not when he was looking at me like I might very well be the center of his fucking universe. Not when I *wanted* to be.

I didn't dare move. I didn't dare try to pull free of his grasp. Not when I could feel the bargain stretched taut between us. Not when he had given me the answer to every question I'd asked myself about him. "Please…"

His eyes flared, and for a breath, his grip on my jaw tightened. Did he see how much I wanted him to kiss me? Would he do it?

He drew in a deep breath, and his hand fell, releasing me. "Go to bed, Cate."

I opened my mouth to protest, but he simply repeated himself without raising his voice. "Go to bed. Please."

I told myself that it was the sudden show of manners that had me fleeing down the hall, but I knew I was running from something else.

I was running from what I'd seen etched in those green eyes.

CHAPTER TWENTY-ONE

The next morning, a jackhammer woke me.

In my brain.

I groaned, dragging a pillow over my head. It would have been a good idea to draw the curtains last night. Then again, last night, as far as I recalled, consisted only of bad ideas. Super bad ideas. Monumentally bad ideas.

Through the cloud of duck feathers protecting my throbbing head, I heard a faint knock on the door.

Lach.

No. *Lachlan*. Boundaries!

My stomach, already mostly liquid thanks to last night's said bad decisions, lurched as I recalled what had passed between us. At what I'd *said*. Apparently, ambrosia didn't erase the memories of the previous evening. In fact, it seemed to sharpen them.

I groaned. Now seemed like a pretty good time to pretend I couldn't hear him knocking...or possibly fake my own death. The knock became more insistent, and I decided that faking my death would be easier.

Before I could construct what I was certain needed to be an elaborate plan, the door opened. Apparently, I had forgotten not only to draw the curtains but to lock my door. Not that a lock meant much, considering everyone here could nip into my room at their pleasure, but it might have bought me enough time to come up with a faked-death plot. As it was, the best I had was to lie very still and hope no one checked to see if I was still breathing.

But a cheery voice called out to me, "Rise and shine, princess."

I screamed into the mattress, which thankfully muffled it. Lachlan's little nickname was spreading faster than a contagious disease, and now even Ciara was using it. I hadn't seen Ciara after Bain's painful speech, but judging from the fact that she did not sound like death warmed up in a microwave, she had not been guzzling ambrosia like water.

The mattress sank beside me, and despite my harrowing condition, I rolled over and peeked out from under my pillow. Ciara grinned back at me, hair done, face made up, looking the picture of fae delicacy, but her eyes were red-rimmed. "Still up for shopping?"

A week had taught me a lot about Ciara, and "shopping" in her language translated to "retail therapy." I pressed a finger to my pounding head to see if I could make it stop long enough to fulfill her request for moral support.

"I was thinking we could hit Canal Place." She started on which designers had released their winter lines.

I wanted to say yes, but the thought of being out in New Orleans made last night's bad decisions slosh in my stomach. There would be lights and noise and other dangerous stimuli that would remind me at every turn that I had gotten colossally, epically wasted last night.

I whimpered. "I can't. I'm dying."

Ciara's soft hand patted my arm soothingly. "Lach said you had too much to drink. He should have warned you."

"He did," I moaned. "I didn't listen."

"The first time I was allowed to go to a Midnight Feast, I was so nervous that I kept drinking ambrosia, and then I puked in bed with three sentries from the Astral Court."

I poked my head out from under the pillow. *"Three?"*

A happy smile slid across her face, and she repeated dreamily, *"Three."* Then she cringed. "Don't tell Bain that story."

"My lips are sealed," I promised and tried to push up in bed, which proved to be the cherry on top of the mistake sundae I had been making since midnight. "I don't think I can go shopping.

Unless we're shopping for caskets."

Ciara bolted up and reached for something on the nightstand so quickly that my head spun. "I almost forgot." She passed me a small cup of red liquid. "This will help."

I stared at the contents suspiciously. "I'm not sure that hair of the dog is the direction I want to take right now."

Nope. I needed Prohibition era–level sobriety. I rarely drank, and this was one of the many reasons why. I suspected that Lachlan had figured out the other reason and greenlit letting loose. He'd said he would take care of me, but his concern had ended the moment my ass hit the floor.

I took a cautious sip, deciding that even if it was poison, I'd probably rather drink it than continue to endure this headache, and swallowed the rest. The room contracted around me like it was giving me a warm hug, and then the pounding ceased in my brain.

"Better?" Ciara chirped.

I stared at the cup, then sniffed it. "Where has this been all my life?"

I felt fine. Better than fine, really.

"It always works," Ciara said. "It's an old witch's brew they make in London. Unfortunately, the Infernal Court refuses to share the secret. They brought some along with the ambrosia. If I ever tracked down whatever grimoire they stole this from, I would be very rich."

I opted not to point out that she was already very rich. Mostly because I couldn't blame her aspirations. This stuff was magic. I couldn't decide if I should send the Infernal Court a thank-you card for this or a fuck-you card for the ambrosia.

"Now that you're all better, can we get going?"

"I don't think Chanel is going to sell out." I threw off my covers and swung my feet over the bed, relieved that I didn't feel the slightest dizziness or slosh in my stomach. "Let me get dressed."

"Hurry up." Ciara smacked the mattress. "Lach made me wait hours before waking you up. It's already noon."

He had made her wait? It wasn't much of a gesture, but it softened me a little. "I'll only be a few minutes."

"I can always glamour you," she called after me.

"You can't use the toilet for me." I paused to pull a few things out of a drawer that was full of my own clothes instead of ball gowns. "What does the Infernal Court have planned next? A ritual sacrifice of virgins accompanied by a string quartet?"

Ciara gripped the foot board. "Today, they issue the first banns. I can't decide if I want someone to object to my engagement or not. I know I agreed to this, but…"

Shit. We were going to need shopping and beignets and probably a box of tissues. "I'll be right out."

Swinging the bathroom door shut behind me, I turned to drop my bag on the counter before using the facilities and found a small cup sitting by the sink. My heart stumbled as I picked it up. I already recognized the red liquid in the glass as Ciara's miracle cure.

Drink this.

The words were written in crisp, bold strokes, and although I'd never seen an example of it, I knew it was Lachlan's handwriting. As was his typical fashion, there were no pleasantries. No "please." No concern. And yet, he'd known how I would be feeling when I woke up. He had not just dropped me on the floor last night and forgotten about me. He had cared, even if only a very little.

I told myself it was nothing, but I drank the second glass for good measure. It settled warm and comforting in my belly, and I couldn't help but wonder why *nothing* felt like *something.*

• • •

Shopping with Ciara Gage should have been listed as an Olympic sport. She approached it with a competitiveness usually only exhibited by professional athletes.

Within two hours of our arrival at Canal Place, she had purchased the entire season's line from Alexander McQueen, a dizzying collection of dangerously high shoes, and not one but two calfskin bags from Chanel. By the time we reached the lingerie that she *needed*, my feet hurt and I was mildly afraid of her. I had never seen such focus dedicated to anything, and I had done a surgical rotation in college.

"You have to buy something." Ciara held up a scrap of lace with an improbably ridiculous price attached to it and smiled. "This would look fabulous on you."

"I can wear it to read in bed," I said dryly.

"No one caught your eye last night?" she pressed, her gaze darting over to me as she passed the scrap of lace to the salesperson Saks had assigned upon our arrival.

Had Lachlan mentioned something? Mercifully, he had not been in his quarters by the time I'd finished getting ready, which meant I had a few more hours to mentally prepare myself for the humiliation of facing him. If he was a gentleman, he would pretend like nothing had happened.

I wasn't holding my breath.

"I prefer that my boyfriends come from books," I said breezily, holding up something that claimed to be underwear. I had my doubts.

Ciara snatched it from me and threw it in her ever-growing pile.

"I really don't need that," I argued with her.

She snorted and rolled her eyes, tossing her glossy black hair over her shoulder. "Not if the only men you sleep with are fictional. But if you come back empty-handed, Lach will kill me."

"Lach?" I choked on his name. He better not know what we were shopping for.

"Did I forget to tell you? He said to buy whatever you want."

I grabbed the lacy nothing from her pile and tossed it back on the table. "I don't want that." Especially not if he was footing the bill. "And I really don't want to be in any more debt to him."

"You're not indebted to him."

"It feels like I am." I crossed my arms and leaned against a display of stockings. "And I don't like being indebted to anyone."

"Because you were an orphan," she said frankly.

I shrugged. So she had sorted out my personal trauma? A college dropout with one semester of Intro to Psychology could have done that. I wished it could have been an easier lesson for me to learn. As a child, it had taken me far too long to realize that most adults, even the ones who claimed to care, weaponized everything from food to shelter to attention. It was a life lesson that had been burned into me like a scar: always be helpful but never need anything or anyone. And never, ever accept a gift. There were always strings attached. My bargain with Lachlan had only reinforced that belief. But the worst lesson…

"Did Lachlan say anything else about last night?" I asked, suddenly very invested in learning about the sizing of Wolford hosiery.

"Only that he caught you in a dark corner with Oberon."

I dropped the package I was holding. "Nothing happened."

"You don't have to explain yourself to me," she reassured me. "Oberon is yummy. If he wasn't such a prude, I might have gone for him."

Oberon had been nearly as uncomfortable as I was, but I wasn't certain if that made him a prude. He had been kind. Funny. Very different than my first impression of him. But even if I was interested, which I wasn't, it wasn't like a relationship was possible. Not when Lachlan owned my nights. Not when he'd made it quite clear that regardless of his claims about wanting me to let loose, he wasn't going to make that easy. Not with the way his eyes followed me, checked me, claimed me.

After a moment, I looked up to realize Ciara was watching me, sadness glinting in her eyes. I forced a smile, and she responded in kind as she scooped the entire contents of the medium thong drawer from Agent Provocateur up and deposited them into her pile of purchases.

"Those better not be for me."

"It's a gift," she said softly. "From one friend to another. I'm buying. No expectations."

I swallowed and finally managed to nod.

"Good." She beamed at me and winked. "Because you're going

to need them. Fae love to rip off a pair of panties."

I did not demand further clarification from her, but that didn't stop me from thinking about it while we finished our shopping. It distracted me almost enough that I didn't hear the absolutely insane price tag attached to our little shopping trip. Almost. But Ciara didn't bat an eye as she passed the salesperson a thin black credit card and signed away more money than I would make in my entire lifetime. But try as I might, and I was *really* trying, I couldn't stop picturing a pair of strong fae hands gripping flimsy elastic lace and snapping it with ease, tattoos swirling over his knuckles as he did it.

I nodded as Ciara debated if we should get étouffée at Galatoire's or take the car to Gautreau's for the privacy. But I was so preoccupied with my fantasy that I walked into a wall.

The wall growled.

I looked up, my hands still planted on the wall, which was not a wall but a broad, hard chest that continued into a breathtaking face and a set of green eyes that threatened to undo me. I jumped away from Lachlan before he could growl again, before I could feel it vibrating under my skin, before it got into my blood and traveled to the deepest parts of me. His faded blue jeans were worn into a work of art that showcased his muscular thighs. I couldn't imagine what they did for his ass. I almost asked him to turn around to sate my curiosity. The rolled-up sleeves of his thin, white Henley revealed his inked forearms, the shirt clinging to every dip and ridge of his impressive upper body. But it was his face, so brutally beautiful, that stole my breath along with every thought in my head.

"What are you doing here?" Ciara demanded as sales personnel carried bags to a waiting limousine. The last twenty-four hours had been full of firsts. My first orgy. My first limousine ride. My first drunken confession that I wanted to lick every square inch of his body.

"You've been shopping for hours," he grumbled. "You spent last week shopping. How much shopping can you do?"

Ciara tossed her hair again, the effect not unlike flipping him off. "What do you care? Didn't you have a million boring meetings today?" She turned to me and rolled her eyes. "He doesn't know how to have fun."

"As a matter of fact, that's why I'm here." He looked me up and down and scowled. I guess I was still lacking in his eyes. Had I really suspected any differently, even if he flirted with me a little? Had I imagined the kiss on the back of my neck, the nose trailing along my jaw, the way his hands claimed my hips and wouldn't let go? "I thought Cate might like to experience more than your rampant consumerism for a few hours."

Ciara flicked her polished nails. "I've spent years honing my rampant consumerism, thank you very much."

He ignored his sister and returned his attention to me. "Where are your bags?"

I shouldered my very non-designer purse a little higher. "I didn't buy anything."

"Didn't Ciara tell you that I'd already arranged for your purchases?"

I had read similar scenarios in books, but the reality was much hotter in person. It took effort to not let that show, because the truth was I was just another item he'd bought. "I don't need anything."

"Actually, we did get a few things." Ciara inserted herself into the conversation with a mischievous grin. "Why don't you show him, Cate?"

I was beginning to question if she was really my friend as I shot her an imploring look.

Lachlan, by some miracle, was not picking up on what she was implying. He glanced to the continuing parade of purchases being Tetrised into the trunk. "Which bag is it?"

"No need," I said quickly.

"Are you trying to steal her from me?" Ciara asked.

"I'm trying to rescue her."

"We were going to go eat," I said. Spending the day pretending like I hadn't basically dry humped him on the dance floor was not what I had in mind.

But Ciara reached over and squeezed my arm. "But Lach is here to save you. Maybe you can model those new—"

"No," I cut her off, my face flaming.

I did not miss the subtle wiggle of her eyebrows behind his back. Apparently, his sister was rooting for me to throw all caution to the wind, hook up with a tattooed bad boy, and hope that some iota of my dignity and heart remained intact—aka *Team Lach*.

Before I could think of another excuse to get out of going with him, Ciara was sliding into the back of the limousine and waving goodbye. She paused with her hand on the door and called out, "We're going to Alouette tonight. Are you two in?"

He frowned. Answer enough.

"I'll come," I said. Even though I had no idea what I just signed up for.

"Great!" she said brightly. And then the limo was off.

He sighed. "Maybe drink a little more water tonight."

At least we were going to tiptoe around what happened. "I think I'm going to skip drinking altogether."

"Good idea." He took my hand and started toward the curb. "Let's go."

Not drinking was a good idea. I had plenty of good ones. The trouble was that every time he touched me, I could only think of bad ideas.

CHAPTER TWENTY-TWO

I didn't know which make of Mercedes it was. I just knew that it was sex on four wheels.

And I didn't even like cars.

Cars were simply a way to get from here to there without getting caught in the rain or melting in the humidity. The Mercedes, with its sleek curves and low-slung body, idling curbside at Canal Place made me rethink that. It wasn't like the comfortable sedan that had toted me through New Orleans in its spacious back seat what now felt like a lifetime ago. This was as predatory and graceful as the fae next to me. I couldn't help but notice two things as Lachlan guided me toward it. One, the car was the same color as his hair—ink black with a hint of midnight blue when the light hit it just right. The other was that he was still holding my hand.

It was a completely normal thing for two people to do when one was leading the other someplace. Lots of friends, family, even strangers, held hands. It probably meant nothing. But that did not detract from how solid and warm his fingers felt clutching mine. Was this the ritual fuckery he'd warned me would happen before I moved into the Avalon? Because it was really screwing with my head.

I wasn't sure when I'd transplanted a bag of hormones where my brain was supposed to be, but clearly I was under the influence of factors outside my control. Yes, I'd found Lachlan attractive from the moment I first saw him. The trouble had been when he'd opened his mouth—and the fact that ever since that moment he said one thing and did another. Hadn't I learned the hard way about romanticizing dangerous men? He was the very definition of dangerous. I'd witnessed it. I knew that behind his polished hotel and limitless platinum card was a body count centuries in the making. I should not find any of it hot. The fact that I did meant I was either suffering from Stockholm syndrome or I was beginning to like him. Or there was a third option: Ciara's comment about fae ripping off panties had chased off any sense I had. I had never had a pair of panties ripped off me, though I'd read about it. I'd just never met a guy who seemed like the panty-ripping type.

Lachlan released me to open the car door, stepping smoothly to one side and offering his hand again. The car, his smirk, and those sinful jeans he was wearing told me he was definitely the panty-ripping type. A car horn blasted across the street, and his eyes strayed to the sound, giving me the chance to gulp down some air as I slipped into the passenger seat. His hand tightened around mine, his other bracing against the car as he leaned in close enough that I caught a whiff of wood and cinnamon. I couldn't bring myself to look at him. It was hard enough to resist his scent.

"Didn't you get the drink I left you?" he asked.

I kept my eyes pinned to the dash like the air vent was the most fascinating thing I'd ever seen. "I did. Thank you."

"You seem a little off." His thumb stroked the back of my hand, and I thought I might spontaneously climax.

There were eight slots on the air vent, and they were pointed toward the window. "I'm fine. Just a little tired, I guess."

He bent down, finally releasing my hand only to place his on my forehead.

I mustered a voice approximately as dry as a bag of sand. "Am I dying?"

"Maybe you should go back to bed."

"No!" My eyes shot to him. "I'm fine, really." The only thing worse than being trapped in a car with Lachlan for the rest of the day was thinking of him in the same breath as a bed.

He chewed on his lip for a moment, which was completely

and *unnecessarily* erotic, before he relented. I couldn't stop myself from staring as he circled the front of the car. Last night he'd been annoyed with me, and now he was treating me like glass. I wasn't sure which one was better. He slid into the driver's seat, and his elbow casually brushed my arm, alerting my entire body that he was within reach. I tucked my hands under my thighs, keeping my arms from the console's danger zone. Was the car a more dangerous option than letting him take me back to the Avalon?

As soon as he pulled away from the curb and into traffic, I discovered it was.

One thing was immediately clear to me: Lachlan had absolutely no fear of death. This was evident in the way that he drove, which could best be described as a bat out of hell attacking Vin Diesel. I had never wanted to google a vehicle's crash-test rating more, but I didn't dare pry my fingers from the seatbelt I was now clutching for added security. I yelped as he zipped around a bus and into a lane of oncoming traffic, narrowly avoiding a pedestrian and earning an impressive array of vulgar gestures from every human in a one-block radius.

"Do you even have a driver's license?" I demanded, clenching my eyes shut, even though one kept darting open to see if we were dead yet.

He only laughed, which I took to mean *no*.

"I'm a little old for a driver's license."

"I don't think that's how it works." I whimpered as one of his wheels bumped the curb and sent half a dozen tourists scrambling in pure terror. Maybe I should throw myself from the car now before we hit a pole and physics did its thing. I choked down another little yelp of fear. "And how old is that, exactly?"

He grinned at me. "If you're trying to ask what I want for my birthday, princess—"

"Watch the road!"

Maybe now was not the time to have this conversation.

Lachlan drifted back into our lane with a dutiful sigh. "In human years, I'm about 244 years old, give or take a decade." He shook his head and added, "And fae can drive blindfolded. No one—and certainly not you—is in danger, princess."

I barely processed the streetlamp we nearly hit as his age sank in. Whatever part of me had hoped finding out he was centuries older than me might be a turnoff did not materialize. Maybe it would when I was not in imminent peril. Somehow, I doubted it. My brain seemed to be out of office where he was concerned.

"Two *hundred* and forty-four?" I swallowed hard.

"And now you're freaked out," he said, tapping the steering wheel.

"What? No." Now I was reassuring him? Which was something he should be doing, given that he had taken my life in his hands the moment he got behind the steering wheel. "But on that topic, now might be a good time to remind you that one of us is immortal and one of us will be killed if you hit that taxi."

He jerked the wheel and avoided it. "Do you want to drive?"

"Can I?" I'd never driven a stick before. I didn't like the idea of this being the first time, but I liked the idea of dying even less. I sincerely doubted fae magic would protect us from a head-on collision.

He didn't pull over.

I twisted in my seat. "Are you worried I'll wreck your fancy car?"

"So, you think my car is fancy?"

I tapped the dash. "I think your car would be better on the right side of the road."

He rolled his eyes and pulled back into our lane.

"What happened to *if I die I'll get out of this bargain*?" He imitated a high-pitched voice.

"Is that supposed to be me?" I snapped, shifting my attention from the road to glower at him. "I'm sorry that I don't want to die splattered like modern art on the side of a bar."

He groaned and slowed the car, but he didn't stop. Instead, he began driving at a normal, non-life-endangering speed, all four wheels within the confines of the painted lines.

I punched him on the shoulder. "Dick! You scared the shit out of me."

My heart flipped a little when he smirked, the car not so much as drifting even with his eyes on me. "Last night, you seemed like you were looking for trouble."

And there it was. The elephant in the room. Or, rather, the car. The car, which left me nowhere to run, nowhere to hide. I suddenly wished I was still being distracted by my imminent death.

"I had a lot to drink." It was a flimsy excuse, but it was all I had.

"I think there was more ambrosia than blood in your veins," he said flatly, his focus back on the road.

"What was I supposed to do?"

"Hang out with Shaw and stay out of trouble."

I threw my hands in the air. "Stay out of trouble. Get in trouble. Make up your mind. Besides, your brother wanted to get in trouble. He's cute and all, but somehow, I doubt you'd be okay with me entertaining *him*."

He scowled and jerked the wheel, sending us down a back alley.

Oh, he didn't like that.

The buildings on either side of us loomed overhead, cutting off the sun. I squinted around nervously. "I don't think we're supposed to be here."

"This is my city. I can go wherever I want." Lachlan stopped the car and reached behind his back. A second later, he tossed a gun in the cupholder. "I don't mind if you get in trouble, princess, but I would strongly prefer you save it for when I'm around. Not my brother."

"Why? So you can mock me? Tease me?" *Drive me absolutely out of my mind?*

The shadows clouding his eyes had nothing to do with the darkness of the alley. He leaned closer, the scent of him making me ache, his breath warm and laced with sweet cinnamon. "No," he rumbled. "So I can protect you."

I shuddered as heat danced across my skin. He'd said it last night, but the gun reinforced just how much he'd meant it. I forced myself to swallow, to wet the tongue that had dried up in my mouth, to not look away from the emerald intensity of his gaze. "I don't need you to protect me."

Because letting him do that was more than letting him buy me gifts or agreeing to a bargain. It was more than indebting myself to him. It was *depending* on him.

For a moment, his eyes glazed and the human glamour he'd worn to walk the streets of New Orleans slipped to reveal the feral fae staring back at me. "Sooner or later, you're going to realize the only person your stubbornness is hurting is yourself."

"Better me than someone else." That was what he didn't understand. It was better this way. It was easier to protect myself and the few people I'd chosen to care about if I kept myself apart. I'd been doing it for as long as I could remember. The key was to keep the list nice and short. Ciara had already wormed her way onto it, but something told me that if I let him on, too, Lach wouldn't occupy a single spot. He would fill up the whole thing.

"You can spend your entire life shutting everyone out, Cate, but don't be surprised when you die alone," he said bitterly.

"That might be profound if you weren't immortal."

A tattoo flared along his temple, flickering in and out of sight until his human glamour settled again. Lachlan pulled back onto the road, carefully signaling and proving once again that I was not in true danger. But as he turned toward a bridge that crossed the Mississippi, he muttered so low that I almost thought I imagined it. "Even immortals bleed."

CHAPTER TWENTY-THREE

We drove until the vibrant bustle of New Orleans faded like a memory, eventually leaving the highway for back roads.

I'd never been this far from the city, and I drank in the wild beauty of Louisiana, more untamed as we traveled deeper into the wilderness. Stately cypress trees, their red-brown bark swathed in Spanish moss, heralded our arrival to the bayou.

The farther outside New Orleans we went, the more I was reminded that I'd left Channing sitting in jail. I'd been able to shake off my nagging guilt before, but there was something about leaving him behind now that made that impossible.

"I need to check on my brother," I blurted out. It was easy to tell myself he was safer in a jail cell when we were in the same city. "I got him arrested, and I shouldn't be going..."

I didn't actually know where we were going. Because, at some point, I'd begun to trust Lach. But now I was being driven away from the only home I'd ever known, from the only *family* I'd ever known. Something cold gripped my guts at the thought.

"It's already handled, Cate," Lachlan said, not taking his eyes from the narrow two-lane road.

My eyebrows shot up. "What do you mean?"

He shrugged without taking his hands from the steering wheel. "The charges have been dropped and he's been set up with a job in the Quarter."

"What kind of—"

His gaze swung to mine, something that looked vaguely like hurt in his eyes. "Bussing tables at a restaurant."

"You...?" I let the question hang between us.

He nodded, confirming he was responsible for this turn of events. "Channing doesn't know it was me. Just that he's not being charged." He cleared his throat. "It's safe work. No weapons necessary, and I have someone keeping an eye on him."

"Oh," I said as he turned his attention back to the road. I should thank him, I knew, but I was too focused on the fact that he'd been thinking of my brother when I hadn't been. Guilt warmed my cheeks, and I silently stared at the landscape as we sped by. I'd done what I thought was best for Channing in a moment of fear and anger. But Lachlan had actually *helped* him. I didn't know what to do with the emotions tightening my chest, so I decided to do what I normally did and ignore them.

But I couldn't help pulling out my phone. I hadn't missed any calls or texts. I even checked my email. I didn't have the heart to ask how long Channing had been out of jail. Not when it was clear my brother was avoiding me.

Eventually, Lachlan pulled the car to a stop, the purr of the engine replaced by the deafening silence between us.

Lachlan climbed out of the car without a word, my pulse ticking higher as he circled to the rear.

I stared out the window at the marshy wetland, searching for a sign as to what we were doing here. He slammed the trunk, and several egrets launched into the air, their agitated croaks shattering the majestic silence. My fingers fumbled for my seat belt as my door opened. He held out a pair of tall, rubber boots. I took them as a hot uneasiness knotted my throat.

"What are these for?" I eyed the black duffel slung over his shoulder.

He crouched and pried off my tennis shoes before reaching for the boots. It took effort to keep my breathing steady as he slipped one on. "It's muddy out there." A strand of dark hair fell over his brow. "And there are snakes."

"I could have lived without knowing that," I muttered as he slid on the other boot.

Lachlan chuckled as he popped back onto his feet. Grabbing my hand, he pulled me out of the seat, hitching his head toward a footpath worn into the dirt nearby. "Come on. I only have you for a few hours."

"You have me every night." The words came out with less bite than intended—almost like I was simply reminding him.

He didn't respond, nor did he offer more information as we started down the trail. He stayed ahead of me, lifting sweeping tendrils of moss from low-hanging branches and leading the way down the sun-dappled path. The briny tang of saltwater mingled with the earthy musk of the wetlands as we approached the slow-moving brackish waters of the bayou. Tupelos outlined the waterway, their swollen bases tapering into towering trunks. He paused, his attention turned away from the marsh, and I turned to find a cabin built against the base of an ancient cypress. Rustic and utilitarian, it blended into the landscape, save for a single plume of smoke curling from a steel chimney pipe.

"Is that—" I cut off as the door banged open, creaking on its hinges, and a male fae stepped onto the cabin's small porch. His hair hung over his shoulders, a few braided plaits nestled against its black waves. He wore a leather vest unbuttoned over his muscled, tattooed chest and a pair of black jeans that faded to gray over his thighs. His pointed ears were each pierced nearly a dozen times. I found myself stepping closer to Lachlan.

"Goemon," Lachlan called, shouldering his bag a little higher. "This is Cate. I brought her out to do some shooting. Thought I'd better warn you."

"Do some *what*?" I hissed.

Goemon crossed his massive forearms over his chest. "Appreciate the heads-up. Stick to the north territory. The egrets are farther south."

I blinked, surprised by not only his lack of deference to the prince but also his concern over...birds?

Lachlan tipped his head in acknowledgment. "Things have been quiet here?"

"Relatively." Goemon searched the sky, frowning at whatever he saw in the clouds. "Even with your city full of foreigners."

Did he mean the visiting courts?

"Don't worry. I'll keep them in line."

Goemon's gaze skimmed to him, a cruel sneer tugging back his lips. "I'm happy to step in when needed."

A chill shot down my spine, but Lachlan shrugged. "I'll let you know." He took my hand with one final nod in the strange fae's direction.

Lachlan strode back toward the forested lowlands, towing me along.

"Who was that?" I asked when the cabin was a speck in the distance. "He acted like he owns the bayou."

He snorted, quickening his stride. "Goemon doesn't own the bayou. He'd probably be offended at the suggestion. He guards it."

"Does he work for you?" There was something off about their interaction.

His brows shot up with another low laugh. The sound slid under my skin and settled into my bones. "Goemon belongs to no court. He's a member of the Wild Hunt."

The term tripped a memory I couldn't quite place. "The Wild Hunt?"

"Mercenaries who live outside the courts," he explained, his boots squelching in the muddy marshland. "They uphold our most ancient laws, hunting down those marked for breaking them."

I thought of the night I met Lachlan. "I thought you meted out your own justice."

"Most of the time." He glanced at me. The shadows hanging in his eyes told me he was remembering the same day. "But there are plenty of fae who ignore the authority of any court. Most live outside them, like Goemon, and avoid entering our cities. There are others who flee to avoid justice for their crimes, but they're delaying the inevitable. Either we will brand them or magic will. Out here, the

Wild Hunt is the law amongst the lawless. They don't care about status or title or influence. They will collect any soul that's been marked without mercy or consideration."

His words chilled me. "By collect, you mean murder them?"

"Execute," he corrected me. "Those marked for the Hunt are dead souls walking. The Hunt cannot be escaped. They are tireless in their pursuit of justice."

"And if someone is innocent?"

"They aren't."

I paused, forcing him to stop. "How can you be sure?"

"Even if I brand a soul, magic must seal the mark."

"Like a bargain?" I asked.

He nodded. "Magic has to deem the accusation to be true. It won't condemn an innocent. It's another way to balance our power."

"But magic can mark someone on its own?" I shook my head. "Why would anyone ever break the law?"

"You'd be surprised how many think they won't get caught. Maybe it's a fault of our nature. But no, magic does not actually brand a soul entirely on its own. That duty lies with me or Roark, as well as the other heirs and their penumbras. There is only one instance in which magic will be called to mete out justice independently." He held up his hand, flashing me the signet he wore. "It's called upon when I cannot meet my responsibility."

The coldness inside me spread until ice ran through my veins. "You mean, if you're…"

"Dead," he said in a clipped tone. "The assassination of an heir or their penumbra is considered a violation of the natural order."

The ice inside me splintered. "If I had shot you that night…"

"Try not to think about it," he advised, "but yes, you would have been marked."

For a moment, I only stared. Then, I smacked him in the shoulder. "You might have warned me!"

Delighted laughter spilled from his lips. "What would have been the fun in that?" He edged dangerously close. "I took the bullets out, princess, but I left your choice up to you."

Another part of the test, I realized.

"And even if it had been loaded, you wouldn't have killed me."

My eyes narrowed to slits until all I could see was his perfect, annoying face. "Take off your ring and let's test that theory."

Lachlan leaned in, leaving nothing but a breath between us. "Why do you think we're out here?"

I gulped, my eyes straying to the bag over his shoulder. He dropped it on the ground, where it landed with a *thump* that echoed in my chest. My heart pounded as he bent and unzipped it. When he straightened, he was holding a heavy black pistol.

"You need to learn how to use this." His tone suggested this was not a conversation so much as an order.

I inched back a step, shaking my head. "I'm not…"

Words failed me as I stared at the gun.

"You are." His gaze pinned me. "You have."

I opened my mouth to deny it but found I couldn't.

His wicked smile taunted me. "You pulled the trigger." His tongue swept over his lower lip like he enjoyed the way the truth of that statement tasted. "And since I prefer to know that you're safe, even in my absence, you need to be willing to do it again."

"I'm not sure…" I could barely think over the blood roaring inside me.

"It's different when you have no choice." Something grim streaked his tone. I caught a fleeting glimpse of sadness in his eyes, but then he blinked and it was gone.

He pressed the gun into my hand.

It was the same one I'd pulled from his waistband the night of the Equinox, but it felt different without adrenaline coursing through my veins. Heavier.

"It's a 9-millimeter. This is the safety." He pressed a small button down on the side of the gun, each word clipped and efficient. "It needs to be off before you can shoot someone."

I rolled my eyes, hoping he didn't notice my trembling hand. "I know that."

"You didn't the night you tried to kill me." His look dared me to challenge him. "Feel its weight. It's loaded."

That's why it felt heavier. He hadn't just relied on me not knowing about the safety that night. I recalled him reloading the bullets in front of me. He'd told me he would teach me how to use it—after I'd earned the right to a weapon. I had no idea what I'd done to warrant his sudden decision that now was the time for me to learn.

Lachlan touched the broad end of the muzzle. "This is a built-in silencer."

I lifted a brow.

"It means that it's not going to blow your eardrums," he explained. He moved behind me, close enough that his body brushed against mine. His arms circled around me, and he took both of my hands, coaxing the gun into position until it was firmly in my grasp and my index finger was curled over the trigger. He drew my arms up and lowered his head over my shoulder. It was harder to concentrate with his warm breath ghosting over my neck, with his hard chest bracing my back, with my body riveted to everywhere it touched his. "Keep both hands on it when you fire. It's got a hell of a recoil." His finger settled over mine, but he didn't force the trigger. "Lock your elbows."

I tried to steady my breathing as I stared straight ahead. We weren't pointing at anything in particular, just a vast expanse of swampland. No wonder he had dragged me all the way out here. I wasn't in danger of hitting anything.

I wondered what the other courts would think of the Nether Prince teaching me how to kill their kind. If that was the real reason we'd driven all the way to the bayou—so that no one could see what we were up to.

"Whenever you're ready," he whispered, his mouth so close that the words felt like a kiss. "Just pull the trigger."

My chest heaved as I stared ahead, everything fading away except the heat of his body, the steadiness of him bolstering me, and the certainty that seemed to seep into me where we touched. I closed my eyes and pulled the trigger. The shot reverberated through my fingers into my muscles, the gun's butt biting into my palm as it jolted me against him. He remained solid, unaffected, an anchor as my entire world shifted and rewrote itself. I held back a gasp as adrenaline soaked my senses.

His lips nipped my earlobe, and a bolt of pleasure barreled down the back of my neck. His body curved firmly around me, and his finger twitched. "Again."

The second shot pushed me even deeper into his arms, and I shivered.

"You like it, don't you?" he breathed. The question was as scorching as where his flesh met mine.

I swallowed. "No."

"You feel powerful." His lips spelled the last word on my skin.

My eyes fluttered closed, caught in whatever spell he was weaving. I softened into his strong embrace, our arms still stretched before us, my palm throbbing from the gun's recoil. This wasn't me, but I couldn't deny that he was right. I did feel powerful. Part of me hated that, but the rest…

He'd read my juvenile record. He'd guessed what was missing from those reports, what I'd been through, how far I might go to protect myself. He'd put a gun in my hand before. He'd been testing me since the first day we met—seeing how far he could push me, honing me into something different, something dangerous.

Something lethal.

A weapon.

Realization dawned on me. He hadn't asked me to move into the Avalon to keep his sister company. He needed me there. Because the other courts were in attendance, the other heirs. This was all about the bargain. "You don't want an alliance," I gasped.

He went rigid. His left hand curled around my wrist, tattoos flickering, like I might turn that gun on him. But I yanked away, and he didn't stop me as I ducked out from under his arms, gun still clutched in my right hand. "You want me to kill one of them."

A mask descended over his face, and the ink on his body settled.

How had I not seen it before? "The test. You wanted to see if I could pull the trigger—if you could use me—because you can't do it yourself. Not without being marked by the Wild Hunt. That's what you want out of the bargain."

For a moment, we stared at each other in stony silence. Blood hammered in my head until it was spinning. The gun felt slippery in my palm. Bile rose in my throat as I looked at it. I dropped it, backing away a step but not daring to let it out of my sight. "I'll never do it," I swore and finally lifted my face to his. "Release me. The bargain is broken."

A muscle worked in his jaw as if he was fighting to hold on to that magic binding us. He looked toward the bayou, but I caught a glimpse of something unrecognizable moving behind his eyes. "I know plenty of killers, princess. I don't need you to do my dirty work."

I felt a twinge at the back of my neck, as though the magic was taking his side and burrowing deeper to prove I was wrong.

"You were ready to shoot me that night." The words were strained as he continued to peer into the distance. "The test was to see who *you* were."

"And you think you know me?"

His head snapped toward me, nostrils flaring. He took a step in my direction. "I know who you are." I couldn't move as he prowled closer. "You chose nursing because you crave that adrenaline rush that was stolen from you. You told yourself it would keep you safe, but you never feel that way. But you are a survivor. There's only one problem." I stopped breathing as he bent and picked up the gun. "You'll only survive if you can protect yourself. Because you won't let anyone else take care of you. So you *will* learn how to take the shot. You *will* be prepared. You *will* know that you have that power—that no one can make you a victim." He engaged the safety and held the weapon out to me. "*You* can pull the trigger."

My gaze snagged on the weapon. "I don't want to."

His fingers tightened over the barrel. "I hope you never have to. I hope I'm always there whether you like it or not," he added when I started to protest. "But my family protects themselves. I will not lose anyone else."

His chosen words dragged my attention from the gun to him. I refused to let them grow roots as I scrounged for proof that he was lying—about his family, about me. It was another trick meant to lower my guard. He'd already proven that he knew me, knew secrets I refused to admit even to myself. "Ciara doesn't—"

"What do you think she carries in those ridiculous purses she buys constantly?" he cut me off. "She can handle herself like you'll be able to."

"I'm not comfortable carrying a gun," I admitted softly.

"Not yet, but you're a natural."

I ignored the forbidden pang of pride that swelled in my chest, focusing on what he didn't say. I wasn't comfortable today, but I would be. Because this wasn't a one-time lesson.

But what was the point? "When I break the bargain—"

"You won't. It's been weeks, and that was your best guess." He closed the remaining space between us. "Face it. You don't want to break our bargain any more than I want to."

The reality of what he was saying sank in as we stared at each other. That my life might have taken a different path if I hadn't stumbled upon his world. Maybe none of this was an accident. Maybe I'd simply taken a detour on my way to him.

Lachlan thrust the gun into my hand as if he already knew all of this. My fingers skimmed the metal before I shoved it away—and stomped off. Back in the direction of the car, back to the safety of what I knew, back to the life I knew.

And left him standing there.

CHAPTER TWENTY-FOUR

The ride to the Avalon was tense. I turned my attention out the window, watching the streets pass by in a blur of color and life. Lachlan stared at the road ahead, and I wondered if he saw any of it. If he saw the city he ran but barely knew. A king outside his kingdom, trying to hold on to control while the world changed, and it slipped through his fingers like grains of sand.

My hands remained in my lap, my index finger stretching as I tried to ease the vibration I still felt from the gun's recoil, but it was nothing compared to the bruising ache in my palm. I hated the reminder that the barrier between life and death was so thin. I hated how violence kept seeping into the cracks between my two worlds. I hated knowing what the decision to pull the trigger felt like.

And I especially hated that part of me wanted to feel it again.

Twilight had fallen when we reached the exposed parking lot attached to the Avalon, overhead stars winking between the thick storm clouds rolling in. He pulled past the gate to a private area where a dozen sleek cars like this one were parked. Range Rovers and Mercedes and Audis, each one of them black. A fleet of vehicles for a shadow court. A single yellow Porsche was the only spot of color in the lot.

He appeared at my door and opened it, refusing to look at me as I climbed out. He hadn't spoken a word to me on the drive home. He hadn't pressed the issue—hadn't tried to force that gun on me, either.

The night had cooled considerably, but the balmy air was heavy with a humidity that prophesied rain. I leaned against the Mercedes and drank in the earthy scent.

He pushed the door closed behind me. "I suppose there's no point in asking you to be careful this evening."

Lach was like a busted faucet—hot and cold and constantly getting me unexpectedly wet. I crossed my arms over my chest. "That is actually a reasonable request." I hesitated for a moment. "Will you come with us?"

He finally looked at me, his gloomy mood slipping a little.

"Not because I need protection," I added quickly before he got the wrong idea. Because maybe he was right about the bargain—about the likelihood that I would break it. I wasn't ready to consider if he was right about whether or not I was trying. "Just so you don't waste your whole night smoking cigars and measuring your dick."

He cleared his throat, glancing over at the hotel as though he had not for one moment considered coming before now. "Just take the 9-millimeter with you."

"God, it's not like there are random villains lurking in every shadow just waiting to snatch me up. Ciara will be there. And Shaw." And apparently, they were both well prepared to handle any issues.

"And you will still be safer if you take the gun."

I rolled my eyes, shaking my head. "I already explained that I'm not comfortable with it." When his scowl deepened, I added, "Yet."

"I told you that you were a natural." He crossed his arms, his shirt pulling against his powerful muscles.

"Being good at it and being okay with that are two different things." I rubbed my bruised palm with my other hand. "I'm a nurse. I'm supposed to save people. Not hurt them."

"Protecting yourself *is* saving someone." His teeth clenched as his glamour lifted entirely. "You have to compromise on something, princess. So which is it—protect yourself or *be* protected?"

A shiver snaked up my spine, like my entire body felt my life being pulled into two directions. It would always be that way with him, I realized, and I had to decide if that was something I could live with if I didn't break this bargain. Or if that division was as inescapable as the deal I'd made in the first place.

"Like I said, plenty of people will be with me. Nothing's going to happen."

His gaze coasted over my necklace, down my body, and landed on my hand, but he didn't speak. Probably because he knew I was right. Eventually, he said, "That attitude is exactly why I'm worried. You have no idea what some of my kind are capable of, and there are dozens of fae from other courts in this city right now. You're not really safe unless—"

"Oh. Here we go!"

"I'm there," he finished.

I rolled my eyes. "Then come. I already invited you."

"I can't," he said through gritted teeth.

"Why? Because people might get the wrong idea?" I fought to keep my voice steady. "I know I'm not your type, but who cares what they think?"

A muscle worked in his jaw. "That's not what this is about. If I'm not around—"

"What? You want me to lock myself inside and cower in fear? Or be prepared to shoot them?" I shook my fists in the air just as the first raindrops splattered my face. I swiped at the moisture. "There's a whole lot of middle ground there!"

"I want you to have fun!" He slammed his fist onto the roof of what I assumed was a very expensive car and dented it. He didn't seem to notice. "I want to know that if I'm not around you aren't being dragged into a dark corner because you take every warning and piece of advice I give you as an invitation to do the exact opposite just to piss me off," he growled.

Because last night he had found me in a dark corner, completely blitzed on ambrosia.

"This is still about Oberon," I realized. Did the divide between the light and shadow courts run so deeply that he couldn't trust any of them?

"What if it is?" He dragged a hand through his hair. "I made it clear that you were not on the table, and he waited until my back was turned."

My eyes widened, a slow smile tipping up one corner of my mouth. "You're jealous," I said. Not annoyed that I'd gotten a little too drunk on ambrosia. Not worried that I'd been in some kind of danger. He was *jealous*. Rain beat down harder, but I wasn't leaving this spot until he admitted it. I would fucking drown here before that happened. "You're mad that I was in a dark corner with Oberon."

He glared at me. "That's not what this is about. You may dance with whomever you wish, fuck whomever you wish, laugh, flirt, as long as you know what you're doing, and last night, you were out of your mind."

He did not get to rewrite this. Not without admitting why he was being a hypocrite. "You told me to let loose."

"I did!" he exploded. "Because I never thought you…"

"What? Finish that sentence, Gage."

He took a step closer, backing me toward the car. "Tell me, princess, how would you have felt if you'd woken up in my bed this morning? Because you were absolutely begging me for it."

I flushed, knowing it was true, and then zeroed in on a new target.

"I guess it's good that I'm not your type." I threw his words back at him. I'd lost track of how many times I had done so. It was childish to cling to it, but for some reason I couldn't let go of what he'd said that first night we met. Even if maybe…he'd known I was terrified that he'd planned to do more than take my soul. Even if he'd said it because there was no other way to ease my fear. Or maybe he was just as riddled with unwanted hormones and feelings as I was. But I was tired of holding my breath to see if he would take it back or if he meant it. "Although, I suppose you've made it clear that you're willing to look past that minor inconvenience."

His eyes went wild, his nostrils flaring. "You don't know when to stop, do you?"

His tone left little room for doubt about what he thought.

The problem was…he was probably right. I lifted my chin. "I

repeat, I guess it's a good thing that I'm not—"

"So help me Gods, if you say you're not my type again," he snarled. I was pressed against the glass now, so close that we were sharing the same breath, so close that my breasts grazed his chest, so close that I could not tell if that was his heart racing or mine. I braced one hand against the rain-soaked car, the other flattening across his lower abdomen, torn between pushing him away and running my fingers over the flat plane beneath them. He didn't break eye contact, his forehead nearly resting on my own as he placed a hand over the one on his stomach and gently encouraged it lower. He didn't force it, and he didn't have to—not when I so badly wanted to touch him. Not when I'd been thinking about it since last night into today, long after the ambrosia was out of my system. Because the tension that stretched between us wasn't the bargain. It wasn't the muddled effects of fairy wine. It was edged and honed as if every moment we spent together had been sharpening into something too dangerous for either of us to ignore. I moved my hand lower, my palm drifting over the undeniably, heart-stoppingly hard length of him.

He gritted his teeth. "Does that feel like you're not my type?"

My entire body heated as my fingers stroked over him, realizing Lachlan could back up every smirking, arrogant, egotistical thing he had ever said to me. I wondered how many cameras the hotel had on the parking lot, on the row of expensive cars, on the one I was pressed against at the moment. How many guards were monitoring us right now. I hoped they enjoyed the show. Because I didn't think I could make it farther than the hood of the Mercedes before I needed him inside me. His lip curled as if he knew exactly what I was thinking.

"I already dented it. Might as well see what other damage we can do."

Apart from showing up at the Avalon, this was quite possibly the stupidest, most reckless thing I'd ever considered doing in my life—and I was already considering doing it twice. He leaned in so close that his dark lashes fluttered across my skin. His mouth slanted, and…the black security door to the hotel banged open.

"Everything okay out here? Need any help?" Roark called over, amusement coloring his voice.

"No." It wasn't so much a word as it was a command—or, rather, a growl.

"I thought you might be having trouble getting back to court, since you're just out here in the rain," Roark continued a bit too gleefully to believe his intentions.

Lachlan never looked away from me, his gaze holding mine. "We. Are. Not."

I was going to drown in those eyes. But whether it was Roark's presence or some latent sense of self-preservation, I managed to tear myself free from them. Lachlan didn't try to stop me as I ducked beneath the cage of his arms. Neither of us was ready to give in. Neither of us wanted to be wrong when our lives were bound together. Not when I still didn't know why he'd made that bargain. Not while my unease grew that I wouldn't like the answer if I figured it out.

But as I raced for the door, trying and failing to dodge more rain despite already being soaked, I knew we were an inevitability—as undeniable as the crash of thunder after lightning shatters the sky.

CHAPTER TWENTY-FIVE

We'd been dancing for hours, and I still hadn't had enough. That might have been because Ciara had talked me into taking one teeny shot of ambrosia when I wouldn't stop pacing in her bedroom. I'd blamed it on my failed attempt to reach Channing. I had tried to call him. I wasn't sure he would call back. But while that bothered me, it wasn't why I was anxious. I hadn't told Ciara what else had happened—or, rather, what hadn't happened—with Lachlan this afternoon. I wouldn't until I decided if Roark had ruined my day or saved me from making a huge mistake. So, I'd taken one shot to get out of my own head, and then another.

The song morphed into a deeper, hypnotic beat, and I swayed between Sirius and Shaw, my perpetual companions for the evening. Mostly because they were the only ones who could keep up with me. But before I could really get the hang of the new rhythm—not that I was a good dancer, just an enthusiastic one—a petite hand closed around my wrist and wrenched me with inhuman strength away from the dance floor.

"I need to sit down," Ciara called over the chaos of Alouette. "Let's go upstairs."

Next to her, Titania continued to ignore me. The Hallow Court princess had sneered when I tried to introduce myself before we'd left the Avalon. She hadn't spoken a word to me during the five-minute car ride to the club or after we'd been shown straight past the velvet rope. Apparently, looks were all she shared with her twin.

I almost wished Oberon was here instead.

"We'll never get through," I shouted as a stranger accidentally hip-checked me. Ciara shoved them away and tugged me to follow.

Alouette was busy for a weekday, bodies packed into the converted warehouse in a writhing mass of sweat and skin and alcohol. We struggled to move through the crowd until our dancing partners got involved. The speed with which Alouette's patrons parted for the incoming fae males, even with their human glamours completely intact, was downright biblical. A few apologized and pressed themselves against the velvet draping the walls. Most simply scattered like the neon-pink light tubes pulsing to the beat overhead.

But they weren't clearing it fast enough for Ciara, especially when a guy wearing a blue suit jacket unbuttoned to reveal a smooth, bare chest danced toward us. He grinned as he slurped down his drink. "Hey, there."

Shaw started to push forward to take care of him, but before he could, his sister grabbed the man's jacket, lifted him off his feet, and deposited him behind us. He stumbled back in surprise, spilling his drink down his front. He cursed at her as he swiped at the liquid dribbling down his abs.

Shaw bared his teeth in response, the neon light making him look like the devil himself. The guy backed away, and we kept walking to the far side of the club.

I lifted my hair off my neck, trying to cool off, as we reached the stairwell. The guard stationed in front of it nodded hello to Ciara and moved to the side. I doubted there was a bouncer in New Orleans who didn't know her. Shaw bumped the guy's fist as we started up the steps. It was at least five degrees cooler on the upper floor and quiet enough to hear the hum of neon illuminating a brick corridor. Shaw and Ciara bickered as she opened a canary-yellow door. I tried to ignore them as I filed in, still fanning myself.

Muffled music seeped inside, the floor vibrating a little beneath us.

"I had it under control," Ciara snapped, collapsing onto a tufted settee.

Her brother crossed his arms, leaning against the closed door. He glanced at me. "Cate, will you please tell her that tiny human females cannot lift two-hundred-pound men without raising some suspicions?" But I shook my head. I was not getting in the middle of this. He sighed. "Lach will flip if someone got a picture of it."

"Who cares? Lach can cover it up. It's his city," Titania butted in. The statuesque brunette seemed to vacillate between being the life of the party and stirring up drama. Or, given what she'd just said, maybe she just spilled whatever bullshit popped into her head without thinking.

Shaw threw his hands up. "Because that guy was an NFL linebacker. It's a lot harder to get a—"

"Blah. Blah. Blah," Ciara cut him off as she slipped out of the pearl-studded Louboutins that she'd purchased earlier at Saks. "More importantly, my feet hurt. Rub them?" She shot Shaw a dazzling smile, but he grimaced.

I refrained from reminding her of my warning that six-inch stiletto heels were ambitious, even for a fae. Instead, I dutifully sat next to her and patted my lap. She grinned as she plopped her feet onto it.

Titania pretended to gag. "I can't believe you would do that."

"This?" I couldn't help laughing. "I'm a nurse. This is nothing."

"A nurse? You have a job?"

"Human, remember?" I held a hand to a round ear. Titania's gaze narrowed on it and lingered, like she might just be realizing this.

Ciara yawned, mumbling a complaint that I'd stopped. "I'm exhausted."

Titania glowered. "It's not even midnight. You can't be tapping out yet."

"I'm probably just tired because I had way too much sex last night." Ciara giggled.

Still safely across the room, Shaw groaned. "I did not need to hear that."

"What were you doing last night?" Ciara called back cheerily, not the least bit embarrassed. Meanwhile, Shaw's cheeks matched his hair. She swung her feet off my lap. "And don't worry, I'm not that tired. Where should we go next?"

"Home," Shaw offered.

Relieved of my duties, I decided to let them debate what happened next and beelined for the private bar. I fished a few bottles of water out of its reach-in and held one against my cheek, still trying to cool down from spending the last hour packed with hundreds of others into the club like tiny, happy sardines.

"Can I have one, or are they all spoken for?" Sirius leaned against the marble bar and pointed to the water bottle in my hand.

"Sure." I tossed him one. Not that he really needed it.

There wasn't a drop of sweat on his forehead, while I was busy peeling plastered strands of hair from mine. Despite Ciara's complaints about her feet and exhaustion, she looked absolutely flawless as well. They all did. It was hardly fair to be blessed with immortality *and* such impressive stamina.

"You look a little tired yourself," he said softly. "Not having fun?"

My eyes strayed to Titania, who had joined in the debate about our plans. "I'm just waiting to get stabbed in the back."

He followed my gaze and nodded. "Fae can be a little weird around humans," he said as I took a swig from the water bottle, "and I don't think anyone expected to see Lach with one."

I choked, spraying the bar with water. Everyone looked over at me, but I waved them off with a weak smile. "Wrong pipe." The others went back to their bickering as I wiped the counter with a napkin. "Lachlan and I are…" I stopped. I wasn't really sure what we were. Finally, I settled on, "Complicated."

Sirius chuckled. "Something complicated between a man and a woman? That would be a first."

"But we aren't together," I said, keeping my voice low enough that I wouldn't attract anyone else to this conversation. "Is that why she hates me? Because I'm human?"

"After the war, things changed between our species."

"War?" This was the first I was hearing about any war.

"World War Two," he said to my surprise. He must have noticed my eyebrows flick up, because he continued, "Officially the last time fae participated in a war effort to help humanity."

"That sounds like a story."

"A long one," he said grimly. "Or I hear it is. I was a baby."

Shaw had told me he was young, and I supposed eighty was relatively so by fae standards.

"Aurora raised me after our parents died in the war." An orphan like me. I wouldn't have guessed, but then I realized that all of the fae royals were orphans. Sisters and brothers but never fathers and mothers. I knew so little about how the crowns passed from parent to child in the fae courts. Maybe I'd been too distracted by their long lives to consider it, or maybe so much time had passed that they hardly remembered, either. But there was something wistful on his face that called to my own grief, to the sorrow of never knowing the most important people in your world.

"She had to grow up very fast," Sirius continued. "Lach, too. I think that's why they get along so well despite everything."

"Do they?" I tried to sound like I didn't care, like I was merely interested. But earlier, when he said he wouldn't lose anyone else, I hadn't considered who he had lost. Maybe not just his parents. Maybe someone he loved. "Were they involved?"

His barked laughter told me enough. "Aurora is too busy with the court to date anyone, but I think friendship is the safest option for those two."

My pulse returned to a steady rhythm. "The Astral court is in Prague, right?"

"Yes." His wide smile was full of pride.

I thought of the picture of Charles Bridge taped to my fridge and understood why. "You love it there."

He nodded. "The history, the city, but especially the alchemy."

"Alchemy?" I raised a brow. "That's not a real thing. You can't really turn things into gold."

"Alchemy is about a lot more than that." He chuckled like the very thought was ridiculous. "It's simply studying the science of magic. We have labs and everything."

"You really study alchemy?" I was strangely impressed.

He scrubbed the back of his neck. "I mean, I'm a bit of a nerd. But take ambrosia, for instance. If you isolate—"

The wail of a siren cut him off. Red-and-blue light flashed through the window. Beneath us, the music stopped. I surged toward the glass on instinct, looking out as a police car screeched up to Alouette's entrance. I was nearly to the door, spurred by a surge of adrenaline, when Shaw blocked me. "Where are you going?"

"They might need help."

"We should stay clear of the cops—"

"Oh, please. Not all of us are avoiding arrest warrants." I started around him.

He moved to stop me, but I elbowed him and shot out the door. Lights flooded the main level as I reached the bottom of the stairs, breaking the sensual spell to reveal floors littered with trash and the dust and tears marring the velvet wall coverings. People pushed toward the side exits as if fleeing the mundane reality before it could infect them, too. Something was definitely going on, but when I began to make my way toward the dance floor, a cop held up a hand.

If Shaw couldn't stop me, neither could this guy. "I'm a nurse. What's happening?"

"Clover overdose. Ambulance is on the way. They're a few minutes out."

Shit. "They'll be too late. I can help."

He hesitated for a minute before jerking his chin for me to follow. He was nearly as effective at clearing a path as my fae companions. People were clustered around the dance floor, some crying, others filming. I froze for a second when I spotted the man collapsed on the floor, recognizing the blue suit.

"Do you have Narcan?" I shouted at the officer.

His mouth twisted. "We used it last night."

"Check the first aid kit at the bar." I prayed that the staff at Alouette were smart enough to be prepared for this scenario. I dropped to the floor, my knees smarting on the polished concrete. The linebacker's arms were drawn to his chest, his lips already turning blue as a breath rattled from him. He had seconds, minutes if I was lucky. I planted my palms on his chest, his skin sticky under mine as I began compressions before leaning over to blow air into his lungs. "Just a little fucking longer." All I could do was keep him alive long enough for the ambulance to come.

Twin shadows fell over me as I leaned to give him oxygen again, but no life-saving medicine appeared.

"Where's that goddamn Narcan?" I barked as I started another round of compressions.

To my surprise, Lachlan dropped to the floor next to me. I had no idea how he'd known what was happening, and this was no time to worry about it.

"What do we do?" he asked as our eyes met. I looked up to find Roark chewing on his lip ring, looking more ruffled than I'd ever seen him.

I tipped my head to where my hands were pumping the man's chest. "Do this as hard as you fucking can without killing him." I glanced up. "And you might want to get everybody out of the VIP room upstairs before the police start asking questions."

Lachlan nodded for Roark to do as I said before taking over. I waited just long enough to make sure he had it, then shoved to my feet, running for the bar where the cop was digging through the first aid kit. Sweat coated his forehead, and he scrambled out of my way. My practiced fingers rummaged through the spilled contents until I found the pouch. I ripped it open as I ran back.

"He's barely breathing," Lachlan said grimly as I knelt next to him. He sat back on his heels to give me room.

Reaching over, I tilted the man's head back and carefully administered the emergency medication. I hovered over the linebacker and said a prayer to whoever was listening.

"What now?" Lachlan asked.

"We wait."

A comforting, warm weight settled on my thigh, his hand an

anchor as I counted the seconds until I needed to give a second dose. The linebacker's eyes fluttered, and I sagged a little as he drew a shallow breath. A few of the people around us began to clap, but I closed my eyes. No one was a hero tonight.

Shouts at the door announced the arrival of the EMTs. Lachlan shot to his feet, helping me to mine. He didn't release my hand as the emergency crew rushed to join us. Nor did he speak as one of them began asking questions, the other starting oxygen. I ran them through what I knew, which wasn't much other than that it had the hallmarks of a trinity overdose. We stepped out of the way as they raised the gurney.

One of the techs paused just long enough to look from me to Lachlan. "You probably saved his life."

Lachlan stiffened.

I pulled away and faced him, questions forming as I realized he was dressed for business but his jacket was off, the collar of his dress shirt undone, no holsters in sight. What was he doing here? I didn't have time to ask questions, so I focused on right now. I didn't know when I'd begun to shake, but now anger unfurled through me. "*That* is what *your* drug does."

I waited for him to say it wasn't his drug or to give me some excuse that he was finding a better alternative. He didn't. He only nodded. Maybe that accountability didn't fix this mess, but it was a start. I was about to tell him that when I looked up to find the police officer studying Lachlan with an intensity that turned my blood to ice. He looked positively rabid, as if he was already imagining the commendations he would receive for nailing Lachlan Gage at the scene of an overdose. Apparently, Lachlan didn't own every officer on the force. I doubted he would go peacefully, and there were plenty of innocent people who might get caught in the cross fire.

"Get out of here," I muttered, stepping in front of Lachlan to block the officer's line of sight.

"I should—"

I cut him off, my teeth clenched. "I'd get out of here if you don't want to walk out in cuffs."

Darkness curled like smoke in his eyes, his mouth pressing into a hard line.

"Before you lose your glamour," I added, worried that more than shadows might slip past it soon.

"I can handle them—"

That was exactly what I was worried about.

"*I* can handle them," I stopped him. "You saved a life tonight. Get out of here before you take one."

Tendons strained in his neck as we glared at each other. Finally, he inclined his head ever so slightly, eyes drifting to my necklace. "You know how to get back."

I waited until he turned on his heels and started toward the back of the club before I spun to the bar. The officer was speaking into his walkie-talkie, and my heart lurched. Taking a deep breath, I strode toward him, mustering a smile.

"Thank you for letting me help him." I fluttered my eyelashes like I'd seen Ciara do countless times.

But he looked past me to the corridor Lachlan had disappeared into. "Where's your friend?"

"Him?" Fluttering wasn't working, so I widened my eyes, glancing behind me like I was surprised. "I have no idea who that was. He just showed up."

His brows knitted together, and he pulled out a pad of paper. "And what is your name?"

"Cate," I said, adrenaline sinking into dread as his pen scratched my name onto the paper. "I work at Gage Memorial."

The pen stopped. He lifted it to his forehead and used the end to scratch under the brim of his hat. "You really don't know who that was?"

I swallowed and shook my head. "Just some guy who helped me save a life."

"He's probably the one responsible for the overdose." The cop tucked the pen into his chest pocket. "I should go after—"

"What?" I gasped loudly, trying to buy a little more time for Lachlan to reach the others, to make sure they had all nipped back to the Nether Court.

The officer frowned, tipping his hat back. "Gage Memorial, huh?" He shook his head a little. "That was Lachlan *Gage.*"

I blinked rapidly as my pulse quickened, realizing it had been a mistake to give him the name of the hospital Lachlan owned. "I had no idea." I wrapped my arms around me and faked a shudder. "I can't believe that monster helped me."

The officer drew a deep breath. "He must be tired of his clientele dropping dead. Nothing ever sticks on him, but maybe if I can catch him on the scene..."

I stumbled out of his way, letting my mouth fall open. "I'm so sorry. Hurry!"

He tipped his hat to me before he dashed off. I was pretty sure I had distracted him long enough for everyone to get away, especially if Roark had given the evacuation notice before the EMTs had even arrived. I headed for the entrance before the cop came back. Pushing out the door, I relaxed as the midnight air coasted over my sweaty skin. I didn't reach for the pendant. I needed to clear my head before I saw him again.

Tonight hadn't just been a reminder of who he was. It was a reckoning I needed to face.

The Avalon wasn't far, and the streets were still crowded with people, some of them staggering out of bars but a fair number lingering by Alouette's entrance. Half looked completely shell-shocked, but I caught snatches of people laughing and figuring out where to go next. As if a man hadn't almost died in front of their eyes. No lessons learned. The shocked ones would find a way to forget. The others would chase down a way. Some would even turn to clover to do it. They might even get a few more good doses and mistake their luck for safety. A tear slipped down my face as I realized Lachlan was right about what people would risk to steal a little happiness, how far they would go to avoid feeling anything at all. And if it wasn't clover, it would be something else.

Hopelessness opened a pit in my stomach. At the hospital, I'd had someone to blame. Then, condemning Lachlan had fueled my anger over the situation. I couldn't look at the people scrolling on their phones or taking selfies for another second, so I darted down a dim side street. I hadn't paid attention on the ride to Alouette, but it didn't matter. I wasn't ready to return to the Avalon. Not with the adrenaline coursing through me, rousing my anger and confusion into a compound that might prove volatile if I had to face him. Not just because of what had happened at the club. But what had nearly happened this afternoon.

He had nearly kissed me again, and I would have let him this time. If only to see what happened next. If he would have had me right there in broad daylight, or if he would have carried me inside like the night before, only this time to his bed. And maybe knowing that was what slowed my steps and kept me from returning to the Avalon. Because I'd just witnessed the dangers of chasing forbidden highs. If I had a taste of him, would I ever want to be free, or would I surrender the rest of my nights for that fleeting, addictive pleasure and let his dark court devour me?

A bulb crackled in the only streetlamp and died. The world plunged into darkness save for scattered puddles of moonlight from the afternoon rain. I followed them forward, somehow more comforted by the shadows than the idea of turning back to the lights of the street that lay behind me. Until I reached a twelve-foot-tall security fence lined with barbed wire and realized this wasn't a street at all, but a dead end. Naturally.

Water splashed behind me, and I whipped around to find a figure moving toward me. It was too dark to make out a face, to make out anything except his sheer size.

Keep it together, I ordered myself and started past him.

He stepped in front of me.

Shit.

He cracked his knuckles against his opposite palm, drawing my attention to a series of red stripes circling his fingers. A flare of panic hit me, but I pushed it aside and changed course again, only to find him standing directly in front of me. He leered at me, his beady eyes wincing as moonlight hit them.

"Are you lost?" As he spoke, I glimpsed two rows of pointed, stained teeth.

Not human. But not like any fae I'd ever seen. Lachlan's words rang in my mind. *Few of us are little...or cute.* Whatever kind of fae the stranger was, I had little hope he was about to escort me home. Footsteps approached behind me, and my panic sharpened to a single thought: survive.

I should have taken the gun, but it was too late now.

Every instinct inside me screamed to run. Probably due to a lifetime of consuming fairy tales. Definitely because I knew that whoever was behind me was with him.

"Don't worry. We'll take care of you." A forked tongue slid along those yellow teeth.

Adrenaline spiked, and the sudden surge in my blood propelled me. I didn't think. Instinct took over, and I ran.

They let me get a couple of feet before a red-striped hand caught me by the throat.

CHAPTER TWENTY-SIX

I was going to die…or worse.

No. Not like this. I thrashed as my feet left the ground, kicking wildly and finding only air. Sharp nails bit into my skin, his grip crushing my throat and cutting off my air supply until I only had enough strength to claw at those deadly fingers. They cut off access to the pendant—the pendant I should have grabbed and didn't in my panic. He swung me closer. Black eyes glinted in the darkness, satisfaction twisting the creature's grotesque mouth into a hideous smile that displayed his barbed teeth. He leaned closer, nostrils flaring as he inhaled deeply. He drew back and looked over his shoulder. "It's her."

Panic seized me as I fought for air, my muscles burning from the lack of oxygen and my heart near exploding. But I refused to go limp, refused to give in, to die like this.

"Sweet nightmares," he taunted, hoisting me higher until I was dangling like a doll, my arms starting to slacken.

No, no, no. Black spots blotted my vision. Not much time. I focused everything I had on my hands, tearing my nails into his fingers, shredding his tattooed skin.

He hissed. "Good. You like it rough. We like it rough, too." He turned, laughing to his companion, and I mustered a final burst of resistance and aimed it into one well-placed kick. He went down in a heap, right on top of me.

I shoved at him and lurched toward the street, toward the people and the lights and safety. If they could see me…

I opened my mouth to scream, but no sound came out.

A hand grabbed the back of my head, nearly ripping the hair from my scalp as the other man wrenched me back. "Leaving so soon?"

He shoved me to the ground, and the other pounced.

Spit sprayed my face as he pinned my wrists against the cold pavement. I couldn't call for help, couldn't beg for mercy, couldn't even cry as he plucked the straps of my dress. "At least this one's pretty. I wonder if she'll taste as good as she looks." His forked tongue slid out of his mouth and slithered down my cheek, his breath rancid and shockingly cold. I twisted, craning my mouth as far from those nightmare teeth as I could manage.

And the pendant slid to my shoulder.

I was never really alone. Not anymore. I'd forgotten.

I twisted beneath him, trying to lift my knee, trying to aim another shot at his groin. Not because I was stupid enough to think he would fall for the same thing twice but because I needed a distraction.

"You've got to be more creative than that." He grabbed my thigh, and my freed fingers shot for the necklace.

Help.

It was all I managed before the other grabbed my arms and held them over my head. "I like it when they fight. It gets in their blood."

Bile rose in my throat, threatening to choke me. I spluttered, managing to turn my head just enough to not suffocate.

"Let's see what we can do about these clothes…and this skin. You'll be even prettier without it." He dragged a razor-shop nail along my collarbone, my skin splitting like a seam, and I cried out, the silent scream shredding my throat as it tried to escape. His face angled over mine, macabre curiosity gleaming as he spilled my blood. I closed my eyes, every muscle in my body coiling with dread.

I prayed they killed me before they…

The world went deathly still, muted like my voice. It contracted in a thunderous rush of wind and shadows that cleaved the night in two and flattened me against the wet pavement, knocking the murderous creature off me. I rolled away from him, gasping, fingers scrabbling to drag my body across the cracked cement. The streetlamp flared to life, illuminating the man standing over me, gun in hand. He looked down at me, and his face contorted with a rage that was ancient and primal.

A prince of death.

I surrendered to the safety of that darkness. My body collapsed onto the street as I drank air into my lungs. Lach cast one lingering look in my direction, eyes narrowing on the throbbing wound at my collarbone. He reached over and chambered a round before stepping forward.

I rolled my head, tracking his movement to discover the monsters edging toward the dead end, excuses pouring from their mouths.

"Stop," Lachlan growled, dark magic lacing the command. He lifted his left hand and cut the air in a circle with his index finger. Both males flipped onto their backs, their hands and feet trying desperately to scuttle away as death approached.

"If we had known," the one that licked me began.

"You knew." Lachlan stalked forward.

The other one shoved at his friend. "He did it. He wanted a snack."

The words snapped me out of my shock as I realized he'd meant what he'd said about tasting me *literally*. I clamped a hand over my mouth, but it was too late. I doubled over and retched.

Lachlan's head whipped around, eyes narrowing on that sound. One of the fae lunged toward the street, and I opened my mouth to warn him before the monster escaped. But Lachlan's eyes narrowed, assessing me with concern as he lifted the gun and fired a single shot without looking. It cut the air and hit the escaping one in his left shoulder with a wet, bone-splintering crack. Not a kill shot, but he went down in a heap, moaning. His companion froze.

I flinched as a tattoo twisted around Lachlan's neck. The air shimmered for a moment, and Roark appeared. His eyes scanned the scene, calculating—collected, unlike the prince he served.

Roark knelt down, and I tucked my knees to my chest as he gently examined my wound. But I couldn't look away from Lachlan as he holstered the gun and reached out with his magic. The magic lifted the fae to his feet, and Lachlan grabbed his arm, twisting it behind his back with a sickening pop. The creature's eyes bulged as he cried out.

"First, I am going to break every fucking bone in your hand," he promised. Something cracked, and the fae arched in agony, mumbled pleas spilling from him. "Then, when I've shattered every single fucking bone, I'm going to cut each finger off one at a time for daring to touch her." The monster sobbed, shaking and squirming, but Lachlan's mouth curled into a merciless smile. "And then, we'll have some real fun. That's what you were looking for, right? A good time?"

I searched for my voice, searched for the words to tell him to stop this, but found none. All I could offer was one small assurance. "I'm okay."

Lachlan's jaw clenched, eyes finding mine, but he didn't let go.

"Please, please, we didn't hurt her. I pray forgiveness." The creature cried out as another bone broke.

"Save your prayers. Your gods are not listening." The cold cruelty of Lachlan's laugh made my heart stutter. "That you touched her would be enough reason, but you made her bleed. There will be no mercy."

Roark helped me sit up, wrapping an arm around my shoulder, but I still couldn't tear my eyes away from Lachlan as he shattered more bones. The creature sagged, his knees buckling, and Lachlan dropped him in a heap on the street. "Stay put."

Neither of the fae tried to escape as Lachlan strode forward, likely held in place as much by his fury as whatever dark magic he'd called upon. Wrath radiated from him as he cut through the night with swift, purposeful steps before lowering to one knee before me. He shot a look at Roark, and the arm around my shoulder dropped.

Muscles tensed in his jaw as Lachlan performed a rapid assessment, his gaze lingering on my neck so intensely that my fingers reached to shield the wound before he detonated.

"What are they?" I whispered.

"Redcaps," he said through gritted teeth. "Murderous fae pricks who are not allowed in my city." Reason enough for him to punish them, but I knew that wouldn't satisfy him. "They will not hurt anyone else."

He paused as if waiting for me to object to what he was saying.

I didn't.

His eyes narrowed, and he pushed the necklace to the side. The cold night air hit the raw cut, and I winced. He sucked in a reedy breath, his eyes flashing to Roark. "Take her to my quarters. *Now*."

I didn't fight it as Roark grabbed hold of me and nipped us back to the Avalon, directly inside Lachlan's private wing. I didn't want to see what was about to happen in that alley, even if the redcaps deserved it.

"You want a drink?" Roark asked me, hovering nearby but not touching me. "Or do you want me to get someone? Ciara?"

I shook my head quickly. I didn't want anyone else to see me like this. Not when I might break at any moment, shattered from within by dredged-up memories. "I'm fine." My lips wobbled, and I forced them to arch. "Would you believe me if I told you I'd been through worse?"

Roark tensed.

"I grew up in foster care," I said softly. "Not all monsters lurk in back alleys."

He softened a little, and I hated the pity that clouded his eyes. "Lach knows..."

Not quite a question, but I nodded. Maybe not the details, but I had no doubt he knew. I didn't have a clue if he'd guessed or if he saw the scars I tried to hide. I suspected the redcaps would pay extra because of that knowledge.

Roark strode to the bar cart and poured me a drink.

I took it with trembling fingers. "Is he going to kill them?"

He hesitated. "Do you really want to know?"

No. I took a drink, swishing it slightly in my mouth like I

could rinse away the memory. I'd seen the murder in Lachlan's eyes, glimpsed the feral rage that he was likely unleashing. He could handle himself, but if the wrong person got in the way, if the punishment spilled onto the streets of the French Quarter... He had already drawn attention to himself tonight, and with that attention, innocent people were more likely to find out what the fae were— something that might get them killed. "Go, before he loses control."

I half expected him to argue with me, but Roark's eyes pinched closed before he nodded once and vanished, telling me that I was right to be concerned.

Telling me that I'd only barely glimpsed Lachlan's power on the street. Telling me that he was in danger of losing control, of letting the darkness that had saved me consume him.

CHAPTER TWENTY-SEVEN

I waited for the guilt to come, waited to feel some pity or remorse for the redcaps who had attacked me. It didn't. Even though I had glimpsed only a sliver of the merciless justice being meted out. It bothered me even less when I braved the mirror and saw proof of their intentions. The bluish hint of fingerprints bruised my neck, sore but not nearly as painful as the cut on my collarbone. It had clotted, but there was a patch of raw pink where my flesh... I looked away. But not before acid burned up my throat and I lurched over the sink. After, I scrubbed my teeth until my gums were raw, until I tasted only mint.

I peeled my filthy dress off and turned the shower on to its hottest setting. I was dimly aware of the sting as water hit my fresh wound, but I didn't care. I needed to wash this away. I scrubbed at my skin under the blistering water until even the hotel's boiler failed and the shower turned cold. My heart had calmed a little by the time I slipped into a silk robe, but I knew it wouldn't settle until he returned, until I saw him for myself.

It was past three when the door to his wing opened. Light spilled in from the foyer, haloing his massive frame as he stalked inside. For a moment, I didn't breathe, didn't move, as I took him in.

He was covered in blood. Black, oily patches of it stained his white shirt, practically dripping off its bloody cuffs. It coated his hands, his neck. I scanned him, looking for signs of injury. There were none. He didn't say hello, didn't even acknowledge my existence as he headed toward his room. I was right behind him, following closely as he continued into the attached bath. He walked to the sink, turned on the faucet, and began to wash his hands, the water running red on the stark porcelain. His palms grated the soap, his head hanging, black hair falling around his face and glamour fading as he scoured. But darkness clung to him, his tattoos reeling across his skin like they were being chased by those shadows.

"That's a lot of blood." The words were barely a whisper. I wasn't certain he could hear them over the running water.

He shrugged. "Don't worry, princess. It's not mine."

There was no hint of amusement. Only flat, endless rage.

"Because that makes me feel so much better." I settled against the wall, studying the blood splattered on his neck, waiting for him to tell me what had happened after he'd sent me home. He kept washing long after his hands were clean, until I finally leaned over and shut off the faucet.

He still didn't look up as he braced his hands on either side of the sink. I stepped closer like I was approaching a wild animal. A copper tang hung from him, from the wet stains on his clothes. Not his blood. Theirs. I shouldn't feel satisfied, not when he'd done something terrible, but I nearly stumbled with relief. It should be proof of everything I'd once believed. That he was a monster. That I was nothing like him. Neither was true. And instead of that making me want to run, it made me want to reach out.

So I did.

His back stiffened as my hand found his shoulder, every muscle tensing. He drew a shuddering breath that made me take another step, bringing my body near enough to feel the heat of his own. One more step was all it would take to close the distance, to press myself against him, to soothe the jagged energy rolling off him and calm my own wicked heart.

"Are you okay?" I murmured, not daring to take that final step.

His laugh was as bitter as nightshade. "I'm not the one you should be worried about." He shook my hand off his shoulder and reached for a towel.

I didn't move, didn't speak.

Lach raised his head, his eyes finding mine in the mirror. A corner of his mouth lifted into something tortured. "Go on. Ask me."

I bit my lower lip and didn't say anything.

His nostrils flared, and he spun around. His hands shot out, bracing against the wall behind me as he leered over me. "Ask me," he demanded again. "Ask me what I did to the people who touched you."

I swallowed, tears lining my eyes as I faced him, faced what he truly was, faced a part of myself I didn't want to believe existed. I could no longer ignore any of it. Not just what he'd done but how I felt about it.

Pleased. More than that—*avenged*.

"Ask me!" he roared.

Tears rolled down my cheeks. "What did you do?"

He exhaled and fell back a step, his hands dropping to his sides. A muscle worked in his jaw while he looked me in the eyes. "What I've always done." He sounded so tired. "Bad things. Very bad things done extremely well."

His cold glare challenged me to question him further, seemed to demand it. He loomed over me, flooding my every sense with him. His massive body, the heat of his skin, his cedar scent mixing with the tang of blood beckoned me. Everything about him called to me from a place I'd long ago buried.

His eyes skimmed lower, lingering on the laceration on my collarbone before he turned away with disgust. Did it look that bad? He reached into his pocket and produced a blood apple. "This will help."

I blinked as he held it out to me, but I took it.

"They're grown with vampire venom. It will speed up healing."

I managed a nod but set it to the side. He had saved me, but his expression told me that wasn't enough to silence the guilt screaming inside me. It was written all over his face.

So, I reached around him for the hand towel. He froze as I lifted it to his cheek and gently wiped the blood there. He watched me warily as I cleaned his skin, not shrinking away from who he was but welcoming the shadows instead. When I paused to search for any missed blood, Lachlan caught my wrist and pulled me closer. His breath was hot on my face. The whisper of bourbon lingering on it told me he cared more than he let on. Had he been drinking before or after... I didn't ask him.

"What are you doing?" Under the gravelly surface of his words, there was a soft edge of curiosity. Bewilderment.

I met his searching eyes, my heart beginning to pound. "Taking care of you."

"You don't have to do that." His thumb stroked across the back of my wrist, igniting something low in my belly.

"Someone has to," I said softly as I spotted more blood. He didn't look away from me as I wiped it off, and I didn't shy away from his stare. Finally satisfied, I dropped the bloody towel on the floor and risked looking into his eyes. "Your shirt."

He straightened ever so slightly. He hooked his thumbs under the straps of his holster and shucked his weapons free. Dropping the holster on the towel, he raised his arms to the side and waited. Not looking away once. My throat slid as my fingers fumbled to unbutton his collar. I tried not to look at the blood. I worked my way down, his gaze boring into mine, stripping me bare as I undressed him. When I reached the final button, I slid my fingers up the seams of his undone shirt to his broad shoulders. I paused to trace a scar, the mottled and knotted skin the only blemish on his otherwise perfect torso. A nearby tattoo fled at the touch, as if his body didn't like to remember what had happened. It must have been horrible if it had left a mark.

He glanced down at where my fingertip brushed the old wound. "As a smartass once said, even immortals bleed—and iron scars."

I didn't want to think about that, didn't want to consider that he could suffer like he'd made those redcaps suffer tonight. He didn't stop me as I shifted my hands under the fabric of his shirt instead, pushing it off his shoulders until it fell loosely around his back. He only watched.

I flushed at the sight of his bare chest, the golden skin and black ink. I wanted to run my fingertips over the dips and peaks of his muscles. His tattoos stilled, as if they were as mesmerized as he was. Instead, I tugged his rolled sleeves free one at a time and tossed the ruined shirt on top of the bloody towel and guns. He did not move as I traced a whorl of ink on his shoulder.

"They're peaceful," I whispered. How could his mind be quiet at a moment like this? I wanted to ask him, but my finger continued to follow the lines and swirls of that strange language. When I finally looked up, his eyes were bright, the intensity piercing through me. Every rational thought fled my brain. "Kiss me, Lach."

Without a word, he took my face in his hands, his calloused fingertips rough on my skin. He paused for a delicious, agonizing second to savor my surrender before his lips crushed into mine, coaxing and dominant as he claimed me. My body curved, softening against his hardness, as I parted my lips to offer more. His tongue swept over mine, licking across the roof of my mouth and along my teeth. Each stroke stoked the smoldering need in my blood toward combustion until my fingers dug into his shoulders to keep me from falling.

I knew then that, bargain or not, I would never be fully free of him.

We broke apart, panting. Lach rested his sweat-slicked forehead against mine and fingered a strand of my hair. "It's you. There's something about you that makes me feel…calm." It took me a moment to realize he was talking about the tattoos. "I don't deserve that peace. Not tonight."

He didn't let me go, and I didn't move away.

"You can have it anyway," I said softly. "It's mine to give." I wondered for a moment how much else I might give this prince. If I might give him everything.

His eyes held mine. "I killed them."

A test.

Not for him. For me.

"I know." That much blood. I swallowed that truth, letting it settle into that long-buried place—and still I didn't let him go.

A reckoning.

His thumb swept over my swollen lips, a battle waging in his green eyes. "I'm the bad guy, princess."

I stroked a hand along the side of his face. He turned into the touch, nuzzling into my palm. "I don't believe that."

His dark laugh rippled through every nerve in my body. "I tricked you out of your soul, your freedom, and I may never let you go. You shouldn't need more proof, but here I am, wearing other men's blood." He gripped my chin and lifted my face to his. "I will ruin you before this is over."

I didn't struggle in his grasp. I just held his stare. Because I didn't want to run from Lachlan Gage anymore. Not while he was looking right into my very soul—to the loneliness and loss, to the mistakes and fear, to all the wounds and secrets I carried.

And he didn't look away.

An awakening.

So I looked back and saw him—the darkness and the grief, the arrogance and the brokenness, all of the beautiful and damned pieces of him. I saw the blood on his hands, the blood that would be on mine—maybe already was. My soul was on the line, and I didn't care. Not when the touch of his skin seared me to the bone. Not when I only felt alive kissing him.

Because if ruin was the price of having him, let him destroy me.

"Then ruin me," I breathed.

His eyes sparked, the words snapping his control. One moment, I was daring him; the next, he had me against the wall. My legs coiled around his waist, his fingers digging into the soft flesh of my hips as he pinned me against it. I gasped when his teeth nipped the corner of my mouth, and he chuckled before his tongue invaded. Savage. Brutal. I yielded to that kiss as his hips rolled against mine, pressing the hard length of him over the wet heat there.

I reached between us to find his belt, but he pushed me harder to the wall, capturing my hands. He drew back, his lips brushing over mine. "We need to stop."

"We do," I agreed, tugging his lower lip between my teeth until he was kissing me again.

His arm snaked up my back, and his hand curled around the nape of my neck. Then he spun me toward the sink and set me carefully on the edge of the counter.

"We can't let this go too far," he ground out, planting kisses along my jawline.

My hands were free now, and he didn't stop me when I reached for his buckle a second time. "Agreed."

He cursed as I slid my hand down the front of his pants and wrapped my fingers around his cock. Something clenched in my core as I stroked that considerable length, savoring him being at my mercy.

He slipped a hand under my robe and found my breast. The rough pad of his thumb circled my nipple until it peaked and throbbed. "It's late. Maybe it's time for bed."

I dragged my hand to his tip and did the same. "Yours or mine?"

He cursed again as I continued stroking him, pushing my robe past my shoulders to dip his head lower—

A sharp rap on the door startled us apart.

"You in there, man?" Roark called through the door, banging on it again.

"Just a second! Fuck." Lach set me on my feet, shoving his cock into his pants.

"Does he do this on purpose?" I grumbled.

Lach avoided my eyes as he tugged my robe over my shoulders.

I gawked. "Wait. *Is* he interrupting us on purpose?"

Roark's impatient voice called through the door. Again. "We've got a big problem."

Lach went to the door, opening it just far enough to glare through the crack at his penumbra. "I'm kinda busy."

I didn't catch the rest of what Roark said, but Lach muttered something and slammed the door shut.

"It's your lucky day." Lach bent and picked up the bloody shirt and his holster. He stared at the shirt for a moment before dropping it again, though he held on to the holster. "I've got to go."

I cinched my robe tightly. "Right now?"

"Yes." He opened the door and stalked into his bedroom. There was no sign of Roark. At least he was going to give us some privacy. Lach slung his holster over the armoire door.

I hung back as he riffled through the wardrobe and produced a clean shirt.

"Where?" I finally asked.

"Does it matter?" He raked his fingers through his hair and shot me a wink. "You just got saved from making the biggest mistake of your life."

I winced as he threw my own words back at me. I deserved that, but this...

His fingers moved nimbly up his shirt buttons, leaving the top open. He reached for his holster, sliding one of the guns free. "Take this."

I shook my head, backing up a step.

He shoved it into my palm and forced my hand to close over it. "You know how to use it now. Safety off." He hesitated as if weighing the next bit. "If you need me, I will come. This is just insurance, princess, and it will make you feel safer."

I inhaled sharply, but I slipped it into the pocket of my robe.

"Good girl." He kissed my forehead. My heart stuttered as he started for the door.

"When will you be back?"

"Late." He stopped with his hand on the knob. "Don't wait up."

I grabbed hold of his shirt. "What is going on? Is it the redcaps?"

"Don't worry about them. This is nothing for you to be concerned about." He studied me for a moment, his eyes lingering on my lips with such intensity that I flushed.

My grip on him tightened. "Don't go."

His hand closed over mine as he leaned in for a swift, possessive kiss. I realized it was a distraction as he pried himself free. "You hate me, remember? It's better if it stays that way, if this thing between us…doesn't happen."

And then he vanished before I could tell him that I knew that.

The problem was that I didn't fucking care.

CHAPTER TWENTY-EIGHT

I paced the length of our quarters, trying to decide if I should just go to bed, even though I knew I'd never be able to sleep. Not until he came back, preferably not covered in blood—his or anyone else's. I cleaned up the bloodied mess in his bathroom, wiped down the sink, and disposed of the towels he'd ruined in a hamper. I even ate the blood apple, surprised to discover an hour later that the cut on my collarbone was now a pale, fleshy pink and the fingerprint bruises on my neck had faded.

That much healing, and Lach still wasn't back. Two hours later, I finally gave up and headed to my room. I didn't bother turning on a light, the fire in the hearth providing enough for me to slip free of my robe and find a nightgown. After debating for what felt like an eternity, I left the door cracked. But just as I had suspected, sleep refused to claim me. I twisted, shoving down the sheets that ensnared my legs, and stared at that open door. Listening for his footfalls, hopeful that he would accept the invitation of that open door and terrified that I should heed his warning.

Tonight had proven two things.

Lach was as deadly as I'd always suspected.

And the world was even more fucked-up than I thought.

Maybe it was that second realization that canceled out any hesitation over the first, but I wasn't sure I could fight this anymore.

I considered finding Ciara to talk this out. I was too stuck in the middle of it to see which way to go. The entire day had given me whiplash. It felt like a lifetime had passed since I'd woken up this morning, hungover and embarrassed. And now everything was different, but nothing had changed. Not entirely. Were we just hurtling toward an even bigger mistake?

Time was running out. He had reminded me of that this afternoon. I had less than three weeks left to figure things out, or the bargain would be permanent. I didn't know if letting him in would doom me or save me, but I wasn't sure I had any other choice. Because one thing was abundantly clear. My entire body warmed, an ache growing between my legs, as I remembered just how clear he had made it. And then in the bathroom...

There was no ambrosia to blame. I was alert after the attack. My head was entirely clear. At least as clear as it could be with the memory of how hard and hot he'd been in my hands—*that* I remembered very, very distinctly. And I was tired of waiting on him to come home.

I curled my fingers around the pendant just like I had done around his cock and let my right hand drift to that hollow ache between my legs.

It wasn't an invitation. It was a challenge.

It took approximately five seconds for Lach to appear at the foot of the four-poster bed.

Was I counting?

He stood at a distance, offering little more than glimpses of his silhouette, but I detected no new bloodstains. His guns were gone, his holster left behind. I bit my lip, wondering if I'd missed him coming in. If he had ignored my open door.

He didn't move from where he stood. Firelight danced across him, casting sparks of red in his blue-black hair. His eyes fixed on the sheets wrapped around my ankles, at my spread legs and the hand between them. We had crossed a line earlier.

Now, I was invading.

My fingers stilled as his gaze narrowed, riveted to them. Lach prowled forward, never looking away, the dark his natural habitat. No hesitation. No uncertainty. I braced myself for him to pounce, but he stopped and planted both of his hands on the footboard. He dragged his glazed eyes from the hand between my legs to my face. "Don't stop."

The command lacing his words sent a surge of arousal slicking my fingertips. I didn't move. I was pretty sure I didn't have to. I could probably climax with one word from him.

He gave me three. Each clipped and punctuated by his perfect lips. "Touch yourself, princess."

I shifted in the bed, eyes rolling slightly, and released the pendant.

"Don't." He shook his head, nostrils flaring as he inhaled deeply. "I want to hear every filthy thought in that beautiful, fucked-up mind of yours."

My breath caught, my body completely at the mercy of that sinful voice, half growl, half promise. I wanted him on top of me, wanted to feel the weight of him, wanted him to fill that ragged, gnawing hunger that grew more demanding with each passing second.

"Show me how you want me." Something desperate edged his words, matching the need I felt.

I was powerless to resist. I dipped my hand lower, sliding a finger inside myself, followed by another, and pumped slowly. I thrust deeper with each stroke, imagining it was his cock, near ready to beg until it was. My hips rose as I rode my fingers harder until my skin was tight and my eyes clenched.

"Eyes on me, princess."

They snapped open and found his peering back, wrenching a moan from my lips. A crack split the air, and my eyes dipped to find his white-knuckled hands clutching the broken footboard. I knew that when those hands were finally on me, no part of me would be left untouched. He would own my body as surely as he owned my soul. And I would let him, if only to see his masterful restraint slip, crumble, *dissolve* entirely.

A dark chuckle reminded me that he was privy to my thoughts, so I let my mind fill with every dirty fantasy I'd ever had. Now all starring him. Teeth and tongues and sweat and skin. I writhed on my fingers as I imagined riding him, never taking my eyes off him as he claimed me without a single touch. My body arched as I splintered like the ruined bed, his name spilling in moans from my lips. I wrung out the last shattering pleasure as he watched, and when I finally sagged in a boneless heap against the pillow, he started toward me.

Lach circled the bed, taking his time as his eyes skimmed over me and lingered on the bunched nightgown at my hips, on the release glistening on my skin. He paused just short of the bed. "Thanks for the show."

The ownership in his voice should have disgusted me. It should have turned me off.

It did not.

He leaned over me, and I sucked in a sharp breath, my lips parting for a kiss that didn't come. He took my hand, eyes capturing mine as he brought my fingers, still soaked with my climax, to his mouth. His tongue curled around them and sucked. It swirled and licked, as if he refused to waste a single drop. The world stopped and re-centered on him. There was only him. He occupied every atom of my being. He owned me. And when he finally pulled away, only to bring his face to mine, air hitched in my throat.

He didn't kiss me.

"Good night, Cate."

He was halfway to the door before I'd pushed up in bed and demanded, "Where are you going?"

But Lach raked one lingering, longing look from my mouth to my bare thighs. "Back to the meeting I was in when you interrupted me."

I should ask him to stay. He waited by the door as if he thought I might. I wanted to, but something silenced me. I didn't know if it was pride or self-preservation. I tamped down on my confusion, not allowing it to turn into something sour. I yanked the sheets up with a shrug and tried to master a simple "good night." All I managed was a nod.

As he slipped out the door, a new ache began in a place *far* more dangerous than before.

...

The next morning, I left my bedroom for breakfast, grateful that Lach's door was still closed. Ciara accosted me in the foyer, grabbing hold of me. Thankfully, my wounds had been entirely healed when I woke up this morning, because she dragged me into a hug so tight I thought my spine might actually crack.

Ciara clutched my shoulders as she released me, worry lining her beautiful face. "Are you okay?"

I pinned a smile to my lips. "I'm fine. It was nothing."

"Cate, you saved someone's life at Alouette, and then two redcaps tried to back-alley Jack the Ripper you." She shook her head. "You are not fine."

There was no way I could tell her that of all the things that had happened last night, the redcap attack had shaken me the least.

"Really, I'm good."

Her lips pursed, and I knew she wasn't buying it. "Did Lach take care of you at least?"

Not exactly. I flushed slightly but nodded. "He gave me a gun."

That was all she needed to know.

Ciara rolled her eyes and looped her arm through mine. "Of course he did."

But she looked a little relieved all the same.

She chattered absently as we headed to the hotel brunch, her babbling a sign that she was as shaken by last night's events as I should be. She didn't release me until we were safely down the stairs without incident.

The breakfast room was already full of visiting fae. My heart stumbled when I saw Lach among them, deep in conversation with Bain and another male I didn't know. Lach didn't look up as I entered, and I wouldn't give him the satisfaction of being the first one to approach after last night.

"Want something to eat?" Ciara asked, oblivious to the fact that I was staring at her brother.

The fifty-seat oak trestle table was laid with bone china and gold flatware. Knowing how filthy rich the fae were, it was probably real. A buffet of sorts had been laid on a smaller table by the arched windows overlooking Waverly Avenue. No one was sitting down, and as usual, no one was eating. Maybe never getting full meant never feeling hungry. That wasn't a problem I had. After last night's emotional roller coaster, I was starving. I took one look at the plates of croissants and pastries, little bowls of butter and jams, and the steaming chafing dishes next to them, and my stomach growled.

"I'm starving," Ciara said and yawned, scooping eggs and sausages onto a plate. "And then there was the whole clover drama last night."

I plopped a smatter of cherry jam on a croissant. "The overdose?"

"Well, I guess that, too." She piled a few beignets next to the eggs.

I reached for a napkin. "What clover drama happened?"

"Lach didn't tell you?"

"I haven't spoken to him this morning." I twisted off a piece of croissant and popped it into my mouth. Any time before sunrise was technically night, according to the terms of the bargain.

She paused and studied me. "I thought he went to talk to you."

I almost choked. I covered it with a cough. "Why would you think that?"

"Because he just vanished in the middle of an argument with the heads of the other families." She shrugged, her eyes darting to my necklace, an eyebrow raised. "I figured you had summoned him."

I turned to get some eggs, hoping my flush wasn't too obvious. That was the meeting he had been in.

"I can't think of anyone else he would do that for." She shifted closer and lowered her voice to a conspiratorial whisper. "And since he showed up to the meeting absolutely drenched in your perfume, I thought maybe…" She was baiting me.

"He was covered in blood. I was just helping him clean up."

"And his pants were unzipped because…?"

That was harder to explain.

A change of subject was in order. "He didn't mention anything about clover."

But Ciara's triumphant smile was blinding. "I knew he was with you." She whooped. "Don't worry. I do not want details, but I was beginning to think you two would never—"

"We didn't," I cut her off before she started planning our wedding. Her face fell a little, and I seized my chance to get her back on track. "What exactly was such an emergency, anyway, that he was in a meeting all night?"

She moved closer, her eyes darting around us like she didn't want to be overheard. "He ordered our entire inventory of clover destroyed and called our men to seize any supply they knew about in the city, including our personal supply at the hotel and what we'd sent to the other courts in their welcome baskets. He'd just given the order when he realized you were being attacked."

My hands were trembling so hard that I thought I might drop the plate. Lach had left the club and immediately done the last thing I'd expected him to do. He had actually pulled clover from the streets. "He didn't tell me."

"He was a lot more worried about you." She had that wedding-planning face on again.

"Yeah." I rolled my eyes. "He was so concerned that he left to go to a business meeting." Twice.

"Bain had a tantrum when they came for his supply and demanded to see our family to call off the engagement. He summoned Oberon and Aurora to witness it all."

My mouth fell open, and I hastily shut it. Why were we talking about clover when that had happened? "So, did Bain end it?"

She shook her head, disappointment tipping her mouth. "No. I convinced him not to."

I hated that Ciara's freedom was the cost of saving lives. She bit into a beignet, sending a cloud of powdered sugar into the air, and smiled gloomily.

"I'm sorry." I meant it.

She swallowed hard. "I do not pretend to understand my brother at all, but I think I understand why he did it."

Before I could ask her more, I felt him.

The air around me seemed to shift, growing thicker and darker as if even magic itself responded to the tension between us. Maybe I'd mistaken that before, but I couldn't anymore. I forced myself to continue what I was doing as he stepped behind me. Not close enough that our bodies touched, only close enough to make me wish they did.

"Did you sleep well?"

Something of the primal creature who had visited my bedroom lingered in that voice, and I turned my attention to the beignets. "I slept great. How about you?"

Next to me, Ciara was not so subtly watching the two of us, her eyes gleaming with barely repressed mischief.

I dared her to say something, but I hoped she wouldn't.

I kept my back to him, afraid to look him in the face, afraid that maybe I had dreamed the whole thing.

"Excuse me. I think I need to talk to Titania." Ciara winked at me as she bustled over to her friend.

Subtle.

"I was too preoccupied to sleep," he told me.

I took a deep breath. *Do not read into that.* "By the clover drama?"

"That?" He shook his head. "I had far more important things on my mind."

"Like?" I swallowed.

He didn't answer. Instead, he stepped beside me and plucked a grape from a bunch in the fruit bowl. He crushed it between his index finger and thumb, letting its juice dribble down them before he sucked the entire thing deeply into his mouth. He licked them slightly and reached for another grape.

Okay, not a dream.

I couldn't tear my eyes from his sensual mouth as he chewed, remembering the wet heat of his tongue on my fingers. I flushed at the dark hunger in his eyes, knowing he was recalling the same thing, and looked at my plate. I was hungrier than ever—starving, even—but none of it looked remotely appetizing anymore. Not when what I wanted to devour was standing next to me.

Lach licked his lips and frowned. "So unsatisfying after I tasted—"

I coughed loudly and cleared my throat. Time to change the subject. "So, not everyone is happy about getting rid of clover, huh?"

His smirk slid into a frown. "Bain is throwing a fit."

I still didn't understand why he would let his sister marry into a court he clearly hated or why they would even care how he ran his. "She mentioned that. I don't know why he needs clover when he has ambrosia."

"We discovered our private supply was tainted, so we had no choice but to ask the other courts for what we had given them, too. It was a precaution."

A prudent one. I nodded.

"Bain accused us of trying to kill him and summoned the other courts to call off the engagement publicly." The look on Lach's face told me that he almost wished it had. "He claimed we knew the clover had been tampered with and had still given it to the rest of them."

"You should have let him end it," I murmured.

Lach's mouth flattened, but he didn't disagree with me. "His spectacle ensured that the light courts will hesitate for a long time before making any new deals with us."

"But you asked for it back. Surely that proves you didn't intend to harm them."

"We didn't tell them why." His mouth twisted into a rueful smile. "And Bain revealing that piece of information is enough to plant doubt regarding our intentions. There's not a lot of trust between light and shadow courts."

There never would be until they learned to work together. But I doubted he would be receptive to this insight.

"Bain made sure the others trust the Nether Court less than ever"—he continued—"which means an alliance with the Infernal

Court is even more important. Bringing them into it is a power play so he can negotiate new terms. The light courts can't fill the clover void. Without it or ambrosia, something worse will find its way onto the streets. Bain knows we need him, and he just ensured that the light courts remain suspicious of my intentions."

Negotiations that would drag on as they all fought for their own agendas. Too busy considering their own priorities to listen to one another—so maybe it was time for someone else to do it for them. If the crown royals wouldn't work together, maybe others would.

I glanced at where Ciara was visiting with Titania and Sirius. Right now, she was a bargaining chip because she didn't know how powerful she was. What about the others? "Bain should be begging to marry Ciara."

"I think he knows she's less than enthusiastic about the prospect."

But if Bain was having second thoughts, maybe Ciara could get out of this. "Maybe you don't need ambrosia."

"There's more at stake over this alliance than our economy," he said darkly. Before I could press him on what, he continued with a sigh. "He postponed the banns to negotiate a handfasting instead."

What ever happened to buying a ring and saying "I do"? The fae made everything so complicated. "Handfasting?"

"Ritual fuckery that used to mean something. Now it's just a magical prenup. It means we'll skip the rest of the banns. It puts our backs to the wall now that he's in a position of power." Lach sighed and swiped a beignet off my plate.

I swatted his hand. "Hey. Get your own."

"Consider it compensation."

I narrowed my eyes. "Compensation for what?"

"Coming to your aid last night."

I knew from the way he smirked that he wasn't talking about the redcaps.

"I have no idea what you're talking about." If he was going to play coy and spend the whole morning spewing innuendo, I would do same. "I don't remember *you* coming at all."

An oversight I was dying to remedy.

He stepped closer and took another bite of his beignet. I was too busy watching his mouth to protest this time. "I probably won't see you for a couple of days."

"What?" I blurted out. "Why?"

"Ritual fuckery, remember? He'll use the handfasting to his advantage, so we will be fighting over terms, with Oberon and Aurora mediating." He shoved the rest of the beignet in his mouth. "There'll be meetings until we reach an agreement everyone can live with, and Bain will do everything he can to work every clause to his advantage, which means I need to be focused to protect our interests."

"And Ciara's interests?"

"Do you really think so little of me?" he asked softly. "Everything I do for my court is in the interest of my family. If the court is weak, they are exposed. She is exposed. Everything I care about is exposed. Protecting what matters comes at a price, princess." His eyes lingered, daring me to contradict him. "And no price is too great. Even personal happiness."

His words drew a line. I had no idea what side I stood on—in my mind or his.

"Even at the cost of what I want," he breathed, "which is why I'm going to need that necklace."

"What?" The question shot out of me.

"Just until a new agreement is reached with the Infernal Court. You no longer need a way to reach the court every night anyway." He paused as if waiting for an objection, but I was too dumbfounded to come up with one. "I've already spoken with my siblings. Someone will accompany you when you leave the court so that there are no further incidents like the redcaps or other distractions..."

Distractions like being summoned to my bed. Heat flooded my cheeks as I unfastened the necklace and held it out. "You didn't have to come last night."

"Princess, I will always come for you." There was no mistaking the sinful promise in his silken voice as he took it from me. The words glided along my skin, activating every nerve, every neuron until my entire being was focused on him. "At least when you're in danger. But for now, I can't be distracted by how much I'd rather just be with you, and since I'm well-practiced at denying myself when it comes to you, I can do it a little longer. But I won't be able to stay away if you let me into that filthy, beautiful mind of yours again. I won't apologize for that, but I'd also prefer not to explain why I'm vanishing out of meetings."

I was going to combust. I swallowed in a pitiful attempt to wet my suddenly dry mouth and tried to respond casually. "No big deal."

"No big deal," he echoed, nodding slightly as he leaned closer, his breath tickling my ear as his cedar-and-spice scent hit me harder than ever before. "If you're going into the city, even with Ciara, I want you to take that gun. Purse or holster?"

Disappointment splashed in my stomach at the fact that the verbal foreplay was already over and we were back to practical concerns. "Purse, I guess."

"That's a shame." His nose touched the shell of my ear, and I shivered. "I would have liked to see where you would hide a holster."

"Maybe I'll change my mind." I shifted my body away and turned to face him, raising a brow. "Too bad you'll be too busy with all that ritual fuckery to find out."

His eyes glazed slightly, and my heart hammered at that naked desire. He raked a considering glance around the room. "Or I could just have you on that table and end their speculation once and for all. Then I wouldn't have to explain my priorities to anyone. Not after they saw how fucking perfect you are when you come."

I should not be so turned on by that option, but I found myself looking at the table anyway. His dark chuckle told me he was seriously considering doing just that when Roark sidled up to the buffet, giving each of us the side-eye in turn.

Lach snarled at him, but I only rolled my eyes as I picked up a new beignet, suddenly ravenous. If he could deny me, I was certainly strong enough to do the same. I smiled sweetly at Roark. "We were just finishing a negotiation."

Lach gritted his teeth. "I think we're far from settling anything."

But he had come when I commanded. So, let him go to his meetings and think about me, want me, crave me, because I decided the terms of *this* arrangement. "We settled it last night. Or I guess *I* did."

His face went utterly feral. I half expected him to pounce and make good on the table proposal.

Roark snorted, shaking his head. "If you two are going to mount each other, don't do it near open flames."

He might have a point.

I was already walking away, pausing to toss Lach a smirk of my own. "Enjoy your meetings."

I didn't bother to turn around. I didn't need to. I knew he was watching every step I took.

Lach might think he knew the only way to deal with the clover problem, and maybe he was right about needing ties with another court. But what would happen if things went south? If Bain refused to negotiate? It was shortsighted to only think in one direction when there were other options.

I dropped my plate off at the table, trying not to blush just at the sight of it, and glanced casually over my shoulder to find him gone—already off to deal with things the only way he knew how. I might be no closer to knowing exactly what Lach wanted out of the bargain between us, but I was beginning to understand what he needed. Giving it to him wouldn't free me, but it would free him. So, I made my way over to where Ciara was chatting with the others.

Titania scowled as I joined them, but I smiled and the sneer faltered. "Someone from your court was looking for you." I pointed over my shoulder, trying to look as innocent as possible so she wouldn't sense the lie.

"Who?"

"No clue." I shrugged. "Brown hair." Since that could be half of the Hallow Court retinue, it would buy me plenty of time to talk to the others before she gave up.

She groaned as she sauntered away. I waited until she was out of earshot before turning to the others.

Ciara's eyes narrowed. "Why do you look like you're plotting something?"

Because I was. I was taking a chance by involving them. "I think I have a solution to all of our problems, but I need your help." I glanced at Sirius. "Yours, too."

His violet eyes widened with surprise, and he looked to Ciara for instructions. She crossed her arms but finally nodded. "We're listening."

CHAPTER TWENTY-NINE

Haley had hesitated to let us work in the underutilized private laboratory reserved for the personal use of Gage associates until she saw Sirius. Apparently, the true gift of the fae was the ability to charm any human with a single smile. I couldn't blame her. I was hardly immune.

So, the three of us had spent the last week feigning shopping trips and lunches while Ciara ferried Sirius to the hospital every available hour and we worked on getting as many samples of clover for him to test as possible. She had even sacrificed her personal, century-old stash to the cause, ensuring we had a base specimen to compare the newer strains against, including the tainted product Lach had seized. I had no idea who she had sweet-talked into giving it to her against her brother's wishes, but I'm sure it was the result of that irresistible fae charm and her resolution to find a way out of her betrothal to Bain.

The morning of her handfasting ceremony—something she willfully refused to talk about—we were no closer to an answer. Sirius had stayed at the hospital, working overnight in a desperate attempt to find something useful. All of us were keenly aware that time was running out when we arrived to deliver coffee. No one stopped us as we cruised past the reception desk, but my heart sped up. I hoisted my new Gucci purse onto my shoulder, grateful no one had asked to look inside it. It was the least flashy option that had arrived at my room a few days earlier, along with a box containing my own 9-millimeter and a very convincing note from Lach. After the redcap attack, I'd decided he was right, but I didn't like it.

But even with the gun weighing down my handbag, I was more worried about Ciara. I stole glances at her every few steps.

"I'm not going to snap," she hissed as I scanned us through the rear security doors that opened into the emergency room.

I schooled my features into mild surprise. "I never said you were."

She huffed. "I know when I'm being watched. I have everything under control."

In fairness, Ciara's yellow Porsche was parked haphazardly in the ambulance bay, so close to the entrance that someone was likely to give it emergency resuscitation. I'd bitten my tongue, knowing no one would tow a vehicle registered in her name. Still, her erratic behavior worried me. The fact that she wouldn't talk about it only deepened my anxiety.

But she paused a few feet from the lab. "I'm sorry. I have a temper sometimes."

"It's cool." I had tried to shoot Lach when he tricked me into a bargain. I had no idea how she was keeping herself this calm in the face of marrying a man she didn't love. In fact, it was increasingly clear that she loathed him.

She let out a rough snort. "Fae *all* have tempers. Luckily, mine cools off the fastest. My mother used to say I was a firecracker and Shaw was a pistol and Fiona was a blizzard."

I couldn't stop myself. "And Lach?"

"Lach is a bomb." Her mouth twisted into a grim line. "That's why he stays away from the rest of us. He's afraid he'll go off."

A wet, dark alley flashed to mind. The only time I'd truly seen him lose control. That night, he'd slipped that delicate—but always dangerous—leash he kept on himself.

"You know he loves you, right? All of you?" I wasn't sure why I said it. Maybe because as someone who'd never had her own family, I couldn't bear to see the strained relationship between them all.

"Oh, I know that. I just wish he trusted us more." Her eyes

darted to me as we continued toward the lab. "After our parents died, it was his job to protect us. He's so worried that he'll lose one of us, too, that he's forgotten how to do anything else."

And the result was crazy ideas, like marrying his sister to another court and telling himself it was a solution when I suspected that the situation in his city made him believe he would eventually fail her, too. I still didn't know how their parents had died. Only what Sirius had told me about the war. None of them talked about their deaths. It had been decades ago, but I suspected that wasn't very long to immortals.

We found Sirius hunched over a microscope, but Haley stopped us before we made it past the lab's threshold. "I would advise you to come back later." She collected the cup of coffee we'd brought him. "I'll give this to him. Later."

"Is something wrong?" I squinted over her shoulder, trying to see what he was working on.

"He bit my head off fifteen minutes ago for saying good morning."

The three of us shared a look. It was impossible to imagine him doing that.

"He's tired," Haley explained. "I know this is important, but he needs a break before he actually breaks." We'd shared enough of what we were doing to secure her support. As far as she knew, he was looking into trinity in an attempt to find a better treatment for overdoses, working to isolate whatever had tainted the strain. None of us had let the word "magic" slip, so Haley thought Sirius was a genius scientist visiting from Prague.

But despite working around the clock in the underutilized lab, we were running out of time to find answers and both of my friends were on the verge of collapse. So much for my brilliant plan.

"And"—Haley continued—"Garcia keeps trying to give him lab work to do. He's going to figure it out, but I'm not sure how much longer you guys have. We're only getting away with it because Sirius is squeezing in the lab work. But if Garcia realizes what Sirius is actually doing, he's going to call Lachlan Gage. So I have to ask.

Does he know what you're up to?"

"Let me worry about Lach." He might be a bomb, but I knew exactly how to defuse him.

Haley and Ciara shared a knowing look. "Still refusing to admit you two are dating, eh?"

"We aren't." Not exactly a lie. I hadn't seen him for more than five minutes at any given time in the last week. Although he'd made very good use of those five minutes each and every time, that hardly qualified as courtship.

Ciara snorted, hitching a thumb at me. "Look at that stupid grin. She crossed that bridge and burned it behind her. She is fucked."

That snapped me out of my daze. "I already told you that—"

"I didn't mean literally." She looped her arm with mine, but she winked at Haley. I'd grown used to Ciara and Haley discussing my sex life like it was a matter of public record. Nothing I said dissuaded them, and it had brightened Ciara's mood.

"Just invite me to the wedding." Haley paused, biting her lip. "Has your brother called you back?"

My stomach began to churn as I shook my head. I'd been calling and texting Channing since I discovered he was out, but he was clearly ignoring me.

She shot me a sympathetic smile. "He'll come around. Don't worry." Haley glanced at the coffee cup she was holding and cringed. "I guess I should try to drop this off. Maybe I'll just slide it on the table and run."

We took her advice and left before she even attempted the delivery. Ciara teased me relentlessly about my relationship status as we returned to her Porsche, but she grew quiet again on the way back to the court. Her driving was erratic and fast—very fast—but, thankfully, she kept her eyes on the road. I checked my seatbelt as she raced past a twenty-mile-an-hour speed limit sign.

She finally broke the silence as the car skidded through a left-hand turn. "Why do you act like nothing is going on with you and my brother around her?"

I blinked, surprised she was worried about my...whatever this thing was with Lach. "Haley doesn't know what you are."

"And what are we? Charming? Gorgeous? Talented?" She flashed a dazzling smile in my direction.

Apparently, egotism ran in the family, but I grinned anyway. "Fae."

"Oh, that." Ciara laughed, glancing out the window with a breezy shrug. "Why does that matter?"

I didn't know where to begin with that question. There were a million reasons why it mattered that he was fae—a million reasons we would never work. But I knew she was talking specifically about why I wouldn't talk about him with my human friends. "Because it's hard to talk about him like he's human. If I slip and say the wrong thing, she'll know something is up."

"So, you're just going to act like you two aren't together." She rolled her eyes, reaching to fiddle with the radio station.

Well, there was no other way to interpret that. "I don't think anything about us qualifies as being 'together,'" I said with air quotes. Nothing had happened. Not really. *Not for lack of trying*, a little voice said in the back of my head, and I told it to shut up. "We just have a bargain."

"I seem to recall something happening last week."

She tossed a saucy smile at me.

"And nothing has happened since." Almost nothing.

"Every time I see *him*, I smell *you*." She scrunched her nose.

"He's always in meetings." I tried and failed to sound nonchalant. "Sometimes we run into each other in the hall."

Her eyebrows lurched up, something triumphant lifting the corners of her mouth. "When you say *run into each other*—is it against the wall, like repeatedly, without clothes on?"

I wished. "I don't kiss and tell."

"Look, I'm all for it. Nobody needs to get laid more than Lach."

I bit my lip, torn between saying something that would only lead to more questions and wanting to ask one of my own. Curiosity won out. "Does he…not…often?"

Her eyes flashed from the road to me. "If you're trying to ask if he sleeps with a lot of women, yes and no."

Only half of that was the answer I was hoping for. I swiveled in my seat to face her entirely. "What does that mean?"

"He goes through periods," she said, shrugging. "Lots of hookups. Nothing serious," she added quickly, as if this mattered to me. "Absolutely no one since he made that bargain with you."

"He must be getting off on pissing *me* off," I grumbled.

"I think that's only part of it," she said with a laugh.

I couldn't believe I was about to go there, but I couldn't stop myself. "So has he had *any* serious relationships?"

Her smile was now saucy with an extra side of sauce. Great. "Not for, like, a century."

My heart clanged at this piece of information—both the reminder of how old he was and how long it had been since he'd cared about someone. "And I thought *I* was having a dry spell."

"He likes you," she said, eyes darting over to me again, "and I think you like him, too."

"I can't decide if I like him or if I want to kill him." That was true, at least.

"Now I'm beginning to wonder if you're in love with him."

I patted her shoulder. "I'm starting to worry about what you look for in a relationship."

"I see the way he lights up when he looks at you," she said, sailing past my joke. "And how do you explain the way he's acting?" She dangled the question without explanation. The trap was obvious. If I really didn't care about him, I wouldn't press her to explain what she meant. It wouldn't matter to me how he was acting. There was only one problem...

I took the bait. "How is he acting?"

She smirked. "Like he's off the market."

Before I could tell her she was imagining things—as much for my benefit as her clarification—a call came over the speaker. My heart skipped when I saw his name on the touch screen.

"Speak of the devil." She accepted the call. "We were just talking about you."

I cringed, sliding down in my seat and praying she didn't tell him why we were talking about him.

But Lach was not in a playful mood. "Can I assume my...Cate is with you?"

My *what*? What was he about to call me? Why had he paused? Had any simple question ever raised so many other questions?

She wiggled her eyebrows at me. "Yes, she is." She shot me a look.

"How far are you two from home?" Annoyance seethed in his voice. "Where are you?"

Ciara cursed, and I knew she was thinking what I was. Had our luck run out at the lab? Because he sounded pissed, and I couldn't think of anything I'd done to upset him today.

"What's wrong?" I cut in. I was already at my overanalysis quota for the day. I didn't need to spend the rest of the drive home obsessing over why he was angry.

"Your brother just walked into the lobby of the Avalon and threatened the first person he saw, who just so happened to be Bain."

Shit.

"In front of every other court."

Double shit.

"I'm on my way home," I promised, suddenly thankful for Ciara's lead foot.

"I'd hurry." His voice was strained. "I might have promised not to hurt him, but I can't vouch for Bain. We're in my office."

What the hell had Channing done now? The call cut off, and I turned to Ciara. "How fast does this thing go?"

Considering she was already clocking eighty according to the speedometer, her blinding smile made my stomach flip. She didn't speed up. "Unbuckle."

"That seems like a terrible idea." But she was already reaching over to do it for me.

"Trust me," she said, clicking the release on my seatbelt. I tried to stop the sash as it slithered off my shoulder, but her hand lifted, fingers poised to snap. "By the way...girlfriend."

"What?" I blurted out, preparing for whatever fresh hell nipping from a speeding car would bring.

"When he said *my*, he was about to follow it with *girlfriend*."

Before I could shake my head, before I could quash the surge of hope I felt at her words, Ciara snapped her fingers. The world warped, and I found myself in front of a familiar desk with four enraged fae staring back at me in the dim, smoke-filled room.

CHAPTER THIRTY

"Cate, thank God!"

I spun to face him as Channing threw his arms around me. Despite our audience, I returned the hug, relieved that he was in one piece. The last time I'd seen him, he was in a hospital bed, and if his behavior was any indication, he was angling for a return trip. He winced, and I drew back, searching him for signs that he had been injured. His T-shirt was slightly wrinkled but clean. There were no visible bruises. It even looked like he'd finally gotten a haircut. The job Lach had gotten him was clearly good for him. I released a sigh I hadn't realized I'd been holding.

"You're okay," I breathed.

"Yeah, but I'm still a little sore." He nodded to his shoulder.

My relief vanished, his healing wound a reminder of how we'd gotten into this mess in the first place. Despite everything I'd done to keep him away, he'd already come back looking for trouble. "Channing, what the hell are you doing here?"

He glanced at the others. "I could ask you the same thing."

"You haven't returned my calls." Although I probably would have avoided telling him where I was if he had.

"Maybe if you had bailed me out—"

"We should give them some privacy," Aurora interjected loudly. She offered a sympathetic smile as she ushered Bain and Oberon out of the room. I wondered if Channing reminded her of Sirius, if the show of empathy was one sister supporting another. I nodded my gratitude to her as she stepped out.

Lach stood and circled the desk, not following them. I glared at him, but he simply raised a finger and sent the door slamming shut. He crossed his arms and leaned against the desk, inclining his head. Apparently, he was staying, but he was going to let me handle this.

"Please tell me that you didn't make a bargain with *him*." Channing threw a finger in Lach's direction.

I already knew this conversation was not going to end well.

"Channing..." I didn't know what to say. I shot a beseeching look at Lach, my eyes flicking toward the door, but his face remained stoic. He knew what I was asking him to do. He just wasn't going to do it.

Channing cursed, and my head whipped back to find him studying us. His shoulders crumpled at whatever he saw, and he staggered to the nearest chair, sinking into it as he hung his head. "Please tell me it isn't true."

I took a deep breath, reminding myself that he was the entire reason I'd made this bargain in the first place. Somehow, remembering that made it both easier and harder to refuse his request. "I can't."

His spine curved, the truth bowing him as he began to shake. I reached to rub his back, but he threw me off with a choked curse. Before I could come up with the right thing to say, Channing popped to his feet, more curses falling from his lips as he began to pace.

Lach straightened, ready to intervene, but I held up a finger of my own. He settled against the desk, tracking Channing's agitated steps.

My brother finally paused, dropping his head to stare vacantly at the floor. "What happened to staying away from the Gages?"

"*One* of us didn't do it," I bit out. Staying composed was the best way to calm him, but I refused to act like I'd done something wrong.

"Why the fuck would you get involved with them?" His eyes were clear as he whirled on me, but something wild moved through them before he resumed his desperate vigil. "I told you I had it handled." He threw a scowl in Lach's direction. "What did you do?"

"We have a bargain." There was no reason to lie to him. There was no reason to believe I would break the bargain with Lach. I didn't have an answer to his riddle. I hadn't even been looking.

He stopped and stared, horrified. "You know what they are." He moaned. "I tried to warn you."

But he hadn't—had he? I thought back to his reaction in the hospital, how he kept trying to say something and couldn't.

I turned on Lach. "He tried to tell me you were fae the night he was shot, but he couldn't. Why?"

"Humans bound to the court through magic cannot speak of it," he admitted.

Channing had known and couldn't warn me, and then he had gotten released from jail—because Lach had intervened—only to find me here with a man he considered a monster. I wrapped a hand around my throat as I considered what it must look like to my brother.

"What is he making you do?" Channing returned his attention to the ground, too disgusted to look at me.

"Nothing, really." The last thing I wanted to do was explain our complicated relationship to Channing in front of Lach.

"Don't lie to me," Channing growled. "That asshole doesn't do anything unless it benefits him."

"*That asshole* is standing right here," Lach reminded us.

We both ignored him. I fluttered a hand, trying to act as casually as possible. "It's nothing."

"What's *nothing*?" Channing demanded. "What did you give him?"

The best thing I could do was convince Channing that there was no issue. The deal was done. The bargain had been made. I belonged to Lachlan Gage, and there was nothing that could be done about it. "I come here at night and stay until morning."

It wasn't the time to explain the banns and Ciara's betrothal or that I slept down the hall from the man he considered a monster. But I wouldn't lie to him.

The blood drained from his face, and he stumbled a step before catching himself on the back of a chair. "You have to spend the night with him?"

I hadn't considered how it would sound to him.

"Not like that," I said a little too quickly.

"What is it like?" Channing asked, suspicion seeping into his voice.

"We hang out." Not exactly. "I make his life a living hell, and he annoys the shit out of me."

Displeasure flattened Lach's mouth at this description of our arrangement, but he remained silent.

A storm brewed in my brother's blue eyes as he scrutinized my face. "That's all? There's nothing more between you two?"

I swallowed. He didn't need to hear that Lach knew how I tasted or that I knew how good his cock felt in my hands. Nope. That was on a need-to-know basis, and nobody, *especially* my brother, needed to know. "I can take care of myself."

Channing winced, pressing his fingers to his temple like he'd heard what I refused to admit.

"For how long?" he asked in a voice so soft it made me go completely still.

"Until morning," I repeated.

He shook his head, panting slightly. "How long do you have to keep doing this?"

I licked my lips, peeking to find Lach silent and stone-faced. "Technically or realistically?"

"How long, Cate?" Channing demanded.

"Until he decides to release me." It was close to the truth, and it was going to be easier for him to swallow than the actual terms of our arrangement.

His breath sawed in and out of him, his chest heaving. He turned to Lach. "Release her and I will do anything—"

"Don't you dare," I cut him off before he ruined his own life. "This was my decision to make."

But Channing shook his head again. "Like hell it was. You did it because of me. Now let me undo it."

I whipped toward Lach. "Stay out of this," I warned my... whatever he was.

Channing turned to him, but he didn't advance. "Let her go." His voice shook, his lower lip trembling. It wasn't a demand. It was a plea. "I'll do whatever you want. I'll live in the Otherworld. I'll do whatever you ask."

I clapped a hand over my mouth, barely choking back a sob as Lach considered for a moment. His eyes found mine, and he shook his head. "Tempting, but no. Your sister is much prettier. I think I'll keep her."

I closed my eyes, a single tear escaping, and begged the universe to intervene.

"You son of a bitch!" Channing started toward him, but Lach just lifted his hand and studied his nails. And Channing froze. From the unnatural position of his body, I knew magic was involved.

I sighed, swiping angrily at my weepy eyes. I should have forced my brother to leave. Of course he was going to make this worse. "Lach, don't," I murmured.

Lach checked his fingernails, not looking at either of us. "Your concern for your sister is admirable, but I assure you, she's perfectly safe with me."

"Bullshit," Channing said through clenched teeth as though even his jaw refused to move. "No one is safe with you."

Shadows flooded Lach's eyes, and I knew the barb had struck. "I have offered her a place to stay, entertained her, and *enjoyed her company.*"

I was going to kill him. There was no mistaking the implication of his words.

When Channing finally dared to speak, every word was pained. "You said you didn't have to sleep with him."

Lach smirked. "She doesn't *have* to—"

"Stop!" I yelled, thoroughly done with both of them. "I have done nothing I did not want to do since I made the bargain with Lach." I swiveled my attention from Channing to Lach. "And stop trying to screw with his head. This is not one of your fae pissing contests, and I am not a prize."

A muscle ticked in Lach's jaw like he was biting back a response. At last, he shrugged. It wasn't quite the acquiescence I was looking for, but it was something.

"Now release him," I said softly.

"Are you going to behave?" Lach asked my brother in a mocking tone.

Channing just stared at him.

Something snapped inside of me. *"Now."*

Lach groaned and waved one hand. "Get out of here before I regret my benevolence."

"What benevolence?" Channing wilted as the magic released him. He glowered at us as he started backing toward the door, his attention bouncing between Lach and me as if he was debating what he should do: listen to the command of the fae prince or look out for his sister.

"Go." I sighed. "I will be okay. I can handle this dick." But Channing hesitated, so I crossed the room and took him by the shoulders. "You don't have to worry about me," I whispered.

His sliding throat told me he didn't believe a word I was saying. He'd made it one step outside, his hand still on the door, when Lach called after him, "Channing, your sister offered her life for yours."

"I didn't ask—"

"That doesn't matter," he broke in. "I will not touch you. That is part of our agreement. But I cannot stop another family from killing you if you're stupid enough to insult them. So before you threaten another fae, remember that your sister will still be indebted to me. Have enough fucking respect to remember that in the future."

Channing blanched as he realized what he'd nearly done. "I wasn't thinking—"

"Precisely," Lach sneered. "So where your sister is concerned, it's better if you let me do the thinking."

I was definitely going to kill him. I pointed at the door. "Channing, get out of here before you're a material witness."

Lach lifted a brow. "We're back to threats?" He groaned as my

eyes narrowed. "On second thought, let me give him a ride home."
He snapped his fingers, and Channing vanished.

I whirled around like my brother might reappear. "Where did
you send him?"

"The best place for him. A jail cell."

I hated that he had a point, especially until Bain forgot the
insult. "You didn't!"

"They'll let him out." He beckoned me with his finger.

I just stared back at him. "What are you doing?"

"Kiss and make up?" he suggested.

My blood heated, but I didn't move. "We have to fight first."

He sighed and picked up an apple from the bowl on his desk.
His sharp teeth snapped its flesh as he nodded.

"You had no fucking right." My voice trembled, but I was past
giving a shit.

His hand dropped to his side, the apple forgotten as his eyebrows
shot up. "No fucking right to what? Save your brother's life?"

"To...*insinuate* that something is going on between us." I paced
the path Channing had worn into the rug—well out of Lach's reach.
I didn't trust him to keep his hands to himself, and I needed to
maintain a clear head.

"Something *is* going on between us," he said slowly.

"Yes, you own my soul," I shot back, "so I'm forced to live here."

His nostrils flared, twin veins straining in his neck. "Any closer
to figuring out my end of the bargain, Cate?" His tongue licked
his lower lip. "Are you trying to figure it out when my fingers are
between your legs? Or when you spend all day with my sister? When
you sleep in the safety of my home? Eat my food? Are you any closer
to breaking it when you kiss me? When you tell me you're coming
home?"

Angry words with an undercurrent of accusation that cut
through me. Because he was right. I had stopped trying and I had
started trusting—the biggest mistake of all. And now, as that sharp
truth sliced straight to my heart, I refused to let him see me bleed.

"So you think that gives you the right to brag to my brother about it? Because you own me? Because you've stolen half my life from me? Tell me, Lach, what choice have you given me?" He shifted, his hands clutching his desk with such force that it splintered like he'd done to my bed. I flinched at the sound, but I didn't stop. "What about Ciara? And Shaw? Can I learn how to love my brother by watching you ruin your family's lives like you ruined mine?"

The words were out of my mouth, flung without thinking and impossible to take back. He flinched as they hit their mark. His knuckles blanched white, the wood creaking under his grip.

Lach released the desk, and I froze, waiting for him to stalk toward me, for him to... I had no idea what he would do to me. But he simply straightened, his voice dull. "I told you I would ruin you." He checked his watch, but he didn't look at me, didn't move toward me. "I have a meeting."

He vanished without another word. I stood there long after he was gone, those hollow words replaying in my head on repeat with my own.

Then ruin me.

I had granted him permission, but I had not realized how he would do it. He had ruined me in a way that I didn't quite understand. Because he was right. I wasn't looking for a way out of the bargain. I was working to help his court, to help him. I slept in a bed he owned, wishing he was in it with me. I laughed with his sister and groaned at his brother's jokes. I came home to this place, to them, to a family, to *him*.

Tears slipped down my cheeks as I stared at the empty space where he'd been moments ago, the fight echoing in the cavernous vacancy he'd left in place of my heart.

We'd ruined each other.

CHAPTER THIRTY-ONE

I avoided everyone for the rest of the day, but I couldn't escape my own head. I'd figured out a thing or two about fae bargains in the last few weeks. Lach had sworn not to harm Channing, but it was stupid to assume that promise extended to other fae, even those under his direct command. And when he'd warned Channing that our bargain would hold even if something happened to my brother, I'd realized how foolish I had been.

Still, no one had touched Channing, even when he stormed into the Avalon and threatened an Infernal Court prince. Because Lach had protected him, even though that wasn't part of our arrangement. Lach had done it for me, and I had thanked him for it by directing the anger and disappointment I felt with myself at him.

Because I'd given up on trying to break the bargain.

Because part of me didn't want to break it, and instead of admitting that to myself, I'd thrown our bargain in his face.

Because the ruin he promised was something more terrifying than I could ever have anticipated. It was a family, a home, a million tiny things I'd never allowed myself to have. He had ruined my isolation, my fear, my ability to see a future where I didn't want *more*.

And while he had clearly stepped out of line with Channing, he wasn't the only one who had been wrong.

So I dressed for the event that evening alone while working up the courage to apologize. All I knew about the handfasting ceremony was that each court would be there to bear witness, so I dressed in Nether Court green. No one had instructed me to do so, and I wondered if Lach would object after this morning's argument. If he would even look at me. But it felt right to represent his court—the one that was beginning to feel like my own.

My gown's filmy fabric, spun from emerald and obsidian threads, was tailored tightly in the bodice to lift my breasts, twin straps woven of pure gold keeping them covered. The dress cinched my waist before loosening into several overlapping panels that brushed the floor while allowing my legs to slip through. I pulled my hair up in a loose twist, applying smoky shadow to my eyes before I swept them with ruthless strokes of coal-black liner and painted my lips crimson. And when I looked into the mirror, I saw a creature fit to stand beside the Nether Court's prince. If he would have me.

Lach had failed to return my necklace, so when the clock told me it was time, I made my way into the foyer of the shared floor. Roark leaned against the table in its center, playing a game on his phone. He glanced up and froze. I cringed, looking down to see what was wrong, half expecting to find toilet paper on my shoe.

But Roark held up his hand, eyes widening. "You're going to be the death of him tonight." He grinned and extended an arm. "I promised I'd get you to court, but I need to stop in the lobby and speak with the guards on duty."

I nodded, looping my arm through his as the lump in my throat swelled. Maybe Lach planned to pawn me off on everyone else this evening, starting with his penumbra.

"Let's take the old-fashioned way." Roark pressed the down button on the elevator panel. The doors slid open instantly, and he held an arm out to keep them open. "After you."

I was holding back tears as I stepped into the compartment.

Roark surveyed me as he punched the button for the lobby. "Want to talk about it?"

I lifted a brow in surprise at his offer. We'd never spent a lot of time together, so either my feelings were written all over my face or Lach had told him why he would be chaperoning my arrival to the Nether Court this evening. I wasn't sure which option sounded worse. "Just wondering if Lach hates me after what happened with Channing this afternoon." Or, rather, what had happened after.

"Hate?" He chuckled softly. "I don't think Lach is capable of hating anything about you."

My heart jumped as I considered if he was right. Finally, I gulped. "I don't understand how he balances it all. The magic, the shadows, the pressure. I can barely handle one confrontation with my brother without wrecking everything."

"Lach fucks up plenty," he promised me. "But our world is light and shadow. *We* are light and shadow. They are the very elements of our magic. One cannot exist without the other. It is in *every* one of us. We have to embrace the balancing act even when it feels impossible. It's harder for those who sit on the throne. The light is stronger in those courts; the shadow's stronger in ours, in Bain's. As Lach's penumbra, I'm supposed to help him with that balance. Help him decide what choices he can live with and pray he's never forced to make one that he can't. But, really, it's all *any* of us can do, and if we're very lucky, we will find someone who helps us choose the right path and loves us when we don't."

I sucked in a breath at the implication of his words, at the intensity of the stare he pinned me with as though he was passing some invisible torch and waiting to see if I would accept it.

"I'm not sure I'm enough," I confessed as the elevator arrived on the lobby floor.

Roark pressed the button to hold the doors closed. "He thinks you are, and even if you aren't, he wants you anyway." He offered me a small smile. "Besides, that balance and acceptance bit works both ways, *princess*," he added with a wink.

I swallowed, digesting what he'd said. "Thank you."

"It's my job to look out for him, for *both* of you."

I cocked my head, realizing that maybe that was why Roark had been keeping such a close eye on us. "Is that why you've been... *interrupting* us?"

He smirked, reminding me so much of Lach that my heart hurt. Had they perfected that look together over their lifetimes? "You two were in way over your heads." His grin widened as I gaped at the fact that he would admit it. "Chaperoning you was all part of the job."

"But you stopped. What changed?" I needed to hear it from him, the person who knew him best, the shadow that was always watching and weighing.

He released the button, allowing the doors to slide open, but as he stepped to hold them for me, he whispered, "The way you two look at each other."

I stewed over his answer while he spoke with the guards stationed in the lobby. I was still thinking about it when we nipped to the Otherworld, arriving outside the Nether Court's ballroom.

The ballroom had been divided into four sections, each adorned with decorations that venerated the unique magic of an individual court. Tables and chairs had been placed for the visiting courts' respective guests. The light courts mingled on one side of the hall. The Astral Court's attendees were gathered around high-top tables and seats swathed in a palette of purples and blues as nuanced and lovely as the night sky that glittered above them. Stars sparkled over their heads, and as I watched, the moon at the center of the enchantment shifted slowly between phases, from waxing to full to waning again. The space next to them was covered in shades of pure ivory accented with gold. Starbursts illuminated the center of each table, lighting the faces of the Hallow Court fae as they visited with one another.

And on the far side of the ballroom, across from the light courts loomed their shadowed opposites. Crimson textiles hung over gold-lacquered chairs and tables, smoldering and flickering like fire. Even the members of the Infernal Court seemed to dance with the dark energy drawn from the molten magic that flowed below us.

But it was the final corner that beckoned me. Flowering ivy wove around the gleaming black chairs stationed in rows, the Nether Court requiring more seating than the others. But its darkness didn't hide the fae assembling there. Instead, the shadows wrapped around them, promising safe haven, shifting and clinging like those twisted vines.

Roark guided me to a seat in the front row of the Nether Court section before claiming the one next to it. The lights dimmed overhead and a hush fell over the assembled guests as a door opened to the ballroom.

Bain strode down the aisle that divided the Infernal and Hallow Courts. He was dressed in all black save for a slip of crimson silk tucked into the breast pocket of his tuxedo. The darkness of his attire accentuated his cold, chiseled features, and with his silver-white hair, he looked like he had been cut from ice. When he reached the open space in the center, another door on the opposite side of the room opened. Ciara and Lach stepped into view.

My friend had chosen a gown more demure than her usual style. Its ivory silk draped her loosely, gliding over her curves. It gathered in a twist at her throat. Ciara wore no jewels, and her face was fresh with only a pale blush swept over her cheeks and a slight shimmer of gold dust on her skin. She'd worn her hair in loose curls that cascaded down her back. She was astonishing, but it was the fae at her side who stole my breath.

Lach's classic tuxedo was cut to fit his muscular torso, the savage, hewn body beneath the fabric impossible to ignore. He'd slicked back his dark hair, showcasing his beautiful face and those glowing eyes. But his gaze was vacant, as haunted as I'd felt since this afternoon's argument.

The pair walked more slowly than Bain, as if both dreaded each step. Lach had mentioned that Bain suspected Ciara wasn't enthusiastic about the betrothal. Few would suspect after tonight. Most would know. But somehow Lach looked even less thrilled about the situation.

"Why is he going through with this?" I whispered to Roark. Looking up, I found his jaw clenched.

Roark's eyes followed Ciara, his voice low and strained when he answered, "Lach calculates his choices through suffering and loss. How much others will suffer, who deserves to suffer, who will lose, and what he can live with. But one person always suffers, always loses the most. He accepted that a long time ago. I think you were the first selfish decision he ever made."

I couldn't look away from Ciara's serene face or the fear shining in her eyes. "Can he live with this?"

"That remains to be seen. The handfasting may be a blessing."

"The magical prenup," I whispered.

He nodded, eyes still tracking Ciara as his prince delivered his sister to her fate.

When the pair reached Bain, Lach stepped between his sister and her betrothed and drew a corded length of golden rope from his pocket. He didn't speak. Instead, he handed the rope to Bain and backed away. As Bain moved forward, Ciara shuffled a bit closer to her fiancé.

A few people were murmuring around us, heads bent together in quiet conversations, and I wondered if I was the only one perplexed by the strangely silent ceremony.

"Okay, what is this?" I muttered. If no one was going to speak, I might need some subtitles.

"It's an old custom, extending back as far as our histories," he said quietly, but a few people around us turned ever so slightly to listen. "Back then, if two fae felt called to mate—"

"Mate?" I nearly choked.

"Mate," he repeated, the word low and gravelly. "Don't worry. For us, it's about more than sex. Mating is choosing to bond your soul permanently to another. If a couple felt compelled to do so, they would handfast." He nodded to Ciara and Bain, and as he did, she held out an arm. It trembled slightly as Bain wrapped the rope around it, crossing the cord several times loosely enough that it draped at her wrist. "Back then, for a year and one day, the couple would live together and wait for the magic to seal. If magic deemed them true mates—if it found their love to be selfless—the binding would become permanent, etched into their skin for the world to see, and their souls would be linked."

"She's linking her soul to his?" I hissed, wondering if I should run up there and put a stop to this, wondering why Lach hadn't already done so. This wasn't the casual, politically driven arranged marriage she'd been promised. What was Bain up to?

But Roark laughed, the sound hollow, as he pulled his gaze from the ritual to meet mine. "That kind of magic died long ago. I've never been to a handfasting that resulted in a mating bond, and I'm guessing neither of them is in danger of committing an act of selfless love."

He had a point. I settled into my seat, my eyes still glued to the wordless ceremony. Bain slipped his own hand past the loose rope he'd placed on Ciara, closing his fingers around her forearm. Ciara did the same to his. The crowd erupted in applause, but I only stared.

Roark grimaced. "And now we hope we find a reason to call this thing off."

I blinked at him. "What?"

"Nowadays, a handfasting is like a trial marriage. If either of them discovers an irreconcilable reason to break their public pledge of intent, the entire thing is dissolved. If they had gone through with the banns and been married, there was no way out for either of them."

It was almost like Bain had done Ciara a favor, although I couldn't imagine why. Maybe he really believed Lach had tried to poison them with that clover. Or maybe he was up to something. But now Ciara had a way out, unless…

"What if magic seals their bond?" I asked, my stomach twisting as Bain untied the rope to reveal fresh tattoos inked where the rope had bound them.

"It won't." He shook his head with a tired sigh. "Like I said, that sort of magic is long dead. There is a spell on the rope, though; hence the tattoos. If one of them declares just cause, the spell will determine if it's true and release them both."

But even with that huge loophole, Ciara looked a bit green as Bain lifted her hand for all to see the marks they bore. More applause erupted, and soon a line began to form, every guest joining it to speak with the couple.

I imagined that the only thing worse than being stuck in a trial marriage for a year and a day was pretending to be happy about it while well-wishers fawned over you.

"Get me up to the front?" I asked Roark. He glanced at Ciara and nodded with grim understanding.

We pushed through the crowd, no one raising a complaint when they saw the Nether Court penumbra at my side. I waited to allow Aurora to finish offering her best wishes before I rushed forward and gave Ciara a huge hug, whispering, "Do you need me to kidnap you? Because I will get you out of here."

She giggled a little and squeezed me more tightly. "I'm fine. Honestly. I have a whole year now." So she did intend to find her own way out of the handfasting. "But can you save my brother? He's in a mood."

It wasn't the time to tell her that I was likely responsible for his melancholy. I pulled away, promising to do so, before I offered Bain a limp congratulations. Roark waited off to the side, chatting with Shaw, so I started toward him to inform him of my new mission, but he nodded to the bar in the corner. Glancing over, I spotted Lach leaning against it. I mouthed a "thank you," and Roark bowed before turning to speak to Shaw.

Each step I took in Lach's direction tightened my nerves. By the time I slipped up to the bar and ordered a single glass of ambrosia, I was wound tenser than a spring.

Lach finally looked at me, but he didn't speak. Quiet but not angry. No, the shadows in his eyes had nothing to do with me. I considered reaching for his hand, but I held back. Maybe I wasn't the person he wanted to comfort him. Who could blame him after earlier? For a moment, we simply stared at one another, daring the other to break the silence.

It didn't have to be complicated. One of us just had to say something. "The ceremony was…"

I couldn't finish the thought, couldn't force myself to act like I was happy about it.

His jaw worked for a moment like he was chewing on his response. "I'm not a big fan of handfasting." He downed his remaining drink in a single swig. "Either way, it delays the inevitable." He glanced around the room and let out a long sigh. "But I think I'm the only one who isn't swooning. I feel like I'm ruining the party."

Maybe it was the honesty of his response that clicked some missing piece into place. Tonight's ceremony was about politics and plotting. Maybe with us, it could just happen. Maybe we didn't have to know where it was leading. And maybe we didn't have to plan for a worst-case scenario. Maybe I could just be here with him and let the rest figure itself out. No magical escape clause necessary.

So, I took his hand, my fingers wrapping around his. "Then let's get out of here."

CHAPTER THIRTY-TWO

I didn't wait for him to agree as I tugged him toward the exit, afraid I would lose my nerve. But as soon as we were in the corridor outside the ballroom, I paused, uncertain where I should take him. I'd spent more time at the Avalon than in the actual court, and this place was a veritable labyrinth.

"I might get us lost," I warned him.

He laughed—not quite warmly, but it was a good sign. "Come on."

My heart pounded as our footsteps echoed through the hall, and I wondered where he was taking me; if he'd had enough of waiting, too; if I would find myself in his bed. But he led us through the winding passages and down a set of spiraling stairs, into a conservatory crowded with towering plants and vines and riotous blooms. Its greenhouse walls were rounded, curving into a glass dome overhead. Moonlight glimmered through it, reflecting off the glass like a celestial crown and casting its sparkling light over the velvet petals and dappled flora surrounding us. The scent of damp soil and florid perfume hung in the warm air, so sultry that I felt sweat bead along my forehead.

Lach continued forward, through the plants, and led us out a set of doors at the far end. He released my hand as we stepped onto a stone balcony. Night wrapped around us, the sky overhead a sheet of inky black without a star in sight, making the sliver of moon at its center all the brighter. He walked to the railing and looked into the endless dark stretching before us.

I moved next to him, curling my fingers over the stone balustrade as he had done. He stared into the darkness with haunted eyes. This was more than brooding. His mind was somewhere else, even though he was right in front of me.

"I'm sorry that I overstepped with Channing."

Surprise turned my head, and I studied him. The ethereal light caught the sharp angles and soft curves of his face, leaching the color from his skin. He looked like a masterpiece carved from the night, a man as constant and ever-changing as the moon itself. My mouth went dry as I considered how much more of him there was to discover, but I forced myself to swallow. "*I* let Channing down."

"By being involved with me." I knew he didn't mean the bargain but rather the undeniable attraction we'd been fighting since the beginning.

"By not keeping my word," I corrected him. "Channing and I promised to stay away from your family, but that promise was based on fear and gossip and hate." I brushed my pinky along his. It twitched, but his hand didn't move to take mine.

"And actions," he gritted out. "You made a promise based on my reputation."

"I didn't know you."

He cast a glance at me. "And you do now?"

Yes, but I wanted to know more. I wanted to hear the stories that shadowed his face. I wanted to memorize his body at night and wake up to his thoughts. I didn't want stolen nights. I wanted every day.

I braced myself and nodded. "I think I know why you helped Channing."

"I wanted to make something easier for you," he said after a moment.

Something fluttered in my stomach. "I don't need things to be easy."

He finally laughed, even if it sounded mildly irritated. He peered across his shoulder, eyes softening. "I know that, princess. I know you don't need things to be that way, but I *want* that for you. I want something to be easy. I know it never has been." He swiveled slowly as though afraid he might spook me. A shaft of moonlight caught his hair, but his face fell into shadow. "I want to take care of you. I know you don't need that," he added, preempting my usual arguments. "But someone should take care of you. You take care of everyone else."

Lach and I weren't so different after all. We gave everything— every ounce of ourselves—for the people we cared about. The realization curled through my body, warm and real and unexpected but not unwanted.

He cared about me. It wasn't just a bargain. It wasn't just a trick. And, in that moment, I realized that at some point I'd started caring about him, too. I drew a trembling breath.

I brushed another finger along his, something electric bolting through my skin. His eyes flashed to mine, his chest rising slightly. But still, he didn't take my hand.

"Why don't you like handfasting?" I asked.

"That's a long story." He tilted his head—an offer to tell that story. I'd spent the last few weeks wanting him, craving him, but resisting. Next to him, I couldn't remember why I'd fought those feelings. And when that resistance had vanished, so had the desperate, frantic urgency I'd felt after the Midnight Feast. I didn't have to steal as much of him as I could before he demanded the same of me. Not that the craving had dissipated. It was still there. The moment he touched me, it would return, as forceful and undeniable as ever. But I no longer wanted pieces of him. I wanted all of him.

The night had cooled, and I shivered slightly. Lach frowned and waved a hand. Instantly, the air around us warmed, as though he'd placed us within our own private, perfect bubble.

"Thank you," I murmured softly. He blinked, relief flashing across his face, as if he'd half expected me to argue to freeze to death.

"I'm really hard to put up with, aren't I?" I asked with a laugh.

"No." He answered too quickly.

"That's a yes." I took a deep breath and offered a confession of my own, hoping it would encourage the same. "It's hard for me to depend on people."

"Yeah, I get that." His smile was careful, like perhaps he also sensed we were on the brink of change. "I tend to decide what other people need on their behalf."

"You don't say?" I teased lightly, playfully. Not to pick a fight, but rather to reassure him.

"My parents made me promise to never handfast without meaning it."

My breath caught at the sudden shift in conversation.

He continued, "They believed in the old meaning of it." He paused as if realizing I didn't know about the custom.

"I asked Roark about it. He mentioned it was a mating thing."

He nodded, looking relieved that I already knew. "They were handfasted."

"Were they...mates?" I recalled what Roark had said about that magic being dead.

"I think so." Lach's eyes clouded. "There was no mark, no proof that magic had sealed them as mates. Sometimes I could swear I remember seeing one, but maybe I'm only imagining it. Maybe I just want it to be true." His brittle smile broke something inside me. "People say that it doesn't happen anymore, that mating bonds are dead, but a glamour could hide it. Sometimes I think they hid their mating bond but that I did see it."

I frowned. "Why?" Everyone in that ballroom had seemed overly enthusiastic about the handfasting, save for the people being joined together. "Why would they keep it a secret?"

"I suppose it's only necessary if you have something to hide, and my parents always had secrets. But I think for them, it was about keeping some small piece of their love to themselves. My father was the heir of the Nether Court and my mother the heir of the Terra Court until they were married. She abdicated her throne."

"Terra Court?" I searched my brain, trying to remember this. The Nether Court, the Astral Court, the Infernal Court, the

Hallow Court. Those were the ones I'd been told about, the ones in attendance tonight. Four courts in total. No one had ever mentioned a fifth.

"It's gone now. Destroyed in the war." He fell silent again, ghosts moving in his eyes, and I resisted the urge to ask more questions.

I had time to get my answers. Every night for the rest of my life.

Because standing with him in the moonlight, I knew that I would never break the bargain—even if I had the answer to his riddle.

I didn't care what Lach wanted as long as it was me.

"Sometimes the war feels like yesterday," he said after a moment.

I stared at him as what he was saying sank in. Despite the warming magic surrounding us, I clutched my arms tightly around my waist as I processed this. "You fought in the Second World War?"

His eyes lifted, set with grim determination. "Wouldn't you?"

I knew I didn't need to answer.

"My parents had moved their court to America long before it started, but when it did... The Terra Court was an earth court—the only one—and it was right in the middle of the fighting." I reached for his hand as he stared into the night. "We were all at the front, except Shaw. He was a kid. But even though my mother had abdicated, she couldn't stand by and do nothing, so my parents went to help."

"Good," I muttered.

A genuine smile ghosted across his face. "She would have liked you. They summoned Fiona home to stay with Shaw. I was stationed in France. I'd taken a bullet during a skirmish with German forces."

Another layer peeled back as I realized the scar on his shoulder was a brand not of iniquity but of bravery.

"I was recuperating at what doctors believed was a miraculous rate when the telegram arrived that Warsaw had fallen, along with every member of the Terra Court's royal bloodline *and* my father. I was called home to the Nether Court immediately, the throne passing to me in an instant. I never returned to the war."

"But *you're* of the Terra Court's royal bloodline."

"That's complicated." He grimaced, scrubbing a hand over his jaw. "When I arrived at court, there was a letter from my father, cautioning me to be careful if something happened to them, and…" Lach hesitated as if the memory was too painful to bear. I knew there was more to this story. He would share in time, and until then, I wouldn't push him for details. "The others wasted no time. Aurora wasn't there. She lost her parents at Terra, too."

Sirius had told me as much, but I merely nodded.

"No one had been happy about two heirs marrying each other. I guess they thought my parents might try to restore the titles of High King and High Queen and rule over every court. I'd barely read my dad's letter when Bain and Oberon showed up and demanded I choose a throne—the Nether Court or the Terra Court—and renounce the other bloodline."

Another impossible choice. No wonder he hated them.

"The Terra Court was in ruins. Everyone was dead. So, I took the Nether Court throne, and I decided I would rule by keeping emotions out of it. I would make the decision that was right for those under my protection." He raked a hand through his hair and released a heavy sigh. "And I've been fucking up that policy ever since. Fiona left because she had too much Terran in her. She never felt comfortable in the shadows. But Ciara and Shaw stuck around, which I've never understood."

Lach drank in the night air. "I've tried to keep them out of things, mostly because it's easier to make emotionless decisions when you don't care. But since I met you, since you begged for your brother's life, I've had to face the truth."

I raised my brows. "And what is that?"

"You fought for him, and I *understood* that. I *felt* the same— something I'd ignored for so long." He dragged a slow breath into his lungs. "I told myself that I listened to your plea because of the Equinox or because my mother would have wanted me to. None of that was it. I listened because you fucking *cared*, and gods, I'd forgotten what that looked like, what it *felt* like."

"But it's not why you made the bargain?" I guessed.

The corner of his mouth lifted, but he sounded hollow when he spoke. "Looking for the key to your freedom, princess?"

"No." I meant it.

"I made the bargain because I liked you *and* because you had something I needed." His eyes darted to mine. "And within fifteen minutes of knowing you, I thought I'd made a terrible mistake."

Laughter burst out of me. "The feeling was mutual." Our relationship had started based on trickery, but that didn't have to continue. It couldn't if this was going anywhere. So I made a confession of my own. "I spent all week thinking about you. I've never let a man get close to me. I mean, I've had sex," I added quickly, biting back a smile when he growled a little. "I kept telling myself that was all this was between us, and when Channing showed up today and called me out, I panicked. Because if it was just something physical, I wouldn't have cared. I guess what I'm saying is that I'm new to *this*."

Whatever *this* was.

He held my gaze. "I've been dealing with a similar problem since the day we met."

I arched a brow, my heart pounding too hard for me to dare speak.

"I like you more than I planned," he confided.

I braced my hands on the railing to keep my legs from giving out. "That feeling is mutual, too."

"Cate, there's a reason I keep a distance from people. It's safer for them. Not everyone believes I won't go after the Terra Court, even all these years later." His eyes skirted to the darkness, looking past it to that faraway place where he had lost some piece of himself. "I can't. I shouldn't. *We* shouldn't. I'm sorry that I made that bargain, that I dragged you into this for my own selfish reasons."

"I don't want you to stay away from me."

He turned to me, something unreadable on his face. Tattoos flashed across his neck, his jaw, as if his thoughts were racing as rapidly as my heart. His throat slid, something desperate and hungry etched in his eyes. We were on very dangerous ground now. One wrong step and…

"You have no idea what you're saying," he murmured.

But I did. I took a step closer to him, and another, until there was no more distance between us. He sucked in a ragged breath, those green eyes searching mine for permission to cross that final line. Not just from me but from himself.

"How many times do I have to tell you I can take care of myself?" My hand fisted in his shirt. If he wouldn't cross the line, I would. "Now take me to bed."

CHAPTER THIRTY-THREE

I didn't have to ask twice.

Lach captured my mouth, a rough hand cradling one cheek, the other wrapping around my neck as though now that he had me, he wasn't letting go. This kiss was different. He clearly had been holding back before. And I gave in to his lips, to the ravaging sweep of his tongue over mine, to the urgency building between us.

His body was hard against mine, and I sank my fingers into his broad, muscled shoulders, urging him closer. With his mouth on mine, I couldn't remember why I had ever resisted him before, why I had ever thought this was wrong when it was so very right.

Lach's hands released my face to grip my hips, sliding lower to cup my ass and lift me off my feet, my legs circling around his waist as the kiss deepened. I was dimly aware of a spinning sensation that I thought was in my head until my back collided with glass. Its coolness made me wince.

He paused. "Do you want to stop?"

I knew he would stop despite the palpable need burning in his eyes. He would end this the minute I asked. I nipped his lower lip with my teeth and pinned him with a lingering look. "I don't want to stop."

He licked that lip like he was savoring the sting of my bite. I was going to devour him.

"Or we can lose the window?" he offered.

"I don't care as long as we start losing clothes," I snapped, earning a rough laugh. He pressed me harder against the window, his hips pinning me to it so his hands could join the fun. I moaned into his mouth, my palms splaying against the window, which provided a means to buck against him and discover he was rock fucking hard. I whimpered despite the layers of clothing between us and dragged myself along his impressive length.

He chuckled. "I thought you wanted me to take you to bed."

"Too far." I began unbuttoning his shirt.

His jaw worked, eyes darkening as my hands slipped under the fabric to run over his chiseled pecs before I peeled the shirt off entirely. "If you aren't careful, I'm going to fuck you right here."

"Here's good." I licked a whirling tattoo on his neck, earning a growl that sent heat pooling in my core. I was through fighting this, and I couldn't wait a minute longer.

His face dipped as he explored my neck with his lips, followed by his teeth and tongue, moving lower to my collarbone until I arched, pushing off the window to offer my breasts. Lach lowered the straps of my gown off my shoulders to free my breasts, and my nipples beaded in the cool night, the only signal that the magical warmth from earlier had faded. I was too on fire to care.

"Fucking perfect," he murmured and closed his mouth over one. A cry escaped me as his tongue flicked its tip before he began to lick and suck, my fingers fisting his hair as he feasted on me. With a low growl, he lifted bright eyes to mine. "I need more."

Before I could tell him that he could have everything, he'd lowered me to my feet and dropped to his knees before me, unbothered by the stone floor. Pushing aside the skirt's center panel of fabric, he groaned when he discovered my lack of panties. Earlier, I'd bemoaned the fact the dress didn't allow me to wear them. With Lach kneeling between my legs, looking utterly feral, I wondered if I'd bother to wear them ever again. The tattoos on his torso shifted slowly as he drank me in, deciding what to do with me.

"Spread your legs for me, princess." The roughness of the command scraped along my senses until I couldn't quite remember how to breathe, but I bit my lip and did as he asked. He finally looked up at me as he slid a finger along my seam, his mouth curling into a smirk at the wetness he found. "I can't stop thinking about how you taste." His tongue licked over his lower lip, and I whimpered. "You have no idea how hard it's been to keep my mouth off of you, how much I've wanted to feast on you."

I sucked in a shaky breath. "Buffet is open."

He grinned, plunging that finger inside of me so deeply that my body bowed off the window. My breath caught as he continued to pump, our gazes locking until his drifted down to watch his finger. I followed, choking back a sob of pleasure as I took in the dark fae prince at my feet, his hand between my legs, his lips so close that his breath whispered over my feverish skin. The finger disappeared, and I cried out in objection.

"Don't worry," he purred, his fingers splitting my seam and urging me open wider. "I'm going to take care of you."

And then Lach lowered his mouth and dragged his tongue up in one searing stroke. My knees buckled, my hands plastered against the glass to stay upright. Wicked eyes glinted up at me, his mouth disappearing entirely as his tongue speared me, claimed me, devoured me. He didn't slow when I began to shake, undone by the sight of him as much as his talented tongue. Instead, his arms hooked my thighs, and he yanked me closer, sucking and licking and consuming until my limbs tightened and I stopped caring about staying upright and gave in to him entirely.

An ache burst through me, splintering and dividing as he coaxed every last drop of pleasure he could. When I finally sagged, boneless and panting against the window, Lach pressed a kiss to me, and I yelped, still tender and sensitive.

He stood, his tongue sweeping the corners of his mouth, his eyes glittering like the night sky above us. "You belong in the Otherworld, princess, because I will never have my fill of you."

And I understood, because my body was ready again, craving him despite the toe-curling orgasm he'd just given me. My hand reached for the buckle of his belt, and his smile widened as he let me unfasten it.

"Has the bed offer been fully rescinded?"

"We're getting there." I freed his cock with a saucy grin of my own and bent to take him in my mouth.

Lach cursed as my lips closed over him, his fingers gripping my hair so tightly that my scalp hurt. "Don't rush," he said through gritted teeth as I circled his tip with my tongue. I lifted my eyes to him as I took him deep in my mouth. "Fuck. On second thought."

A moment later, I was in his arms. Gold shimmered around us, and then we were in his quarters at the Avalon. We only made it as far as the living room rug. Lach laid me across it and waved a hand at the hearth. A fire blazed to life, and I watched its light dance across him as he kicked off his shoes and reached for his pants. My heart pounded at the sight of his naked body, at the tattoos that covered him but didn't flash and change, as if his mind was finally completely quiet and he was acting purely on instinct. I'd had him in my mouth, but seeing him…his muscled form, the cock jutting out and ready, had me reaching for the zipper of my gown.

Lach was faster. He tore it clean down the front. "I'll get you a new one."

Apparently, panties weren't the only thing the fae liked to rip off. His mouth found mine as it fell away, and my skin sang as it met his, every nerve firing and throbbing where we touched. His fingers skimmed between my breasts, circling my nipples and pausing to flick them with a masculine grunt of satisfaction before they descended lower and he pushed two inside me, moving them slowly in and out, preparing me.

"Should I…?" He paused, his eyes meeting mine in question.

I could barely think with him touching me, barely process anything but the overwhelming need to have him buried inside me. But I knew what he was asking. "I'm on the pill."

"Thank the gods," he muttered, pulling his hand back and slicking himself with my wetness before moving between my thighs.

I wrapped my legs around him, gasping as his cock nudged against me. He paused, bringing his eyes to mine before sliding inch by glorious inch inside me. I arched into him, hooking my arms around his neck and welcoming him deeper.

Lach snarled his approval as he began to thrust slowly. "You feel even better than I fucking imagined."

His words sent a thrill shooting through me. Not because he'd hidden his desire—no, he'd been blunt about that for weeks—but because I felt it in his touch, saw it reflected in the way his eyes pierced straight through me.

"Kiss me," I whispered, nearly breathless as he thrust slowly in and out, each stroke deeper than the one before.

"You only have to ask." His mouth angled over mine, claiming my lips as he claimed my body in a steady, punishing rhythm. I'd never been with someone like this, so wholly that the entire world fell away and there was only him and us and nothing else mattered.

Lach's hand slid under me, holding me against him as he shifted back onto his heels until I was seated on top of him. His first thrust hit so deeply that stars wheeled in my vision, and a moan of pleasure broke free. He growled at the sound and unleashed himself, pounding into me as pleasure twisted my body into a knot, each stroke coiling me tighter and tighter until I unraveled around him. He buried his face in my neck and followed me, his hips thrusting up as he emptied inside me.

We collapsed into a pile of sweaty limbs, arms and legs and bodies still entwined. "That was…"

He kissed my forehead. Answer enough.

I snuggled against him, shivering slightly as my sweaty body cooled. His eyes narrowed, and he frowned. "You're cold."

"I'm perfect," I murmured dreamily. I never wanted this moment to end. Mostly because it was perfect, too. But also because I had no clue what happened next. It was exhilarating and terrifying, but in his arms, it didn't seem as scary.

For a few minutes, I lay there, tracing his tattoos with utter fascination. Lach detangled himself from me and pushed onto his feet. I was about to protest his sudden absence when he scooped me into his arms. He carried me to my room, laying me across the bed before disappearing into my closet, and I sprawled across the sheets, still shivering but hardly caring. Lach reappeared with a silk robe. He beckoned me to sit up. I groaned and pushed myself up, my languid limbs resisting the request for movement. He chuckled softly as he helped me into it and cinched the sash at my waist.

I climbed back into the bed, burrowing under the covers, but he remained standing.

"Stay," I said softly.

He hesitated.

"Unless I wore you out," I added dryly.

He snorted. "You just let me know when you're ready. I can go all night."

All night? I might test him on that.

Lach circled the bed, slipping in beside me. He rolled on his side, and I followed suit. For a moment, we just stared at each other, our hands creeping closer until his fingers swept over mine. His thumb paused on my ring. "Should I be jealous of whoever gave you this? You wear it all the time."

It was a tentative, guarded question, but something more than curiosity laced it.

"Nope. Unless you find dead women intimidating."

"Actually..." He flashed me a smile.

"It was my mother's. It's all I have from her. Gran told me to never take it off. The woman who took me in when I was a teen," I explained at his questioning look. "Other than Channing, she's the closest thing I ever had to a family. I kept it hidden in a bag before I came to live with her, but I think she knew I needed to finally feel safe enough to wear it. It's hard to explain."

"It wasn't safe to wear it?"

Another careful question. I took a deep breath, wondering if I wanted to wade into such deep waters tonight. But Lach had opened up to me. He had trusted me. He'd earned the same. "Before Gran, I'd been placed in a lot of homes. Once I hit my teens, I started staying out, getting into trouble, and it got harder to find someone who would take me. But somehow they found another family who was willing. They seemed completely perfect when I moved in." I drew a shuddering breath as unwanted memories resurfaced. Lach went very still, and I forced myself to continue. "I'd been in some rough situations before, but there was something about him that creeped me out. I thought if I just caused some more trouble, they would send me away like everyone else did. But when they found out, he decided to show me what happened to girls like me. He said I was asking for it. His wife found me after, begged me not to tell, but I told a teacher the next day. She didn't believe me, but she had to report it. They removed me to investigate and discovered the woman had covered up her husband's past."

Lach's breath sawed out of him, his eyes blazing. "What happened to him?"

"He went to jail for a while. He got out a couple of years ago. They felt the need to inform me." My voice cracked a little, and Lach pressed a hand to the side of my face, solid and reassuring.

"I'll kill him."

I knew he meant it. I swallowed, waiting to feel fear or resistance, but I felt nothing. I shook my head. "I made peace with it a long time ago." I had, but I'd never been the same. I bit down on my trembling lower lip before forcing my eyes to meet his. "No one in my life knows. Not Channing. *No one.* I don't want it to define me."

He remained silent for a moment, and I surged ahead, sniffing a little. "My case worker told Gran what had happened when they called to find a new placement for me. She made them bring me straight away. When I arrived, she took one look at me with such understanding. Later that night, she showed me to my own room with my own dresser. She tried to help me put my things away, but... that just felt too permanent. But something made me trust her—I think she might have been the first person I ever trusted—and eventually I showed her the ring. This one small thing I had left of my parents. Someone had taken it from the scene of the accident and sent it to the hospital with me." I swallowed. "Gran said I could choose to see it as a reminder of what I'd lost or proof that I had survived. I knew she wasn't just talking about the accident. And I decided to wear it."

A single tear slipped down my cheek. Lach caught it with his thumb, and I forced a smile that felt too fragile to trust with anyone but him.

"After that, I stopped getting in trouble, scared that I would get sent somewhere new, somewhere that I wasn't safe. Then Channing showed up and turned our world upside down, but it almost felt like having a family. I focused on school and got a scholarship. I spent my first two years of college reclaiming my body, deciding who I wanted to share it with." I paused. "That probably sounds stupid."

"Not at all," he said softly. "I'm honored you told me."

I scrunched up my nose. "Did I kill the mood?"

"No. You did not. I guessed, but knowing…" He stroked a thumb across my cheek and up to wipe away another tear. "I want to know if I cross a line."

I turned my face into his touch, kissing the palm of his hand and finding it salty with my tears. "I will, and you haven't." I meant it. I drew a deep breath. We were teetering on the edge of something serious again—something that required me to trust him no matter how much it scared me. "I feel safe with you."

He tensed. "You are, even if we met in unconventional circumstances."

That was putting it mildly.

His eyes lifted, the smile on his face so boyish that it stole my breath. He had never looked this unguarded, this vulnerable. A hand cupped my cheek, his thumb stroking my skin and igniting a different fire inside me. "That night you showed up here and demanded to give your life for your brother's, I think I wanted to help you. Help you in a way I sensed no one ever had, and I knew they hadn't, because I had lived so long in the same position. But you weren't afraid to cry, to show how much you fucking cared. You just let all of it show—your heart, your soul—and it was beautiful. I thought I was just listening to an Equinox request." He chuckled as if the idea was ridiculous to him now. "You drove me so out of control, I nearly forgot that sometimes. And then, at the Midnight Feast, you were drunk on ambrosia, and I wanted you so badly."

I frowned at the memory of being dropped onto the floor—albeit at my own demand. "Could have fooled me."

"Believe me, not taking you to bed that night was pure torture. I'd rather be shot again." I preened a little, and he rolled his eyes. "Does the thought of me preferring agonizing pain to saying no to you please you, princess?"

"A little," I admitted. "I thought you hated me."

"That was a mutual concern, I believe. But no, I could never hate you. You infuriate me and you challenge me and you make me…" He paused and looked me in the eyes. "It was never a fool's bargain between us, but making it was selfish. I wish I could tell you that I did it entirely for you, but I didn't."

Somehow, I'd always known that. Always known that I would never be free of him. I just hadn't expected that a day would come when I wouldn't want to be freed.

"And now?"

"I like you more than I planned. But the bargain between us…" He trailed off, shaking his head. "It needs to be broken."

I reached for him, tilting his face up to meet mine. "Don't. I don't want you to break it."

His eyes closed, shuttering against my words. "And if I don't, will you ever truly believe this is real between us?"

"What about what you get out of the bargain?" I asked, holding my breath, wondering if he would finally share all of his secrets. "What you wanted from me when you made it?"

"I want you more." His lips skimmed along my jawline. "I won't steal a night from you, not when I want you to give them all to me."

My words jammed in my throat. This was what I'd wanted from the beginning—to be free of the bargain. But somewhere along the line, I'd begun to want him more. I swallowed and swung my leg over his body, rocking myself over his hardening cock. "You can have them," I whispered, "and you can have me."

I untied my robe, letting the sash flutter to my hips. He reared up, capturing my nipple between his teeth as I ground against him. His hands shucked the robe from my shoulders, a mischievous gleam in his eyes when he grabbed the sash.

"I'm never letting you go," he warned me, wrapping the fabric around my wrists—a different, darker sort of handfasting, one meant only for us. "Bargain or not." He looped the sash around his wrist and yanked me closer, his lips brushing over mine.

His eyes hooded as he reached between us with his free hand to aim his cock. An aching need spread—permeating my blood, burrowing into my bones, soaking into my skin, into every inch of me—and narrowed as his tip breached me. I bit my lip as I sank over him, moaning at the way he stretched me. It was nearly too much, and when he was sheathed so deeply that I wasn't sure where I ended and he began, he lowered us back to the bed, still holding my tethered hands.

"I'm never letting you go," he whispered again and thrust his hips up, over and over as if he could seal the words physically. I cried out, meeting his demanding rhythm, need swelling into a near frenzy inside me. A guttural snarl tore from his chest, primal and animalistic, and he flipped us over, drawing my bound hands over my head and slipping his beneath the binds of the sash to twine his fingers with mine. He angled his hips to drive deeper, his lips on mine, tongue spearing into my mouth as though he needed to claim more of me.

I wanted everything he had to give. Pressure mounted in my core, and I was gasping against his lips as it built and built, tiny shivers of what was to come splintering through my veins even as I continued to rise.

"Come with me," he urged. His bright eyes riveted to mine, breathing hard and fast.

Pleasure burst through me, radiating through my body like sunlight breaking through the clouds. His hand tightened around mine as he shouted my name, tensing and spilling inside me.

My legs, boneless and trembling, slackened and dropped from his waist, but he didn't roll off me. His forehead pressed to mine, and he brushed his lips over mine. The kiss, so sweet and soft after our frantic lovemaking, sent a new and unfamiliar pang through my chest. The hand holding mine relaxed, and he slipped it free of the sash before loosening my makeshift binding.

"What happened to never letting me go?" I asked breathlessly, half wanting to stay under his control forever.

His mouth crooked up. "I hadn't meant it quite so literally." That fucking smile... Devastating. "Although I could be convinced to tie you up again."

"I'm yours," I whispered, meaning it. "Tie me up as you see fit."

His grin spread, lighting up his entire face. "In that case..."

CHAPTER THIRTY-FOUR

A kiss woke me the next morning. My eyes opened to a muscled male chest, and for a moment, still half asleep, I burrowed into it, drinking in his warm, spicy scent. Lach's arm curled around me, drawing me closer, and instantly my blood heated along with my cheeks. He'd stayed the night, and while I wasn't sure how to process that exactly, the closest feeling I could name was...pleased. We'd figure out the rest one day at a time.

"You snore," he told me softly, tracing the tip of my nose with a long finger.

And the moment was over.

I propped myself up on my elbow and tried to haul a sheet over my body. "Careful. I might die from being over-romanced."

"It's cute." He batted my hand away from the sheet. "Don't. I was enjoying the view."

I snorted and yanked it up anyway. "You're shameless."

A *dozen* shameless memories of last night flashed to mind, and I bit my lip.

"Proudly." He twisted a strand of my hair around his index finger. "I'm sorry to wake you, but I couldn't wait any longer for breakfast."

"Does that mean I have to get dressed?" I wasn't quite ready to share him with the world.

He laughed, the sound oozing from him as slowly and sweetly as honey. "That won't be necessary."

He flipped me onto my back, shoving the sheet completely out of the way, and began a slow descent from my neck to my breasts, where he paused. Sunlight caught his face as he lifted it to me, illuminating a fleeting tattoo, and my breath hitched. Last night had been like a dream, but seeing his beautiful, brutal body hovering over mine in the daylight was a fucking fantasy. A low throb pulsed between my legs when his mouth curved up on one side.

"After last night, I'm famished."

Oh.

He kissed my navel before circling it with his tongue.

Oh.

He urged my knees apart, and I let them fan open, earning me another cocky grin as he continued to lick and kiss his way down. My eyes shuttered when he reached the apex of my thighs, my breath catching in my throat. I stretched my arms overhead, reaching to grip the headboard to brace myself, and my hand brushed something hard and cold under the pillow.

I pulled out one of Lach's guns and frowned at it.

He paused, his breath hot on my skin and his eyes on the gun. "No need to resort to violence. I'm not going to stop."

I realized I was accidentally aiming it at him and dropped my hand to my side. "You slept with a gun under your pillow?"

He chuckled. "I always sleep with a gun under my pillow."

I started to push the weapon toward the edge of the bed, but Lach planted his hand over mine to stop me. "You're always safe with me."

Before I could tell him I knew that, he urged my fingers more tightly around the pistol and rose to his knees. Something primitive gleamed in his green eyes. Lach yanked me closer, guiding one of my legs around his waist and lifting the other to his shoulder. He paused as the tip of his cock nudged against me. "You're always in control, even when my cock is buried inside you." I moaned as he slid in an inch, and his eyes narrowed on my mouth. "*Especially* when my cock is buried inside you."

My grip tightened around the pistol, its cold steel anchoring me as he plunged into me. Lach drew out languidly, and I whimpered in protest. He murmured my name as he guided the leg braced at his shoulder to his waist, planting his hands on either side of me to angle himself impossibly deep. I groaned, hooking my ankles against his back as he fucked me with deliberate, measured restraint that underscored his claim.

I was in control. I was safe. Even when I let my guard down, even when I was vulnerable, even when it felt like my entire being was at the mercy of this man—because he would put himself at *my* mercy.

"No matter what you've gone through." His voice strained as he thrust, rolling his hips until he hit a spot that sent arrows of fire shooting through me. "No matter where you've been." He glanced at the gun I held and snarled, the sound bolting to my core. "From now on, no matter what, no one will touch you without permission, or they will answer for it. Even *me*."

The promise cleaved me, breaking open a deep, hidden void even I had never found. My body arched as I reached for him, the gun forgotten in my desperation for him to fill it, to fill me. I coiled my arms around his neck. "Kiss me."

His mouth crushed against mine as he bore down, driving faster and harder. The kiss shifted to something frenzied and urgent. I was drowning, and he was oxygen. My nails dug into his shoulders as I surrendered entirely to the desperate need propelling me, to our undeniable connection, to this man.

The world fell away around us. My limbs tightened, my hips rising to meet his thrusts as if I could compel him into my very soul. And when I unraveled, he followed me over the edge.

After we both caught our breath, Lach gathered me into his arms, drawing my body against his. We laid in silence, his lips pressed against my hair as I traced the strange language of his tattoos.

"What is this?" I asked, my finger following the four symbols that had settled on his breastbone.

"Theban," he murmured. "One of our ancient tongues."

I peeked up at him. "Do you actually speak it?"

"Not well. It survives mostly in writing."

"And tattoos," I said dryly. I pointed to the one on his chest. "Do they mean something, or do you just enjoy being in pain?"

A shadow moved across his face. "They write themselves. No needles necessary."

I tilted my head to see him better. "Ciara doesn't have any."

"I know." His lips brushed my forehead.

I opened my mouth to ask more, but he rolled on top of me.

"Now, about breakfast." His grin made my heart skip.

The door to my bedroom rattled on its hinges, jolting us apart. "Are you in there?" Ciara's muffled voice called. "I need you."

So much for breakfast.

"Just a second!" I yelled.

I pushed him off me and scrambled out of the bed, looking for something to wear. My silk robe was on the floor.

"Tell her to come back later and get back in bed," he said, watching me from where he lay with amused eyes.

I shushed him. "You need to leave." I looked around. "Where are your clothes?"

He pushed up with a frown. "In my closet."

"Go get them."

He scowled, but he climbed out of the bed. I nearly forgot why I was kicking him out at the sight of his ass. I shook myself free of my daze. Ciara was in the hall, and he was naked. I threw the robe at him. "Put this on."

Lach stared at me like I'd grown another head.

"Ciara is out there."

"So?" He shrugged into the robe. It stopped several inches above his knees, the silk straining against his broad shoulders. He looked absolutely ridiculous, but at least he wasn't naked.

"So!? Do you really want to be naked when she breaks down the door?" I grabbed a pair of random sweats from a drawer, nearly tumbling over as I tried to pull both legs on at once. "This isn't... proper."

His lips pressed into a thin line, and I got the distinct impression he was trying not to laugh. "I think we passed *proper* around midnight."

But Ciara would see him and have questions, and I personally didn't feel like following last night with an interrogation. I yanked a shirt over my head. "Just nip into your room or something."

His amusement fizzled, his pressed lips setting into a hard line. "I've never done a nip of shame before."

The door shook on its hinges again.

"Cate, are you alive?" Despite the door between us, I could hear Ciara's annoyance.

Lach gestured to the door. "Just open it."

I groaned, wishing Lach's default setting wasn't *difficult*. "Just nip!"

He opened his mouth to protest again, but I cut him off with an exasperated glare. He threw up his hands and vanished.

I gulped down a deep breath, raking my hands through my hair and hoping that I wasn't a total wreck. Throwing open the door, I feigned a yawn. "What's up?"

"Up?" she repeated, her brows jumping an inch. She peered over my shoulder. She was in satin pajamas, her hair piled in a messy knot on top of her head, and she still looked gorgeous. "Were you talking to someone?"

"Nope." I stepped to the side and let her see my empty room. Her eyes narrowed on the bed as if the askew sheets were a clue.

She leaned against the wall and crossed her arms. "You disappeared last night."

"I didn't feel like a party."

She studied my face, and I wished I'd had time to check the mirror to see what condition I was in after being up all night. But I must have passed muster because she scowled. "I tried calling you. I had to get Roark to let me in."

"Sorry. My phone probably died." In fact, I had no idea where it was.

"I can't find Lach, either." She glanced around my room again, like she knew he'd been here.

"Oh. Did you check his room?" I walked out of mine and headed toward his.

His door was wide open.

"I did. His door was unlocked, and he was nowhere to be found," she said suspiciously, following after me. She grabbed my arm and tugged me toward the living room. "Come on. We can't keep them waiting."

"We? Them?" I repeated weakly.

In fact, three people were waiting for us in the living room. Roark and Shaw were lounging in the twin set of leather club chairs by the fireplace, both eyeing the other person in the room with a mixture of curiosity and wariness. Sirius waited on the couch, and he looked relieved to see us. He pushed to his feet, and my heart stuttered when I saw the folder in his hands.

"She lives—for now," Ciara announced ominously.

I ignored her, focused entirely on that folder. "What did you find?"

"Shouldn't we wait for Lach?" Shaw asked.

"This can't wait," I told him. Not if Sirius was holding what I thought he was.

But Shaw studied me. "Do you know where Lach is? We thought maybe you two took off together last night."

"No clue." This was true, since he wasn't in his room.

He tilted his head. "We just figured if you…"

"Give it a rest," Roark muttered.

Shaw rolled his eyes. "You just want to—"

"Would you just try again, Roark?" Ciara interrupted her brother.

He sighed, but he straightened a little, an intense concentration settling on his face.

"What is he doing?" I whispered to Ciara.

"Calling Lach. He's been trying to reach him all morning."

"Does he need a phone?" I asked slowly.

"He's using the signet, but Lach must have taken his off…or he's just ignoring him." She rolled her eyes.

The signet ring *connected* them? Roark had admitted last night that he had been purposefully keeping us apart, but he hadn't said *how*. I had no idea if Lach had been wearing his last night—or, for that matter, ten minutes ago. But he was definitely taking it off in the future.

Roark finally relaxed. "He's on his way."

"So, can you hear him?" I asked carefully.

A smirk played on his mouth. "Only if he wants me to."

I was going to have to speak with Lach about that.

"But he was radio silent last night," Roark said meaningfully, his gaze locking on mine.

The relief I felt was short-lived as Lach appeared in the living room, hair an artful mess from where my fingers had gripped it through the night, a smug smile on his perfect face, and *still wearing my silk robe*. He shrugged at my incredulous look.

Ciara blinked. "Where are your clothes?"

Shaw hitched a thumb toward the fireplace. "Over here with Cate's dress—or what's left of it."

Ciara crossed her arms, brows raised, a slow grin splitting her lips.

Embarrassment stained my cheeks as they all looked between us. "I plead the fifth."

"Sorry, princess." Lach winked as he strolled over. "They probably smelled me on you anyway."

And he'd gone there.

I sighed and covered my face with my hands.

"I told you they would bang before Samhain," Shaw said, grinning.

"Shaw!" Ciara hissed. "We all knew that."

I glared at her, but she only laughed.

Sirius cleared his throat, and we all looked at him. He shifted uncomfortably, holding up the folder. "Should I come back later?"

"Why is he in my apartment?" Lach asked slowly, as if he'd just realized there was an Astral Court prince sitting on his couch.

"Don't ask me." Shaw shrugged and pointed in our direction. "Ask those two."

Lach looked between me and his sister. Ciara hesitated, and I jumped in. I had no idea what news Sirius would deliver, but this had been my idea. "We've been studying the alchemical makeup of clover. An older batch as well as the trinity strain. Well, Sirius has been studying it. We mostly bring him coffee."

Lach studied me for a beat. "You have been doing what?" His voice was lethally soft. "Why?"

I swallowed, reminding myself that I was safe even now, that I was still in control of my life and my actions. I met his stare. "I thought if he could isolate what's changed in its magic, you might be able to fix it." I took a deep breath and glanced at Ciara. "And then you might not need ambrosia."

Lach fell silent for so long I wondered if he was having a medical event. Finally, his gaze flicked to Sirius. "And what did you find?"

"Something that shouldn't be there." He tapped the folder. "Shadow court magic."

I deflated at the revelation. Nothing. He had found nothing.

Lach scoffed. "Of course there's shadow court magic. It comes from the Nether Court."

"I'm sorry. I should explain," Sirius said quickly, rubbing the back of his neck. "I thought the same thing at first, when I only found shadow court magic. I was about to give up when I remembered that there are two shadow courts."

Shaw leaned forward, bracing his elbows on his knees. "Holy shit. Are you saying…"

Sirius glanced between all of us, looking slightly unnerved by his own findings. "So, I analyzed a sample of ambrosia. There are traces of Infernal Court magic in the newer batches. Have they been involved with clover production?"

"Apparently," Lach said tightly, "but not with *permission*."

Ciara clapped a hand over her mouth. Shaw stayed quiet this time. Even Roark looked shaken. But Lach…

I closed the distance between us and took his hand.

His eyes met mine, a rueful smile forming on his shapely lips. "That son of a bitch. Bain thought he could hide it in plain sight."

"And he would have gotten away with it," I said in a soft voice, "if we hadn't trusted the Astral Court."

There was a flicker of surprised pride in Lach's eyes, and he nodded once before looking at Sirius. "Thank you."

"What now?" Ciara dared to ask.

Lach squeezed my hand before smiling at her. "Ready to break your handfasting?"

CHAPTER THIRTY-FIVE

I t was noon before we successfully summoned the other fae royals to meet with us. Both of the light courts were already preparing to leave following the successful handfasting. Only Bain and his retinue had intended to stay past this evening. After we were through with him, he would probably be the first to go—and likely by force. There had also been extensive debate regarding whether to host the meeting at the Avalon or in the Otherworld, whether or not weapons should be allowed, and if attendees should be limited to heads of court.

In the end, practicality had won out. Since Sirius needed to back up our claim that the Infernal Court had tampered with our clover supply, we'd extended the invite to every royal family member. That had necessitated somewhere larger to gather than Lach's office. We'd opted for a conference room in the Avalon, since Lach was unlikely to allow Bain to ever step foot into his home court again. I'd lost on the issue of guns, which was why there were twin 9-millimeters holstered under Lach's Armani suit jacket, but the jade-green Birkin bag he'd presented to carry mine was sitting on the nightstand in my bedroom.

Since I had never attended an official business meeting between courts, Ciara had helped choose my outfit. I had foregone the usual ball gown in favor of a close-fitting, high-neck blouse that might have been modest were it not entirely tailored from forest-green lace. I had paired it with a black pencil skirt that hugged my hips before narrowing to my knees, a pair of sheer black stockings, and Gucci pumps with gold heels so tall and pointed they could double as daggers if I regretted leaving the gun behind. She had glamoured my makeup and hair to save time, taming this morning's frizzy mess into lush waves before darkening my lashes and shading my lips scarlet.

Ciara had inverted her handfasting look, opting for a tight black jumpsuit that left nothing to the imagination. She'd magicked sharp cat eyes and bloodred lipstick. If anyone doubted where she stood on ending the trial marriage, one look at her would suffice.

Each court took a side of the square conference table, royals and penumbras sitting with their attending guards behind them at a close distance. We waited for the others to sit before Lach and his retinue took the side stationed in front of the entrance. A reminder that he controlled who came and went in this court and this city as well as a quick exit if things went south. The Nether Court royals sat, Roark speaking quietly with the men he'd positioned at the conference-room door. I stayed back, nervously fingering the phone in my skirt pocket.

"I thought we were done with meetings," Titania complained as soon as Lach had settled into his chair.

Lach ignored her, opting instead to hold up a hand. He nodded to Roark's empty spot beside him. "We will begin in a moment, when *everyone* is ready."

Roark moved to my side, sweeping the room one final time to assess any potential threats, but he didn't continue to the table.

"I think they're waiting for you," I muttered.

Roark flashed me a wicked grin as Lach's voice rose over the hushed conversations starting around the conference table. "Cate?"

I blinked as Lach extended a tattooed hand to the seat at his side. He couldn't possibly expect me to join him, to assume the chair meant for his penumbra. The message it sent would be complicated. Worse than complicated. I glanced at the table, looking for another seat as if it was a mistake.

I was still processing Lach's request when Roark touched my

elbow. "Go on. He's making a statement."

A statement I wished he had cleared with me, especially since his penumbra appeared to be in on it. I lifted my head, aware that every eye in the room was watching me, but I strode forward to join him. A few members of other courts shared glances as I took the empty seat, their faces a telling mixture of curiosity, amusement, and, in Titania's case, disdain.

As if to answer the unspoken question hanging in the air, Lach reached over and placed a hand on my knee. A few brows raised, but the statement was now clear to everyone, including me. He slid a quick glance at me, as if assessing how much trouble he'd find himself in over his show of affection. There was a time when I might have cared what the others thought or what they would assume. But right now, there was only one message I wanted to deliver, so I edged closer to Lach and planted my palm high on his strong, muscled thigh. My place might be at his side, but I wasn't his pawn any more than he was mine. The corner of his mouth twitched, his head inclining ever so slightly.

Message received.

"Exactly why are we here?" Aurora asked, folding her hands on the table. "While we appreciate your hospitality, I confess I'm eager to return home and see to the business of my own court."

Lach leaned forward, resting his chin on one hand, the other still marking his newly claimed territory. "I will be brief, as I think we're all through wasting time with this business."

The others shared concerned looks, but Bain chuckled uneasily. "Is the honeymoon already over?"

Thankfully, the honeymoon hadn't even gotten started. Ciara had shown the good sense to insist on separate bedrooms until the final details were concluded, telling Bain she wanted to wait until they returned to the Infernal Court.

The flicker of Lach's eyes—lethal and cold—toward Bain might have been answer enough, but he cleared his throat. "We received disturbing information this morning that forces me to reevaluate my sister's marriage to Bain."

"What the hell?" Bain jumped to his feet, knocking his chair over in the process. The other royals began whispering among themselves as he planted his hands on the table. "On what grounds?"

I couldn't decide if he was overplaying his innocence or genuinely surprised.

"Manipulation, deceit." Lach spoke so calmly that I knew he was in danger of detonating. I squeezed his thigh gently, a reminder that putting an end to this was the first step in setting things right. "You negotiated a trade agreement—a marriage—to replace a product that you were tampering with."

Oberon shifted forward, eyes narrowing. "That is a serious allegation."

"And a fucking lie," Bain added. "I have absolutely no clue what the hell you think is going on, but your sister is mine by law and custom for the next year."

Ciara stood, glaring at him. "I don't belong to *anyone*."

"You do without proof of this unfounded allegation," Bain shot back. He looked like he might cross the room, throw her over his shoulder, and drag her to his court. All around the room, hands moved slowly toward jackets in anticipation of what he was going to do next.

I stilled. I'd known allowing guns was a bad idea, but no one would listen.

"Sit the fuck down," Lach ordered him. "You are in *my* court, and you will act like it."

MacAlister placed a hand on his prince's arm, but Bain shook it off, righted his chair, and sat back down.

"Do you have evidence?" Oberon pressed, and I wondered how often he got stuck with the role of mediator. As the oldest, he was probably tired of it.

Meanwhile, Aurora and Sirius were speaking softly to each other, the crown princess beginning to shake her head as she listened. Finally, she straightened with a sigh. "My brother has something he would like to say."

The shared surprise of everyone in the room was a testament

to how rarely anyone considered the other royals in line to their individual thrones.

Sirius cleared his throat, tugging at his buttoned collar before he flipped open the folder in front of him. "I've been analyzing different strains of clover against older ones, as well as ambrosia."

"You little—" Bain growled.

"Do not finish that sentence," Aurora warned him, her amethyst eyes flashing. "Or you won't only be answering to Lach."

He fell mostly silent, muttering under his breath while he glowered at the rest of us, particularly the young Astral Court prince bringing evidence against him.

Sirius continued, undeterred by Bain's attempts at intimidation, laying out the science behind his discovery. Glances between the other assembled royals told me that they believed what he was saying, perhaps because he was a light court prince. A fact that shouldn't matter but one that I knew did. When he finished, rage mottled Bain's face.

"None of that is true. You're lying."

Sirius looked up from the folder, blinking. "Alchemy doesn't lie. Someone used Infernal Court magic to taint the supply of clover. That's a fact."

"I've seen the evidence, watched Sirius work. He's not lying, but a prince with something to hide might," I added coolly, eyes narrowing on Bain.

He aimed a sneer at me, but I didn't shrink. "Are you accusing me of not only tampering with another court's product but also lying about it?"

Lach flourished a hand, sounding a little bored. "Yes, precisely. Try to keep up."

Bain zeroed in on him, hands curling into fists on the table. We hadn't just lost an ally today. We had made an enemy. "Regardless, it's not up to you to end the handfasting. It's up to your sister." He finally looked at Ciara, and for a moment, he softened. "You don't really believe this."

She glared back at him, her throat sliding a little. "Alchemy

322 FILTHY RICH FAE

doesn't lie." She sucked in a breath and held up her hand, which still bore the tattoo from last night's handfasting ceremony. "Let's leave it up to the magic. If Infernal Court magic was used to hurt my court, I am well within my rights to call off this trial marriage."

For a moment, Bain just stared at the ink on her wrist, on her hand. We all did, and as we watched, the mark faded until not a trace remained. Bain snarled, his eyes flashing when he discovered his matching one had gone as well. Ciara sank carefully into her chair, her drooping shoulders the only hint of her relief.

Bain looked around the room, holding the gaze of each of us in turn. His eyes paused on me. "You're going to regret this."

Lach's grip on my knee tightened. "Take care with how you speak to her."

Bain simply shook his head and buttoned his jacket. "I suppose we've dodged a bullet. If the Nether Court is so easily swayed, you would be poor allies."

I suppressed a laugh. Barely.

"You have until nightfall to get the fuck out of my court." Lach rose, glaring back at him. "Gather your people and get out, because when the sun sets, you are forbidden to set foot in my city or my court ever again."

Bain held his gaze, snorting slightly. "You're going to regret this." He snapped his fingers and vanished; a moment later, MacAlister and the other Infernal Court retinue followed.

As soon as he was gone, Aurora whirled on her brother. "Can you give me a little warning before you pick a fight with another court?"

He flashed her a sheepish smile, but I found myself jumping in. "He did it because I asked him to. If you want to be mad at anyone, direct it at me."

Lach remained silent as Aurora surveyed me.

"Fine. But a word of caution," she said as she looked between him and me. "You just made an enemy. I hope you know what you're doing."

So did I.

The Astral Court took their leave, Sirius promising to be in touch with Ciara and me after he spent more time studying the clean sample of clover he had. We promised to visit him in Prague when he was finished. The Hallow Court followed, except for Oberon, who remained.

"Aurora is right," he warned us. "Bain holds a grudge."

"I can handle him," Lach said tightly. "I'm sorry that you wasted your time on this business." There wasn't an ounce of sincerity in his tone.

Oberon simply shrugged and smiled warmly. "I rather enjoyed myself." He beamed at me, letting that smile fill his face. "Until next time. I hope we meet soon."

A growl slipped from Lach, but I shushed him. "I'll look into those shirts."

He chuckled, tipping his head once at Lach, who scowled in response, and disappeared.

"I think I need a drink," Ciara announced, slumping in her seat.

"Me too." Shaw nodded, scrubbing his chin. "Care to join us?"

Lach shook his head. "Celebrate after the Infernal Court is gone." He nodded to Roark. "Have our men do their best to make Bain uncomfortable. The sooner he's out of here, the better." Then he looked at Shaw. "Take our sister to get a drink. I don't trust Bain to behave himself."

"What about Cate?" Ciara pouted.

Lach's attention was now aimed at me, something feral prowling in his shadowed green eyes. "Cate is occupied."

"They're going to be occupied a lot now, aren't they?" Shaw muttered.

Before anyone could get another joke in, Lach snapped his fingers, and I found myself standing with him on the stone balcony. It looked different in the day, the Otherworld no longer hidden by shadows. An orchard stretched before us, the trees soaking up the final moments of light as the sun descended on the horizon. Their branches were laden with blood apples, and butterflies, so delicate they were nearly translucent, fluttered from fruit to fruit.

Lach's arm wrapped around my waist, drawing me closer to him. "I'm sorry I put you on the spot."

I frowned before I realized what he meant. Then I rolled my eyes. "Fae and their pissing contests." I picked a piece of lint off his shoulder. "I guess this means we're official."

"I think that might have been obvious to everyone else for a while." He smiled, but it faded like the setting sun over his shoulder. "I want you to stay here until nightfall or until it's confirmed that they're gone."

I raised my brows. "Is this because I didn't take a gun to the meeting?"

"I don't expect him to go peacefully. I will feel better—"

"If your fragile human girlfriend isn't around?" I finished.

"If my *girlfriend* isn't around. There's nothing fragile about you, princess," he corrected me, brushing his lips over mine. Even the soft kiss was searing, and I slipped my hand under his suit jacket.

"And what am I supposed to do while you're vanquishing our enemy?"

"Our?" Delight danced in his eyes. "I do like the sound of that." He kissed the hollow beneath my ear, and I shivered. "Make yourself at home? Preferably by getting naked in my bed?"

I reached absently for the pendant, then frowned. "And how will I summon you to said bed? You never returned my necklace."

"You won't have to summon me to our bed," he promised darkly. "My nights belong to you now."

I swallowed, his words dashing a white-hot line through me. "I guess I could take a bath. I do miss that tub."

Preferably a very cold one before I burst into flames.

"Use mine." His eyes drifted lower. "It's big enough for two."

"But you have to go play big, bad boss," I pointed out.

His gaze skimmed lower and lower, his teeth sinking into his bottom lip. "I'm sure I can speed things up."

I drew back so he was forced to look up. "Without getting shot, please."

"I'll do my best."

"That's so comforting." I sighed, looking around us. "And which way is your room again? I'm going to need a map for this place."

He chuckled. "The wraiths will show you. Just ask them."

I thought of those disembodied howls following me through the halls and cringed. "Do I have to?"

"They answer to you, princess." His arm tightened around my waist. "There's no need to fear them."

"Debatable," I muttered. I wasn't sure that being Lach's girlfriend earned me royalty status, especially where the wraiths were concerned.

His raspy laugh was cut short, fading as his eyes grew distant. A second later, he frowned. "Roark says the fighting has begun." He gave me a swift kiss. "I'll be back when I'm done kicking their asses out of New Orleans."

He released me, and I fought the urge to grab hold of him. "Seriously, don't get shot."

His smirk did nothing to reassure me as he nipped to the Avalon to end this once and for all.

After he was gone, I wasted five minutes trying to remember my way around the Nether Court before I gave up. "Can you show me to Lach's room?"

I felt even sillier than I'd expected, talking to an empty hallway— until a hollow moan answered. Icy dread dashed that feeling, but I paused and waited. Another moan sounded a few steps away as if the wraith was traveling. I turned toward the sound and froze as a shadow moved. The moans shifted and changed as it continued down the corridor.

It was guiding me.

I took a deep breath and followed, trying to ignore the way my hair stood on end at the keening sound. "Thank you," I said when the shadow finally paused in front of a familiar door.

There was a soft moan, and the wraith splintered, dispersing into curling shadows that melted into the hallway's black walls.

Lach's room was more cluttered than I remembered, his crammed bookshelves in utter disarray. If he didn't hurry, he was going to return to find them alphabetized. I scanned the room, picking up a few abandoned shirts and jackets as I tried to ignore the siren call of his bed. It was unmade like the last time I was in here, even though as far as I knew, he always slept in his quarters at the Avalon. But I suspected the black silk sheets smelled like him. I forced myself to turn away before I peeled my clothes off and dove in to find out. If the bed was giving me dangerous thoughts, I wasn't certain I should risk looking at the bathtub. Not until he was here to join me. The thought stoked the fire already burning low and deep inside of me.

A bath might not be the answer, but a book might do the trick. I continued to the nearest shelf, bypassing books written in what I now knew was Theban. The door creaked open, and I fought a smile. Wouldn't have to summon him indeed. I'd just thought about getting naked, and he had shown up. "That *was* fast."

I pushed the book I was holding back into place and turned, but it wasn't Lach.

"Making yourself at home, *princess*?"

CHAPTER THIRTY-SIX

I stared at MacAlister's oily smile as he slithered into the room, my brain trying to process what my racing pulse already had. He paused in front of the door to block the only exit. I reached for my pendant, muttering a curse when my fingers found bare skin. I had no way to call Lach.

"What the fuck are you doing here?" I demanded, my voice catching slightly.

He let out a low whistle as he peered around the room. "These are his private quarters, aren't they? You have dug your claws into him." MacAlister flicked his nails. "I'm impressed. I never thought I'd live to see Lachlan be fool enough to let a woman *distract* him. I thought he was heartless, and then he showed up reeking of you. He overplayed his hand. He exposed his heart."

My own heart hammered in response, my chest constricting around it like a vice, but I planted my feet.

"Leave," I commanded.

"Perhaps his little show earlier gave you the wrong impression." Disgust curled his lip, and he bared his teeth with a rabid snap. "You are not in control. You have no power here. But you do have one use."

A thin sheen of sweat broke over my forehead as my mind began to race. But I did have power. I had control. And I wasn't going to let an asshole like MacAlister take it from me. "What do you want? Let's make a bargain."

I would find a way out of it. The Infernal Court penumbra wasn't nearly as clever as he pretended to be. No, he was cruel, and cruelty was a fragile thing. I could break him.

But he shook his head. "I already have a bargain of my own to fulfill," he explained. "I made a promise to bring Lach to his knees, to prove I could be his penumbra."

My locked legs rooted to the spot, my stomach seizing as he stalked a couple of steps closer. I shook my head slightly to clear it. I fumbled for something to say to keep him talking. "You want to be Lach's penumbra?"

MacAlister rolled his eyes. "What good would that do me?" He was speaking in riddles, but each prowling step he took betrayed his intentions. I forced myself to back away as he advanced on me. "I've lived long enough in the shadows. I just want to be free. We all do, even your friend Roark."

"Roark is free." My hands fisted at my sides as I swept the room, looking for a way out, for a distraction. I'd never get through the window. I had to get past him and out the door, find the wraiths, find *anyone*.

"No one is free in these splintered courts." The bitterness in his voice chilled my blood. "We are all imprisoned by broken magic. Even your precious Nether Prince. I'm really doing him a favor."

"Doing him a favor?" My laugh dripped venom. I raised my chin, meeting his poisoned glare with my own. I edged along the wall, toward the large window instead of the door, knowing there was no way I would get past him. Very carefully, I kicked off my heels. I'd never make it in those. "I doubt he'll see it that way when I tell him how you tormented me. Who do you think you are?"

"I am the one who breaks him," he hissed. "I am the one who will carve his heart out from your chest."

A lost future flashed before my eyes at his words. My thumb fumbled over my ring as I realized he was going to kill me.

I was a *survivor*.

He pounced, but I was faster. I threw myself behind a velvet chair, my knees hitting the wood floor with a *crack*, the fabric of my skirt splitting several inches. Pain shot through my legs, but I ignored it as adrenaline pumped through my body. I wouldn't die at the hands of a maggot like MacAlister. I reached down and ripped my skirt to my upper thigh. Lurching to my feet, I aimed for the door. I'd made it halfway when he caught me by the hair, wrenching me backward and into a shelf. Books tumbled around me, the shelf teetering from the impact. I threw myself as far away as I could as it crashed down.

"You're making a mess," MacAlister complained, prowling toward me. "Just do what humans are good at: *die*."

"Go to hell!" I hissed.

"You first." He pitched forward, diving to catch my foot.

I kicked at him, but his sharp nails dug into my ankle. I reached for another book, but my fingers came up empty. MacAlister laughed, using my leg to yank me closer. "Do you put up this much of a fight when Lach screws you? Or am I just lucky?" With his free hand, he reached inside his jacket and drew a pistol. "I can't decide if I want to choke you to death with my own hands or just shoot you and get it over with."

It didn't matter that I wasn't fae; those bullets at close range were just as deadly for a human.

"I bet those redcaps loved you," he sneered. "He knew you would be a problem, but I kept telling him that penumbras solve problems. And honestly, he won't be able to disagree after today."

I ignored his babbling as I grappled, straining toward a volume of Shakespeare's collected plays. My fingers brushed its edge. "Yes, you deserve a fucking raise." I finally got a corner of the book and launched it at him, clipping his shoulder.

MacAlister snarled, lifting the gun. "Decision made." He released my ankle. "I'll give you a running start. Might I suggest how poetic it would be to die in *his* bed? Devastating." He cocked the hammer as something clicked for me. "On the count of five." He held up a finger with his free hand. *"One."*

I was already on my feet. I didn't let myself think. I just acted.

"Two."

I bounded two steps, reaching the edge of his bed.

"Three," he crooned, on his feet now. "And truly, a romantic choice."

I dove, my arms stretching until they burned toward the headboard.

"Four."

My fingers slid under the pillow, brushing the cold barrel of a 9-millimeter.

"Five." His shadow fell over the bed. "Would you mind turning over? I think it will be more impactful if he can see your face."

Safety off. I flicked it with my thumb as I flipped over, swinging my arms over my head. MacAlister tilted his head, blinking rapidly as I aimed.

Just pull the trigger.

And I did.

The recoil shook my arms, but I got off two more shots. MacAlister stumbled back a step, his gun clattering to the floor as crimson seeped across his white Oxford shirt. His head fell forward, stunned, for a moment before his legs gave out. He crashed to the ground, eyes lifting to stare at me. His mouth opened, a bloody gurgle foaming on his lips instead of words.

Horror spilled through me, making my hands tremble so hard I nearly dropped the pistol. I tamped down the next one, refusing to let my mind process what I'd just done. It was like the hospital. Life or death. Use the adrenaline. I slid from the bed, holding the gun in front of me as I approached him slowly. MacAlister stared at me, a smile twitching on his mouth.

I kicked his weapon across the room before crumbling to my knees, Lach's gun stretched between us.

MacAlister wheezed a laugh, reading my face. "You...still... die."

He was right. I knew what these bullets could do, and with that amount of blood, I knew I'd hit something *vital*. I had killed a penumbra. Not even Lach could save me.

"No one is dying," I muttered. MacAlister's eyes widened as I dropped the gun behind me, out of his reach, and crawled closer to him. Ripping open his shirt, I discovered an entry wound in his upper abdomen. The bullet had likely hit an organ and, judging from the amount of blood, multiple arteries. I choked down a sob of fear as I pressed my palms to the wound.

"Where's your phone?" I asked through clenched teeth.

He answered with another bloody laugh. "Too late. For both of us."

I leaned to wipe my sweaty brow on my forearm. MacAlister seized under my hands, his limbs jerking as his body went into shock. Minutes. I had minutes.

"Help," I whispered, but there was no one to hear me. He was going to die, and there was nothing I could do to stop it. A moan rose in the room, keening and hollow as if the wraiths were calling to the Wild Hunt themselves. I dropped back, wiping my bloody hands on my torn skirt before struggling to my feet. I'd barely managed it when Lach appeared.

"How?" I choked.

But he didn't answer. Another moan did. The *wraiths*. They'd been watching out for me, as he'd promised.

Shadows rippled in Lach's eyes as his gaze swept to MacAlister, face tightening as he reached the same conclusion I had. A heartbeat later, the weight of what I'd done collapsed on me. I stumbled a step, and he caught me. He pressed a single kiss to my forehead before steadying me by the shoulders.

His eyes sought mine, forcing me to focus on him. "He's dying. I'm so sorry about that."

I nearly crumbled at the reminder, but he held me upright.

He closed his eyes and drew a shuddering breath. When he opened them, they were cold and calculating. The prince of the Nether Court stared back at me. Lachlan Gage. The monster I once hated.

"We don't have much time." Another searching glance. "When he dies, his signet will mark his killer and summon the Wild Hunt. I can't stop that now. Bain doesn't know; MacAlister must have blocked him before he came after you, or he would already be here."

Tremors racked me, but Lach's hands remained steady on my shoulders. I stared into his eyes without seeing him. I wanted to tell him that Bain had sent him. That MacAlister had said as much. But my voice refused to work.

Shock. I was in shock. And that wouldn't help either of us. I forced a nod.

"Bain will come after you when he discovers what's happened. I'll stall him as long as I can, but you need to get out of New Orleans." He glued his eyes to mine until I nodded. He reached into his pocket and pulled out a key fob. I stared at it. He didn't have a choice. I'd compromised the court. If I stayed, I would put all of them at risk, and he knew it. Behind us, MacAlister rasped. "Shit. We don't have much time. There's a phone and money in the glove box."

Would he be punished for this, too? What would happen to the court? To his family—to my friends? To *him*? My lips wobbled, but I made them move. "Lach, please—"

"There's a phone in the glove box," he repeated, silencing me. "Plug it in and start driving. Get the fuck out of New Orleans. After today, do not step foot in fae territory. Ditch your old phone on the way out of town. Leave it there. And as soon as you're away, call the only number in the new phone. They'll know what to do. I can't risk coming with you now or using my magic to get you farther than that." He shook my shoulders. "Do you understand?"

I managed to nod, but he had to know that it didn't matter. The world spun around me, but I focused on his instructions. I would leave. I would keep trouble from the Nether Court, from him, from my home. That's what this place would always be to me—what he would always be to me—and I would protect both at all costs.

"Destroy the new phone as soon as you make that call." MacAlister was seizing again. I couldn't breathe. I wasn't ready to let go yet. I just needed a few more minutes. I would bargain with the devil himself for more time. I fought to inhale as the full weight of what I'd done pressed down on me. Lach gripped my chin. "This is the most important thing. Do not take off that ring, Cate."

"What?" The question tumbled out of me. He grabbed my hand, brushing his thumb over the emerald. "I don't understand."

"Neither did I. But—" MacAlister rattled, and I clapped a hand over my mouth to smother a sob. "It's what I wanted." He continued, panic edging into his voice. "Swear that you will never take it off and that you will never give it to me."

I stared at him. How could he be worried about something so insignificant while the world ended around us? I opened my mouth to ask him, to beg him to stop trying to save me and just be with me in these final, stolen moments.

Lach shook me. *"Fucking swear it."*

"I'll never give it to you," I choked out. Tears spilled down my cheeks, and then something tingled on the back of my neck—hooking and digging before fading to nothing. My eyes flew open, a sudden coldness flooding through me as I recognized that sensation. *"No."*

My fingers flew to the spot as if I could stop it, but it was too late. Somehow, I knew not a trace of the bargain remained. "I don't understand. How—"

"It doesn't matter. You're free. I should have done it sooner. I should have done a lot of things sooner." His hand wrapped around the one still holding the back of my neck, and he dragged me closer. MacAlister let out another wet, gurgling breath, and my questions faded as I realized time was slipping away.

"We didn't have enough time," I whispered, tears blurring his face. I blinked, desperate to memorize it.

I could see the tears shimmering in his green eyes as he pressed his forehead to mine. "There would never have been enough time with you." His mouth found mine, salt mingled with longing and regret, with what might have been and never would be. The kiss tasted like goodbye. When Lach finally broke it, he paused for one final look into my eyes. "You need to go now."

He released me, the sadness of his smile shredding the final pieces of my heart. He turned, and I waited to be swept away, but instead he took a single step, pausing to watch MacAlister fighting for his final breaths.

Seconds. We had seconds.

There was so much I needed to say to him.

"My nights still belong to you," I blurted out. That would always be true, bargain or no. No matter how many I had left. I swallowed. "I belong to you."

His eyes closed for a second, momentarily shutting out the man dying at his feet. He reached into his jacket, the fingers of his other hand twitching like he couldn't quite stomach sending me away. The smirk he flashed didn't reach his eyes. "Always have. Always will, princess."

His words pierced me as he pulled a gun from his holster. I blinked as he lifted it, realizing a moment too late what was happening. His fingers snapped, but I lunged as he pulled the trigger, the world sweeping away beneath me as Lach shot MacAlister in the head—taking the kill shot.

CHAPTER THIRTY-SEVEN

Darkness greeted me first. I fought the urge to dissolve into it, to let it swallow me whole. It couldn't be worse than the agony of facing what Lach had done. But before I could surrender to the shadows, strips of green neon hummed to life, racing to outline the walls of a garage and illuminating a sleek black SUV, its hood emblazoned with *Sentinel*. I stared around me, my brain kicking on with the lights.

He had sacrificed himself for me. It felt like my chest was caving in, collapsing on the empty space left behind where he'd been ripped from me. Another bleeding wound I couldn't staunch.

The pain was too much, too heavy to bear. I couldn't move. I couldn't think.

"Focus." The word echoed back at me, summoning his instructions.

One step. Just one. I took it. Then another until I reached the SUV. I fumbled for the door handle. It unlocked automatically, and I climbed in, gripping the steering wheel. I rested my forehead on it and tried to remember how to breathe. But all I saw when I closed my eyes was the grim determination on his face as he killed MacAlister. As he took the final kill shot, claimed my fate, gave up everything—his family, his court, his *life*—to save me.

And I would not sit here while he died for me.

I would not just give up.

Sitting up, I dashed my tears with the back of my hand and

reached for the glove box. It fell open to reveal a black leather bag. I unzipped it to find rolls of money, a handful of papers, and a few passports, each labeled for different countries—and at the bottom of the bag: an old Nokia phone.

He'd given me instructions. I only had to follow them. I only had to do the next thing he'd put in front of me. But I couldn't, not with emotions bottlenecking in my throat. So, I screamed.

It tore out of me, clawing and primal and raw. And when I finally pried my white knuckles from the wheel, my throat ravaged, I went back to work. I found the power cable and plugged the phone in, knowing it wouldn't charge until I opened that garage door and drove out of New Orleans.

Until I left this city.

Until I left him.

Maybe I would always belong to him, but I wanted to be with him more.

But he had freed me in those final moments so the bargain wouldn't fester between us as *he* ran from the Wild Hunt, not *me*. He'd done so instinctively, acting compulsively, as though he had always had this plan in place. Looking around me at the secret, outfitted garage, I realized that he had. That he had known one day he might have to run. But instead of him nipping to this car and his money and passports and that help waiting on the other end of a single call, instead of choosing to flee before the Hunt tracked him down, he'd sent me. Maybe because he knew Bain would come for me when he discovered MacAlister's failure. Maybe because that's what he'd promised he would do.

Protect me.

I gripped the wheel, my eyes focusing on my ring. On proof that I had survived again, but only because he would not. On the linchpin of our bargain. This stupid ring that he somehow knew I would never give to him willingly, especially after he'd refused it first. After he'd told me that it was worthless. That its only value lay in what it meant to me, so I would never think of offering it again. Such a simple, clever trick. Something howled inside me to take it off, unable to stomach the sight of it. Because it no longer meant I'd survived.

It carried the weight of loss. It always had, but I'd chosen the easier story to swallow. I didn't remember my parents, so maybe it had been easier to believe it was so simple. Black or white. The past or the future. But now I knew exactly what I'd forfeited. The loss of the life I'd only tasted, the family I had glimpsed, the man who might have very well always known what I needed—because he needed it, too.

It was all gone, and I'd vowed to wear this ring like a scar for the rest of my life.

I wanted to crumble into my grief, but I didn't have time to break down. That would come later. And suddenly, I was grateful for all of those double shifts, for the chaotic pace of Gage Memorial. I ignored the twinge of sorrow I felt at leaving it all behind. But my job had taught me to focus and follow instructions, so I knew what I had to do next.

I fumbled in the dark until I found a garage-door remote in a small overhead compartment. My pulse shot up as the door rose, revealing a worn-down New Orleans street. Judging by the plants growing in the cracked brick of nearby buildings, it was a long-abandoned industrial district. I had no idea where I was. I just had to follow the signs out of town, make that call, and convince the person on the other end to point me in the right direction—the only direction I was willing to go.

The one that took me back to Lach, because if he thought I was going to leave him to run, to die...I sensed another argument in our future.

Our future.

A future I was not willing to give up on.

There was just one thing I had to take care of first.

I pulled out of the garage, my eyes squinting in the afternoon light. The sun caught the emerald stone of my ring, twinkling at me like a message. I had no choice but to leave without goodbyes if I had any chance of helping Lach next. I only hoped Ciara and the rest of the Nether Court would understand, that Haley wouldn't worry, but there was only one other person I couldn't walk away from, and if I had to ditch my phone on my way out of the city, this might be my last chance to use it.

I took it out and prayed Channing had been paying his bill. Because I couldn't leave my brother behind. I wouldn't lose anyone else.

"What?" Not the friendliest greeting, but I nearly sobbed with relief that he'd actually picked up.

"You answered." The words were as raw as my throat, and I had to swallow before I broke down.

"Cate, what's wrong?" No longer angry with me after our fight. Just worried. Just *family*.

I stopped the car and began punching an address into its navigation system. "I don't have time to explain. I need you to meet me at my house in twenty minutes."

"Twenty minutes? What the hell is going on?"

"Just do it. *Promise* me."

He paused and finally sighed. "I'll be there."

. . .

I drove like the Wild Hunt was chasing me, and when I pulled up in front of my quiet, empty house, I saw Channing sitting on the doorstep. I jumped out of the car, grabbing Lach's mysterious phone and the leather bag. I swore under my breath when I realized I didn't have my house keys—and Channing kept losing my spare.

He popped onto his feet, drinking in the expensive car I'd just arrived in. "Is that a Range Rover?"

I ignored the question and grabbed his hand. "I need you to break into my house."

His eyes bulged. "Cate, what the hell is going on?"

"I'll explain, but we only have a few minutes." I had no idea how Lach planned to buy me time or how much of it I had before Bain came after me—and every second I spent before making that call was another second with Lach that I lost.

"I can't—"

"It's not illegal if I'm asking," I cut him off. My landlord might disagree, but what choice did I have?

Channing studied me for a minute, his brows nudging together like he was assessing my state of mind. "I can pick the locks."

I had never expected such disconcerting information to be so comforting. Channing went to work while I held up my phone's flashlight. Each lock took two minutes, and then we were inside.

"I just want to grab a few things." I tossed him the bag and the phone, trying to ignore the now very overdue library books on the coffee table. "Keep an eye on that."

"Why?" He stared at the Nokia. "This thing is an antique. Does it even work?"

"It's supposed to." It had charged long enough to power on. "It's going to connect us with someone who can help."

"Help?" he repeated, the color leaching from his face. "Why do we need someone to help us?"

"I'll explain later," I promised him. "Just don't break it."

I booked it to my room to grab the little clothing I'd left behind when I made my temporary move to the Avalon. I'd never expected that I would be leaving here for the last time then. I shoved the clothes into a backpack and paused to look around the room for anything else I wanted to bring with me. But all I saw was secondhand furniture and little else. Things that meant nothing to me. As if this life was those borrowed library books—always waiting to be returned.

Channing was digging through the leather bag when I returned to the living room. Rolls of cash were strewn on the couch. "You aren't going to believe this." He tossed me one of the passports.

I opened it to find a blank page, but as I frowned, my photo appeared, along with a stranger's name and information. A magical escape ticket.

"Cool, right?"

I forced a smile. I didn't know if it was a spell or a glamour. I wasn't going anywhere, but I could get Channing out. I clung to that.

"I told you I would explain on the road. Get that back together—we're going to need it. And don't forget the phone."

He reached for the money, nodding. "Look, I'm really sorry, Cate."

"What do you have to be sorry for?"

"I got you mixed up in this." He gestured to the leather bag, the money, the magical passports. "But I'm going to get you out of it."

"Great." I shouldered my bag higher, tapping my foot. I didn't need to be reminded that Channing had been the reason I'd tracked down Lach, that I had made that bargain to protect him. I didn't know if I hated him for introducing me to the world I'd lost or loved him for giving me even a short time with it. And thinking about it now was a waste of time.

"I'm going to fix it," he swore, rising to his feet.

"Channing, I'm not really worried about that right now. It's not safe for us here. I'll tell you in the car."

He lifted his chin, squaring his shoulders, and pressed on with the apology. "I'm sorry I couldn't keep you safe."

"I'm your big sister. It's my job to protect you, remember?" I hitched my thumb toward the open door behind me.

But he didn't budge. "Not anymore. He'll protect you now."

"What are you talking about?" I asked slowly, dread skittering up my spine at the determination on his stony face.

"You'll understand."

I opened my mouth to demand an answer, but before I could speak, a rough hand clamped a rag over it. I jerked as a sweet aroma bloomed in my nostrils, thrashing wildly as darkness blotted the edges of my vision.

The last thing I saw was my brother's stricken face.

CHAPTER THIRTY-EIGHT

Lach

It had been decades since I dumped a body in the bayou. I drove to the northern territory, away from the egrets Goemon had warned us about but nowhere near the spot I'd taken Cate. It felt like a lifetime had passed since that day. Maybe because my own life was now on borrowed time. Maybe because of everything that had happened, because everything had changed.

Her. Me. Us.

Everything.

The sinking sun cast an orange glow on the glassy surface of the slow-moving river as I parked and popped the trunk. Some said dead bodies were heavier to carry than people, but they always felt lighter to me.

I'd wrapped MacAlister, along with a few stones, in a Turkish rug from my bedroom to keep my upholstery clean. A sentimental gesture, since I'd probably never see the Mercedes again, but I couldn't stomach the idea of losing anything else today. Not after seeing the look on Cate's face when I nipped her away, when I took that shot. I'd needed her to understand what I was doing, but I couldn't let her stop me, couldn't risk that she might wind up wearing the same mark now branded on my neck if I let her stay.

FILTHY RICH FAE

My boots squished into the muddy bank, saltwater and decay hanging in the thick air as I hoisted the body higher on my shoulder. Getting rid of the body would ensure no one could confirm Cate's involvement. I'd charged the wraiths with silence—one of my last official acts as ruler of the Nether Court, but a command they would follow. Although she hadn't been the one to kill him, I doubted Bain would care. It wouldn't matter that he had been the one who'd sent his penumbra to assassinate her. Blood spilled was blood owed. And if it had been her blood, I would have spilled every drop from every soul at the Infernal Court and not been satisfied.

But she was alive. With any luck, she was already safely in New York. I tried not to think about it, tried to ignore the relentless urge to follow her, to check on her, to see she was safe for myself.

Because she wouldn't be if I was anywhere near her.

So, I'd followed through on my promise to buy her time, praying that it would stem my need for her long enough to get my head on straight. Considering I hadn't managed a clear thought since the moment I first saw her in front of the Avalon, I doubted it would work. But I had to try. I had to do everything I could to keep her heart beating, because the thought of a world without her…

I heaved MacAlister into the river, his body shattering the bayou's serenity with an ominous splash. For a minute, the bloodied carpet bobbed on its surface until water soaked through the fibers of the rug and it slowly began to sink, as heavy as my own heart. A ripple cut across the water in pursuit of the bloody bounty. If the body didn't settle to the bottom, the alligators would see there was little to find.

I half expected them to continue to the shoreline in pursuit of me, half expected that the pain in my own chest seeped blood like the body in the water. And as I backed away from my dirty work, the ache deepened, the need to go to her so acute that I stumbled, nearly tripping in the marsh grass.

I was so preoccupied that I didn't hear anything until a shotgun cocked behind me. I swiveled slowly around to find Goemon aiming at me.

"Most people run from us." He spit on the ground and resumed his target.

I swallowed, keeping my hands in front of me. There was no point reaching for my own gun. He'd felt me the minute I stepped foot on his land. He had likely known the moment MacAlister's signet burned its badge of shame into my flesh, the other members of the Wild Hunt sensing it as well. They would have all been pursuing me soon enough. At least it was going to be quick.

"Who was it?" He jerked his head toward the bayou.

"Bain's penumbra." There was no point in lying to him. The truth would come out eventually, or my version of it—the one that carefully skipped over the two bullets Cate had delivered herself.

Goemon grimaced. He studied me over the barrel, his eyes mere slits in the bright sunlight. Then he shouldered his shotgun. "I've always liked you, Gage. Unlike that asshole Bain." He shook his head, black hair streaming behind him. "But rules are rules. I don't make them."

"I know," I said warily. I scratched the brand on my neck. It was surprisingly itchy, but I supposed being marked for death wasn't meant to be comfortable.

His mouth dashed into a thin line before he sighed. "I'll give you a running start, won't even let the others know I saw you, if you answer one question."

"Shoot." I sighed, pinching the bridge of my nose. "On second thought. Just ask."

Goemon barked a short laugh, but something primitive gleamed in his squinted eyes when he turned them on me. "Was it worth it?"

A smile curled my mouth, my fingers already twitching to snap as I answered, "Yeah, *she* was."

· · ·

Cats scattered, hissing and arching their backs, as I appeared in my sister's living room. The feeling was entirely mutual, maybe even a little more so today. The witch on the couch scowled at me, dropping knitting needles into her lap, before she bellowed, "Fi, your asshole brother just nipped into our living room." Romy glared down at my muddy boots, her dark eyes flashing at her dirty floor. "And he is making a fucking mess."

Even on days when I didn't track half the bayou onto her wooden floors, there was no love lost between me and my sister's girlfriend. But today, I ignored her, searching the apartment for Cate. I shouldn't have come. I knew that, but I couldn't run yet. Once I knew she was safe, I could let her go. But not before I told her everything. Not before I told her how I felt.

There was no sign of her, and I whipped in Romy's direction, ignoring the finger of panic tracing my spine. "Where is she?"

"Not having a freaking heart attack like some of us." Romy glared as she picked her needles back up, and that casual annoyance made my blood run cold. She shouldn't be acting this unnerved by my sudden appearance. Not after that phone had rung.

"Where is she?" I demanded, not waiting for an answer I feared wouldn't come. I thundered into the adjoining kitchen, continuing past its cluttered counters to the hall.

Romy was on her feet now, padding behind me. "Fiona! Remind me why your family is allowed past my wards again."

My sister finally appeared, wearing her usual disdain, but it slid from her face when our eyes met.

"Where is she?" My words softened, pleading with my sister, with the gods, with whoever might be listening. "She called, right?"

Her gaze cut to Romy, who subtly shook her head. Fiona pursed her lips before waving me on. "Come with me."

Each step felt heavier than the last as I followed her back to the kitchen, a pit opening in my stomach. She should have been out of the city by now. Maybe she'd gotten lost.

Fiona twisted her hair up, tying it off in a messy knot. Always good in a crisis—that was why she was the only number saved on that emergency line. She sifted through a few takeout menus until she unearthed the phone from the pile and plucked it free of the charger. "It didn't ring." She cocked her head as she passed it to me.

"And there are no missed calls."

My eyes fixed on the screen, willing it to light up now.

"What's going on, Lach?" Fiona's eyes probed me, her breath uneven. "Is it Ciara? Shaw?"

"They're fine." I shook my head. "Roark just checked on her." Fiona hadn't spoken to me since I'd phoned her about our sister's betrothal to Bain. There wasn't time to catch her up now. I would explain everything she had missed when Cate got here. Things had progressed too quickly, going from possibility to certainty with the breathtaking velocity generally reserved for stupid ideas like picking fights or falling for the one woman you shouldn't even touch.

But her fist banged the counter, the cat at her feet darting to safety. "Will you tell me what the fuck is going on? Why would someone be calling that phone?"

There was a rush of air, and Roark appeared near the table.

"For fuck's sake." Romy clutched her chest.

Fiona moved to Romy's side, stroking soothing circles on her back. She shot a look at Roark as she dragged Romy toward their bedroom. "He's expecting a call. Good luck."

But he already knew. He always did, even though I'd blocked him as soon as I felt Cate's panic bleating in my own chest, shielding him from what I'd found when I arrived in that room and realized what I had to do. I'd reached out for a split second as I left the bayou, asking him to check on my family and telling him where I was heading.

I didn't bother shutting him out now as I paced into the living room, waiting for the phone to ring, as I replayed those desperate minutes, my instructions to her, that final, inexorable choice. Where had things gone wrong? She was good in a crisis, trained for it. Even after shooting MacAlister, she'd tried to stop the bleeding. She was thinking clearly despite the shock. She had followed what I was saying. The memories ratcheted my steps faster, my instinct beckoning me to return to New Orleans. She was still there. I wasn't sure how I knew, but I felt it.

Roark moved into my path. "Everything is secure in New Orleans."

But it wasn't—*she* wasn't. My arms curled over my head, my palms covering the mark of the Wild Hunt. I'd sent her to that garage, knowing everything was in place for her escape. I had acted to protect her from them, but I had miscalculated something. Panic gripped me, as unshakable as that new tattoo.

His eyes skirted the brand, his face stony as he saw the memories through the signet ring connecting us. "You protected her. You did everything you could in the moments you had. She will be fine. Give her time." Rational, collected words that called to a control I no longer possessed.

I didn't give a shit what he thought. It had happened too fast, and there was more she needed to know, more I needed her to understand. She needed to know why she had to follow those instructions. She needed to know that she would be safe if she listened, if she stayed out of fae territories and let that ring keep doing its job. I should have nipped her sooner instead of stealing that kiss. I should have sent her directly here.

Roark shook his head. "You had a split second."

Because I'd hesitated, unwilling to let her go, and there hadn't been the time it would have taken to travel the distance to New York. I'd left myself no choice but to send her to the much closer garage. If she was still there, if she was still in fae territory—even the Nether Court—she wasn't safe. I had to go back.

"No!" He grabbed me as if he could physically hold me back. But I could—I *would*—return. What choice did I have? Roark's grip crushed my shoulders. "We *will* find her, but you can't return there. The Wild Hunt is on, and you don't stand a chance if you step foot back in New Orleans."

I'd left my city unprotected. I'd abandoned my throne. I was a dead man walking.

And I wouldn't change a thing if it meant Cate was still breathing, but I wouldn't rest until she was safe.

Certainty heated my blood until it prickled and throbbed, until it coiled and snaked from that aching absence in my chest across my skin. Roark was speaking, reasoning with me, *bargaining*. I couldn't hear him as a new weight settled over me—a beckoning, demanding tempest brewing as it cried out for her.

"You can't—" The shrill ring of the phone in my hand cut him off.

Fiona nipped in, summoned by that sound, but I wrenched the door to the balcony open as I accepted the call.

"Where are you?" I gripped the balcony railing, relief surging through me despite that strange, new magic smoldering inside me.

"He said I could trust him." Channing's voice gasped.

The magic ignited my blood.

"What did you do?" I seethed.

"A bargain."

His rasp dredged up the memory of another rattling breath. A blood-soaked chest. MacAlister's triumphant glare as I took that final shot. Succeeding even in death by dooming us both. I knew the sound of imminent death when I heard it.

"He swore he would take her away, so when she called, I phoned him like I was supposed to, but..." Channing coughed, choking and gurgling. "He...he shot me."

"No shit." Killing him was a much easier way out of a bargain.

I didn't bother with a goodbye as I crushed the phone to dust in my hand, destroying it like she should have done to the one Channing had just used. I stared at the remnants of it as a new plan began to form. Magic glimmered on my skin, attempting to settle into place, to bind me to life instead of death. I brushed it off, blowing the dust of the phone off the balcony before I stalked inside to find the others gathered. The stricken look on Fiona's face told me Roark was filling in the gaps for her. Romy clutched her hand, and my heart strained at the love in that touch. My sister scanned me as I entered, probably looking for the mark of the hunt, but her eyes paused on my left hand and went wide. I shoved it into my pocket and directed my attention to my penumbra.

"Call Garcia," I ordered, "and have an ambulance sent to Cate's place before her stupid brother dies." She would never forgive me if he did, and while Channing was a fool, he had led her to me. He had delivered the one person I wanted. She'd been right under my nose the entire time, in *my* city. I'd given up the search so long ago, and then she had walked in and made that demand. Called me a monster and offered me that *esmeraude* ring, tugging it just far enough from her finger to stifle its magic—

"We should call Ciara." Fiona snapped me out of the recollection.

"No," I said firmly. "Someone has to run things now. We need Ciara in New Orleans, but Shaw should come here." He would throw a fit, but I could only protect one of them, and he was my baby brother—whether he liked it or not.

"Ciara won't be safe," Roark argued as Fiona went to make the call.

But she would be with Roark to guide her. He'd kept me alive, a miraculous fucking feat.

"*You* will keep her safe." Not an order. A fact. I slipped off my signet, the twin to his, and the magic prickling on my skin flared, searing across my hand, over my wrist as I surrendered that final shred of my old life to my fate. The magic sealed around me, binding my flesh, my life, my soul into something permanent and irrevocable, and on the other side of that bond, I felt the faint, beautiful beat of Cate's heart. Nothing more bled past the other magic protecting her. It wouldn't get past that glamour concealing what I already knew from the world, concealing the truth from even her. The stifled bond felt like a cruelty, as though even my selfless act demanded some retribution. But, like breaking our bargain, if that was the cost of keeping her safe, I would pay it. Because she was alive, even if Bain had her, even if she was in danger every moment. My heart still beat only because hers did.

I held the signet out to him and gave one final order. "Protect your princess."

But he didn't take it as his gaze fell on my palm. Not on the ring but on the glimmering gold tattoo that laced it, crossing to my wrist and over the back of my hand. "What is that?"

Something impossible. Something inescapable. Something worth fighting for.

He continued to stare until I reached over and thrust the signet into his hand. "Your duty is to the *throne*. It was never to me. Go to Ciara."

Roark finally lifted his eyes to mine, his brows lowering as he tried to hear me…and failed. He shook his head, dazed. "Did you know?"

Yes. No.

How could I have ever known?

How could I have ever not?

And perhaps it was the lifetime we had shared, but Roark nodded even without the signet linking us, understanding what I couldn't say, what I couldn't quite comprehend myself.

"If Bain finds out that you two are…" He drew a long breath before his shoulders squared. "He'll summon the Wild Hunt for her, too." His fingers closed over the signet as he accepted his new charge.

"Then let's hope she keeps that *esmeraude* on her finger."

He nodded grimly.

Roark tugged his lip ring, a tattoo snaking across his temple. "The second you step foot in London, it won't just be the Wild Hunt gunning for you. I don't suppose there's any point in suggesting that you keep your distance."

There was not. Not with this sacred and unbreakable new magic binding me to her. Not when every breath without her burned like I was drowning. Not when she was in my enemy's hands. Not when she was mine.

And if I had to walk into hell to get her back, let me burn.

EPILOGUE

"You'll understand."

Light seeped into my dream, and I blinked to discover a buttery shaft of sun pouring through the open window. I bolted up, staring at the white curtains fluttering on the warm breeze sweeping through the room. I clutched the soft sheet over me as I scanned my surroundings. A gold clock ticked faintly on the nightstand, a glass of water resting next to it. My fingers drifted to my dry mouth. A cloying sweetness lingered on my parched lips. The memory of a hand pressing a chloroform-soaked cloth flashed to mind, and I ignored the drink.

Throwing off the sheets, I hauled my heavy legs over the side of the foreign bed. My heart stuttered when I saw the white cotton nightdress I wore. Where were my clothes? I scanned the bedroom's paneled walls, their serene white continuing to the furniture. Everything was bright and calm and lovely.

Everything was a lie.

I rose on unsteady feet and walked slowly to the door. I said a silent prayer as I reached for its crystal knob, my pulse speeding up as my gaze fell on the emerald I wore.

"Don't take it off."

I winced as Lach's voice filled my head, an ache spreading through my chest, threatening to send me to my knees. I forced myself to turn the knob, deflating with relief to find it unlocked. Bracing myself, I stepped into an airy lounge. Columns held up the high ceiling, the walls punctuated with arched doorways. The glossy marble floors were cool against my feet as I tiptoed through the open space. There were no guards. No staff.

I wasn't a prisoner.

I followed the breeze moving through an arch. It drifted out of the palace and into a courtyard. I paused on the threshold, drinking in the lush, manicured hedges surrounding the stone palace. A blood-apple tree rose from the center of the immaculate gardens. I was in the Otherworld, but where? My eyes studied the rolling hills in the distance, their brilliant green peppered with golden flowers.

The clink of metal on china drew my attention away from the distance, and I turned to find a table laid with crisp linens and expensive china. A small bounty of fruit and pastries waited along with a familiar face. Not Bain, thankfully, but a friend waiting for me. I waited for relief to find me, but something locked me in place. I forced myself forward, ignoring the cold creeping up the base of my spine. He didn't look up from the paper he was reading as I approached. I paused at the edge of the table.

He ruffled his newspaper and turned the page. "I hope you slept well."

Was he the person on the other end of the phone Lach had left me? Had Channing made the call? I turned in a full circle as if my brother might appear from somewhere within the palace.

But my host gestured to a seat across from him. "Please sit."

I did, still processing the rolling countryside that surrounded us, peaceful and lovely, so perfect that it almost hurt. *Gnawed*. Like underneath the idyllic beauty, something festered.

"Please eat something." He pushed a tray of pastries toward me, but I stared at the gold-rimmed china before me.

"How did I get here?" I asked.

A frown tipped his mouth, and he picked up a scone. "I apologize for that unpleasant business." He slathered clotted cream on it and placed it on my plate. I didn't touch it, and the frown deepened. "It's not poisoned. I promised you would be safe here. I always keep my word, Cate."

I folded my hands to hide my trembling fingers. "Did Lach send me here?"

"Have something to eat," he urged, ignoring my question.

Maybe Lach thought sending me to a light court would protect me from Bain, but I didn't belong here. I belonged with him. I didn't care about the Wild Hunt or the danger. I wouldn't sit around eating scones while Lach fought for his life. I moved, bracing my palms on the table to rise. "I want to go home."

He picked his paper back up. "The Nether Court is not your home."

And this man was *not* my friend.

Numbness spread through me, my hands slipping as I slid into the chair. "Where is he?"

He shrugged, eyes skidding over the newsprint. "Holed up somewhere, but he'll come out soon enough."

"He's not that stupid. The Hunt is after him."

But he snorted. "Don't underestimate how stupid love makes you. Look what he did to save you."

I opened my mouth to deny it, but the words choked in my throat. Lach had saved me, chosen me over his court, taken the final shot to keep the Hunt from marking me. The truth splintered through me. My heart hammered wildly against my breastbone, trying to escape the confines of my chest to seek him.

For a moment, the world fell away as every ounce of my being cried out to him as if he might hear me. I gripped the edge of the table to keep from crumbling. The light caught the ring I wore, casting golden ribbons over my skin. They swirled and shifted. I blinked, and they were gone—but something soft soothed the ragged need. Maybe it was the magic of the court playing tricks on me.

"With any luck, he'll destroy the Infernal Court before the Hunt catches him." He continued in an easy, friendly way that made every word more cruel.

I had trusted this man. *We* had trusted him. "What are you going to do with me?"

"I haven't quite decided yet," he confessed. "Eat something."

But Lach had known. I swallowed and lifted my chin. "No."

The friendly face slipped to reveal the monster below it. *"Fucking eat something!"*

I flinched, cowering from his sudden, violent rage. I broke off an end of the scone but didn't put it in my mouth. I'd learned my lesson about fae food. But he settled again, mollified by my feigned obedience.

"Really, I can do whatever I want with you." He poured tea into a waiting cup and saucer. "Your brother isn't terribly bright, and he's a disastrous negotiator. He left me so much to work with."

I stiffened, my fingers edging toward the butter knife next to my plate. He tracked the movement.

"I'm not uncivilized, Cate." He clucked a disapproving tongue, and the knife slid across the table to him. "I'm not like those monsters in the shadow courts."

No, he was something worse. A devil with the face of an angel.

He shrugged at my stony silence. "And you only have to be here to serve my purpose."

I swallowed. "And what is your purpose?"

The appearance of his sister interrupted us. She was even lovelier in her own court, her skin glowing like she was lit from within. Her warm amber eyes cooled as they landed on me, a sneer curling her upper lip as she dropped into the empty chair between us. "Does she have to eat with us?"

I could only stare at her.

"Cate is our guest, for now," he added, his teacup settling with an ominous clink on its saucer. Oberon turned back to me. "As to your question—what is any king's purpose? War."

ACKNOWLEDGMENTS

This book was a journey—a long one with a lot of pit stops and sleepless nights and surprises. It kept me on my toes, and I could never have written it without the support of an amazing team behind me.

I am forever grateful to Liz Pelletier, who called me up out of the blue and said three words: "Filthy Rich Fae." I'd been debating what direction to take the Filthy Rich world, and your call was like a light in the darkness. Thank you for being endlessly supportive of this project, always being there for me when I was stuck or confused, and never losing the faith for both of us. This book is here because of you, and I look forward to writing many more books together.

Thank you to Louise Fury for always being my champion, for talking me through the dark moments, and for being a friend through life's unexpected twists. I'm so honored to be represented by The Fury Agency.

My endless thanks to Becca Syme for keeping me grounded and helping me see the big picture. Thank you for helping me embrace my dreams in an authentic way, for making the unknown less scary, and for listening, even when I'm just vomiting my insecurities. You are the GOAT.

I owe so much to the Entangled Team for bringing this book to shelves. Huge thanks to Jessica, Heather, Lizzy, Rae, Nicole, Lydia, Bree, Meredith, Brittany, Ashley, Brittany, Lauren, Curtis, Mary, Britt, and the rest of the Entangled family for everything you do. I don't know how I lived without you all. Thank you to the team at Macmillan for all your hard work! A special thank you to Hannah Lindsey for making me laugh during copy edits—a feat I never thought possible—and for just being an excellent human in general.

Thank you to my foreign agents for bringing my books to readers all over the world. And thanks to the team at Tantor for bringing the story to life in audio.

When I started writing over a decade ago, I could never have imagined the path I would take. I'm so grateful to have had Elise and Shelby Lynn along for so much of it. Thank you also to Geneva Lee's Loves for being my safe space on the internet through it all.

I am so blessed to have so many talented writers in my life. Thank you to Rebecca Yarros and Tamara Mataya for always being a phone call away. Special thanks to Cora, Robyn, Kim, Audrey, Angel, and Ruby for being people I can always count on. You inspire me every day.

And to my family: you are the reason I do this. You are my why but also my how. Thank you for sitting through dinners when Mom has a bad case of word lag. Thank you to James and Sydney for laughter and inside jokes. I wish you weren't growing up so fast, but I'm honored to be at your side while you take on the world. To Sophie, thank you for reminding me to slow down, for afternoons swinging at the park, for being my sunshine on the cloudiest days. I will treasure these days for the rest of my life. And to Josh—my first and last and everything—what an amazing story we're writing together. I can't wait to tell the rest of it with you.

Filthy Rich Fae is a dark and sexy urban fantasy about obsession, captivation, and sacrifice. As such, the story contains elements that might not be suitable for all readers, including death, violence, blood, injury, dismemberment, criminal activity such as shootings and drug dealing, gun violence, sexual activity, dubious consent scenarios, substance and alcohol use, overdose, medical treatment and emergencies, and physical assault on the page. Loss of family, child abuse in a foster home setting, rape, and genocide are discussed in backstory. Readers who may be sensitive to these elements, please take note, and remember: don't take a bite of the apple, no matter how tempting...

an imprint of Entangled Publishing LLC